Once Human : STORIES

Once Human : STORIES

Steve Tomasula

TUSCALOOSA

The University of Alabama Press
Tuscaloosa, Alabama 35487-0380

Manufactured in the United States of America

FC2 is an imprint of The University of Alabama Press

This book is made possible in part by support from the Institute for Scholarship in the Liberal Arts, College of Arts and Letters, University of Notre Dame.

Cover design: Lou Robinson

Typeface: Several typefaces were used throughout this publication.

∞

The paper on which this book is printed meets the minimum requirements of American National Standard for Information Sciences—Permanence of Paper for Printed Library Materials, ANSI z39.48–1984

This book has been cataloged by the Library of Congress.

For Maria, Alba & Ava

hu·man /ˈ(h)yo͞omən/ NOUN: A HUMAN BEING, ESP. A PERSON AS DISTINGUISHED FROM AN ANIMAL OR (IN SCIENCE FICTION) AN ALIEN.

individual |ˌindəˈvijəwəl| NOUN: A SINGLE HUMAN BEING AS DISTINCT FROM A GROUP, CLASS, OR FAMILY

person |ˈpərsən| NOUN: A HUMAN BEING REGARDED AS AN INDIVIDUAL

Once Human : STORIES

The author would like to thank the editors of the following magazines and anthologies in which some of the stories collected in this book first appeared:

"The Color of Flesh" in *Mandorla: Nueva Escritura de las Américas/ New Writing from the Americas.*

"The Risk-Taking Gene as Expressed by Some Asian Subjects" in *The Denver Quarterly* and *The Year's Best Science Fiction* (Eos/Harper Collins).

"The Color of Pain and Suffering" in *Chelsea.*

"Self Portrait(s)" in *The Iowa Review.*

"The Atlas of Man" in *McSweeney's.*

"C-U See-Me" in *The Iowa Review* (Awarded the Iowa Prize).

Portions of the novella "Medieval Times" have appeared in *Ninth Letter*; *American Letters and Commentary*; *The Western Humanities Review*, and the anthology *Not Normal Illinois: Peculiar Fictions from the Flyover.*

"WeKIA" in *Quarterly West.*

"Farewell to Kilimanjaro" in *The Pannus Index.*

Grateful acknowledgement is also made to the designers and artists who helped make this visual-edition what it is: book design and art direction by Robert Sedlack, with contributions from: Graham Ebetsch ("The Risk-Taking Gene as Expressed by Some Asian Subjects"); Erin Prill ("The Color of Pain and Suffering"); Mark Cook ("Self Portrait(s)"); Tom Walker ("The Atlas of Man," "Medieval Times" and "WeKia"); Crispin Presbys ("C-U See-Me"); Maria Tomasula (art in "The Color of Flesh" and "Medieval Times"); Lauren Halleman McCarthy ("Farewell to Kilimanjaro").

Wave with text in it (with "Beyond, the open ocean" copy): Charlotte Lux Typewriter illustration: John Traub

Once Human : STORIES

The Color
of FLESH

On top of everything, she cut herself.

"Shit!" Yumi yelled, dropping both X-acto knife and
the glossy gun catalog she'd been cutting in the kitchen.

"What's the matter?" Jerome called from his studio.

"Nothing," she yelled, ambulancing her finger from kitchen table to bathroom,
telling one of those white lies we all tell when we're too busy, or too blue—when
we're preoccupied, don't care or are unaware; too harried, polite or green, dulled
by routine, too livid or 'don't want to deal with it'; too 'I don't have time for
this'—too stuck in our rut—simplify, simplify—too yellow or don't want to
fight—just yet—or maybe too pissed to explain.

"His fault," she muttered, holding her finger under the bathroom faucet; her
wound—as rends in flesh are called—stung—the stream of cold water turning
rosé (red, Jerome would say) before swirling down the drain. After patting her
finger dry she put on a Band-Aid, and here is where our story really begins.

Slowly she raised her finger into the bright white of the mirror above the sink, her
attention arrested by how little the flesh-colored Band-Aid resembled the color
of her flesh. The sight of it, the sound of Jerome hammering in the bedroom he
used as his studio, then his heavy grunting—with a sexual rhythm—made her
want to cry. But she didn't cry. She looked at the wan face looking back at her
from her bathroom mirror, at the quiver in her lip, and resolved to be stronger
than that. She had always been stronger than that. Then she sat down on the
toilet to think.

How had she not noticed this difference before, she wondered, running her hand over what she already knew to be the answer: her prosthetic leg—and how closely the Band-Aid matched the color of its smooth skin, that is, matched her. Or so it might have been natural for her to say, she thought, given the continuum between this moment, this Band-Aid, this leg, and the series of legs she had had, going back to her childhood, back to when her mother would take her to the shop that sold such things and she'd get fitted; the day they returned to pick up her new leg was always a festive occasion—mother and daughter out on a shopping excursion that always included a new pair of shoes—and ended with her *walking* out of the store in them. It was like buying a new school uniform at the start of each year to replace one that had grown alien, had begun to chafe and squeeze, had begun to click. That is, a leg wasn't a uniform. Or a pair of shoes. It was more intimate than that. More intimate than even dentures. Almost a part of her even though it was apart from her. Or maybe it was more correct to say its apartness was a part of her. Which isn't to say that she ever confused the leg she wore—is that the right word?—with herself. There was her leg, then there was her other leg. Her not-leg. And her not-leg, like the Band-Aid, was always a pale shade of?—what?—not white, not the white of a ghost or a dead person, but not the color of flesh either, not if her other leg, her non-prosthetic leg, was the color of flesh. Whatever that meant.

On one of those outings, she'd sat in the shop, reading a comic book as she waited her turn, dozens of legs in all styles, sizes, and stages of repair, retrofitting,

alteration, dangling from the ceiling—Gepetto's workshop, they told kids, as if that was comforting—while another girl was fitted for a charity leg: a black girl, as they were called then, even though everyone knew blacks weren't black any more than whites were white. Rather, the girl's skin was more coffee-colored while Yumi's own skin was, well, coffee-colored too. Or call it tea. Or bamboo, if that helps you imagine it more. But trying on the new, old donated leg with its straps and buckles, the girl looked black because the leg was white, that is, a vinyl, orangey color. Nevertheless, she was so happy about getting a new old leg that she seemed completely oblivious to the mismatch in color. Or maybe the new old leg was so not her that it didn't matter. Or was so much a part of her that it didn't matter. In any case, Yumi had been so moved by the girl's unflinching nature that she resolved to be like her.

Despite the protests of her mother, when it came Yumi's turn to be fitted, she chose one of those new stainless steel legs, a leg that instead of skin evoked things modern: space ships, or chrome, abstract sculpture like Constantin Brancusi's *Bird in Space*, but most importantly, that black-not-black girl, that is, a girl who wasn't embarrassed for her other leg, her leg-not, and so avoided dances, roller-rinks, pogo sticks, hopscotch, sack races, any situation that would call attention to it.

Perhaps this is why, years later, she fell so hard for Jerome.

From his studio came a murderous scream. "I'll kill you, Bitch!"

Jerome was a performance artist of sorts and was rehearsing the script he was to stage in a few days. The scream was followed by crashes, then Jerome swearing at the top of his lungs, first in his own voice, then in his other own voice, the voice of the female lead, which he also played in the one-person dramas he created.

She loved him for his sense of humor. For his looks. But most of all, she realized, recalling how quickly she had moved in with him, she loved him because he loved her in spite of her leg/not-leg: the antithesis, she had thought, of that joke she met on-line, the grin he wore in his on-line photo collapsing in real time as he entered the restaurant they'd agreed to meet at and he caught sight of her leg. "I'm sorry," he coughed before running away. With Jerome, though, the transition from the prosthetics aisle of the medical supply store where they met, to lunch, then dinner, then bed, had been so smooth that she had to struggle to remember them as discreet events. It was only afterwards, after she was living in his apartment, that she began to notice things. Small things. Like the Band-Aids that had been as invisible as the air she moved through but now, now that Jerome polluted this same air with doubt, bothered her as much as— Well, as much as she'd been bothered by birds.

That is, after stumbling upon his collection of pornography—a whole drawer full—she'd begun to notice lots of things she never had before, the first being how radically different the thing a hummingbird had to do to stay in the air

was from what a hawk did to stay in the air. Or a jet. Or hot-air balloon. And yet it was all called flying. The same with walking. After finding more, and worse, porno mags in the closet—graphic, vulgar things—she couldn't help but remember how radically different what she did to go for a stroll was from what people with two natural legs did. If stairs were involved, what she did was closer to swimming. Yet both acts were called "walking."

Walking. Which morphed yet again under the gaze of people gawking as though watching a parade go by….

Her thoughts began to trip over themselves for if things as obvious and fundamental as legs and walking could be so disjointed what of the unseen? What of ideas? Or feelings. How large could the gap be between what one person felt and what another called…. Love?

Enormous, she realized. And it was the freak-factor of his magazines that told her so: magazines with cheesecake shots of white women wearing corsets so tight that their waists could have been squeezed into napkin rings. Some of the women in these magazines were missing a limb. Some both legs. All of them were missing clothes. Naked. All that skin, she'd thought, turning one flesh-colored page after another, sheer repetition bringing home the fact that everyone had skin. Men and women. Bears had skin. Snakes too. Tomatoes and potatoes and grapes. And yet….

When she heard Jerome coming home from the medical supply route he worked, she quickly hid the magazines back in his dresser, back where she had found them, and she kept her peace, trying to figure out what all those white women, and his owning them, could mean.

Judging from outward appearances, nothing had changed. Jerome kissed her as he often did when he came home to find her already there; their evenings were spent as they spent many evenings with her reading or drawing anime-eyed girls, rampaging robots, up-skirts and explosions, using her X-acto knife to cut from hardware or gun-lover magazines the pictures that she added to the girls to create the cyborgs who fought injustice in the manga world she authored while Jerome worked

at what he thought of as his real job, his calling, his art, making life-sized puppets, building the sets, incorporating the crash-test dummies or CPR manikins he bought at employee discount for the avant-garde puppet burlesques he put on in whatever gallery or warehouse would have him.

The new one-man production he was working on was to open in a few days so he was very busy, retreating into his studio as soon as he got home. So she bid her time, worked on her manga, and waited for a good moment to bring up his collection, not sure how to bring it up.

Inside, though, she was all turmoil. The thought of living with someone who was really in love with her leg-not, grew increasingly unsettling. Mortifying. Even sick. Her mood teeter-tottered as she sifted their six months together for clues to what he really felt about her. She had no memory of him even mentioning her leg unless she brought it up first but she couldn't decide what this might mean. After all, she'd never brought up his. Or the color of his flesh for that matter. Still, she couldn't shake the feeling that he was acting (as she

was now acting), that she had trusted him with no real reason to trust him (unless that's what trust was), and that he had pulled the rug out from under her. From under them. From under whatever it was that they had had. Or what she had thought they had had or what she had thought he had thought they had had and that was the most dizzying thing of all—the idea that what they had actually had was a nothing. A void. An absence—at best a gap between what she thought and what he meant by "love," a disconnect because he hadn't lied to her, no, but because he was telling the truth when he said he loved her, meaning something like arousal, or desire, something like what he felt toward all those nude and limbless women in the magazines—or that he felt about her in some other way that shared only the most cartoon of outlines with what she meant when she said she loved him—or even that he felt something like she felt toward him only to a different degree.

There were degrees as well as kinds of love, weren't there?—a mother's love as well as puppy love. Pure love—as well as impure love. A 17% pure love but love nonetheless. The newly-minted love she and Jerome had shared. Nature's Second Sun. Mutations and animal passions. Zoos of love—and those were just the loves that had labels. Yes, she realized, as surely as there was no one color of skin, there must be loves that fell between labels, between words, rivers of loves—*the wine of love*—that went right through the finest mesh of letters: more loves that had no name than loves that did and each one being itself just as the crayon labeled "Flesh" could itself be neither true nor false. If there was a lie, it was on its wrapper, in its name, what was said about the crayon, and the same was true for all those things that were called love—*My love is a red, red rose*—the labels for loves no more unfailing than those for colors.

Still, philosophy didn't buy her much, she realized. Not if friendship could be a shade of love. Not if curiosity could be a color. Not if some perv's itch could be a love. Worst of all, there was pity.

Her instinct was to haul his magazines out into the light and demand to know his true feelings. But she was afraid to have her worst fears confirmed and the dream she'd been living popped like the bubble it was. Wouldn't you? Then, preoccupied over what to do, she'd cut herself. Now, sitting on the toilet in the bathroom, she knew she could not go on this way any longer.

She rose and took a hard look at herself in the mirror. Her body was still young even if tiny crinkles had begun to appear at the corners of her eyes; her chin was slacker than it appeared in the manga-style drawings of her face that she sometimes included in crowd scenes while the angular, samurai contours that made the heroine of her strip look semi-machine-like increasingly illustrated by contrast how quickly real bodies, like hers, lost their edge. The thought of another round of first dates sent a shudder through her. Equally repugnant was the idea of having it out with Jerome over this, the two of them slipping into some absurdist, *shoujo* manga—that is, girls' manga—about their true feelings or whether

what they shared had been a lie, or if the fog she had entered was the true delusion, an illusion cast by some evil Pokémon or Emotion Alchemist who could only be defeated with a flower. Or a song. But what else could she do? Resigned, afraid, full of dread, angry that she—that no one—could escape their own human comedy—it's hard to find words for the complex of emotions raging through her though mostly she was afraid that she was about to lose what she thought she had had by discovering that it had never been there to have—she took a deep breath, opened the bathroom door, and went out to face whatever twist life deemed to place in her plot.

She found him in his studio, back to her, adjusting the cape of the life-sized crash-test dummy that he had dressed for its role as Mr. Invincible. Arranged as a crowd of gawkers were his other cast members: naked store manikins, all bald and as genital-free as Barbie though with varying degrees of nipple realism; there were also CPR Dummies, their mouths open Os like the mouth of the Inflatable Suzie beside them but made for paramedics to practice clearing blocked air passages. He'd switched their arms and legs around so none of the skin tones matched, then positioned the crowd so that their painted faces appeared to be shocked by the rubber butt that was mooning them, that is, by his Prostrate Exam Simulator, realistic penis and scrotum dangling, while three other Disease and Burn Victim Medical Training Manikins stood in the poses of See, Hear, and Speak No Evil.

She braced herself. "Jerome," she began, "why do we call our bedroom your studio?"

"Hmmm?" he asked absentmindedly, bending over the pride of his collection, a Geriatric Care Manikin that was more fully jointed than those pose-able manikins carved from blonde wood and sold in art supply stores. The vinyl this one was made of had been molded to give it an old person's wrinkles. It could be converted from a man to a woman and it came with fully functional cavities, if by functional you meant, like the manufacturer, that its nostrils could be suctioned, enemas and catheters applied…. Jerome was at the point in the play where Mr. Invincible is reincarnated as Old Mother so he was switching the genitals of the manikin.

"I said why do we call our bedroom your studio?"

"We only have one bedroom," he said, gripping the plastic penis like the handle of a pump. Enough leverage and the whole genital area snapped out. "This is the only room we have with space for my work. You know that."

"But why do we call it that? You could still work here even if we called it our bedroom. It is the room where we keep our bed. And sleep. And make love. It's our boudoir. I mean, I make my strip in the kitchen but we still call it the kitchen."

He stood and faced her, dressed in plaid boxer shorts. Over his bare chest he wore a Breast Self-Examination Training Vest: a realistic, flesh-colored, silicon casting of the front of a woman with C-cup breasts. "Is something bothering you?" he asked. The breasts were white, alabaster headlights in contrast to his bronze skin, which was bronze in contrast to their whiteness.

"Jerome," she said, steadying her voice, "I found your magazines."

He stood there, the bathing beauty's symmetry of the breasts strapped to his chest pointing out everything she wasn't, a stunned stupid look on his face asking for an explanation, and to give him one she marched over to his stack of appliance manuals and pushed, sending them to the floor. The covers of a dozen of his porno mags fanned out like paint samples in a hardware store, a rainbow of pink tones.

"They're for my work," he said icily. "I use them as…. Reference material."

She had expected a little truth. A little humility or apology. Not some chicken-shit dodge, not some bullshit attitude, so she strode to the dresser where she had first discovered a few magazines hidden among his underwear, growing more angry at him for lying to her than for having the magazines to begin with. "Oh yeah?" she yelled, jerking the drawer open to expose them; but she did so with such force that it came

out of the dresser and fell to the floor. There, in the cavity beneath where the drawer had been, were more magazines—hardcore, cripple-fuck magazines she hadn't known about—and the sight of them flash-flooded her with the rage of having caught him in the act, in bed with some other— How many more?

"Liar!"

She threw open the closet and with a yank brought down a cascade of magazines. Years worth of subscriptions. Yes, subscriptions that he must have continued across moves, using the change of address cards to remain faithful. "Lies and acting! You don't hide all this other shit!" she yelled, indicating the stuff he brought home from the medical supply house he worked for: Mr. Budget Intubation Head; Baby Blood-Pressure Arm; the Bleeding-Wound Variety Pack and the rest of his freak show—his cabinet of curiosities that she—its jewel—had been living within, thinking all the while that it was their home! She fought to hold back the tears she could feel coming on, hold back her anger as well as stand against the loss, waiting to see what he would answer. Waiting to see if it was her not-leg that he was in love with, no not love, in lust with. He cleared his throat to speak. This better be good, she thought.

But it wasn't.

"I did put them there," he admitted, "but I didn't hide them. Not if by hide you mean lie, not if by lie you mean mislead, not if by mislead you mean veil…"

The more he skated, the faster she slewed through the subtle put-downs she endured each time she left the house— "…not if by veil you mean mask…" —strangers who, upon seeing her leg, offered to guide her onto the subway as if she were blind, or begin talking louder, as if she were deaf, or— "…not if by mask you mean act…" —or talk slower, explaining sports to her as if her mind couldn't keep up, each slight in itself a single drop but together an unrelenting torture that some days made her want to scream. Kiss off! "…or con, or color, or cover up, or cloud…" But of course she never could say what she thought; no, not to them, not to people who did think they were helping; she could only murmur 'No thank you,' or remain mute and take it, take it, take it, take it. Until— "…not if by act you mean deceive instead of tell a poetic truth or protect—"

"Protect?"

The drop too many hit:

"Protect?" she yelled—

morphing as she never had before, entering a zone where she was beside herself watching herself swell into one of the gigantic robots of her strip, the size and weight of her anger taking on a momentum of its own, a life of its own that was also

strangely liberating as she clobbered the nearest of his manikins. It toppled into the next; Hear, See and Speak No Evil fell like dominos. The sight of the chain reaction was liberating. His toolbox was next, with her getting her legs into the lifting.

"Stop!" he cried, his rubber breasts slapping about as he rushed to catch his props, the non-acted concern he had for his manikins—but not her!—fueling her robot's rampage. "Stop it!"

He begged her to stop trashing the months he'd spent creating his show while she screamed at him for the lie, for always it was a lie. "You mean protect yourself!" Oh, she'd had it with the hypocrisy, their myopia—and now him!—acting like they were protecting her, holding a door for her then standing far enough aside to let a leper pass. She grabbed Mr. Invincible by his cape and flung him out the door of the bedroom. He crash-landed into one of the end tables in the living room. Her life was a saga of everyone doing everything for her "Except just acting normal!" she yelled, their argument

and the limbs of his puppets spilling into the living room, the narrow rooms too small to hold her rage. Then, as quickly as her robot had blasted through his laboratory, it exhausted itself.

She flung herself onto the couch and let go a heavy sob. When she managed to choke it back, calm down, she buried her face in the cushions as she laid out for him wounds she had thought were forgotten: winning the Silver at an all-school art show because, as she later learned from the mother of Bronze, a judge felt sorry for her. She told him about being one of those girls who could walk into a dance and turn every man's head—away—a chaperone coming up to offer a sympathy dance. She told him about girding herself for brave happiness, about guys from the on-line dating service, about the monumental scale of staircases in government buildings, their giant-sized flights designed to make mere citizens feel humble and people like her less than citizens....

After the longest time she opened an eye. Jerome was still standing there, still wearing his Breast Self-Exam Vest. But instead of the sorrow, or remorse, or even the speechless empathy she expected, he was staring at her. At her legs. Both of them. And at her ass, yes, that was the only word that fit the way he was looking at it and the rest of her body, like a man who'd been too long in prison, or at sea, too long alone, no matter what he said, his body affirming that only the flesh didn't lie. Except for faces, she knew—a poker face to hide excitement—or eyes, shut to mask emotion; or hips, or hands, or legs too—the way they could be crossed to say 'no' while allowing a skirt to ride high up a come-hither thigh. Is that what he thought? She tugged her skirt down.

"If you prick us do we not bleed?" he said, his voice thick with passion. "If you tickle us do we not?—"

"Oh, get off stage—"

"Off stage?" He gave a bitter laugh. "In my very first play in college, I came off stage to police who wanted to talk to me because a bike was stolen and someone said the thief looked like 'Othello.' With black friends I have to pretend to like basketball; I wear polo shirts when working with other whites, pretending, as my mother said she believed, that the Golden Rule really could be colorblind, by which she meant body-free—even though we lost a doctor last month because, to the cops who stopped him, a wallet in the hand of a black man was a gun. I never knew why she clung to that myth until one winter after school, when a bunch of kids who *said* they were my friends held me down, copping feels, pretending to ass hump me," he said, holding out the rubber, Caucasian-colored breasts to her in supplication, their brown nipples growing like big, dilating eyes as he squeezed, "the way my daddy must have done my white mamma." Unlike real breasts, when he let go, these didn't show the trace of his grip.

"When I managed to turn my face out of the snow, I could see two teachers watching—from a window high up in the school, like an audience in a balcony, or overseers looking down into the yard, seeing no evil being done, hearing no evil— Maybe because black-on-black riding didn't hurt if it was mixed with white-on-white—which hurts less than white-on-black or black-on-white. Who knows?—but not *doing* anything."

"Nothing. Lay there and play the possum that understood how well my mother knew that colors had bodies, who realizes—only after the fact, after he's sworn 'never again,' then worked through all that—that while the play's the thing wherein we catch the conscience of the king, it's also how we catch the conscience of the players. And the Queen, and the peasant in the last row, and the salespeople at the mall where I buy my costumes," he said, pointing at the polo shirts in the drawer she'd yanked open, "who *say* thank you as I hand them my cash, but lock their car doors as I walk through the lot out to my own.

"Or not. Otherwise, to suspect every handshake, every smile, every gift and gesture....

"You must be blind to not have seen any of this in the plays I write," he said, sweeping his arm to indicate the stuff of his performance: the manikin arms and heads and wigs scattered about the living room, the white penis he'd been removing from his Geriatric Care Manikin when she started throwing his props and puppets everywhere. But also, she saw, he meant to accuse her gun catalogs, drawings and cutouts of cyborgs, fighting for the right to be human, as if injustice was something that could be defeated, on the kitchen table beyond. "Or to read the way I've always treated you as anything but what it was."

She stiffened at his attempt to turn this, to blame the victim, her. "Right," she said sarcastically, remembering what had started their fight, "you're trying to tell me you don't get turned on by those naked—" She caught herself before she could complicate them beyond hope by saying—amputees?—

"I admit to being a man," he said, that look coming back over his face as his eyes ran down her body. "No," he added sincerely, bringing fingertips to chest in that stage gesture actors often used to convey sincerity. "I admit to being human."

There was a knock on the door. "Who the fuck could that be?" she muttered, and they stood there motionless and silent, silent and motionless, waiting for whoever it was to go away. The knocking became a pounding. "Open up—" A gruff voice.

The both of them wiping back tears, Jerome took a few steps across the tiny living room and tore open the door.

Two cops stood there, a woman cop and her partner: white faces, blue uniforms and authority. Much later, Yumi would realize that the male cop was actually caramel-colored, his dark blue uniform, she'd figure, being the thing that turned him white as she got up from the couch and saw his and his partner's official eyes turn in unison to the rubber breasts Jerome still wore.

"Good evening...sir," the cop said, "a neighbor reported fighting in your apartment. Can we come in?"

"Oh for Christ's sake," Jerome said, "No." He tried to close the door but the cop stuck his baton inside, jamming it open.

Jerome opened it the rest of the way, trying to explain. "Look, I'm an actor. Someone must have heard me acting. There's nothing here to see."

...nothing to see, Yumi felt like parroting—this originality from someone who wrote plays. Instead, agitated, she bit her lip, knowing that just because Jerome said what was expected, just because the woman cop at her door had the expected P.E.-teacher's haircut, prison-matron expression, that is, just because the human comedy was a burlesque they'd all rehearsed didn't mean it was any less real—or dangerous—and looking over Jerome's glistening bronze shoulders, seeing the cops' impassive expressions, she also saw him as she never had before: a black man explaining himself fast to two white cops. Then she noticed how much destruction she had done to the apartment, crying surely having left her own face puffy, her eyes red. Manikin limbs were scattered everywhere.

"...NO CAN DO," THE COP WAS TELLING JEROME. JARHEAD HAIRCUT; HIS JARHEAD BODY FILLED THE DOORWAY LIKE A SQUAD CAR. "WE GO AWAY AND YOU OR YOUR WIFE OR WHATEVER ENDS UP HURT, THEN OUR SUPERVISORS...."

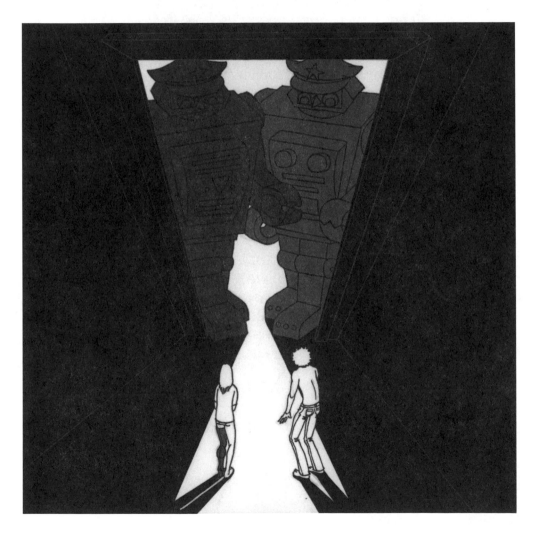

"Oh let them in," Yumi said, seeing that the quickest way to get rid of them would be to go along. "What are you afraid of?"

THE INSTANT SHE SAID THIS SHE SAW THAT THE COPS TOOK IT THE WRONG WAY—NOT AS SHE HAD MEANT IT, THAT JEROME HAD NOTHING TO HIDE, BUT AS A TAUNT, CALLING HIM YELLOW FOR WANTING TO QUIT THEIR FIGHT NOW THAT SHE HAD THE MARINES ON HER SIDE. SHE ALSO SAW THEM TAKE IN HER PROSTHETIC LEG—THEN LOOK BACK TO JEROME AS THEY DID THE CALCULUS FOR A FAIR FIGHT, AND IN THAT INSTANT SHE HATED THEM FOR THE ASSUMPTIONS THEY WERE MAKING ABOUT HIM, ABOUT HER, BUT WAS GLAD, IN SPITE OF HERSELF, FOR THE ADVANTAGE.

THE COPS WERE IN THE APARTMENT NOW, AND THE WOMAN COP HAD WORKED HER WAY BETWEEN YUMI AND JEROME, SAYING SOMETHING TO HER, TRYING TO GET HER TO GO INTO THE KITCHEN. SEPARATE THE COMBATANTS, YUMI KNEW FROM WATCHING *REAL COPS* ON TV. "THESE YOUR DOLLS?" HER PARTNER WAS ASKING JEROME.

YUMI DIDN'T WANT TO GO INTO THE KITCHEN. THERE WASN'T ANY REASON FOR HER TO GO INTO THE KITCHEN, AND WHILE SHE TRIED TO EXPLAIN THIS TO THE FEMALE COP SHE HEARD THE MALE ONE BEHIND HER SAYING, "A GUY BEATING UP ON HIS CRIPPLED GIRLFRIEND ISN'T GOING TO LOOK GOOD IN COURT." THE C-WORD FLOODED HER WITH ADRENALINE JUST AS JEROME BEGAN TO RAISE HIS VOICE: "I'M *NOT* GOING TO ANY JAILHOUSE...."

THE WOMAN COP HAD A HOLD OF YUMI BY THE ELBOW AND WAS TRYING TO LEAD HER BY IT TOWARD THE KITCHEN. YUMI STAYED PUT. THE GRIP TIGHTENED. THE INSTANT YUMI YANKED HER ELBOW FREE THERE WAS A CRASH BEHIND HER—LIKE DISHES BUSTING. WHEN SHE TURNED TO THE NOISE SHE FOUND JEROME AND THE COP WRESTLING, ROLLING AROUND IN CRUSHED FLOWERS AND PIECES OF BROKEN VASE ON THE FLOOR.

JEROME'S RUBBER BREASTS WERE IN THE COP'S FACE BUT JUST AS QUICK THE COP ROLLED HIM OVER, AND JEROME'S OWN FACE WAS MASHED INTO THE CARPET. WITH THE FINESSE OF A RODEO COWBOY, THE COP GOT INTO A SITTING POSITION ON TOP OF JEROME AND PUT HIM IN A HAMMERLOCK. EXCEPT THE COP KEPT TWISTING JEROME'S ARM UP, SO HIGH, AND AT SUCH AN UNNATURALLY PAINFUL ANGLE THAT HIS CRIES MADE IT SEEM AS IF HIS ARM WAS GOING TO COME OFF.

"Stop it!" Yumi yelled. "You're breaking his arm!"

JEROME HAD ALREADY STOPPED FIGHTING AND WAS JUST LYING THERE IN PAIN WITH HIS FACE GROUND INTO THE WHITE CARPET. THERE WAS A SMEAR OF RED AT HIS NOSE AND YUMI REALIZED SHE WAS SEEING HIM AS THOSE TEACHERS MUST HAVE THAT DAY HE WAS BEAT UP IN THE SNOW, THE PANG OF EMPATHY THAT WENT THROUGH HER SO STRONG THAT LOOKING BACK AT IT LONG AFTERWARDS, SHE WAS CERTAIN THAT IT COULD NOT BUT BE AT LEAST SOMETHING LIKE LOVE AS HE JUST TOOK IT, THE COP WHIPPING OUT HIS HANDCUFFS—NO, IT WASN'T HANDCUFFS AT ALL THAT HE RETRIEVED FROM HIS BELT, YUMI REALIZED IN THE INSTANT IT TOOK HIM TO GET OUT HIS STUN GUN: AN EVIL-LOOKING DEVICE LIKE ELECTRIC HAIR-CLIPPERS ONLY WITH ELECTRODES FOR JAWS THAT THE COP WAS ABOUT TO DIG INTO JEROME'S BACK WHEN YUMI YELLED *HEY!* AND KICKED HIM. NOT WITH HER GOOD LEG, THAT IS, HER NATURAL LEG THAT WAS GOOD FOR BALANCE, BUT HER OTHER GOOD LEG, HER ARTIFICIAL LEG THAT WAS BETTER THAN A BILLY CLUB FOR BLOCKING CLOSING DOORS, CRACKING BRAZIL NUTS, OR KICKING OVERLY-WHITE COPS RIGHT IN THE BALLS.

AGGGGGGHHHH! HE SCREAMED. EXCEPT NO SOUND ACTUALLY CAME OUT OF HIS MOUTH. THOUGH HIS MOUTH OPENED WIDER THAN INFLATABLE SUZIE'S, HE WAS BEYOND SCREAMS, BEYOND WORDS OR SPEECH OF ANY KIND AS HE CRUMPLED INTO A FETAL POSITION ON THE FLOOR. JUST AS SHE WAS ABOUT TO GIVE IT TO HIM AGAIN, YUMI WAS WRENCHED ABOUT BY HER PROSTHETIC LEG— AS THOUGH IN MID-KICK THE AIR FROZE SOLID AROUND IT—AND BEFORE SHE COULD SEE WHY, SHE FOUND HERSELF ON THE FLOOR BESIDE THE WRITHING COP, BESIDE JEROME, THE FEMALE COP STANDING OVER THE THREE OF THEM, HOLDING THE LEG THAT HAD COME OFF IN HER HANDS WHEN SHE GRABBED IT TO SAVE HER PARTNER FROM THE SECOND BLOW.

Months later, Yumi stood before the bathroom sink, looking at herself in the mirror. On one finger was a fluorescent-green Band-Aid with smiley faces that looked nothing like skin; the cut on her other finger was completely healed, if by healed it was meant that she no longer had to think about it, tend to it, stanch its flow. As she marveled at the smoothness of the scar, Jerome came in beaming. The paperwork on her court decision had arrived and he had made a frame for it: a silver frame with a pattern of interlocking rings that reminded her of the Olympics. Or one of those frames that newlyweds sometimes use to frame their marriage certificates. She joined him as he hung it over their bed, the bed in their bedroom:

Yumi Song v. The State of Illinois.

An altercation with Officers Mike Garcia and Meg Leary led to the arrest of Yumi Song and Jerome Williams. Said officers seized Ms. Song's prosthetic leg to hold as evidence and the State Prosecutor's Office detained said prosthetic leg for 5 months pending trial.

At a hearing called for by Ms. Song's attorney, the Prosecutor's office claimed that Song's artificial leg should continue to be held as evidence because Song used it as a weapon in an attack against Officer Garcia. Song's attorney did not deny that his client used her leg in the assault. He maintained, however, that the leg should not be classified as a weapon and to hold it as evidence for such an extended period constituted a form of punishment before a verdict of guilty.

Presiding Judge Rosemarie Grey concurred and ordered the release of the leg, finding that while Song's leg may not be an actual leg, as maintained by the Prosecution, she did in fact use it in ways wholly consistent with kicking.

Story: Steve Tomasula | Art: Maria Tomasula | Design: Robert Sedlack

Now we see but a poor reflection, as through a glass darkly; then we shall
see face-to-face. Now I know in part; then I shall know fully,
even as I am fully known.

—I Corinthians 13:12.

C–U See–Me

06:12:00:13:12

Pecker hopping. Bare chest and thighs shiny with sweat. Nothing they hadn't seen before, thought Luke, making out through the glare of an apartment window across the courtyard someone watching him as he jumped rope naked.

He kept up the rhythm while the someone—a woman?—a man with hippie hair?—settled in, watching. Steady as a camera.

1011 1101 0110 1111 1100 1101 0101 1100 1101 1....
—a choreography of bytes....

Standing before glossy grins on the magazines in Gas-N-Go, J. felt eyes on her. Instinctively she looked up—a bowed mirror collaged her own bowed face with the reflections of two men behind the cash register, watching.

Odd, thought Luke, skipping rope in his living room, that he, an investigator for Family Pharmacy and Foods, Inc., a person who knew how surveillance could turn anyone to glass, could be so untroubled....

Name:_____

$13.13

Voice of the cash register instead of the cashier.

Webs of laser light parse melons and cupcakes. Then the cashier scrutinized F.'s signature—an X that he had purposefully made illegible—

1011 1101 0110 1111 1100 1101 0101 1100 1101 1....
—a choreography of bytes to and from massive data banks....

The cashier handed back his card.

The system always gets you in the end, F. thought, needing a shower for giving in, for admitting by using the card that if a tree fell in the forest and there was no one there to watch, it didn't exist. At least he'd goosed Big Brother by getting plastic *after* he'd been canned. He returned the card to the wallet chained to his jeans, hoisted his paper grocery bags, then left, puzzling out how he'd lost that job.

An electronic eye opened the door.

Calls to OSHA were supposed to be anonymous.

Find out the names of everyone on your block: http://www.anywho.com

From up here, he could see everything: luscious melons, a rack of cupcakes....

This is stupid, J. thought, eyes weighing on her in that old exhausting way.... She didn't want a magazine, was only buying one because—

Just because she hated having to *ask.*

Stan said the name on the cashier's Gas-N-Go uniform. She placed a copy of *Look* on the counter, fished around in her purse—eyes unbuttoning her blouse—

1011 1101 0110 1111 1100 1101 0101 1100 1101 1....—to and fro and up into the card reader of the cash register.

On the monitor below the counter, *Jane I. Smith,* and other info linked to the credit card he'd just swiped appeared across a video of her face.

Approved.

After paying, J. stared straight ahead as she asked, "May I use the key to your restroom?"

Store 03513
06:13:08:31:57

...firm melons....

Luke pressed up on a ceiling panel to expose the grid of video cabling suspended above the aisles of Family Pharmacy 02830. Was it the casual way his neighbor spied on him? Was that why he was so casual about being spied on? He plugged a palm-sized camera into one of the jacks that fed a VCR housed deep in a locker, deep, deep in the manager's office.

Name:_____

The *infanta* in the painting looks out through 400 years of yellowing varnish at the viewer, looking back at her being looked at by the *menina* who is seen by the viewer who is looking at the dim mirror in the background which darkly reflects the king and queen looking back at the viewer standing where they should be, gazed at by Velázquez standing before an easel in the painting, looking out at the viewer looking in at him….

The only one who isn't giving their eyes a workout is the dog…..

The cookie-cutter architecture of every Family Pharmacy was as comforting to Luke as the contours of his own living room. To get to Store 04902 he navigated a landscape tagged by gangs—*¡Latin Kings!* The chrome and glass of Store 02786 mirrored mini-vans and condo landscaping. Like some oddly-shaped congressional district, his territory encompassed customers in mechanic's coveralls and customers in tennis whites. And yet, the Great Equalizer, the identical nets of video cables that hung above all, the identical one-way mirrors and surveillance software lulled him, as he climbed a ladder, the way the blind must feel returning from the bustle of streets to their own home.

He hummed as he worked, inserting the needle lens of a camera through a ceiling panel. He trained the camera down upon the spot where the cashier's hands would be after the store opened, his thoughts drifting all the while to his neighbor. Who hadn't been trying to hide his spying. If so, the guy could have easily peered out from behind his blinds. But no, he'd stood full faced in the window—as if to make sure Luke saw him seeing him.

Back on the floor, Luke checked his handiwork—the lens was a pin-head, lost in the pebble-grain of ceiling panels molded for just such purposes. Identical in every store. Identical to the ceiling in his living room.

Now he had to find a new gig.

In the privacy of the Gas-N-Go washroom, J. lifted her skirt.

Name:_____

Nice legs and firm buns—probably a jogger. Or belonged to a gym.

The museum line inched forward bringing another suit and all the other tourists, children, and art students down the velvet rope that channeled them toward the exhibit—and me, N. thought, speeding through her thirty-sixth hour without sleep. Behind her was the gallery she was guarding, bare except for the single painting that the line was waiting to see: *Las Meninas*. Every time the Art Institute mounted a traveling old master, it was hunks on parade, and N., dressed in her museum-guard's uniform, took up her position at the doorway to get a better look at the suit that the line was now offering up: older than the college guys she usually dated—even a hint of gray. Trim bod. Unless that was the cut of his Armani talking.

Should she smile at him?

Transit Authority Driver Application.
Name:_____.

In the janitor's closet adjoining the women's washroom, S. stepped up on a chair to reach the rolls of toilet paper on the top shelf. Noiselessly, he moved them aside, one by one, until a pinpoint of light shined out from the peephole he had drilled through the wall. He pressed his eye to it.

Name:_____

Loose strands of hair, face flushed, squinting out from under him, his back dough-pale in the mirror on the ceiling….

Name:_____

Toilet paper trailing from her heel, J. emerged from the Gas-N-Go washroom, got in her car and pulled away from the pump, a camera filming her license plate.

55.7 said the radar gun of the first speed trap she drove through, she knew.

53.4 said the second.

102.5FM said the scanner making a survey of the radio stations being listened to in every passing car, no doubt.

Just then, the truck that had been tailgating her roared past and cut her off. "I'll fix your wagon, mister," she muttered, using her cell phone to dial the number stenciled across one cargo door: *How's My Driving? Call 1-800-2-ADVISE.*

A half hour later, she pulled into her reserved parking space, cameras the size of bazookas panning the lot from the roof of the office building. Her efficiency evaluation was coming up, she remembered, walking by them. Surely Mr. W. was compiling data on her for his report—no matter what favors she did him—and she made a mental note to look in on the e-mail of her subordinates—just to make sure they weren't goofing off.

NY officials propose national warehousing of not just the DNA profiles of criminals, but of everyone, beginning with newborns.

View people at work in an office in England (or pick from 62 other countries): www.camscape.com

Grunting?

Modulated by the squishy sound of suck?

Monitor #5 showed J. get out of her car. Monitor #4 showed her walk across the parking lot. Monitor #3 showed her enter the lobby where K., the receptionist, was watching rows of banked monitors. "Have a good meeting, Ms. Smith?" she asked, and J. answered in sync with her gray-scale video puppet, "Very good," hurrying by to an open elevator.

Monitor #1 showed Mr. W., her boss, already in another elevator, unbunching his crotch.

In the privacy of the elevator, J. adjusted her panties. Probably better shadow a few of their cases too, she thought, just to make sure that they weren't padding their time sheets. The elevator opened onto the glass facade of her office suite: *Employer Information Services.*

View what other people are searching for on-line: http://google.com/trends

The door swings open so smartly that at first you believe it: *Welcome To Family Pharmacy*. But then there you are, framed like a criminal on a wanted poster that was a 21" monitor. As he did whenever he transferred buses at this stop, he walked quickly to the liquor department. He grabbed a bottle of gin, stepped to the blind side of the cameras, took a deep draw, then recapped the bottle and put it back on the shelf

In the ceiling mirrors she could see a bald spot on the back of his head, shiny with sweat....

06:12:17:23:59

Melons.

Rendered in the grays of black-and-white surveillance, the Family Pharmacy cashier looked older than the nineteen years recorded in her file, the angle of the ceiling-cam exaggerating her cleavage.

"Rigggggght—now!" Luke pushed the pause button.

Freeze-frame held the cashier's arm midway between the till and the apron of her

Family Pharmacy smock. Using his laptop, Luke ran the history generated by her cash register one more time, and one more time the software alarm that had alerted him to her in the first place went off. Time and date stamps on both video and receipt log confirmed the aberration: she'd rung up $13.13. Family Pharmacy didn't sell anything for $13.13. Even so, even though she'd rung up $13.13 three times that day, he still might have passed over it as an honest mistake if she hadn't done that thing a lot of the guilty did in the videos he made: as the tape continued to play, she glanced up at the camera, even though it was impossible for her to know a camera was there.

Guilt. Melons. Guilt. $13.13.

He bit his knuckle; six billion people on earth and everyone but him had some reaction to being watched:

Store 02830: Embarrassment:

The teenage girl's giggles dampened into tight-lipped silence as she realized Luke really wasn't going to let her go until she emptied her purse. Her face went scarlet as she did so, a home pregnancy test tumbling out.

Store 03033: Anger:

"Are you calling me a thief?"

In answer, Luke laid out the employee time sheets that had been short-changed in order to make the store look more profitable. The shift manager suddenly lunged at him from across the table.

What was his problem?

Say YES! to Caller I.D. and see who's calling before you pick up the phone!

"Hey, the Candy Man's here." The pharmacy technician stepped off the bus and into the grip of four Kings. From behind, one tore his backpack from his shoulders. "You're late, Candy Man." They shook out homework, textbooks and smock....When the Ritalin he'd pilfered from work also spilled onto the sidewalk, they dove on it as if a piñata had burst. Fighting each other, they stuffed the pills into the folds of the red ski masks they all wore as berets. Then they were off, hooting and bobbing away. "See you next time, Candy Man...."

Slowly, he picked up scuffed papers, books, and his own red ski mask. *Family Pharmacy, Inc.*, said the bronze nametag pinned to his smock. His theft but not theirs would show up in inventory and seeing his face reflected in the dull metal, *Timo Garcia, Pharmacy Technician*, he wondered how he was ever going to cover it up....

E. spread her legs to give the camera a better view....

If five years in the FBI and another four as an investigator for Family Pharmacy had taught Luke anything it was that six billion Homo sapiens eat and shit and react to being watched in so few patterns that it had to be the heritage of some deep-seated animal instinct. Yet here was another case, underlining his own apathy at discovering that he himself was being watched.

...Baby E. coming into the world at http://www.video.google.com/videoplay?docio=-8304491341610181767

He switched off the monitor and its screen went black, reflecting the longing in his face for the cashier's fear. Oh yes, it was fear. Every time she rang up $13.13 she put a hundred dollars in the till. And whenever he caught someone putting extra money in the till, it was because they were actually putting it back—covering up a previous theft after the wee of their suspicions began to swell with the presence of a data double, caught forever in an embarrassing moment like the poor slob on *Real Cops*, hauled out onto the front lawn in his underwear, over and over, the cops wrestling down his buttocky girth in the forever of rerun syndication—just because he'd had the bad luck of being drunk enough to fight back on the night cameras were out cruising with cops, looking for just such a spectacle.

So why was the only bump in his night the fact that he didn't care someone was spying on him?

He closed his eyes to see the hippie's expressionless face watching him exercise naked. If only he could hate that face. If only he could summon embarrassment. Or shame or violation or….

Nothing.

Back in the FBI, there were shrinks for agents who had burned out. Who had dealt with so many lying punks that they couldn't see anything but deceit, even in the mirror…. Had something similar happened to him?

> The video showed the employee check the hallway, then turn back into the lunchroom and piss in its coffee pot.

It wasn't like he never gave a damn whether he was watching or being watched. When he'd first jumped companies, he'd actually felt cheezy using all his high-powered government training to expose the criminal nature of stock boys, setting up cameras in washrooms and lunchrooms to do so…. Now he knew better than even portrait artists that when a person looks in a mirror, the 'life sized' reflection they see is only half as big as their actual face. But anymore, he couldn't even pretend it mattered.

Store 03484: Denial:
"That's not me." In slo-mo, the tape showed the pharmacist forging a prescription for himself.
"I swear to God, that's not me."

The bus-driver applicant slid open a tiny slot in the wall of a dim, pocket washroom and was shocked to find an expansive lab on the other side, bright with fluorescent lighting. White-coated technicians bustled about. "Thank you," one said as a command, sitting right there, hand out for his urine sample. Humbly, as if in a confessional, he passed her the Dixie cup.

The bus lurched and F., juggling a gallon of house paint, collapsed into the nearest seat to keep the paper grocery bags he also held from bursting. A chick dressed in the uniform of a museum guard giggled. She held one of those bags with handles—a plastic bag from Family Pharmacy that would still be choking the earth a thousand years after the paper ones he used had decomposed. Go ahead and laugh, jerk, F. thought. Plastic bags—just so she could get her deodorant and whatever other shit she had in there home a little easier.

Was that a gun sticking out?

The driver's eyes switched to them for a moment, filling the big mirror above the windshield—the mirror used to watch passengers, not traffic.

"Well, where are they?" Luke sighed, going behind the camera counter in Store 02834.

"Right here." The photo-counter guy pulled out one of the yellow envelopes used to return photos to customers. Usually, when an employee reported that a customer had turned in kiddie porn or other illegal pictures for processing, they turned out to be just naked baby pictures. Or naked husband and wife pictures. Or naked boyfriend or girlfriend pictures—sometimes screwing—but always a waste of time. Still, he had to check out every report because the company was worried about lawsuits.

The first ones she showed him were just what he'd expected: blurry photos of naked bodies, shot from the ceiling, a balding guy puffing away on top of a young girl, loose hair obscuring her face, contorted by laughter. Or was it a grimace? He shrugged. But the photo-counter guy said, "There's more." He shuffled through the birthday snapshots of another customer until he found a photo of a teenager wearing a red ski mask and pointing a gun at passengers on a bus. A Smith & Wesson 9mm semi-automatic, from the looks of it.

"See, I told you."

"Yeah, I'll check with the police to see if there's been any car-jackings lately. Sometimes punks like to reenact their crimes for their friends. You have the customer's address?"

As T. slept, his mother crept into his room. His book bag and Family Pharmacy smock hung on the door—such promise—and as she brought her shears near his neck she grieved for the rumors Raul had told her about gangs and her son. Last week she had even found a gun hidden in his underwear drawer and she crossed herself—how complicated the world had grown. Her mother would have simply taken a few of her son's hairs to a *curandera*, but she....

She snipped off the hairs she needed for a home DNA test. If he had a drug problem, she had to find out—before his father did and beat him for the overtime, for the tons of flock, even, that he had heisted from the paper factory he slaved in to pay the boy's tuition.

As T. slept, his father crept into his room. Why couldn't he just let sleeping dogs lie? he wondered, standing over the boy's snoring form. T. was in college—to be a doctor. Had a good job, a girlfriend.... Then he remembered the boy's sneaking mother. Neighbors gossiping. She and Raul, her old flame, still whispering together about?— What? *Hijo de mi esposa es suya,* went the saying, *pero mijo?—quien sabe.* With a Q-Tip, he swabbed up drool from T.'s mouth for the home DNA test that would confirm whether or not they really were father and son.

Name:_____

Call 1-800-DNA-TYPE

The world conspires to make you conform, F. thought, wishing he still had the hemp bag one of the Mexicans at his old job had given him. Weary from riding the bus from job application to application, he clutched the plastic bag that held his paintbrushes and rollers. The hardware store didn't even offer paper bags and the plastic ones they did have gave off a sickening petroleum smell. The bus lurched—new man at the wheel—the smell of the bags and the smell of the bus beginning to make him nauseous. He closed his eyes against the motion. Tried to sleep, tried to imagine himself in one of the jobs he'd applied for that day. But his mind turned as it always did before sleep to his last day at Williams Paper Products. He'd been running the machine that ground up mis-made tissues and Kotexes and turned them into Christmas tree flock when the employees' toilet backed up—again. Making sure his supervisor was at the far end of the plant, he'd slipped into the lunchroom and called OSHA to report it. As he'd done the week before. And the week before that. And had been doing since a heart attack put Old Man Williams in the hospital and put the plant in the hands of William Jr., the balding yuppie son who refused to do anything about the toilet.

> Net Detective: the easy way to find out anything about anybody: www.net-detective.net

The bus lurched. As it groaned along, the stench of the clogged toilet seemed to waft to F., the one employee john just off the dirty little closet that served as a lunchroom. It wasn't the stench so much that had put him on a crusade. It was—dare he use the anachronism?—being treated like a serf, William Jr. with his Armani suits and art collection, and brass and paneled office where he didn't have to breath the dust of ground-up Kotexes. Where he didn't have a hole to shit in, ten minutes in the morning, a half hour at lunch, and ten in the afternoon to do so....Then Junior fired him—for taking home a pound of flocking for his own tree—Everyone did *that!*—convincing F. that Junior had somehow found out he was the one who kept reporting them to OSHA. But how? Were the phones tapped? It wouldn't surprise him. The fuckers would jam a telescope up your ass if they thought they could make a dime by examining what you had for lunch. Yet whenever he tried to pin down the moment he was seen, his mind went spinning out of control, the question too big to handle, like thinking about God or Infinity—

The bus lurched.

Is someone barfing?—that fucking hippie in the back of the bus!

"Hey," yelled the chick in a museum uniform, "don't do that shit in here! Hang your head out a window!"

The bus driver's eyes scowled in his mirror.

"Don't worry man, I got a bag," the dude said, holding up a plastic bag, pendulous with vomit.

> You are on a video camera an average of 10 times a day. Are you dressed for it?
> —Kenneth Cole Clothing & Accessories, Fall Catalog.

"You see the vomit in that bag?" one black woman told another. "He ain't foolin' me. That was *gin* vomit. There weren't no food in there. Nu-uh, not one single chunk."

The window across the courtyard remained empty as Luke uncoiled his jump rope. He turned on the TV for the noise. Slowly, he unbuttoned his shirt. He dropped his pants. The window across the courtyard remained empty. He stepped out of his BVDs and the breeze hit his pecker. Should he close his blinds? The window across the courtyard remained empty. He pulled on gym socks and laced up gym shoes. Already he'd broken a sweat and if he closed the blinds—

Suddenly—a flash of movement—

The hippie appeared in the window.

Not wanting to tip off that he knew he was being watched, Luke began to jump, telling himself that he was simply willing to pay the price for the fresh air. Yeah, everything had a price.

After work tonight, instead of putting up with drunks on the bus, maybe she'd ask him for a ride home.

Candy Man Special: pink Tranxene t-tabs, capsules of Darvocet, Seconal.... She chugged a Vicodin to iron herself out. She had to get it together, especially the giggles. The last time she babysat, Mr. W. had looked at her kind of weird—suspicious-like....

The next night, the hippie was already there when Luke got home. He had pulled a recliner up to the window and was sitting in it, hands clasped behind his head. Watching. Waiting for the show to begin.

I call on NASA to build a satellite that would provide continuous, live images of earth from space....
　　　—Vice President Al Gore

Compared to the taut college boyfriends she'd had, his body was surprisingly soft. She squeezed her knees together to see how far she could make them sink in, the effort gritting her teeth in the mirrors above....

What a hotel! He wouldn't have never brought her here if it weren't so close to his father's hospital that he could visit afterwards. But the mirrors! Mirrors on the walls, mirrors on the ceiling, a slight convexity making him look thinner in them, younger. Even with her. Didn't the size of his meat-injection grit her teeth!

Plus the walls were thin enough to hear through.

W. got up off his knees.
　　He closed the cabinet to hide the video camera he'd bought to spy on the baby-sitter.
　　Odd enough that she showed up last time in her museum-guard's uniform—as if she'd forgotten to change—but when he pointed it out to her, she couldn't stop giggling. At first he'd hesitated about spying on her in his home. But it was her place

of employment, after all. And on the coffee table was a baby monitor, and through its transistorized speaker came the sucking sound the baby made whenever it lay in innocent sleep and if the sitter was doing dope he'd fire her—as quick as he'd fired that fuckup at work.

Unless.…W. felt a stirring in his groin over the thought that he could do her right there on the couch. Right in front of the camera as the baby slept.… It's me or the narcs, baby!

"You sly fox," he chuckled, sitting down with the warranty card of the new camera. Name:_____. As he waited for the sitter to show, he began to fill it out, warmed by how slick he'd already been at work, comparing the minute-by-minute operation log of the paper-grinders to the log of the pay phone in the employee lunchroom. Click-clack, just like that the trap snapped and he'd bagged the fuckup who'd been stealing flock to clog the toilet in the employee's break room.

Own a computer? Skis?… The list of questions was longer than a loan application. Everything is more complicated these days, he sighed, continuing. Between work and home, he had six places to check for messages.… *Birthdays of Children:* _____. Now why did they need to know that? For a moment he considered leaving the line blank. But if he didn't tell them everything they wanted to know, couldn't they void his warranty? *Tiffany*, he wrote in, *Age 10 Months.*

White House Debriefing, 1806: Upon completing the Lewis and Clark Expedition, the 19th century equivalent of landing a man on the moon, Lewis met President Jefferson to report on all they had discovered; there were no tape recorders, of course, and since neither man bothered to write about the meeting, nothing is known about what was said.

White House Debriefing, 1998: Monica Lewinsky: Can I be Assistant to the President for Blow Jobs? President William Jefferson Clinton: I'd like that. *—The New York Times and 1,273 other newspapers world wide, not including Internet coverage.*

1826: President Thomas Jefferson sighed a dying breath, comforted by his life of public service, monumental enough to warrant carving a mountain into a likeness of his face even though his private life… Well, as he'd said about secrets when Lewis confessed his own improprieties with Shoshone squaws, that's what graves were for.…

"Mr. W., could I have a ride home tonight?"

You sly old cock master.….

1998: DNA testing reveals that President Thomas Jefferson fathered children by his slave Sally Hemings.

Back in the FBI, Luke had had teams to help him shadow suspects. One team would follow the rabbit while two others traveled up parallel streets. That way, if the rabbit turned, one of the other teams could pick him up without arousing suspicion and the teams would leapfrog each other, taking turns being the shadow, or traveling a parallel route, waiting for the rabbit to turn their way.

Pouring over the drug inventory for Family Pharmacy, Luke felt an adrenaline rush similar to the one's he'd get on those hunts. Did you want to know which cashier worked slowest? It was all right there in the volume-against-time summary report. Were you more interested in which pharmacist filled the most Xanax prescriptions? Or who had last touch? Again, the numbers told the tale. No matter which way a rabbit dodged, their shadow would turn up in another parallel data stream.

ABERRATION REPORTS
Region 0008   District 0389
Scoring Type: All Cashiers

NUMBER	SCORE	TITLE
Report 1	3	Cash Return/Sales
Report 2	3	Avg. Check Returns
Report 3	4	Returns to Same Acct
Report 4	3	Exchanges
Report 5	3	Post Voids/% Sales
Report 6	3	Cash Post Voids/Sale
Report 7	4	Post Voids/No Sales
Report 8	3	Post Voids/5 Trans.A
Report 9	4	Voids Employee Purch
Report 10	4	Transact. Voids
Report 11	3	Line Item Voids
Report 12	4	Price Modifications
Report 13	4	Sales Not Scanned
Report 14	3	% Sales Keyed
Report 15	4	% Credit Card Scan
Report 16	3	Gift Certificates
Report 17	4	Payouts
Report 18	2	No Sale Transactions
Report 19	2	Sign Off Transaction
Report 20	-	Cashier Profile

Then suddenly the trail went cold. For weeks he'd been tracking cashier 00000501, Maria Martinez, following the money, a pattern beginning to emerge: often, a woman in some kind of usher's uniform would show up at her register with a prescription she'd gotten filled in pharmacy. But the pharmacy inventories showed no aberration.

Then just when he asked the store manager to rotate the schedule to see if he could get any flags to pop by letting the data play out through a new configuration, it stopped.

Had he been spotted?

Back in the FBI, the only rabbit they ever lost was that spy for Airbus. Not shackled to the politics of purchasing committees, the rabbit's corporate-backed counter surveillance team had used the latest in de-encrypting scanners to trump their counter-counter-surveillance, outfitted with an old administration's government issue, and the first thing that occurred to Luke now was that he had stumbled onto a bigger, more sophisticated operation than one nineteen-year-old cashier.

ACTIVITY ABERRATION SCORES

STORE	CASHIER	SCORE
02830	00000501	35%*
02798	00000402	22%
03489	00000470	20%
04902	00000312	20%
03142	00000300	19%
02786	00000201	17%
03065	00000233	16%
03153	00000550	16%
03098	00000781	16%
03241	00000250	15%
02799	00000342	14%
02952	00000215	14%
03065	00000482	14%
03486	00000550	14%
02792	00000874	14%
02830	00000208	14%
02931	00000340	13%
03045	00000203	12%
02076	00000339	12%
02789	00000348	11%

In

Out

Huffing

Puffing loose hair from her face, her camera aimed at
the mirrored ceiling. Pinned to the mattress by his weight, she squirmed for leverage,
grimacing with the effort. If only she could roll him to the bottom, the picture would
be of her bare ass and his face, and she'd have all the evidence his wife would ever need.
Then the two of them would be free. Free forever....

Withdrawal.

Withdrawal.

Withdrawal.

J. sifted the ATM data and saw by the locations of his withdrawals where William
Williams Jr. had traveled in Europe last summer. Lots of lunches at art museums. This
month he'd been spending a lot of time at Memorial Hospital. And the Paradise Hotel.

As she worked, merging data bases, her mind wandered back to a marketing class
she'd had as a sophomore. Sales of televisions had been originally stunted, they'd
learned, because people were afraid that the TVs could be used to watch them. The class
had snickered at that naïveté. But she now smiled at their own, the bit stream that came
back from William Williams's digital TV allowing her to create a pointillist portrait of
him out of what, how and when he watched, the bookmarks in his silicon memory—
no porn, no Jesus channels, lots of golf—a gold mine of demographic information, his
activity while surfing detailed enough to reconstruct even the movement of his eyes.

As a sophomore, such nakedness would have made her blush. But his home was her
client's store, after all, at least while he was logged on, and she now understood that she
was only helping him get the products he wanted. And anyway, no one could copyright
their own name so what did he lose if she sold it to others? A double-click on *Daughter
Tiffany* and the infant's file opened up, already two screens long.

1951— The Miracle of Television: Viewers from coast to coast are amazed at the God's-
eye view offered by the first national broadcast—*See It Now*—bringing together on
one screen both the Atlantic and Pacific Oceans. Live!

Before Luke could turn on the lights in his own apartment, he saw that the
apartment across the courtyard was lit up unusually bright. In darkness, he went to his
window, not believing—

The window across the way had been stripped bare.

The man had moved out. Even the walls were bare. Luke couldn't remember what had hung on them, but there had been something, Indian dream catchers, family portraits, something other than the bare wall he could now see through the curtainless window.

Then the man appeared.

Paint roller in one hand, he was bending and straightening, painting the wall, flood lights in the emptied room making the swatches of red paint he laid down brilliant.

And he was naked.

1999— A God's Eye View: Intervention Specialists simultaneously monitor from a single "command center" hundreds of office cleaning crews, stock rooms, cashiers, customers, ticket booths, clerks, alleys and pedestrians scattered from coast to coast. Westec, *We're Automating Management*. 888-947-8110 (www.westecnow.com)

01010101010010101010101111010110111111001101010101011111001010101
010.... UPC codes streamed through bundled wires, transforming the slow procession of granola, goat cheese and other groceries on the conveyor belt into multiple packets of information, their prices adding as on an abacus run at the speed of light, generating a personalized coupon for F., collating the purchases into a profile of F., reporting F.'s name back to a cat-food manufacturer, adding F.'s name to a mailing list for the health conscious—but then, as cupcakes broke the web of laser beams, taking it off again—setting a marker that would also drop from inventory F.'s organic apples for being too far off the great bulge in the bell curve of volume.

National Identity Card, she snickered, Thy name is VISA....

"I'd like to report that my sex is being harassed."

Luke had gotten so used to seeing cashier 00000501 as a collection of data that he had to work to get over the disorientation of seeing her in the flesh. Profoundly alive. Eyes shining, hair a black no monitor could match, flesh tones without raster. A work of Nature. Each breast a ripe pear, between which a tiny gold man was wrecked, crucified from a neck that had been caressed by?—lightly brushing hair, and hair heavy with a shower's wetness. Shoulders, tummy, knees: bone and flesh bearing the memory of exhaustion, and also goose-bumped suspense, her legs a wonder of utility and sensuousness. In black nylons. And a miniskirt, Ace-bandage tight, that made the Family Pharmacy smock she also wore into the habit of a corporate nunnery.

"Tell me about it," he said, switching on a tape recorder under his desk, and she began what was obviously a prepared speech about David White, the store manager: how he kept wanting to have sex with her, how he had started by telling her that she had nice melons, that before he was married, the girls used to call him The White Lightening Rod, and Davie Cracklick. In his office, he went weepy because his wife didn't appreciate him. He began calling her at home, telling her he could take care of her—in every way. In the break room he tempted her with promotions. Then he threatened to fire her, insisting that it was her choice and he kept threatening until finally she did it.

"You had sex with him?" Something didn't sound right.

She began a dry cry. "Where else would I find a job with benefits?" Luke sat silent, an image of the doughy middle-aged manager and the young girl.... Then from nowhere, she continued, "Timo, my boyfriend is a technician in pharmacy. He's not a thief. He's just.... He's going to college. He wants to be a doctor but a gang in his neighborhood, they make him steal for them. Every week he got to pay their toll to get home. When the manager found out, he said he'd have Timo arrested and kicked out of school if I didn't have sex with him. So I did. But it wasn't enough. I had to keep doing it or he'd tell Timo. Then, he wants a piece of the drug money too. So he sets it up so that Timo fills the "prescriptions" of customers that Mr. W. sends him; I ring them up and he makes sure the records keep everyone clean."

"You were scrubbing the books right at the register?"

"It's all that motherfucker's fault. He made us do everything."

Luke leaned back, trying to figure out what didn't sound right. When he couldn't, he asked, "Will you wear a wire?"

Every night now, he skipped rope naked, lights on, while the hippie painted naked, lights also on.

Static, then the wet suck of sex....

He massaged his prick, one of the *Victoria's Secret* catalogs he regularly received open to buttercup panties. It had begun with the thrill of saying "buttercup panties" to the female operators who took orders. But then during one of these dates, he discovered that he could use the cordless phone to eavesdrop on neighbors. Then he got a scanner so he could zero in on active cell phones. Now he sat below the antenna he had strung across the ceiling of his living room to improve reception of the neighbor—which one was it?—who was into phone sex every Thursday at eight.

But this!— Moans became squishing, crosstalk, multiple connections—he sealed his ear to the receiver—the sucking continuing even as a fourth voice moaned, "O Willie, do me!"—

W. hated making love with the baby monitor turned on, the sucking transmitted by the baby in the next room a Viagra antidote. He suddenly had a horrible thought: Was the Candy Man selling him placebos?

Was that a death rattle? W. leaned in between the wires and bio-sensors that cocooned the hospital bed his father lay dying on, a moist suck coming from the tube in his throat.

Why couldn't he get organic apples from the store any longer? F. wondered.

For quality control and training purposes, your call may be recorded.

How did my life become so murky, T. thought, breathing so heavily he sounded like that balding manager. Below, his girlfriend kept working, kissing and licking even though he just knew he couldn't do it—not with that radio turned on.

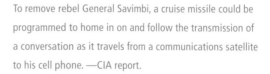

To remove rebel General Savimbi, a cruise missile could be programmed to home in on and follow the transmission of a conversation as it travels from a communications satellite to his cell phone. —CIA report.

Wearing a wire was pure theater, Luke knew. The tapes he made would never stand up in court. But he wasn't a cop so didn't have to worry about that and employees were still somehow more moved by photos and other low-res cloud formations of their crimes than the hard-edged portraits that could be composed from ones and zeros.

He turned back to the fine-grained profiling program running on his laptop, Timo's life so crystalline in it that it was a thing of beauty.

J. thumbed through *Look*, glancing up from time to time at the alphanumerics filling her screen with the herky-jerky rhythm of a human typist. The cursor slid Ouija-board smooth to a new field, the profiler that she was monitoring using it in an office two floors down to compile data on a job applicant, one Fred C. Johnson, for Ever Ready Security. Along the bottom of the screen, a counter tracked keystrokes per minute as the woman applied various demographic slucers, massaging the data on 300,000 names. Fred's profile was blurry due to a scarcity of data, which seemed odd these days until M. called up his college files and saw that he had majored in being poor: i.e., philosophy. She skimmed a long list of books that he had paid fines on only after the college turned his account over to a collection agency. Weird stuff from ex-commie countries—Dostoyevsky, Kafka—countries that had recently become less secret but were still iffy. What was he applying for? She scrolled up to *Position: Night Watchman.* Did their warehouses ever store explosives?

1826—James Fenimore Cooper publishes *The Last of the Mohicans* under the name "A Gentleman from New York" because it would have been vulgar for his family's name to appear in the news.

Luke skipped rope faster, adrenaline kicking in—Tomorrow it would all go down, manager, cashier, pharmacy technician. He'd even coordinated the police so they could grab their most regular customer—that girl in the video who was always dressed like an usher.

1996—Jenny Ringly, a junior at Dickenson College in Pennsylvania, becomes the first to put her life online by setting up the *Jenny-Cam*, a camera that allows anyone to see into her dorm room 24 hours a day, whether she is doing homework, making out, not there, talking on the phone, taking a shower....

Catalogs for pre-assembled log-cabins.

The Utne Reader.... The slick catalogs that had begun to arrive since F. started using his charge card avalanched into his lap when he sat down at the kitchen table. A new John Denver CD played instead of real folk music; Robert Redford's Navaho Dream Catcher hung from the ceiling instead of the *Ojo de Dios* made by the wife of that Mexican at his old job—to watch over their machines, he recalled wistfully. When he'd been fired, Timo Sr. had given it to him. *Para suerte.* But it now lay where he had tossed it when he'd begun to paint, its shabby yarn sticking out from under slick brochures for organically-fed steaks.

He cradled his head. What a burlesque of himself he'd become, running up debt for junk instead of living off his charge card, as he had planned, to read. To write a little poetry. To take up the didjeridu, even painting. The mural he'd begun on a wall of his living room wasn't even half finished: a cartoon landscape peopled by thousands of stick figures: cave dwellers and soccer teams wearing jet packs. Dervishes ascending into heaven. He'd wanted to create the mother of all landscapes. Of canyon vistas, but also of NASA-eye views of earth, travel posters to Holland, TV footage of suburban sprawl, Jackson Pollock's abstract *Summertime*.... So he'd rendered the sky as a nude woman, one breast the sun. The other breast a sun too. But between fell the shadow, and his Ur-landscape captured the essential no better than the words "bow wow" mirrored the sorrow of a dog. Which the Turks pronounce "how how." The Jews "huf huf." The Danish "vow vow." The French "wah wah." The Dutch "woof woof." The Italians "bow bow." The Thai "hong hong." The Koreans "mong mong." The Chinese "wang wang." The Swahili "wow wow...."

> *The unexamined life is not worth living.* —Socrates, and www.homecams.com, the site that lets you see inside 1,024 private homes....

Then he'd run out of paint. And he didn't dare risk maxing out his card for more.

He picked up the classifieds again. How could he have gotten so far from the one thing he learned in college?—That the only honest man is a naked man. When a daily reminder?—

Looking out the window, a sickening thought occurred to him. Had he simply misread the dude across the courtyard as well? For weeks now, he'd been assuming that the naked rope jumping was an act of philosophy by an honest man, unafraid to exercise nude in the free air—like the ancient Athenians. But was it more base than that? Was it possible, even, that the dude was just coming on to him? He moved back into a shadow. Gratefully, there was no one across the courtyard now and he collapsed into his recliner to think.

> 1999: A multinational effort (code named Echelon) attempts to monitor all phone, fax and e-mail transmissions worldwide and sort them by keyword and voice print.

He blew a mournful note from his didjeridu. To be or not to be.... Hard to believe, what with the way everyone went around parading their thinks, that there once was no such thing as a soliloquy, that Shakespeare had to invent it, and F. longed for the solitude to think soliloquy thoughts instead of worrying about the rent.

Bus Drivers Wanted...

Again, the want ads offered no relief.

Ready-Men Now Hiring. No Experience Necessary....

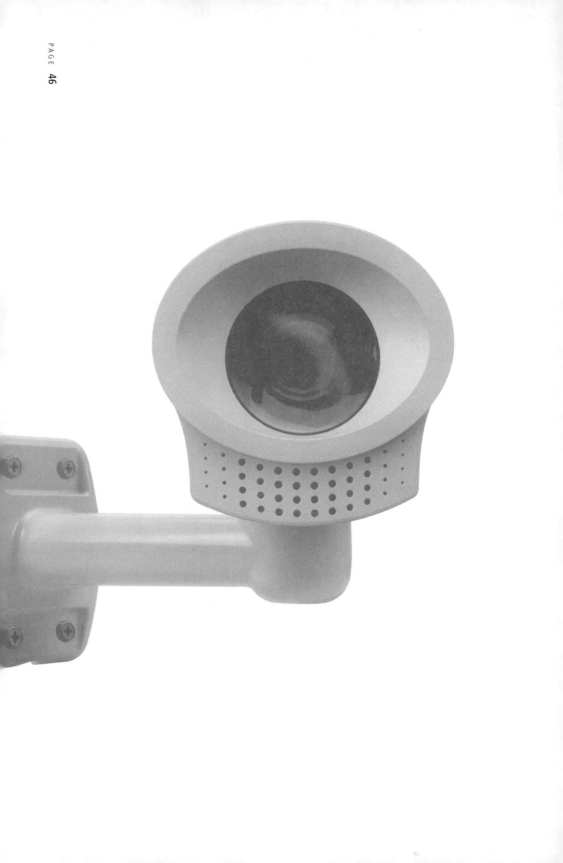

If only he could find a dream job like he'd had as a philosophy student. Working in the bowels of an all-night bowling alley, he'd been able to live like a hermit, reading, and reading, *Don Quixote*, Orwell, Russian novels—*The Overcoat*, Kafka—the only time he'd had to do anything was when one of the automatic pin setters got stuck. And even then he could usually fix it by rolling a ball down the gutter....

A classified suddenly grabbed F. by the short hairs. It was so obvious, he couldn't believe he hadn't thought of it before:

Wanted: Night watchman for midnight shift in warehouse....

...iffy reading habits; iffy credit; complaints to OSHA; fired for stealing, she wouldn't even have to tie into the data banks of urine analysis for this one.... Sure enough, the profiler that J. was shadowing typed, *Employer Information Services recommends that the candidate NOT be hired for the position of Warehouse Security Guard because he distinctly matches the following profile: Malcontent.*

But instead of going on to the next case, she milked her report for an extra thirty-five minutes.

"Every computer can be a window open to every company in the world."—President Bill Clinton

The Ritalin wearing off, N. looked from the meninas in the painting to the bored expression of another museum guard—"Please, don't touch"—to the coy smiles of the meninas, to the tourists she was watching, to the back of the guard in the next salon, who could see the back of the guard in the next, and that guard seeing the guard after that and so on all around the museum until the guard in the salon behind her could see her back, and sure enough, when she turned around, there he was, looking at her.

The revelation gave her a chill, warning her, for some reason, to not stop by Family Pharmacy today on the way to her baby-sitting gig.

"We're ready to go, Luke," said the undercover narc. "You want us to take along these two as well?"

The cashier and the pharmacy technician cowered on the couch in the manager's office like the two scared kids that they were. Let them sweat a minute, Luke thought. Let them shit a brick. In a squad car outside was the manager—probably still screaming that he had been set up, that the little gold digger had wanted him to leave his wife, and when he wouldn't she said she'd get him. But Luke knew better. He had it on tape.

"I'll take care of them," he said at last and the technician went limp, whispering, "Thank you, thank you…."

"Suit yourself," the narc said. "If you have a change of heart, you know where to find us," and he waved a goodbye salute.

The kid buried his face in his hands but the girl sat upright, blinking back, expectant, as if it could have gone no other way.

Finally alone with them, Luke allowed himself the satisfaction of the moment's taut minimalist logic: bare office, metal office desk, single video monitor on the desk. And the rabbit. Outside, bell-clear skies; inside, clammy palms and the buzz of fluorescent lighting. He took a breath, then began: "There is something that people have that no one can take away. A gang can beat you up, steal your money. But even if they kill you, they can't take away this one thing." He paused for effect. There was none from the girl. "But you can give it away. You can give it away because that one thing is your reputation. Sometimes when we're young it's easy to make a mistake. You might want to do something later in your life, though, like go to med school—"

"I do!" the boy interrupted. "How did you?—" Recognition sobering his features, he turned to his girlfriend. She took his hand—patted it the way an older sister might quiet a child.

"Well," said Luke, "a conviction for stealing drugs would ruin that forever." Looking at the girl now, he continued. "We do what we think is right at the time, but later we see that it's very wrong. An older guy comes along, he takes you to a grand old hotel…." Then dropping a name the manager had sworn by, Luke finished, "Like the Paradise—"

The boy's head snapped toward his girlfriend. "You never went to the Paradise," he said, some bigger story flashing between them.

"Yeah," the girl protested, following another's lead for the first time, that high-strung tone that said, You ain't got nuthin' on me, copper, creeping into her voice.

For her benefit, Luke arched an eyebrow as if she'd just claimed that the earth was flat. He wanted to tell her of corpses, back in the FBI, with bruises on the backs of their hands that told how they had given their last trying to shield a face from blows; he wanted to tell her how even a field mouse bends the grass; how a person walking down a sidewalk leaves infrared hot spots; how e-mail could be recovered from a hard-drive that had been totally erased….

Instead, he began a slow show of stacking blank videocassettes on the desk, as he did whenever he didn't have any evidence. Often, just the sight of cassettes was enough to make the guilty ones confess—the ones, at least, who were basically good.

Or at least still had a conscience, even if in a way, those tapes were their conscience.

As he suspected, the girl was basically a good kid. She fell silent when he switched on the monitor and remained mute as a saint, eyes transfixed in its blue glow. "There's nothing you can do that doesn't leave a trace of some kind," Luke continued, "and the memory of data banks is long, unforgiving, and worldwide. Wherever you go, whatever you do, no matter what you say, your digital shadow will always be there and believe me, not even a philosopher can jump over his—or her—own shadow."

Turning away from his girlfriend, the boy mumbled, "I guess that makes us all deep thinkers."

Shadows long in a late summer sun, Luke practically skipped home, happy over how well everything had gone. True, the buyer, the usher, didn't show, but she was just a lagniappe anyway.

A wind shivered the trees that lined his street and he buttoned his collar. A futile gesture. But that was okay. A time for all seasons, autumn coming so gradually, if relentlessly, that a lot of people wouldn't even notice until some trees were bare.

As he entered the courtyard of his building, a new surveillance camera stared down at him and he couldn't help but smile. One of the reasons his ex had left him was because he kept bringing the office home. But she would have been proud of the way he gave those two kids a second chance today, letting them resign.

Find out the location of this story's author by going to the Global Positioning Homepage (www.stevetomasula.com)

Like the eyes in a painting, the gaze of the camera seemed to follow him as he came up the walk. It was installed because there'd been a rape in the courtyard a few months back, he knew, and it made him wonder why he had been so uptight because he didn't care that he was being watched. Why had his ex been so uptight about him not being able to shut off his watching others? After all, this place, this courtyard, was his home too, wasn't it?

The micro lines of the camera looked absolutely millennial against the ponderous Victorian limestone and ironwork of the rest of the building. A Hitachi C-U 24X. The same kind of camera that was used outside banks, and over the drive-up lanes of Taco Bells, aimed at customers as they ordered their burritos; it had a wider field of vision than the cameras they used in Family Pharmacy, mounted so that a customer's video double was the first thing that greeted him or her as they entered—unlike the dummy cameras that simply gave the appearance of watching. Its optics were coated—when

the courtyard was bare in winter, the brightness of snow wouldn't white everything out; with 0.3 lux illumination, its circuitry would be hot enough to see by the sodium-vapor lights that flooded the courtyard at night; its weather-proof housing would allow it to operate in rain or summer's heat as reliably as those indoor cousins that watched people shop in the weatherless weather of malls; or work in factories, or play in parks, in hospitals...newborn infants or those dying under observation....

Anyway, Luke thought, only a schizo could be one person at work and another at home.

Then he was before the doorway that led to his neighbor's apartment.

While looking up at the camera, he had taken the path that led to the apartments directly across from his own. Realizing that he was before his neighbor's vestibule, an urge came over him to get the guy's name from his mailbox....Why hadn't he done it before?

He pulled open the door, heavy with leaded glass, and a motion sensor switched on a light inside the vestibule. Rows of locked mailboxes gleamed, burnished by generations of fingers. A matrix in brick and brass. Third floor, middle apartment.... A finger push and the doorbell would ring upstairs. Should he introduce himself? In a way, Luke realized, he had his neighbor to thank for making him see that he wasn't nuts. Remembering how preoccupied he'd been with seeing a shrink was like remembering another person: a nail-biter who had pined to regress to a life behind closed doors even though closed doors had become as quaint as the skirts Victorians once used to hide the legs of chairs.

It wasn't that there was something sneaky about what he did; rather everyone just did what they did in front of his eyes, in front of everyone's eyes. May as well curse the sun for making all grass grow.

Footfalls suddenly pounded down the steps; the inner door opened and a man burst into the vestibule. *The* man—the watcher, bowling shirt, long hair pulled back out of his eyes. In that instant of recognition, Luke saw in those eyes that he had also been recognized and that the man had also seen how wrong it was for them to be standing face-to-face. How doing so undermined...whatever it was that they shared—or at least—

Awkwardly, Luke stepped aside to let the man get his mail: high-gloss catalogs and a computer-generated letter that Luke couldn't help but notice—a pay stub?—from **Ever-Ready Watchmen**. Was the guy in the same biz? Was that why they both understood that seeing the other naked deserved no more notice than yesterday's weather? He wanted to say something, but everything that came to mind was too forced and before he thought to ask about the mural, the guy mumbled "Excuse me," and was bounding back up the stairs. Skinny, hairy legs, flip-flops flipping....

Luke stood there a long time. If he turned to the names on those boxes, he realized, it would be harder to go home to his workout. And yet how could he not be curious about the man who watched him exercise naked? He drummed his fingers on the heavy outer door. Courtyard before, mailboxes behind. Was it just as well?

The building he stood in with its dark oak moldings, its doors opening onto doors, was built in another century. It was only much later, and gradually, that tenants had lost their taste for heavy drapery. That the privacy hedges had been cropped to improve visibility from the street. That the night of the courtyard had been turned into halogen day....

He pushed into the open air. From where he stood he could see that the shades were up in not just his apartment, but in lots of apartments. A wall of windows. Through them he could hear a mournful, aboriginal *wa-waaa*—someone playing a didjeridu?—then a man and woman having an argument. Or was it that poor slob on the *Real Cops Show?* The flicker of two or three other TVs played more momentous moments, no doubt: ex-commies pouring onto the techno-color side of the Berlin Wall. And smaller moments: secrets of incest blooming across the electronic skies of talk shows, masturbators, the overweight, adulterers, the lonely, the angry, the happy, the sad and other plain folks calling in from home, all of them going about their lives while he.... Cured, a shrink might say, if being normal only meant acting like your neighbors, and he took a step toward them. Home. For the first time in months he felt at home.

His shadow rose up to meet him, clinging to each step with a fierce, animal tenacity, though it was now being cast by the light that had switched on automatically as he approached.

THE COLOR OF PAIN AND SUFFERING

To get flesh right, Tomasz used to mix his own on-screen colors: a touch of red to make cheeks ruddy, if the drawing was for the defense, or maybe a tincture of gangrenous green, if the illustration was for the prosecution, what was right for the prosecution being wrong for ruddy, and visa-versa. Obviously. But no one worked that way anymore. Not at Medical Illustrators, Inc. Instead of the millions of colors that came with the paint program he was using, the company had reduced the palette on his and the other two computers in the studio to a standard set of premixed colors. Then they'd assigned them names like "Bone"; and "Internal Organ"; and "Flesh: 2nd Degree Burn...." As if giving them those names could make it true. As if a burn from a malfunctioning tanning booth was the same as a burn from a Molotov cocktail; as if blood from a hunting accident was the same as blood from a death squad. And to remind himself that blood wasn't just red, Tomasz liked to think through the projects in the old way—or maybe even as that surgeon from America's own civil war who made charcoal drawings of skull fractures, works of 19th century science that were also *memento mori*.

It was getting harder to do so, Tomasz considered, selecting "Right Leg," from a pull-down menu; a cartoon outline of a leg like from an uncolored coloring book appeared on screen. Already he was forgetting some of the old ways while the space he had to continually carve for himself became increasingly diffuse. He selected the airbrush tool, then brought up the pallet and mixed a little "3rd Degree Burn" with "Organ: Internal" to get an orange that could be used to alter the standard set. At least a little. Even if it was so little that it was almost a state of?—

He had another look at the photo he was working from: a young thigh with a gash puckered by suture and skin grafts. His IN box held other photos, x-rays and post-op reports about one bodily trauma or another, each calling for illustrations that would be used in one lawsuit or another, the words, bodies and pictures all somehow blurring together. *Sika* was the name on the deposition he was working. There was no such name as *Sika*, he knew, at least not until its old-world parent had gone through that ethnic cleansing lots of names went through once uprooted, Byzantine consonant combinations streamlined, umlauts abandoned more quickly than wooden shoes. But Tomasz knew. As would anyone who had been there. Sitkovac—it was Bosniak. Unless it had been Sikavica: Croation. But the boy could be Serbian gypsy. Sitoîević. Or Albanian. Albanian Muslim. Or Christian—hundreds had died for less—unless an ancestor had merely married into the name once transplanted here, in which case the boy would be more gypsy than any other. Or at least his name would be.

Only the body didn't lie, even if, according to the company, skin only came in one of three colors—Caucasian, Af.-Am., and Other—and Tomasz smiled at the clucking his *tetke* back in the old country would erupt into if they could see him here in

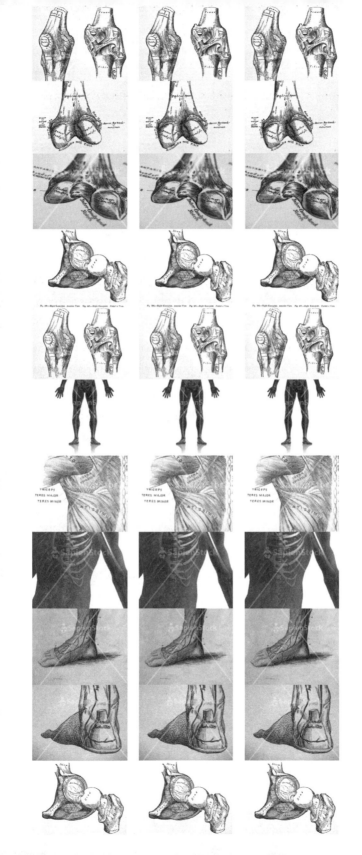

America, sweeping away all of their curses, evil eyes, histories
of revenge and blood feuds with the click of a mouse.
Flesh: Caucasian.

When his family had sent him to Germany—*go!* his *tetke* had
insisted—such a thing would have been incomprehensible to him
as well. Instead of Croatia, where everything mattered, how you
baked your bread, whether you crossed yourself with two fingers
or four or said *sela* as SAYla or SEEla, in Germany it seemed as
though nothing mattered. Except, he learned, some of the things
that seemed to not matter—whether you were Serb or Croatian—
mattered the most—whether any immigrant in Germany would
be given asylum. Contorting his hand to hit the control keys he
needed to paint the leg, his body remembered those German
desks and how after an exhausting day of following the thread
of his Croatian dictionary through the labyrinth of his teachers'
German, he would happily wave *dovidjenia* to classmates,
mistaking their guttural calls for goodbyes till he got home and
his uncle explained through the smoke of his cigarette what was
really meant by the words "go home foreigner." In bed, Tomasz
had wished he could go home—despite the fighting—just click
his ruby slippers and be there like in that American movie. But a
home gutted by shells was nothing like one ruined by a tornado,
they insisted. So evenings were spent in that cramped Hamburg
flat, twisting his tongue to learn the labyrinth while his uncle
smoked for a way to get Tomasz's parents out, and when the
fighting only kept sweeping them before it—*you're deserting us!*
his *tetke* were said to have shrieked—Tomasz knew that whatever
country he found himself in, it would be even harder to escape
the cartoon view.

"Knock, knock."

Tomasz looked up from the aneurysm clamp he was drawing to see Alice standing in the doorway of his cubicle. Short professional hair, arty glasses, petite body in a suit from one of those boutiques where working women got their costumes: Victorian collars for bankers, Bauhaus lines for women, like her, in advertising—with a bicycle cuff on one pant leg. Since she couldn't drive she rode her bike everywhere. "My blonde American girlfriend," he'd explained by e-mail to his mother back in Croatia—though he knew American women like Alice wouldn't want to be thought of that way. Even if he had been seeing her steadily enough to make her his girlfriend. Which he hadn't. Still, his mother, his mother back in a shell-pocked country, worried about him way over here in Chicago—*where everyone has a big house, big car and tommy gun.*

"I'm sorry," he said, "I lost track of time." He really was sorry. Like most Americans, she had very little tolerance for waiting and he could tell she was peeved for having to come inside to find him. But already her face was softening, and he knew she was amused by the way he'd said he was sorry. Monotone. The way he said everything, according to her. She'd told him so the time he'd fallen into a long complaining monologue about a Build Bosnia program that had constructed a highway ramp onto a pasture. When he noticed her grinning at him and asked why, she'd answered by calling his flat delivery of every emotion cute. Cute, just as all the other Slavs she'd met through him, according to her, described every absurdity and outrage in the same even tone.

"Let me back this up and I'll be right with you."

She nodded, smiling patiently—Mr. Monotone, gathering up his horror show.

"Yech," she said, looking at the printout of the boy's leg he had created earlier. "What happened to him?" A Post-it note on the file said Dial Up P&S, office shorthand for Pain and Suffering, so that's what he'd been doing, adding highlights that would make the wound appear to radiate pain, sharpening the edges of each stitch so that they would work on a jury as subliminally as jewel-like coloring and hazy, sfumato paint handling worked on the viewers of Renaissance Madonnas, the most moving paintings of Madonnas, he'd learned in art history, often being portraits of the artist's mistress since only a lover could know what details on canvas would convey the intimate sense of her hair, the warmth of her body....

When he was a teenager—after losing his German visa to
Mittlere Reife—graduation—he and his father had accompanied
his father's sister along with a new water closet back to the flat
she had fled during the war. While putting the flat back in order,
his father had sent him out to buy some *povitca* whereupon
he had been called upon to help a boy who had chased a
baseball—courtesy of US UN troops—onto a field and stepped
on an unexploded bomblette, lying there all that time, maybe
stepped on by dozens of other people or animals. Lucky boy,
they all said later, a small, anti-personnel bomblette, and not
an anti-tank mine. They had used Tomasz's belt as a tourniquet.
When Tomasz's father made him go retrieve it—one of the few
things he had acquired in Germany—he'd been directed to a
room where a doctor was cleaning the dirt and bone fragments
that had been blown up into the stump by the blast. Tomasz
stood in the doorway, held by amazement over what the inside
of a leg looked like. The doctor motioned him closer, and as he
worked, he asked Tomasz many things, his name, his age, his
family's region— At that point Tomasz fell silent, realizing that
the doctor was probably Bosnian. Yet he seemed to be doing
the best he could for the boy who appeared to be Bosniak.
Still, to be safe, Tomasz only mumbled that he'd been away.
"It's good to travel," the doctor had said in a very disinterested
manner. The boy winced, and the way the doctor was only half
listening to the noise of language to help distract his patient,
enduring the ordeal on a minimum of morphine, no doubt. So
he answered his questions, and each answer led to another
question about why he had fled to Hungary, about why he had
left Hungary for Germany, his school there.... Art class was best,
Tomasz told them. The boy bit his sheets and Tomasz felt his
own face grow hot, the stupidity of the words, the irrelevance
of what he did or didn't like in this situation making him squirm

even as he continued: in art, words were not so important so that was the only subject he had done well in.

Washing up afterwards, handing him his own belt to replace the one that had been lost, the doctor asked him, "Have you ever heard of medical illustration?"

The doctor had done a one-year trauma fellowship at the med center of Ohio University. Which had a technical communications department. A church on campus had a sponsorship program. Now, whenever Tomasz had to alter his illustrations to accentuate pain and suffering, he would think of the glossy redness of that boy's leg—the one real wound he had seen outside of a textbook or dead Ohioans in the anatomy lab—splintered at mid-shin, getting into his medical diagrams enough subtle information so that the viewer would wince, at least a little, not enough to know why, just enough to remember what it felt like to touch the point of a needle. Or imagine the needle enter, then exit their own flesh as the doctor pulled the stitch tight. He had to be subtle: the illustrations he drew were supposed to appear as dispassionate as the E-Q-Zs of an optometrist's eye chart, as dryly objective as a tax form, and therefore as authoritative as the Surgeon General. The best of all propaganda.

Judging from the disgusted look on Alice's face, his sleight of hand had worked, and he showed her the x-rays he'd been working from. Displaced scapula. Multiple Lacerations of Flexor/Extensor Tendons. "It's a liability case. A construction company was doing some work at a school and the plaintiff says they didn't mark off the work zone adequately." A photo showed the yellow tape used around construction or crime scenes, broken down by a fallen basketball backboard and pole. "The boy got into it after school

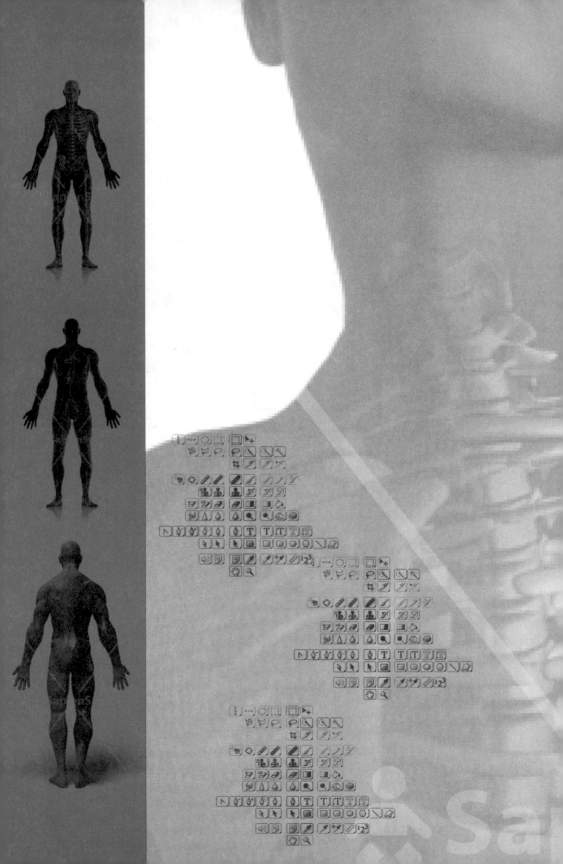

and that's when the backboard fell on him. "Multiple operations, possible nerve damage, rehabilitation, pain and suffering."

Alice stared at the photos with a sickish expression till he took them from her and put them back in their folder. It wasn't so much that Slavs were monotone, he knew, as that Americans were squeamish. And he couldn't help but feel a pang of resentment, at least a little, at her—and himself—for not being used to things like this. For finding it ever harder to imagine boys back in *Bosna i Hercegovina* dreaming to have a normal life like theirs. The boy who had the basketball backdrop fall on him was probably going to get, what? Half a million dollars for his pain and suffering? One million?—while there were so many hobbling around *Bosna i Hercegovina* who..... While he, the son of teachers, had seen none of the fighting at all and escaped even the rebuilding.... It wasn't her fault, or his, that some lives were worth more than others.

"Let's go."

"Ugg, do you have to own that truck today of all days?" she asked as they walked her ten-speed toward his Ford Explorer, white and big as a small elephant in the company lot. The bike rack he'd mounted on its roof since meeting Alice was so far from the ground that it underscored the vehicle's inhuman dimensions. And also his rashness in buying it. After landing his first real job, he'd wandered rows of stereo equipment, then cars, just to amuse himself with ways he might spend his sudden wealth. Then he'd come across the Explorer—Red-White-And-Blue balloons fluttering under car-lot lights—its huge tires, its enormous boxy white body and fenders making it look like one of the UN vehicles that used to awe him and his teenage friends back in Croatia—a gleaming three-ton contrast to the donkey carts and flimsy Yugos his countrymen had produced with their oil-burning, two-stroke economy that couldn't go twelve miles without breaking down, and when a grinning salesman emerged to shake hands—balding like his *Tetka* Josef, and wearing what could have been one of his cheap Soviet suits—he couldn't help but think of his other *tetke* and *ujake* and friends back home imaging him here behind its wheel, blonde American girlfriend by his side. Though he hadn't met Alice yet. Though she wasn't blonde.

She swung her bike up above her head, holding it there like an Olympic weightlifter. Elbows locked, she stepped up onto the Explorer's running board. The bike had an ultralight frame, so holding it like that wasn't difficult; it was the height of the SUV's roof that inspired this maneuver, and she had to stretch on the tips of her toes to lift the bike the last few inches into the rack where it snapped into place, its wheels languidly turning air, spokes catching the light.

He got into the driver's seat; a turn of the key and the massive engine roared to life, the voice of a news commentator surging from the radio. Alice climbed up into the passenger's seat, smoothing her linen pants. "You really would look good in something snappier," she said, switching the radio to one of

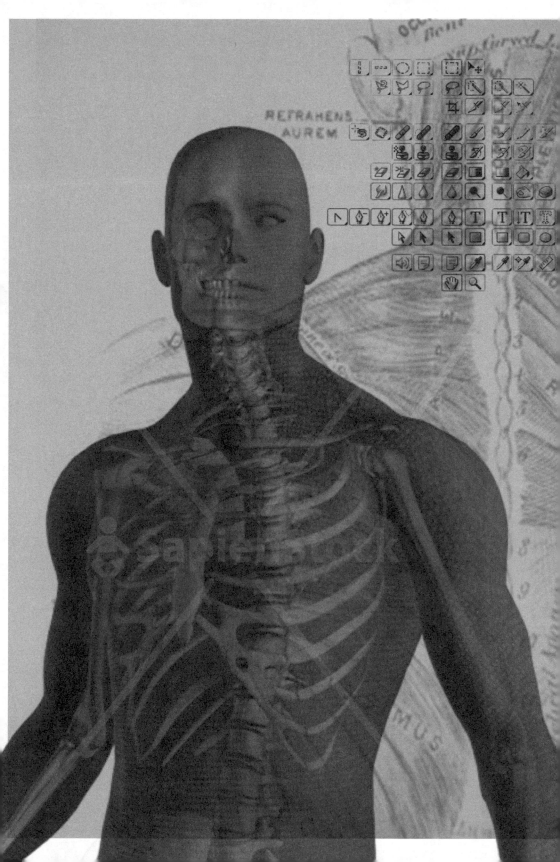

the country-and-western stations that ran ads for Monster Truck rallies.

She was around those flashy advertising types all day so he knew there was an element of real dissatisfaction in the jokes she made about his SUV. And his clothes. And his haircut. And in the way she just switched stations on his radio—when she knew he'd want to check on the latest from the Milosevic trial. He switched the radio back to NPR, even if she was having her own crisis at work. "Everybody at work was talking about your problem today so you're going to take it out on me," he said. The moral high ground. He craned to look around the SUV beside him so he could back out, stealing a glance at her: pouting as she buckled her seatbelt.

"Yeah, everybody was talking about it," she said by way of apology. Then she proceeded to tell him the latest in the flap churning her agency: they'd been hired to make a commercial for Volvo and her boss had been the one to push for a thirty-second spot that depicted a Monster Truck running over but failing to crush a Volvo sedan. Safety doesn't sell, the competition insisted; car crashes scare off customers no matter how depicted. Then the president of some Monster Truck club was tipped off by the driver that Alice had hired for the shoot; he'd surreptitiously made his own tape of her crew filming the commercial, then waited for it to air before putting his tape into the hands of a local news show—for a segment called *News You Can Use*—which made a big deal about car companies and their lies.

As Alice spoke, the radio commentator began to talk about the Milosevic trial and Tomasz wanted to hush her so he could hear, but she was on a roll about clients and Monster Trucks so he let her go—

"...and now they're threatening to pull the account...."
He noticed that her agitation didn't extend to her boss for
skipping town during the trouble and leaving her to answer
questions. And feed the two pampered cats that lived with him in
his rich house. The destination they were headed for.

🖈 ✐ 1²³ ◎ ⊤

Lake Shore Drive was Tomasz's favorite road in America partly
because its name really did seem to come from the land and
not just the American impulse to keep the grid neutral: Main and
34th Street, they'd say; that is, there were no plazas named after
the massacres that had occurred in them. No trolley stops named
for particularly bloody dates in glorious revolts. It was springtime
now so the beaches were deserted, but driving along Lake Shore
Drive in the summer it was easy to see where the impulse came
from: during warm weather, the strip of beach between the drive
and the lake was perpetually populated by young professionals
like him and Alice instead of the saggy-teated old men one
would see on the gravel beaches back home, or wheezy matrons
in housedresses, their nylons collapsed around thick ankles as
they set up canvas, Soviet-era camping paraphernalia.

Like Croatian roads, which only ran where nature allowed
them, this one also followed the contours of water: past the
frozen public beaches, beyond the city's edge, even a series
of picturesque, hairpin curves had been left un-straightened
despite the fact that he himself had seen among them a couple
of those white crosses people sometimes placed on shoulders to
commemorate the spot where a loved one had died—in the fog
that came off the lake, no doubt, as several yellow signs warned.
Slippery When Wet.

"...brani Slobodana Miloîević a ili njegovu nacionalistiiku politiku..." began streaming from the radio and Tomasz felt an adrenaline rush at the sound of home. Just as quickly, the fog of the translator's voice descended, blanketing the woman's Croatian in an English that blunted the outlines of what lie beneath. He turned up the radio, straining to pick out snatches through the gaps as she described the days that led up to Yugoslavia's disintegration into warfare and hatred. Why? Tito himself had been, like Tomasz, half Croat and half Slovene while his memories of trips to see his aunt in Bosnia came to him as a hazy fairytale. Had he simply been oblivious to the wolves in the forest? No one could paint a picture in words that made any sense, as the witness speaking on the radio admitted. As even some of the murderers now professed.

Tiny white flowers—like those that appeared in spring throughout the Neretva Valley—grew along the guard-rails they passed. In Croatia, no one would put a guardrail along a slippery spot no matter how often people died there and Tomasz wondered if that was ultimately why the country had come apart. To catch a flight from Hamburg, he had traveled by Eurobus from Belgrade to Budapest, tensely watching the edge of the precipices that the bus groaned along as it wound up mountain curves that were sometimes so crowded with Christian Crosses, as well as the Crescent Moons of Islam and Stars of David, that they served as a sort of makeshift guardrail, though in fact they'd never be able to save anyone.

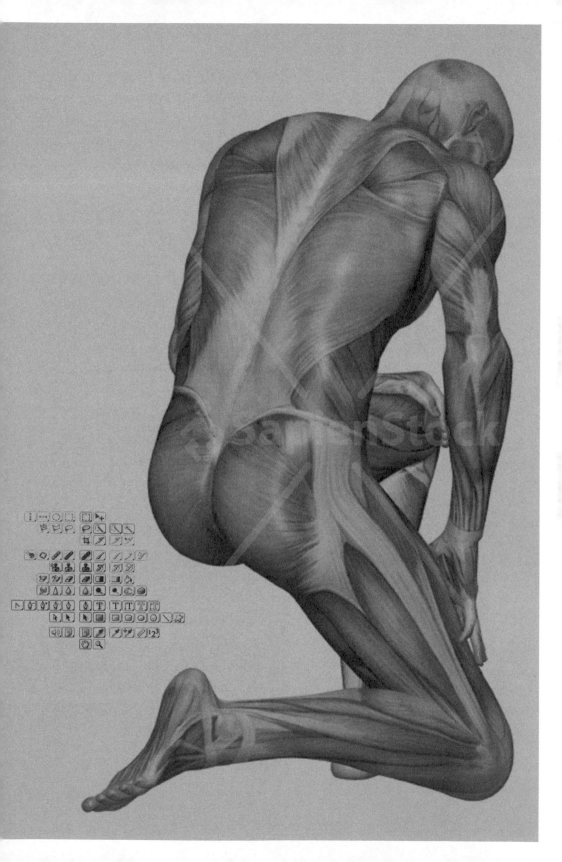

Alice's boss lived in that wooded area populated by the rich just north of the city. As they neared, the houses became more upscale. One looked like a French Château, the next a space station with a stainless-steel sculpture in its front yard. The further north they went the more property each estate had, the homes themselves more secluded. When he'd first gotten his Explorer, before he knew Alice, Tomasz used to drive up this way on his own. He remembered wondering who lived in these mansions, and then the disorientation of seeing three in a row being torn down—one a beautiful home with bay windows and a patio. It had been dollhoused, as his *tetka* and others in Bosnia referred to buildings that had avoided direct hits during shelling but had been so structurally damaged by the force of the explosions that the outer wall eventually collapsed, leaving the inner floors exposed as in a child's dollhouse. Not far from where cousins lived, a whole block had been dollhoused, the people crawling out of the rubble to go about their lives as best they could, not having anywhere else to go and no money to rebuild, living in full view of passer-byers on the street.

When Alice explained that these houses had been dollhoused by the wrecking ball, destroyed to put up more expensive homes, he hadn't believed her. Who would? Why? "The owners don't have any choice," she insisted. "With the demand for lake-front locations what it is, it makes no sense to have a $250,000 house on a $500,000 piece of property when you can rebuild in line with property values and resell the whole thing for $1.5 mil."

"Huh?"

"It's all relative."

"That's it," Alice said, referring to a private
road that headed up through dense trees.
He kicked in the four-wheel drive—his first
chance to use it—though he was disappointed
to find that the road was only a driveway that
spilled onto a wide concrete apron before
a modern glass and metal house. Sand and
dune grass landscaping. Low-slung roof line
to not jar with the panoramic horizon of the
lake beyond. Alice used the remote her boss
had given her and one of three garage doors
opened with the solemnity of a drawbridge.
He wouldn't be able to pull in with her bike on
the roof so she hopped out, not waiting for
him to help her get it down as a woman back
home would. If a woman back home would
own a bike. Which she wouldn't. The Explorer
rocked toward Alice as she stepped up onto
the running board on his side where the rack
was, her bare waist exposed by the reach and
pressed against his side window.

He looked up to the house through the
windshield. Lines as clean as an umlaut-
less name. Back in Yugoslavia, only Soviet
ministries could imagine an architecture
without filigrees on top of curlicues. A house
this far out in the country—that is, a peasant's
house—would have the name of its husband-
and-wife owners ornately carved above the
doorway, along with the year their farm had
been established, that is, the year of their

marriage. But her boss had already been divorced twice, Alice had said. And the only plaque on his house said *Protected by EVEREADY Security*.

Alice grunted, the momentum of the bike swinging her through a wide arc as though she were a Chinese acrobat about to pop up into a handstand on its seat.

Inside, the house seemed too clean for anyone to actually live there. Gray leather conversation pit, gray walls so the framed stills from glossy ads would stand out—lots of empty floor space like in an art gallery or museum, one glass wall looking out onto the lake: blue, of course, with a blue sky making the window look like a wall-sized, blue abstract painting. The two cats—fluffy white Persians—came walking out, meowing complainingly, and Alice dropped to a knee cooing, "What's the matter, my babies, my babies?..." She carried on scratching them, the cats rubbing against her, marking their territory by getting hair on her suit. "Tomasz," she said, "I'd like you to meet High. High, this is Tomasz. And this is Life," she added, indicating the other cat. The two cats looked identical to Tomasz but Alice had been able to tell them apart as quickly as a roommate, and Tomasz continued to stand there awkwardly, waiting for her to finish as he had that time they'd run into her boss in a bar near her job, Alice introducing them—Winston—before going off into office talk Tomasz couldn't possibly join, her boss lowering his voice, drawing her closer, arm around her waist till Tomasz was standing behind them by himself, hands in his pocket. Now, as he waited for her to finish again, he looked around at the framed stills, a bookshelf of golden Ad Age trophies.

#1 Huggies Diaper Campaign. A framed photo caught his eye—
it was of them—Winston and Alice—Hawaiian leis around their
necks, coconut drinks in hand, cheek to cheek as though on a
honeymoon—at least that's what people in Croatia would think.
Here, according to Alice, it was no big deal. Co-workers. He
knew where the picture had been taken. Co-workers, or at most
friends on a business trip: the campaign Medical Illustration
had been subcontracted for, and the reason Tomasz had met
Alice. A pharmaceutical company had hired her agency to put
together the presentation they were going to mount for doctors
invited into a captive space, in this case a cruise ship: Doctors
who might prescribe their drug would be given a free cruise if
they would sit through an informational meeting about a new
antidepressant geared toward the teenage market. Alice, in turn,
had subcontracted Medical Illustration to do animations and
illustrations about the pill, and they in turn had put Tomasz on
the job of creating graphics for the power-point portions: lots
of sad faces on depressed, beautiful young girls. She'd asked
him to dinner to talk about it and he had wondered what he was
supposed to make of a woman asking a man—him—to dinner. In
Croatia they would know. *Co-workers—ha!* A few weeks later, as
they lay in bed near the end of the job, she told him that she was
going on the cruise too, a perk from her company. Her and her
boss. Friends on a business trip. No big deal.

Tomasz didn't like it. Still, he hadn't wanted to sound like one of
those pug-nosed youths in black, knee-high soccer stockings,
singing nationalist songs about the Eagle of Freedom shrieking
as a Croatian/Bosnian/Serbian/Albanian youth fell defending the
Motherland against the Albanian/Serbian/Bosnian/Croatian Hun.
"You seem very familiar," he said now.

"Oh yeah," she answered, "We're—" Looking up from the cats she saw that he'd meant the photo. "Why don't you get us a couple of beers," she told Tomasz, "they're in the wine fridge behind the bar."

He didn't know there were refrigerators for just wine but filling in blanks had become so common for him that he just went and, sure enough, there it was: a squat refrigerator as small as those in Croatian flats only with a thermometer built into its door and nothing inside but racks for wine, one of which was filled with green bottles of imported beer. When he came back, she was sitting on the couch with the cats, and he sunk into its deep leather beside her.

"Didn't you bring one for High and Life?"
He sat up—the cats had an automatic machine to feed them, and to clean their litter box—there really wasn't anything Alice's boss wanted her to do other than keep the cats company—he was worried about their loneliness. But then she laughed, and he realized what a stunned stupid look he must have had on his face.
"It's a joke," he said flatly. "You were making a joke."
"Come here, you monotone Slav," she said, hugging him to her.

🔣 🖉 🔢 🔘 🔤

The next day at work, Tomasz put the finishing touches on the illustration. Public Radio was carrying the Milosevic trial so he had it turned low in his cubicle as he worked, sweeping his digital pen through an arc to airbrush a torso the color of a Barbie doll. It was hard to concentrate. He had watched the war compulsively on TV but there had been no pictures of the bayonet rapes these witnesses were describing at the trial; not even blood, or shop-

keepers shitting themselves out of fear and the contradiction between what was said and what the pictures had shown made him realize that the more he had looked, the less he had under-stood. Or had he? Death was always aesthetic, whether it was in a clinical autopsy report, a slasher movie, or the voices of chil-dren singing *Ring Around the Rosy* about everyone falling down with bubonic plague. Still, the question made him confused. And ashamed for being in a position to pass judgment from afar. A tourist to their suffering. At the parties Alice took him to, he had given his opinion of the war between talk about the best bands. "Yeah, like what was that war thing all about?" Alone, when he tried to imagine what that war thing was all about, all he could see was the stump of that boy. An image with no caption.

An hour later Marsha, his project manager, popped in and said, "Geez, a little heavy on the red, don't you think." It was only then that Tomasz saw what he'd done: the chest wound on his screen had the appearance of raw hamburger, the transparency he'd made illustrating not so much the injury he was supposed to draw as the traumatic amputation he'd seen in Bosnia. "Yes, I'm sorry. I'll fix it."

Marsha looked from the illustration to Tomasz, then back. Then she looked at him again. Her brow furrowed. Then she did it again. "Okay," she finally said. Then her voice lightened to that tone reserved for office banter: "Have you seen this?" she asked, opening the newspaper she'd had folded under her arm.

In the weekend section there was a photo of a trucker with his foot on the hood of a Volvo as though he was a big-game hunter posing with his kill. A semi-circle of Monster Trucks had been arranged behind him, all logos and flame decals, a driver scowling beside each, tattooed arms crossed over pot bellies that reminded Tomasz of the way the stomachs of SZUP goons back home always seemed to strain the buttons of their uniforms. *It's time we put American value against the car of choice for foreign-beer drinking Wall-Street yuppies,* said the caption. *We're going to give this car a dose of NON-virtual reality....* It went on to announce the sale of tickets to a rally where the smashing of the Volvo by the Monster Trucks in the picture would be the high point.

"...talk about making a B.F.D. out of nothing," Marsha was saying, continuing on into a sympathy rant about commercials with mermaids shaving men underwater or the pseudo science in diaper comparison tests. Tomasz recognized this last as an ad Winston had come up with. "...only a moron would take that stuff seriously...." But Winston took it seriously and he wasn't a moron, Tomasz knew. Lots of people took it seriously. They'd given Winston that plaque displayed behind his bar for coming up with the idea: an actor in a white lab coat pouring a beaker full of yellow liquid on Diaper Brand X to show how it ran all over the place while the blue liquid he poured into a Huggies diaper was completely absorbed. Only the thing was, if you watched the commercial frame-by-frame, as Alice had shown it to him, you could see that not only did the beakers have numberless scales, but the one used to test Brand X was larger than the beaker used on the Huggies; also, the unnamed diaper had been shaped into a water-shedding dome for the filming while the Huggies diaper had been pressed concave, a bowl. "No one said the actor was a scientist or that the comparison was an experiment so it wasn't like the commercial lied," Alice had said, "in fact, its beauty is that it doesn't actually say anything."

"Give Alice my condolences, would you," Marsha finished, patting Tomasz's shoulder as she headed back to her office. Tomasz nodded, then sat there looking into his screen. Last night, every time he broached the subject of her and her boss, she didn't say anything. He'd ask her how long she'd known him and she'd answer, Long enough. Long enough for what? They'd ended up having an irritating evening because of the verbal dance. Maybe that photo of her and Winston was, as she said, a nothing. To her. But if it was a nothing to him, would he frame and hang it with the rest of his trophies? And if it wasn't a nothing to him, what was its somethingness? How comfortably she moved through it all— his house, his cats, his life. Maybe she had been to his house for office parties as she had said, but would a woman who'd been to a man's house for an office party know where to find his tweezers? Seeing her mix fertilizer in an atomizer to water his plants or the familiarity with which she brought out the sugar bowl was like watching her shape a portrait from thin air. A family portrait.

Oh, so what? he thought, returning to his drawing. So what if they'd fucked each other silly before he'd met her. She was his now, wasn't she? His. She'd never put it that way, of course, and when he thought how she would put what they were to each other, he wondered if she and Winston really were just that much more sophisticated than him. Sophisticated enough to see nothing wrong with having it both ways.

⬙ ✐ ⒓ ⊙ ⓣ

While they watched the *News You Can Use* segment Alice had taped for Winston, Tomasz took the moral high ground with her: "That's just a lie," he said as the hidden camera showed her crew reinforcing the Volvo by welding extra braces into its roof and trunk. She shot him a look. But what was wrong with speaking bluntly? Wasn't honesty always straightforward?

"No one ever shoots a commercial in one take," she'd alibied, "we were simply making sure that the car would hold up all day." A Monster Truck approached the Volvo and began to climb its rear bumper; jump-cut to a close-up of an enormous tire slowly rolling onto the Volvo's trunk, then across its roof. "The whole idea was to simulate what might actually happen, not shoot a documentary." The roof only bowed slightly under the massive tire. "Haven't you ever heard of poetic truth? Making up a fiction to tell a truth?" But in the home video that the Monster-Truck aficionado had shot of the making of the commercial, a wider view reveals that the massive tire rolling over the roof of the Volvo wasn't even on the Monster Truck: Alice's crew of five or six men had taken an extra, loose tire that was identical to those on the truck and were rolling it by hand over the Volvo as their own camera zoomed in, framing the shot so it would appear as if the truck was driving on top of the car. "What were we supposed to do?" Alice said as though accused, "Smash up a hundred forty-thousand dollar cars to make one commercial?"

"You find these gray areas very easy to live in, don't you?"
"What's that supposed to mean?"

After sending his files to the print server, Tomasz opened the new folder Marsha had left in his IN basket: photos of a lacerated leg. Pictures of a basketball court that he was supposed to diagram. It looked like the same court he had

drawn a few days ago. Downed basketball hoop. Bulldozer. It was the same court. And the same plaintiff: Sika. The case he had already finished. He gathered it up, then went to see Marsha, a row of snap-apart eyeballs that Janice had made for a laser-surgery defense staring at him from their pedestals on top of the flat files. He found Marsha with David, one of the other illustrators, going through the details of a complicated settlement negotiation involving the difference between a tumor and a cyst and a chinstrap on a motorcycle helmet. "Marsha," he said, "excuse me but there must be a mistake here. You gave me the file for the Sika case I finished last week."

"Same case, different client," Marsha said, "check the affidavit." *Zakaria, Zakaria & Associates,* it said. "The plaintiff switched lawyers?"

"No, these are the illustrations you're supposed to make for the defense."

It took Tomasz a moment to register what she'd just said, then he asked, "You want me to make the illustrations for both sides of the case?" Even as the words came out, though, he could see the truth of it: these photos of the basketball court had been shot from the opposite side of the playground. The warning sign looked much closer to the basketball hoop and the construction equipment than it had in the photos he'd gotten from the prosecution. In those photos, the sign had been a dot in the distance, seen from the back, while the backboard that had fallen on the boy dominated one picture, heavy as a guillotine blade and embedded in a dark stain on the asphalt that looked like blood though who knows what it really was—engine oil. Or just water. The photo had been taken from a ladder, he now realized, its height maximizing an optical illusion of distance while to take the photo used by the defense, the camera had been placed low, and fitted with a telephoto lens to optically collapse the distance between warning sign and accident. Had the second photographer done a better job or simply had more truth to work with?

Already in his mind he could see that the site diagram he would make from this set of photos would imply that the accident was much more the fault of the victim. Without even looking, he knew what the note from Marsha would say: Minimize P&S.

"...and since you're already familiar with the case," she was explaining, "you'd be the one to do the best job."

'Best' in this case, Tomasz knew, meaning 'quickest,' i.e. most cost-effective, i.e. most profitable for Medical Illustrators, Inc., the color of pain and suffering always tinted green.... "But it's for a big construction company," he tried, not knowing what else to say.

Marsha's eyebrows arched.

"So," he continued, "I don't mind helping some injured boy claim damages but to help a company get out of paying for their negligence...."

"That's for the courts to decide."

"But I'd— I'd—"

"What? Feel like a prostitute with a paint program?"

That wasn't it at all. Being a prostitute or a hypocrite or anything like that never entered his thoughts though the quickness of her answer, its edge, gave away that it had entered hers. Or at least had come up. But for that, he knew, you had to believe that the world was the way it looked while ever since he began contributing to the way the world looked in America, the more he felt that slipping, sinking feeling he'd had watching his old country on CNN, the thousands, maybe millions of pictures he'd sat transfixed before each night as they poured out of the war becoming dream-like—a whole way of life slipping into memory....

Marsha sighed, being patient with a child. A foreigner—having a hard time believing that pictures could lie because he couldn't believe that they could tell the truth any more than the color green could be true or false. If there was a lie, her face said, just to move on, it would be in the caption, the claim made for the picture. Yet if that was completely true, then what of the boy's pain and suffering? What of the bleeding his belt had been used to staunch back home? Then there was Alice. A flood of captions came to him, and when it came to captions—the claims lawyers would make for the pictures—all he was doing was following orders. He didn't want to think about it....

"Couldn't you at least put David or Janice on?—"
Before he could even finish the sentence David appealed to Marsha: "I'm already humping Ludlow vs. MediCorp."

"They're just clients," Marsha said, slipping into that managerial tone that announced 'discussion over.' "And anyway, you're the only one who could get it done in time." Then, as if to placate him she added, "Think of it as a kind of neutrality. If they're the

Germany to each other's France then that makes you Sweden."
Switzerland, he thought. She meant Switzerland.

⚏ ✎ ⒓ ⊙ ⓣ

Alone in his car, driving to Winston's lake-shore house, Tomasz
tried to remember the outline of Switzerland. Was it large
enough to hold cars as big as his? With bigger payments and a
radio leaking tales of pain and suffering from homeless Croatians
as he drove to a mansion to pamper cats. As a favor to a
girlfriend who wasn't his girlfriend. But who might or might not
have been the girlfriend of the man who owned the mansion, and
was her boss. Who might or might not have been sleeping with
her. Or still was. Or was at least trying to. Or not. If he brought it
up, Alice would act like he was imagining things. But he had keys
in his pocket. Real keys not imaginary keys and he touched them
to make sure they were still there, on a ring with the remote to
the alarm system. Alice had given it to him since today she was
wining and dining clients out in the high-tech corridor west of
the city so wouldn't be meeting him until much later. So what?
she'd mock if he brought it up, you think I'm sleeping with them
too? Still, he didn't like it. Didn't like it so much that maybe she
was right, that he was just being juvenile. Or backwards. A DP
fresh off the boat. A lack of sophistication, as she'd called it.
Words. Without the words husband and wife, she had once told
him, there was no such thing as adultery. Only sex.

She had meant it about them, he had thought, a fun thing.
Liberation. But the more he thought about it now, about her
other euphemisms and evasions and what had happened at
work, the more he felt like he had entered that political movie
he'd once seen back in Croatia that ended with a worker in a

state-owned rifle factory disguised as a plant that made vacuum cleaners. His job was to deburr each part as it came past him on an assembly line and he truly believed that his one small job contributed to the assembly of vacuum cleaners. So he began to steal one for his wife, taking home a different part each day and he couldn't understand why, when he put the parts together at home, he ended up with a rifle. The man who lived in the next flat, a political agitator, saw what was going on so took a job on the line to prove it. Like the first man, he stole a different part each day but every time he tried to assemble them for members of the opposition, all he ever got was a vacuum cleaner.

Tomasz pulled up before Winston's house, his rifle factory. He left his Explorer outside so Alice could see that he was here when she arrived. He used the remote of the SUV to lock it, then the remote of the house to disarm its alarm, and went in. It was still a little unsettling how in America you locked up everything but walked right into the heart of every home. In Croatia, every house, even small flats, had an entranceway because of the *tetke*, but even more so because the Muslims would be appalled by the lack of discretion, by a brutishness that allowed strangers to walk right into your private business where your daughters and underwear might be.

The cats came out meowing, but there was no way Tomasz was going to play along with that stupidity. From deeper in the house he could hear a high-pitched beeping. A smoke detector? He began walking toward the sound, looking for it. Then he remembered: when Alice had given him directions for disarming the alarm, she'd said that if he heard a beeping to not worry about it—it sounded like the warning given off by the security

system but if he'd already disarmed it, it would be the warning
the answering machine sounded when it was full. He went to the
bedroom to see if there was a way to silence the annoying thing.
There it was, a red light flashing on the phone by the bed. He
pushed a button and the messages began to play. "Hi Alice, this
is Winston. Listen, Stacey booked our flight to Cancun, but we're
going to have to leave on a Wednesday instead of a Thursday..."

Cancun?

"...the client says its real bikini weather down there so bring
a swimsuit...."

Then Tomasz saw earrings on the nightstand, behind the phone.
Alice's earrings? If she had worn them on the first day they'd
come here he would have surely noticed, wouldn't he? But if she
didn't leave them here that day, then when?— He stood there
looking at them, the red stones glistening in the palm of his hand,
the bed a pure white square beside him, his stomach knotting.
He was sure he'd seen her wearing these in the past. He put them
back on the nightstand then went out in the living room and
sunk into the conversation pit to think. The lake was before him, a
deep purple. A cat hopped up into his lap. After a while he went
back into the bedroom and picked up the earrings. Definitely
not cufflinks as his imagination had begun to irrationally hope.
He stood there looking at them until that sensation of being
watched made him turn around and he was startled by a man. A
man standing right there. Dark uniform of the SZUP Police, hand
on a holstered pistol.

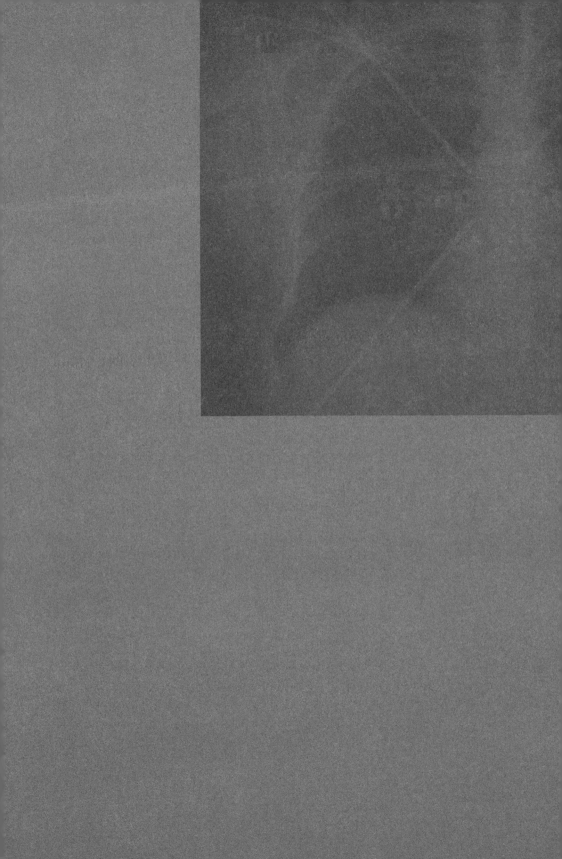

Alice thought that his being held for breaking into Winston's house was a big joke. He was supposed to have pressed and held the button on the remote control to disarm the alarm system, not just press it the way his Explorer's remote worked, and they had fought about whether or not she had told him this detail. The security guard who answered the call found the front door open, came in and found Tomasz standing in the bedroom holding jewelry. Tomasz had been made to stand, right where he was, hands on head and facing the wall—which was glass and looked out onto the lake—as the guard exchanged staticy chatter over his radio with police. An hour later he was sitting, face in hands, in the small cell the exclusive suburb used as a holding tank, along with two black men who claimed they'd only come out from the city to look at the houses but had been picked up because the cop who stopped them didn't think that looking was reason enough for them to be there. *You'll end up in prison, Tomasz heard his tetke warn. In America they put all young men in prison.* By the time the security company managed to contact Winston, and he had managed to talk to Alice, it was after midnight and Alice and Tomasz had fought all the way back to Winston's house where he showed her the earrings, and demanded an explanation, and she said the explanation was that he was paranoid, so he played the message, and she called him crazy, and told him to get off her case, to give her some space, and exhausted from fighting, they'd gone to sleep at opposite edges of the bed.

⚒ ✎ 1²³ ◎ ⊤

The next morning they dressed in different bathrooms and stayed in different spaces even together in Tomasz's SUV as he drove them to their jobs in the city, patches of fog swirling before the windshield. "Slow down, you're driving too fast,"

Alice complained. Tomasz stepped on the accelerator, whipping the SUV around one of the curves that followed the lake, growing angrier, picking up the fight where they'd left off the night before as if there'd been no interruption.

Alice continued, "I didn't tell you about Cancun because I knew you'd make a big deal out of it."

"And having horns on my head is not a big deal?"

She didn't answer. But when he glanced over at her, she was fuming, her eyes shiny with anger, not guilt it seemed.

He should have backed off but he had her down and something inside made him want to finish it off so he said,
"You didn't answer."

"I don't even know how to answer something like that," she said, her nose beginning to run. "Why do you think I'm with you?"

"How would I know? For the ride."

"If that's how you feel just let me out. Let me out now," she said louder. "We're close enough for me to bike the rest of the way in. Let me out now. Right now!" she yelled.

Fine. The road was narrow here, the shoulder not much wider than the SUV but he pulled over anyway—to talk, he would later tell himself. He'd never meant for her to get out. But she was already out, slamming her door behind and he'd hesitated, checking his side-view mirror for traffic.

By then she was already on the running board of the SUV, stretching to bring her bike down from its rack on the roof of the Explorer and so he couldn't open his door without knocking her off. "Alice," he said through the glass. She worked purposefully to free the bike, ignoring him.

"Alice," he repeated to her torso, pressed to the side window. Then it was gone. It happened so quickly he couldn't tell what had happened other than the sudden movement of her body, the simultaneous screech of tires.

⬚ ⬚ ⬚ ⬚ ⬚

Tomasz had never been to any of the trials that used his illustrations but he made a point to go to Sika vs. O'Mally Construction, the trial that would swing on illustrations he had made for both the prosecution and the defense. After creating them in the solitude of his cubicle, it was disorienting to see his drawings argued over so publicly, displayed one after another in the fluorescent glare of the courtroom, first to lay the entire load of guilt on the doorstep of the defendant, then to absolve the company of any wrongdoing whatsoever. The lawyers did the talking for the illustrations, of course, which stood mutely on easels as their meanings were battled over, the lawyers wrestling words into convincing, if contradicting stories, and Tomasz was surprised to see that what he had created was the most concrete evidence they had of what had actually happened. Throughout the trial, he watched the faces of the jury members, trying to judge from them which version of his drawings was winning. It was impossible. Eight men and four women sat there stoically looking on with expressions that were nothing like Alice's face, beaming happily from the state I.D. he had found while fishing

around in her purse for her insurance card that day at the emergency room. She smiled in the I.D. as no one did in their identity photos back home and the contrast seemed to be a portrait of two peoples as well, one confident all would be made right, the other standing there waiting for the camera to click as if they already stood before the immigration/police/interrogator machinery that would decide their fate. Because they knew the reason such photos were taken, they couldn't show more enthusiasm than was displayed by these jurists, their faces blank. Or maybe they were just weary. In that, Marsha had been right, he was sort of a Sweden, or Swaziland, or Suzhou, trying to put into words the view from Switzerland without ever having been there. Or at least come up with some caption that could be lived with even if everyone knew it would really explain nothing.

🖬 🖉 ⁱ²₃ ◎ 🍨

His palms went clammy from waiting in the hallway with the others for the jury to deliberate. As if he was the one on trial, he became as nervous as he'd been in the surgery waiting room, trying to sketch in his mind a cartoon of the sequence of events that had happened, trying to fill in the blanks of 'what.' Forget the why. Even so, the closer he came to the thing itself, the sketchier his panels became, the last depicting all he could come up with for what she might be feeling on the other side of the wall, an unimaginable, white nothing....

Down the hall, the lawyers themselves joked around with a familiarity that showed there was nothing personal between them. That they had done this before and would probably be back in court tomorrow, maybe with their roles reversed in another case. Even the boy who had been injured was there, shooting pretend baskets at the far end of the hall, the accident

having happened so long ago that by
the time it came to trial he seemed to be
completely recovered.

On *News You Can Use*, Monster Trucks
crumpled a Volvo like a tin can. The rally
was presented as a great victory for Truth,
Justice, and the American Way. But despite
what the commentators said, the pictures
showed that it took those trucks seven or
eight tries to do so, the roof of the Volvo
withstanding the first truck just as it had
appeared to do so in the video Alice's
crew shot. Then it withstood a second
truck driving over it, bending only a little,
giving in completely only after a fifth truck
demonstrated the fiction she had created
for Winston's commercial to be more
truthful than the actual un-doctored reality
shown on the news. Still, the crowd at the
rally roared for the victory of the trucks, and
the news show ended with a spokeswoman
for Volvo apologizing to the public, then
reading a statement about pulling the ad
and canceling their contract with the agency
that had misinformed them of the manner in
which their company would be represented.

100

stroke

stroke

stroke

stroke

stroke

stroke

stroke

stroke

stroke

stroke

stroke

stroke

stroke

stroke

stroke

stroke

stroke

stroke

stroke

stroke

stroke

stroke

stroke

stroke

stroke

stroke

stroke

stroke

stroke

stroke

stroke

stroke

stroke

stroke

stroke

stroke

stroke

stroke

stroke

stroke

Self Portrait(s)

The neck of a mouse is easier to snap than a pencil, Mary had said.

Hundreds of necks later, it was the ease of the words that most bothered Jim.

He laid the mouse stomach-down on the lab bench, whiskers twitching, the mouse curious about what its nose was against, though of course, oblivious to the big picture descending from above. Like all of us, Jim thought, wishing he hadn't been so quick to tell Mary he'd help her make an embryo.

He stroked the mouse for a five count, the minimum time one study said was necessary to calm small animals enough to prevent fear's adrenaline rush from skewing the hormone measurements he'd later take. Then he held the rod he used against the base of its skull, close to the C1 vertebrae line as Mary had taught him, twining its tail around a finger. A stiff yank and the mouse twitched, dead.

After "Hello," how to euthanize a mouse was the first thing Mary had said to him. It was the reason they'd been introduced, so that first impression partly explained why he remembered her voice so clearly, her tone casual, familiar, the same way she'd later tell him she was borrowing his lighter. The same way she'd later ask to use his semen.

Still, waving away the fog of sublimating dry ice he used to make the mice docile, he knew he didn't need Mary to see how anything could become familiar. Even invisible. Once, Dr. Woo had gone off at him for allowing a batch of mice to die slowly. The carpenter who rented space below Jim and Mary's loft had called to complain that water was leaking from his ceiling and Jim had biked over to shut off a faucet, he'd thought. When he got there, though, he found steam billowing from that radiator that never worked right. It streaked windows and six months of art that Mary had been making for an upcoming show—he couldn't leave—and by the time he got back, Dr. Woo, the Primary Researcher on most of the studies Jim pulled, was angrily incinerating the mice, along with the three months' worth of now-useless data that they carried in their cells.

The board that policed the treatment of lab animals could have made trouble. And as Jim signed a paper stating that he under-

stood the protocol for harvesting livers, or hearts, or bone marrow, or whatever material a study called for, he knew to not say
what he was thinking: that there were plenty more where they
came from. Even so, working with so many mice it was hard to
not know what he knew as he lifted the next by its tail. Its white
body emerged from the cold fog like a Popsicle from one of those
carts Mexican vendors pushed around his parents' old neighborhood.

Laying the mouse down, Jim let his mind wander as he often did
while he worked, putting the bar behind its skull, yanking its tail,
getting into a zone like a basketball player finding his rhythm, he
imagined, lifting another mouse, calming it—three, four, five—
yank; grab the tail and yank; grab the tail and yank; three, four,
five, yank; grab the tail and yank; grab the tail and yank, in one
fluid motion yank, hard enough to jerk the spine from the base of
the skull, yanking hard enough to kill instantly but not so hard as
to break skin, a touch thing, like shooting a basketball, grab the
tail and yank, till an hour later, when he was going good, there'd
be a pile of white bodies in the basin of the stainless-steel sink,
his trigger finger sore from the yanking.

Everyone was shaped by their world, at least a little, he knew,
pinching a flap of skin in one mouse's stomach. Still, though
he'd been a premed major and never bothered by the dissect-
ing, the killing always got a reaction from him. Holding the soft
underbelly of the dead mouse between thumb and forefinger, he
snipped it open with surgical scissors. Not a big reaction; but
a little one, like anyone might get when it was their turn to gas
the used rats, or do anything unpleasant. Two more snips and
the liver was free from the purse he had made of the body. But
with her, an artist who only majored in bio because her parents
wouldn't pay for an art degree, bodies were something so not to
flinch over that it was weird, her words not spoken in a tone that
could be called matter-of-fact, or clinical, or even cold. No, she
was on a curve so far ahead that he couldn't even see what direction she was going though he knew that if he could, it would
explain a lot.....

·

Jim often went up to the eleventh floor of the research center so he could eat his sack lunch with Mary. The elevator opened onto a floor that looked identical to his because they all looked identical: porcelain-white corridors, a ring of labs around shared equipment like the million-dollar spectral photometer that his floor shared. The people came from all over—Taiwan, the Philippines—but even they looked the same: the techs, like him, dressed in jeans, tennis shoes and white lab coat, photo-ID clipped to the pocket; the PIs older, their postdocs already starting to take on the serious, preoccupied look of their mentors. A Korean doctor passed by discussing something with his black intern, and Jim couldn't help but imagine Mary going to one of them if he backed out.

Today he found her and her assistant Pamela, a tech like him, doing rabbits on the opposite side of the window that separated the operating theater from the rest of their lab. Coming upon the two women dressed in their scrubs, blue caps and surgical masks covering all but their eyes, Jim often suffered a moment of disorientation—who are you?—sizing up the shape of their bodies before the boyishness of one gave its answer. Mary Elizabeth Smith. But who was that?

As he entered she teased, *"How's it hangin' Dr. M.,"* glancing up from the incision she was making. It was a joke they shared—him being Dr. Moreau to the Mice—and he answered back, *"Yo, Dr. R.,"*— the Dr. Razor to the Rabbits—hopping up on a lab bench with his lunch.

Artist? Lover? Someone's Daughter? Friend? She was also Dr. Razor to pigs. And to the rats, and the dogs: all of the large animals used in studies that required a lot more surgical skill than he could provide. The bypasses, gene therapies, and other trial procedures she performed were more complicated. They took longer so when she could she worked in stages, opening the chest of one rabbit while the anesthesia was taking affect on another, while Pamela helped a third come out from under. Today they were juggling six operations, three chests clamped opened at once.

snap

"Hey," she said, tying off an artery to simulate heart disease, "Laura scheduled a late meeting today so I can use the microinjector while they're out," meaning she was going to skip lunch. So he unwrapped his peanut-butter-and-jelly sandwich on his lap and watched as he ate.

snap

She was good. Seeing her this way, working on her rabbits, it was easy to picture her in a MASH unit, operating on shot-up soldiers, or earthquake victims. The arteries of a human were way larger than those of a rat so he was sure that technically she could pull it off. To do open-heart surgery on rats, she worked by looking through the telescoping lens of the headgear she wore. The arteries themselves were no thicker than red thread while the 10-0 suture she had to use was so fine it was invisible to the naked eye. Yet even working at this microscopic scale her movements were sure. "This is nothing," she'd tell people, "Do you know how hard it is to draw a straight line without a ruler?" And it was true. Her ability with a scalpel was at least partly the result of her art training. Not long after they'd begun living together, he'd unrolled a bunch of her old canvases, her juvenilia she called it, that he'd found stuffed in a barrel. They were nudes and still lifes from her undergrad days, self-portraits so detailed that she had used a brush with a single hair for some highlights. The paintings were marvels of draftsmanship, but they embarrassed her now for their lack of ideas, and the whole while he looked at them she kept insisting that he roll them back up. She hadn't made a painting in years; no artist she took seriously did. And her ability to draw would never even come up if it didn't live on in her scalpel work, or in the delicate maneuvers she could make with a cell in the microinjector. Still, eye-hand coordination wasn't the main reason she'd make a good surgeon. Once, he had joked that if they were ever on an isolated camping trip and he needed an emergency appendectomy, he'd want her to be the one to do it. He thought she'd make some crack about removing the wrong organ, the anatomy of a man being different from a rabbit, after all. Instead, she'd only said, "Okay." Without hesitation. Without a hint of irony. He wished he had her balls.

snap

snap

snap

snap

snap

snap

snap

"There. That should do, little one," she said, finishing a stitch, then turning the rabbit over to Pamela. In a few weeks she'd try to cure the rabbit's heart damage by injecting stem cells that earlier studies said could be coaxed into becoming new blood vessels. But of course the rabbit didn't know that part, what with a ventilator making its open chest work up and down. Finally turning her clear brown eyes fully on Jim, she asked, like always, "So you going to come along?"

·

Mary brought out a tray of petri dishes labeled with the names of PIs and other clinical i.d.s., then opened the one marked *ART: Rat blastocysts*. It was another inside joke, the initials usually standing for Assisted Reproductive Technology, not the literal way she meant the label to refer to the blastocysts inside, the fertilized rat eggs she was using.

While she positioned them on the platform of the microinjector, he took a seat on the stool beside her and adjusted its second binocular microscope to his eye height. All a blur.

"Like a virgin...." Mary softly sang to herself.

Jim liked watching her make art more than he liked watching her operate. She had to do a lot of it on the sly, using the expensive equipment for personal use as she did, so only he and a few others at work like Pam and Laura knew she was an artist—it was a link between them. Plus he liked going to Microbiology. Its test tubes and cultures gave the department more of the feel of what he thought was a real lab.

A turn of the focusing ring, and the blur he'd been looking at resolved into blastocysts floating like amoebas in the medium. Or nebulas. Nebulas that were actually half the size of a period. They swam away from the even finer pipette Mary controlled with a joystick. She had made the blastocysts earlier; the male and female protonuclei wouldn't fuse for a while, and before they did she was trying to inject the male protonucleolus with the DNA of a third rat. The idea was to make a rat whose DNA fingerprint would show that it was a mosaic of three parents. The technique was common. Most of the mice used as disease models and all of the custom animals were now created this way. She'd gotten the idea to use the method to make a work of art from the lab mice that carried a jellyfish gene; the gene caused their tumors to glow a green that reminded Jim of the brilliant blue or orange stripes on some tropical fish, and allowed the tumors to be studied without killing their host for an autopsy. But a Brazilian artist had beat her to that one, creating a green-glowing rabbit. So she thought she'd leapfrog them both by using the technique on one of her own eggs. It was an outgrowth of an earlier work of bio sculpture she'd made, *Self-Portrait:* an egg she had encapsulated beneath a bubble that functioned as a magnifying glass, placed in the frame that used to house her high-school graduation portrait. To make the portrait she had in mind now though, it was important that she use an embryo that was viable. "My egg, your sperm, and some junk DNA of a third person," she'd told Jim. It wasn't as mechanical as Mary had hoped, though, and this was her fourth attempt to make it work with rats. "It's a touch thing," Laura had said when teaching her how to work the controls, so Jim knew it wouldn't take Mary long to ice it.

She brought the glass pipette, her easel, up to the egg and the suction at the pipette's polished tip held it fast. Operating the other joystick, Mary took up her brush, an even more microscopic hypodermic needle. As she maneuvered the needle into a position that would allow a clean stab into the male protonucleolus, he felt himself squirm, thinking of his own protonucleolus semi-fused with hers under the light of the microinjector.

"...doing it for the very first time...."

When she'd first brought up the idea, he'd agreed right away. It was only going to be an art work—not a baby. Religious art. She was going to call it *Trinity*. She had no intention of implanting it in a womb or allowing it to become a fetus, even if it was important for the piece to have that potential, at least for a while. "Integrity of materials, and all that," she'd said, explaining how it wouldn't have the same impact if she only faked it with Silly Putty or something else that wasn't real....

The idea of his sperm mingling with her egg had been a powerful aphrodisiac, making him hard, horny. A powerful link between them. Or so it had seemed. Then her conception of the piece began to evolve. Mary changed its name to *Resurrection*, thinking that if she could use the junk DNA from a third party, mitochondria that would serve no function other than to give the potential child's DNA fingerprint the trace of a third parent, why not use junk DNA from Christ? Jim's real importance in the project began to show as she became consumed with tracking down the thirteen churches that claimed to have Christ's tissue, his foreskin, removed by circumcision since he was Jewish. Supposedly, the rest of his body ascended into heaven. After failing to find anyone who could get her a piece that wasn't totally iffy if not an outright scam, though, she decided to settle for any garden-variety saint with good provenance. She didn't even care which, even if she was being picky about the relics that showed up on e-Bay. Way more picky, it seemed, than she was about the guy who filled his spot.

"Do you know how easy it is to get sperm?" she laughed when, to see how she'd react, he'd joked that getting a sample from him was the only reason she'd let him move into her loft. But he was afraid to ask if she meant get it—$100 per dose—from the fertility clinic she'd contracted to harvest her eggs, or get it herself. Either way, it didn't exactly make him feel vital.

The needle punctured a dark spot on the jellyfish, the male protonucleolus. "Damn," she said. "Do you think it went all the way through?" He couldn't tell. But it didn't look like it. So she syringed in a tiny gray stream, a trillionth of a liter of solution containing the junk DNA from the third rat. "Looks like the membrane held," she said. She pressed a button on the first joystick, cutting off the suction and the egg floated away. Then she moved the microscopic glass pipette to capture another one. If this trial worked, she'd have all the pieces: injection technique down; a fertility clinic to harvest her eggs; she'd set up an account with one of the dozens of commercial labs in California to purify and multiply junk DNA from a tissue sample. They'd FedEx it to her overnight. All she had to do was come up with a saint. And have him jerkoff.

"So that's what you'll do with my little guys," he said, watching her inject the next protonucleolus.

Silence. Then, "That's what I'll do," she said, her tone suddenly flat. They'd been down this road before.

She continued to work in silence till he said, "Will it hurt?"

"No one's making you," she said, the edge in her voice telling him that this wasn't the time.

•

She eased her naked body onto his, kissing him. But the condom he had on, the non-spermicidal kind used to capture semen samples—a test—made him self-conscious, like he was on a microscope slide, and though they went through the same motions, did all the same licking and biting, he was so aware of the difference from what it was like when he first moved in that he knew she must feel it too.

She was six years older than him and had sworn off men for a while after her divorce. He'd just dropped out of pre-med—still a horny college kid, bottled up by books—so when they met, the chemical reaction had been exothermic. The first time he picked her up at her loft, they didn't even make it to the movie that was the pretext for the date. Dressed in a skinny summer dress instead of the scrubs he always saw her in at work, she'd offered him a joint, then ten minutes after that they were fucking, her clogs and panties on the floor, her thin dress hiked up around her waist, him in the condom she'd had at the ready as they went at each other on the mattress she then used as a bed.

They'd stopped using condoms after the results from a date for AIDS testing came back negative—an era of STDs brings into existence courtship rituals like that—but now, after having gone through the motions on the queen-sized bed they'd bought to replace the mattress, he wondered what she saw when she looked into their future. If she even looked.

Sure enough, a moment later she gave him a pat and was up. A lot had changed since he'd begun to stay here, he knew, watching her pull on the oversized sweatshirt she used as a bathrobe. She carried his sample to the corner of the loft she used as a kitchen. The two of them used to walk around the loft naked without giving it a thought. But no more. Bed sheets hung across its big industrial windows so construction workers rehabbing a neighboring factory into condos couldn't see in—just as a lot of other incremental changes had become second nature. The dirty mop heads she'd been weaving into sculptures when she got her divorce—so important to her then—were now pushed against one wall, the loft big enough to just push things off to one side and forget about them. Even a heap of mop heads six feet high.

"So far so good," she called back, looking through a jeweler's loupe.

In a way, though, it was as if nothing had changed.

"Was there ever a doubt?" He tried to sound enthusiastic. Except for the bed, his bicycle and a few other things, his own stuff seemed to just melt into the junk—materials she called it—that she used to scavenge from dumpsters and demolition sites on her way home from the lab.

"Never a doubt," she said, smiling, coming back to bed. She pulled off her sweatshirt and her pink nipples dangled before him as she bent to put the loupe on top of the bedside TV. She switched the set on, then lay back in his arms. Now that she wasn't examining him any longer, it was easier for him to see her body and from it he could tell she was more relaxed as well. Glad because what could have been a hard decision for her had been defused? He pushed a hand up her back.

"Mmmmm," she murmured, warmly, her register deepened by age—her body, like his, like everyone's, a portrait of a life lived. Gray peppered what he guessed had once been jet-black hair, her hair short as a swimmer's so she could easily get it in and out of a surgical cap. The first time he saw her naked, he'd been surprised by how much older her body looked from the other girlfriends he'd had—students like him, mostly younger. There'd

been tufts of hair at her armpits because she'd been a girl at a time when some mothers still told their daughters that things like that didn't matter while the smooth girlfriends he'd had, if they knew that story at all, would have thought it a relic of old hippie weirdness, or just plain gross. When he dug his knuckles into her back, she gave a little gasp, the flesh wrinkling before

the plow of his palms instead of snapping back even though the muscles below were firm, her calves more muscular than some bike messengers. A mole on one shoulder. Earlobe piercing closed from nonuse. The imperfections and idiosyncrasies struck him as— As particularly her unlike the thousands of glossy fashion models who were so unreal for their symmetry—

like the plaster casts of Everyman or Everywoman they used to use to teach anatomy—everyone's ideal, and therefore ideals of no one. Especially those old enough to not be mistaken for kids. Time's winged chariot at my back, as an epigram to a chapter on aging said in a biology book he once owned.

"Oh gag," she said, groaning at something in a commercial. "That joke's so old."

Or did coming home to him feel more to her like the routine of laundry day? The last thing she wanted after her divorce, she'd said, was to jump into another relationship. And she never really gave him permission to move in. It's just that he had been coming over, then sleeping over, then sleeping over and coming back later in the day so often that after a while, without either of them pointing it out, he had begun to stay. Now her project and whether or not he was going to go through with it was pointing it out. And the thought of her finding someone else to help her seemed too much like moving out even if he had never really moved in.

"Jim, do you think we're doing the right thing?" she asked, as though she'd been reading his mind. She leaned out of his arms to twist the coat hanger that was the TV's antenna, its picture wiggling back into form. "I'd hate to do anything that could wreck what we have here."

Her question surprised him, and he hugged her for finally coming around to at least consider his reservations. "I don't know, Mary," he said. "I mean at first I didn't think it was any big deal but now that it's starting to seem more real...."

"Maybe we should have just thrown that flier away."

"Flier?" She was talking about getting cable TV, he realized. When she'd first rented the loft it was supposed to have been for studio use only. She'd needed its space for the video cameras and welding equipment she used to use to make art from junk and heaps of mop heads that her then-husband wouldn't let her bring into their apartment. The loft was in an old, MaidenForm bra factory with a tar roof that got blistering in the summer and made the place impossible to heat in the winter. It was against code for anyone to live there. But when she fell out with her ex for good, she'd gotten a microwave and moved in. When the surrounding factories and warehouses had begun to be converted into luxury condos, Paul and Mary sort of figured it was only a matter of time before they'd have to get out even if they both said doing so would kill them, the difference between the loft and the sterile research center, the chance the loft gave them to live apart from the grid, an oasis from the lab's controlled atmosphere. Still, when a flier arrived announcing that cable TV was now available in their area, they debated whether to get it and risk alerting the landlord to their presence.

She sat up in bed and looked at him, the bemused look coming onto her face showing that she realized what he had been talking about. Then she hit him with a pillow."Would you give it a rest!" she said in mock disbelief.

"What? Why is it so hard for you to put yourself in my shoes? I mean, you're going to do it anyway, right? If not with me, then with some other guy."

She shook her head and laughed one of her exasperated laughs. "We've been through all of this. I'd do it without anyone else if I could, but eggs don't keep. Sperm freezes—that's why it's so cheap—embryos freeze, but not eggs," she said, referring to the way she wanted to display the art embryo: in liquid nitrogen—the way another artist displayed the bust of his head he had sculpted out of a block of his own frozen blood. "If you don't want to help me out, just say so and I'll get a dose from a male donor when they harvest my eggs. I'm not doing 'it' with anyone, if that's what you're worried about. Then she looked at him hard. "Is this a Catholic thing?"

Whenever her logic found no corollary in him, she went back to the fact that he'd been brought up by religious parents. "No!" he said, trying to explain it for her, and himself, without lapsing into sperm competition among apes, or any of those other theories of domination through sex that they learned in animal biology. This to someone who had sold her eggs to make ends meet while getting her master's in art. When he could think of nothing to say other than the fact that he didn't want to think of her eggs in a tube with another man, he said,

"Oh, forget it."

•

"You could use a new set," the cable guy said. He sat on the bed, adjusting the controls of their old portable TV. The channel control worked okay, if you knew how to use it—a touch thing. But the guy didn't know how to use it. No one would ever have to know again, so Jim wedged a toothpick in the control to make the set stay on the channel that the cablebox needed to work. "*Showtime, HBO...*" The guy used the new remote to surf the channels in the package Mary had ordered, demonstrating that they were all there. "...and *Court TV*," he said, leaving it on the channel Jim had asked about. Mary liked the reality-TV shows, the channels that just put on footage of murderers confessing, or surgeries being performed, so he wanted to have one of those playing when she got home.

"You been putting in a lot of systems around here?" Jim asked as the guy packed up.

"You kidding?" he said, motioning to the rehab going on across the street. "I bet the only reason this building hasn't been sold to developers is because someone's holding out for more cash. I remember when the hospital was in the middle of a ghetto. No more," he said. And it was true. The hospital that Jim and Mary worked in had been an island in a war-zone part of town that ran up to the mostly empty industrial area they lived in. As recently as two years ago when Jim met Mary, riding his bike the couple of miles out here had been creepy. Now he stopped on his way in to pick up a coffee from the Starbucks in one of the condo buildings that a lot of interns lived in, the pockets of new condos and student housing that had sprung up growing so numerous that they had begun to connect. "The world's changing, my man," the guy said, hitching up his tool belt. Then he was gone.

Jim found a couple of TV dinner trays among all the junk Mary had accumulated. He opened the freezer in the corner of the loft that was her kitchen, and got the TV dinners he'd bought to surprise her with. Behind them were some of her cultures, and behind those a box with a Korean label. It was the frozen squid they had bought at a Vietnamese market when they'd just begun dating. They had these plans for making an Asian dinner in her loft, but back then it seemed like all they did was screw, and the squid had remained frozen there all this time. He pulled it

stroke
stroke
stroke
stroke
stroke

stroke
stroke
stroke
stroke
stroke

stroke
stroke
stroke
stroke
stroke

stroke
stroke
stroke
stroke
stroke

stroke
stroke
stroke
stroke
stroke

stroke
stroke
stroke
stroke
stroke

stroke
stroke
stroke
stroke
stroke

stroke
stroke
stroke
stroke
stroke

out, imagining the look on her face when she saw what he had cooked. Was it still good? Behind it, in the deepest part of the freezer were more sealed baggies—had they bought other stuff that day as well? *Joe, Korean 2.5.00.000S* was written in magic marker on one. Inside was a brown bottle that Jim at first thought was the kind Asian markets used to sell rhino horn and other potions. But then, scraping away the frost, he saw that it was one of the bottles used for samples in Microbiology. *Luke, Afro.-Am. 2.15.00.000S* said the next. There were some seven or eight others.

The plodding of someone laboring up the stairs sounded out in the hallway.

When he saw *Jim, Caucasian* on one of the vials, he knew what he was looking at.

A scratching of keys, the door swung open and Mary was there, carrying her bike on one shoulder.

"Who is Korean 2.5.00.000S?"

She stopped, her mouth open in mid-hello. Then she put her bike down. "Just some guy I knew before I knew you."

"And Afro.-Amer. 2.15.00.000S?"

"Look, they were all just guys. You don't know any of them."

"I—"

"And even if you did, this was before we met. You didn't think you were the first, did you?"

He could feel his blood quicken while behind his eyes there was a flash, a prom date's mother snapping pictures as he posed grinning in a living room decorated with framed photos of his date in other corsages, arm-in-arm with other guys. "And you

snap

snap

snap

snap

snap

snap

snap

snap

were saving their jizz? Like some kind of memento?"

"Not a memento," she said sarcastically. "I thought I was going to make art out of it."

"What?"

"Nothing came of it." She crossed her arms. "I really doubt if that old beater of a freezer even keeps them cold enough to be viable."

"That's beside the point!"

"I knew I should have thrown them away," she said more to herself than to him. "I didn't mean to—"

"I mean, you harvest their sperm, my sperm, then keep it on ice until you could get around to making art out of it? Without telling anyone?"

"It was just an idea. Nothing came of it. Maybe I should have said something but it's not exactly like you guys were so concerned about what happened to your sperm when you came over here."

"Who the hell do you think you are!"

•

He hadn't meant to make her feel like dirt.

GENETIC BACKGROUND in which the Transgenic Mice Will Be Made? Jim clicked on the radio-button beside F2(C57B16 X CBA). As he continued to fill out the on-line form, placing an order for the genetically altered mice Dr. Pashvani needed for one of the lab's studies, he wished he hadn't gone there. That is, he wished he hadn't yelled, "Who the hell do you think you are?" and then continue to spray gasoline on the big, blowing oil-rig-fire of a fight they had until she was screaming back, "All right, all right, I feel like dirt! Are you happy!"

Alpha 1 (IX) collagen; Alpha 1b-adrenergic... He scrolled down the long list of genes that could be knocked out of a mouse's sequence till he found *Vascular/endothelial-cadherin*, and clicked its radio-button. Mary had issues about who she was, he knew. Serious issues. When she'd been in college, she'd gotten an e-mail from someone claiming to be an unknown sister who said that both of them had been given up for adoption when they were infants. Mary had told the woman she was crazy, but when she searched birth records to prove it, she couldn't find her own. It turned out that she wasn't related to the woman, but her parents denied she was adopted right up until she laid the DNA evidence before them.

Charges for Blastocyst Injections, per targeting (2 clones) $3,000.

After she'd told Jim that story, how she might never have discovered the lie she'd been living if she hadn't seen a billboard—Call 1-800-DNA-TYPE—set up by a bio-tech company that helped settle paternity cases, he understood a little better how she could sell her eggs. For the longest time she didn't want anything to do with her parents, treated them like kidnappers who had made her major in something practical, something she wasn't. She didn't talk to them through the rest of her senior year, which meant that she had to pay for it herself. When she turned to the ads for waitressing at the local IHOP or Big Boy, she also found the other ads that periodically ran in the school newspaper, ads for healthy coeds to become egg donors, or to rent their wombs. A friend had already volunteered for the first and had been paid a $12,000 gratuity. On the psychological screening portion of the application that asked prospective donors why they wanted to do it, Mary didn't have to lie: she was glad to help other women have their own kids, she wrote, rather than have to adopt someone else's. But he couldn't stop wondering how many of them were out there—those women with their kids. The thought of her eggs mingling with the sperm of different men—the connection she would have with those men, and women, and kids—gave him a pang of jealousy. If the fertility drugs every donor had to take allowed her to give up twenty to forty eggs, how many other e-mails would Mary be getting in the future? And that's assuming she only sold her eggs once. The egg she used in *Self-Portrait* came from those days, she claimed. But that would mean she'd kept it for years. When there were more where those came from, as she put it, and had needed money while going through her divorce. No wonder she couldn't get her mind around his reaction. He must seem like a dinosaur sometimes, he thought, clicking on the bookmarks of his browser to reveal all the links he had saved to tomatoes that carried codfish genes so they would be less susceptible to freezing; blue cotton that didn't have to be dyed to make jeans; synthetic skin, ears and noses grown in petri dishes; cow embryos that were part human; goats that gave steroids instead of milk; Dr. Pashvani, Dr. Woo and thousands like them asking if all plants, animals, cells—all nature—could be used as rearrangeable packets of information, while he, Mary, and thousands of techs like them did the grunt work of stitching together answers....

•

"...remember also, Father, Your servants Alfred Wiesoki..." The priest was getting to the part Jim came for so he began to pay attention. "...Stanley Stodola, Martin Zwoboda; Dolores Szyarak, Jose Garcia, and James and Jean Krygoski"—Jim's parents— and when the priest finished intoning the names of the dead, Jim and the few others in attendance at this weekday mass murmured, "And let perpetual light shine upon them." It was a mass of remembrance. And though it seemed like so much voodoo to him, his parents had both bought masses for their parents, had attended regularly each and every anniversary of their deaths, or birth into Christ as the church put it. So for each of the six years since their deaths he had paid to have their names said at mass, if for no other reason than to remember.

Scattered around the dark church were a few old people: his parents' generation, too set in their ways to move away when the neighborhood began to go Hispanic. An icon of the Virgin of Guadalupe now hung in an alcove where Jim knew an inscription in Polish remembered those who had died in The Great War, as people called WWI before world wars had sequels. A woman his age sat in a side pew—stylish business suit, arty glasses—on the periphery like him, and here no doubt for the same reason. It was a connection between them. She also looked a little lost, but tried to go through the motions, following the lead of the others who were not just remembering someone dead but were literally praying to save their souls.

Seeing the old people finger worn rosaries, Jim was always struck by their belief in words. How they thought words could cure disease. Resurrect the dead. Determine whether a soul burned in eternal hell or basked in perpetual light. Like the woman, he had also tried to pray along at his first mass of re-membrance. He could have done it easily when he was a kid and attended the grade school attached to the church. But he hadn't been to mass in years since then, and he felt foolish, like a person trying to sing the second verse of a Christmas carol they could only half remember. But why not? he thought, glancing at the woman mumbling along. What could it hurt?

Even so, his mind kept wandering to the communion railing and altarpiece, a marvel in carved oak that no one would even try to duplicate today. Had Mary been born 500 years ago, she might have worked at carving communion railings like this one instead of making the art that she did. Had she been born in Europe, that is. Had she been born into the right guild, that is. Had she been born a man. He remembered how excited she'd been to see the stained-glass windows the time he'd brought her here. He knew about her interest in tribal art so wasn't surprised that she also liked religious art. Still, he hadn't thought she would actually make any till she returned with a camera to shoot the church's rose window in different light. It was its blue at dawn that she wanted to use she said. And its shape reminded her of a petri dish.

Looking at it, a deep blue circle now protected by bulletproof glass, he remembered the stories he'd heard about it as a kid. It had been made in Lithuania, the master stonemasons, glass ar-

snap

snap

snap

snap

snap

snap

snap

snap

tisans, and other craftsmen needed to make a church like this all back in Europe, the connection between the new and old worlds straining from the start. And it did look like a petri dish. He'd never noticed how much body stuff there was in the church till Mary started asking about the cannibalism of their rituals: "This is my body, take and eat?" she had said when he tried to deny it. "What's up with that?"

As in other churches, the body of an emaciated God/man hung crucified at the front of this one. But the thing that struck Jim after all these years, the thing that had most made him think it was all a lot of B.S. and voodoo to begin with was the way they all thought water could turn into wine, bread into flesh. That a man could simultaneously be a dove. Virgin birth. But now, going through his catalog of mice with tobacco genes, his bookmarks to test-tube babies, infants with baboon hearts, and the rest, none of it seemed so farfetched any more.

"This is my blood," the priest said, raising a chalice of wine above his head. A Mexican altar girl in dingy tennis shoes and a surplice as white as a lab coat rang the chimes, just as he had as a kid, to mark the moment of the wine's transformation. It was about words, but also about bodies. Always the body. Even if bodies were becoming as permeable as words: him standing here because twenty-six years ago his forty-year-old parents, good Catholics to the end, bet rhythm against chemistry; his mother's Polish mother before them marrying his Lithuanian grandfather because his first wife had died in childbirth, all three of them coming here after The Great War from different parts of a torn-up Europe on the basis of rumors that the Middle West—as if it were a hamlet—was where they'd find people from their village. The rumors themselves had been based on the construction of this church, they later realized—the windows from Lithuania, the communion railing from Poland, and when he thought of the web of words and bodies that had been needed to bring him into existence, he couldn't help but wonder?— Who were any of them?—5,000 generations back to the African Eve, the last wom-an genetic reconstruction said all people now walking the earth

stroke
stroke
stroke
stroke
stroke

stroke
stroke
stroke
stroke
stroke

stroke
stroke
stroke
stroke
stroke

stroke
stroke
stroke
stroke
stroke

stroke
stroke
stroke
stroke
stroke

stroke
stroke
stroke
stroke
stroke

stroke
stroke
stroke
stroke
stroke

stroke
stroke
stroke
stroke
stroke

stroke
stroke
stroke
stroke
stroke

were descended from, as few as fifty of her descendants walking out of Africa and into Europe to continue a web of chance and circumstance so old and interwoven that it almost seemed as if it was his one true creator, the number of accidents and chance encounters—a world war had to have been fought—and miscarriages, and births that it took to get to him too large to hold in his mind—like thinking about god. Or infinity. No wonder words like 'race' were supposedly going the way of words like 'miracle.' If a person counted back 120,000 generations to Adam, the first amoeba, even words like fish and mammal began to blur—forget about monkey/man. Yet in the free fall he understood for an instant how his grandmother could have gotten on a boat to come here. Penniless. Not a word of English. Unknown continent before but an understanding deeper than marrow that she was part of something larger than herself. And as water seeks its own level, she had found his grandfather here in this church.

Trim, aerobicized bod: the lawyer, or ad exec or whoever the woman his age was shot him a frowning glance—as though she'd caught him checking her out. But really he was trying to look past her, to the dark side-chapel where votive candles flickered before relics: bone chips or bits of flesh from dead saints. Among the relics, he knew, was the dried blood of St. James, the saint his parents had picked to be his namesake and patron, housed in a silver heart

·

They were supposed to be celebrating tonight. A piece Mary had made two years ago, *In A Beginning*, had won the Tokyo Prize for techno art and this was its opening. They lay in bed looking at a projection of it, taken from the web, routed through a projector plugged into her computer's video output and cast on the bed sheet that hung across one of the windows of their loft: creases in the sheet rippled the live image, a deep-blue circle speckled with dots that reminded Jim of the night sky seen through a telescope. But instead of the night sky, the circle was a petri dish, and instead of stars, the dots were E. coli bacteria. Mary had contracted a lab to infuse their cells with a synthetic gene whose sequence of amino acids carried a message: LET MAN HAVE DOMINION OVER ALL THE PLANTS AND ANIMALS OF THE EARTH. The actual petri dish was set up in Tokyo, but anyone could see the same view of it that he and Mary were looking at by going to her web site. Once there, they could use their mouse to trigger an ultraviolet flash on the bacteria. When they did, the projected circle flashed whitish, then returned to its deep blue glow, the blue of the rose window in the church Jim's parents had been buried in. The idea was that each flash of the UV light would cause the bacteria to mutate a little, corrupting the message in a way no one would know until she translated the genetic coding back into English.

The loft lit up again, as from lightning, the sheet going momentarily white. Someone somewhere in the world had clicked their mouse. In the flash Jim could see Mary's face, serene, and he took her hand, glad their fight was over. Living in a loft with no walls, it had been hard to avoid each other. Slowly they had begun to talk again. First in clipped answers to clipped questions, then more naturally. What the hell, he thought, beginning to understand what the project meant to her. And wanting the fight to be over before this, her biggest opening, he'd bought a bottle of massage oil—a peace offering—to place on her pillow with an IOU for a back rub as a way to say, if the project meant so much to her, he'd go along with it, even if he didn't know what it all meant. Entering the loft he found a woman-sized pillar of mop heads in the chair where Mary normally sat. She'd made a video of her lips, then connected it to a motion sensor and Watchman buried in their strands so its tiny screen appeared right were her lips would be if she were the mop heads. Whenever he came near, the video lips said, "I'm sorry." When Mary showed up, they made up, and backs rubbed, egos massaged, he told her his IOU had another meaning. Instead of being happy, though, she only said that she wanted to think about it. That she wasn't sure what it all meant either.

Right after that she'd found out that *In A Beginning* had won the Tokyo Prize, and she'd be getting 500,000 yen. And right after that they got their eviction notice.

"What will you do with the money?" he asked, refilling her paper cup with champagne.

"I don't know. Maybe buy a dress. Or a new pair of shoes."

After the success of *In A Beginning*, a knockout project like *Resurrection* would really put her on the map, he knew, at least among the artists who used plants and animals, living tissue, or palettes of bacteria as their medium. And she knew it too. And that the prize money would pay for the harvesting of eggs, if she decided to keep them all instead of donating the ones she wouldn't use to the clinic that was going to do the job. It would also pay for the purification of DNA she'd extract from a tissue sample, as well as its cloning and amplification. Even so, she still hadn't said she'd go through with it. Even though her rats had tested positive for poly-parentage. He knew it had something to do with him, though he wasn't sure what. Though they'd both said they were sorry, though they knew they had to get out of the loft by the end of next month, they still hadn't made any plans for moving elsewhere and he was afraid it was because she was thinking about going on without him.

She hadn't said anything to make him think this. They just didn't talk about it. Or her project. And that's what worried him. That out of courtesy to him, knowing how he felt, she wasn't going to involve his body before they split. She didn't want that tie.

The projected petri dish lit up again illuminating the loft. In the flash he tried to read her face. What was she thinking? Was he in or out? In a way, he couldn't blame her. The thought of giving up the loft for a regular apartment with white walls and a real kitchen was depressing. The kind of depression that made him feel older, like he was turning into his parents shopping for linoleum. How much more so would it be for her—signing a lease with a guy as if she was stepping back into another marriage.

He should have known, just coming and staying as he did, that all along he'd been living on borrowed time. Still....

"You know my parents' church?" he said, bringing the length of his femur to hers, knee to knee, hip to hip, skin to skin. "I never showed you that time we went to look at the window, but a side altar has the relics of a few saints."

"Oh yeah?" she said, an eyebrow raising.

"Yeah. One of them is St. James. The patron saint of pilgrims, refugees and other travelers to new lands."

"I like it," she said.

"It's in a silver heart just screwed to the wall. And the church is open twenty-four hours a day. In case someone going by gets religion in the middle of the night. It's a Catholic thing."

His words gave her pause. "So what? You're saying we just go in and steal it?"

"Not steal. Borrow. After you amplify the DNA, there'll be enough relics for a million churches."

She studied him for the longest time, then said, "You're serious, aren't you?"

•

GeneTech. The FedEx package arrived as they were packing to move into their new apartment. Most of the junk—her mops and auto fenders—they decided to just leave behind. But the other stuff, her cultures and sheets and towels, they had boxed up or put in big garbage bags. The boxes and bags and tools and pots formed a pyramid by the door with the FedEx package on top so Mary could hand carry it. Which she did, when the time came, cradling it against her waist as they went out.

stroke
stroke
stroke
stroke
stroke

stroke
stroke
stroke
stroke
stroke

stroke
stroke
stroke
stroke
stroke

stroke
stroke
stroke
stroke
stroke

stroke
stroke
stroke
stroke
stroke

stroke
stroke
stroke
stroke
stroke

stroke
stroke
stroke
stroke
stroke

stroke
stroke
stroke
stroke
stroke

stroke
stroke
stroke
stroke
stroke

snap

snap

snap

snap

snap

snap

snap

snap

Friday night. And we are in search of a table. An IKEA table that we found online—It is in a store that never closes though we must travel out of the city—even beyond the airport—to reach it. In the sky above, planes crisscross the night, making it easy to imagine the map we'd once seen of FedEx routes, every point sprouting colorful bouquets of arcs that end on every other point on the map, a plane flying along one of them carrying our table to the store ahead. Or maybe it came by ship, the shipping lanes that crisscross the oceans as braided as the FedEx routes in the sky, an enormous container ship loaded in Sweden gliding along one on its way to America and passing an enormous container ship from America en route to Sweden, and both loaded with furniture. Or more likely, our IKEA table was designed in Sweden but made in China, a stream of emails along similar webs connecting armies of inventory managers and sales managers and orderers and shippers and suppliers and accountants and clerks and all their databases linking financial systems to mines to mills to factories that will transform ore into steel into wire into screws that will arrive just in time with the plastic pegs and varnish and felt and glue arriving from other nodes connecting other webs to be assembled as ours and others' tables and packed, with Styrofoam peanuts, as they come off the assembly line, into boxes (which, like the peanuts, also arrived just in time) that will be stacked onto pallets to be lowered into enormous ships that are manned by Greeks, docked in Ireland, but registered in Eretria, and will pass, as they steam toward San Diego, other ships that have been loaded in San Diego and are en route to China, and all loaded with furniture in boxes on pallets in identical steel containers that have been designed so that they can be stacked like Legos once they've crossed the ocean (no translation problems here), trains carrying them to regional distribution warehouses where the shipments are divided among trucks that are placed on highways that crisscrossed the country beneath the crisscrossing of planes in the sky, the truck with our table inside already having circled the cloverleaf that we wind around as we exit the expressway onto this plain where buffalo once roamed but is now a land of big-box stores—CIRCUIT CITY and HILTON GARDENS (who stays there? we wonder—and why? a hotel in a field)—a land of giants that are big boxes themselves separated by miles of prairie since giants need lots of space. A link to Google Maps has shown the way. Though there are no houses or people there is lots of traffic (where does it come from, what is it doing out here?—is the whole world buying a table tonight?) on freshly laid roads that connect the giants, their dotted lines so white on new asphalt that they look as though they'd just been extruded from a giant pastry chef's piping-bag, the roads making looping patterns whose logic must be apparent on some blueprint of the future, or could be seen from the air the way those ruts ancient Indians carved in fields were discovered to be, once modern men could rise high enough to see, the outlines of giant spiders and scorpions, but to us with our ant's eye view appear as a maze does to its rat. HOME DEPOT. TEXAS ROADHOUSE. Their parking lots are so large it takes many minutes to drive past. Then there it is: a big white cube on the horizon, like a block of Lucite, glowing white from within except for its blue and yellow IKEA logo along its top, the building growing as we approach, its lines so clean they also seem to have come from the drawing board of a Scandinavian designer, like an IKEA lamp itself but made the size of an iceberg, the way some artists take ordinary objects—a beach ball, or spoon—and duplicate them on a gigantic scale, a pencil, say, as tall as a tree, or a bowl of cherries large enough to fill the plaza of an office building…. Yet rather than stick out as those sculptures do, the store is as harmonious with its landscape as that Frank Lloyd Wright house built to hang over a waterfall, the stream that tumbles out from under the house flowing, before it falls, right through the living room. Here, the flat Midwestern horizon is epic, so must be its stores, no building smaller than an airport terminal, and in tune with its neighbors the way that the fake Egyptian pyramids and faux Eiffel towers and medieval castles of Las Vegas are all of a fabric, or rather, *are* the fabric, each store here separated by a mile of blacktopping (no sidewalks), like an archipelago of stores protruding from a sea of corn, each, like IKEA, the size of a stadium though they bear the names JOE'S CRAB SHACK, and BUBBA'S BACKYARD BAYOU BARBEQUE, and seem like crab shacks, and roadhouses inflated to the size of a balloon in the Macy's Thanksgiving Day Parade and made of materials and methods used in industrial architecture. They bear tokens of their namesakes, also rendered at industrial strength: a crab shack, decorated with what looked like, from the highway, fishing nets though as we near we can see that they are woven steel cables thick enough to support a suspension bridge; a roadhouse is adorned with auto license plates and yield and stop signs that one might well find on the walls around the pool table inside a real roadhouse if they weren't the size of billboards; FISHERMAN'S WHARF has a faded pier though the sea and the salt spray that weathers wood is 2,000 miles away. MEXICAN HACIENDA, THE GOLD RUSH, JOHNNY ROCKETS, evoke as we drive by, Old Mexico, a Prospectors' Saloon, the Space Age, the way that book *Learning from Las Vegas* claimed that the marquees and fake pyramids and Eiffel towers give a coherence to the landscape, and that by adopting the style of Las Vegas to sprawl everywhere, we could enrich our landscape with symbolic meaning. We have, apparently, learnt well from Las Vegas.

How well, we could not imagine until we found a parking place, maybe a quarter mile off, and began to walk toward the IEKA building, passing, we note, cars with license plates from every neighboring state, thus, the logic of the cloverleaf is revealed, explaining why this landscape has given rise to big-box stores as surely as mountains create their own climates—our trek joined by one then two, then dozens, hundreds, maybe thousands of other shoppers from all parts of the vast plain of cars, converging like raindrops into rivulets, rivulets becoming a watercourse heading as inextricably as water runs downhill toward the glow of the building where shoppers, who had arrived before us and so were now at the end of the journey, were streaming out. Most are carrying their purchases: desk lamps, and salad bowls, as we can see from the pictures on their boxes. The front of the store—which in a bygone day would have been department-store windows decorated for President's Day, or Christmas, or whatever holiday was imminent, trying to attract the eyes of window shoppers, tourists, and others lingering on lunch hours or rushing to catch cabs or make other appointments—is instead a loading zone (there isn't even a sidewalk): dozens of cars are backed up to the building where other shoppers are loading purchases too large to carry, using dollies to roll out boxes containing beds and bookcases (or so the pictures claim though it seems impossible to get a bed or bookcase into the large, flat, stackable boxes being loaded into cars). We have seen our future, we think, as we enter, and are immediately funneled onto an escalator, carrying the stream of shoppers we are part of up. Do we need to go up? we wonder as we are carried away, one escalator carrying us up to another as bodies are transported in meat processing plants where sides of beef are carried on hooks to stations for further butchering. Wouldn't the tables, like the sofas and other heavy items, be on the ground floor? We had been expecting to enter a showroom of sofas, or Lay-Z-Boys, then look for a directory that would tell us where to find the faux kitchens wherein would be found the table we were in search of, but IKEA, as meatpackers to cows, has done this thinking for us: the escalator channeling our bodies where they need to be, and where they need to be is the top of the store. This Way, the sign says. There is only one way. UP. (If you bend the body into a prayerful position, medievals thought, prayer would follow.) But then, once there, we flow like water trickling downhill through forests of bookcases, media cabinets, floor lamps, end tables, fabric sofas, leather sofas, sofa beds, modular sofas, chaise lounges, armchairs, footstools, TV stands, speaker cabinets…. The river of shoppers we had been divides into tributaries that continue on through other forests of DVD racks, tie racks, shoe racks, umbrella stands, sideboards (oh, look at that), end tables, rugs, wine racks, bookshelves, bookcases, towel racks, storage boxes in every size, lamp shades (it had never occurred to us to change the shades on our lamps), curtains, blinds, curtain rods, cushions, blankets, sheets…. In reverse of the way we shoppers coalesced to become a single stream as we entered the store, the stream continues to divide into rivulets of shoppers trickling through forests of chandeliers, lamp cords, ceiling fans, office lights, desk lamps, track lighting, lights with green shades that evoke library reading rooms, funky psychedelic lights, spotlights (that's kinda cool), lamps to hang over paintings or place under plants…. In the middle of the store we come upon a food court: BUS YOUR OWN TABLE the sign informs us. THIS IS WHY YOU ENJOY LOW PRICES. (It seems a threat.) We continue on, for to get to the lower floor, where in fact the table seems to be located, one must walk through the entire store, just as in Las Vegas, to go to the washroom, you must walk through the casino. To get to the bar you must walk through the casino. To get to the theater, parking garage, restaurant or anywhere, you must walk through the casino. So we continue on through other forests of filing cabinets, IN & OUT baskets, wastepaper baskets, kitchen garbage cans (we could use one of those), bathroom garbage cans, laundry bags, hampers, wastepaper baskets, magazine racks, racks for letters and spices and bikes, stereo-cable management solutions—YOUR RESOLUTION: A SUPER ORGANIZED REFRIGERATOR—closet solutions and pantry solutions (we didn't know our pantry had a problem) and entryway solutions…. (Look at that: an old wine barrel used as an umbrella stand. How clever.) Then there it is: the table we saw online. One. The last one, we think. How lucky no one in this entire mob has taken it. We inspect it. It seems less angular than it appeared in its online photo. Its legs do not all seem to be exactly parallel. And its grain somehow seems a bit too regular, like the pattern in wallpaper, or linoleum. It is made of wood-like particles. We hesitate. But we have driven so far. We lift it. It is heavy. Heavier than it looks, but of course particleboard and glue is denser than real wood. What made us think it would be real wood? We decide to get it. But we are not allowed to buy this table. A sign tells us that we are to take one of the numbered tags beside the table and proceed to the lower lever. Ah, we think, where we thought the table would be from the first. So we take a tag with the number and continue down, winding our way through forests of woks and pans and pots, vases, plastic flowers, baskets for newspapers, baskets for letters, baskets for fruit, and baskets for dirty underwear, nestled baskets that just seem designed to hold other baskets, baskets with odd shapes and no discernible purpose, bowls, cups and saucers, stackable stools, patio furniture, (Look!—that same wine barrel now fitted with seat cushions to turn it into a chair!), patio umbrellas, heaters, racks for wood; scented candles to facilitate romance, candles to mask smells, candles to repel bugs, candles for emergency power outages; cork boards, tacks for cork boards, African animals made of papier-mâché, bronze baby shoes from someone else's baby; refrigerator magnets; ceramic pitchers, clear plastic pitchers suitable for a picnic, (Look—now that wine barrel is an ice bucket!), and matching cups, picnic baskets too, wall cabinets, throw rugs, and throw pillows, bed pillows, and pillow cases, knitted throws, sheepskin throws, throws made of bamboo, outer cushions, inner cushions, cushion covers, wicker chairs; beer mugs, champagne glasses—let's not even get started on the different kinds of glasses—clocks that could have come from an office, a train station, the London Tower, Mars....

Though the store has been designed so we must walk past every item in it, we are not allowed to see the table we are actually buying, we learn, when we arrive at the ground floor: a warehouse, with a concrete floor and a metal ceiling two stories above us, floor-to-ceiling shelving filled with boxes. Its architecture, and the sight of others looking from tag to aisle markers makes us understand that we are to locate the aisle and bin number on the tag we obtained upstairs, and there we will be invited to help ourselves to a box that contains the table we wish to purchase. Aisle 97, 98, 99, 100.... There are so many aisles they seem to extend to the horizon. ...111, 112, 113... They seem to bow with the curvature of the earth. ...128, 129, 130.... Finally we locate the aisle, then the bin, but it seems a mistake: how could the table we wish to buy fit into a box so small? But yes, the numbers, and the picture on the box match. So we take the top one from the dozens stacked up there, load it onto the trolley provided, and wheel it back to the opposite end of the warehouse where signs say the cash registers are located.

There is a sea of other shoppers here, all funneled from different parts of the warehouse, each pushing a cart with brown boxes like ours only in varying sizes. At the far end we can see a cashier ringing up people in line. She is the first employee we have seen. There must have been others, but she is the first we have seen. Before us, where the lines are shorter, are self-service checkout stations: we find the barcode on our box, pass it under the web of laser beams; the price appears, and a robotic voice says to select payment method. Please insert Charge Card. When I pull the card out, the magnetic stripe on the card, a series of 1,300 magnetic dots, actually, passes through a detector so that each dot generates a series of on or off voltages, like flipping a switch or telegraph key on and off thousands of times a second, a string of 01010101001001001001s, computer code—a kind of Morse Code—for my card number, my name, our agreement's expiration date, along with the store's identification numbers, purchase amount, my information, our information, racing through wires outside the store at 2,400 blips per second to a computer that connects me with 20,000 banks, 14 million other stores, and 600 million other shoppers reserving rooms, renting skis, buying tables, lamps, and chairs around the world—as well as movie tickets, Slurpies, hotel reservations, shoes, fashion's hot new yellows, clocks in the shape of a Sphinx, pogo sticks, and god knows what else—to see if my card is where I am, and being used in a pattern that indicates I am who I say I am (in the past, I have stumbled into patterns—e.g. cash advance, liquor store, gas-station purchase—that indicate to the system a theft of my card, triggering its denial); it checks to see if I am using it in patterns that indicate I will in the future be able to pay the price of my purchase as I have in the past (e.g. continue to use it as I have in the past to buy things like groceries or that cool jacket I found at Goodwill, without any sudden aberration or blip in the pattern, e.g. Tiffany's), the entire system humming at the speed of light, generating other 1s & 0s that will be warehoused (they tell me) in other data bases, that will make it possible to make ever more precise portraits of exactly who I am (fine-grain portraits they call them), and how I live (to better serve me, they say), before returning its verdict: Approved. I have the machine's approval, for my behavior has matched my pattern: Groceries … Goodwill … Ikea; and not Groceries … Goodwill …Tiffany's. I am my pattern and my pattern is me so I am awarded the machine's approval. I make my mark with one of those pens that writes on an Etch-A-Sketch-like screen. I always make my mark—the name my mother taught me to write with a personal flair, a mini work of art, really (I am very proud of my signature)—indeed, one could say I make a point to make this beautiful, artful signature crude and illegible on those cash-register signature pads. It has never seemed to matter. What seems to matter is that someone is there to make a pattern on the computer's pad, the pattern I make with the stylus one with the pattern the machine reads on its screen, we two, for a moment, one, the way the fingertips of God and Adam touch, the machine's pattern giving my pattern the spark of life—Approved—but also my pattern contributing to those that make up the machine the way tiny thumbnail-sized portraits can come together to form a much larger portrait, the bald heads or black pompadours of the sitters in the tiny portraits allowing each of them to appear from a distance as a pixel with a certain shading in the much larger portrait, the particular way one of the sitters in the thumbnail-sized portraits might have combed her hair, or the nerdy style of eyeglasses another sitter might have on his face, or the big ears or small nose of others only relevant to the larger portrait in the way they contribute to the pattern, just as any one vote, snowflake, or grain of sand is meaningless but in the aggregate can elect Nazis, shut down airports, turn gardens into deserts, the behavior of many individuals acting in certain ways, each for their own peculiar reasons, giving rise to larger patterns, mass migration in Europe, ethnic neighborhoods in America, fashion trends, riots, these larger patterns combining to form even larger patterns, climate, café society, rock 'n roll, the rise of China, the fall of Rome, the computers we use having more and more influence in the patterns we form, they say, the patterns that we are, even, computers suggesting which books we might like to read, which movies we'd want to see, or which men or women we might like to share our lives with…. How else could the machine know the sequence of purchases your typical charge card thief—or lover or reader or you—will make?

Moments later we are back out in the night, Scandinavian-designed, Chinese-manufactured, Greek-Irish-Eritrean-delivered table-kit in a box designed to fit into the backseat of one of those standard compact cars sold around the world, that is, our car, driving to the final station on the assembly line—our home—where the final workers—us—will assemble it with the wrench thoughtfully supplied in the box. As we pass BAYOU BARBEQUE we wonder if the diners inside had come to BAYOU BARBEQUE by way of the highway system we used to come to IKEA, if they have driven out here for the food or because this is where the highway led, funneling cars like ours, from homes like ours, in towns like ours, scattered about states like ours, into the BAYOU BARBEQUE parking lot, as others had poured into the IKEA lot, maybe some of the diners having met online, as we had, funneled toward each other without even knowing it, going on a first date, as we had, which had seemed to be at the time so much our own idea but in retrospect somehow seems to be the outcome of some algorithm—even Predestination, as Calvinists might call it—before moving in together as we had, and finding ourselves in need of a kitchen table, as we had, an online search suggesting the table that was now in the back of our car just as a different online search had suggested the other to each of us, those diners in BAYOU BARBEQUE who might be on their first date unaware, as we had been, that they are on a different part of the same journey, using forks and knifes that had arrived by routes similar to the one our table had taken, and eating off of plates that were washed by immigrants unseen, back in the kitchen, delivered to their sinks by other unseen patterns, likewise the lettuce, like the waitresses who bring the hamburgers to the tables via routes of their own, the lettuce and onions and waitresses arriving like the ketchup, that is, just in time, to the hamburger arriving to its bun from animals that remain unseen though to get here we have driven by many fields where they might have grazed, the meat arriving instead by plane and train and truck from industrial feedlots and holding pens and slaughterhouses in other parts of America, and Argentina, and Australia, a single patty composed of beef from 14 countries, as they point out whenever there is an e-coli outbreak and they are unable to explain the source of the animal, let alone its bacteria, which makes us wonder what we are, if as they say, you are what you eat, eating animals we never see, spending money we never touch, traveling paths mostly in the dark, the beef and plates and ketchup and people and so many other variables coming together from so many different paths that it's difficult to say how we, who were once known as humans, got here from there, or where here is, for that matter, or where there is, for that matter (the two being relative, so to speak), driving by cars going in the opposite direction from which we've just come, our phones, which had supplied the directions, reversing them at the push of a button, as well as offering alternate routes: three alternate routes, the possibilities being multiple if not infinite. And as we had done when deciding which route to take to come out here, we choose the route that our phone says we would think is choice #1.

the Atlas of Man

A single photo of a nude man is mute. But photograph
50,000 nude men, nude women also, and just as celestial
bodies divulge their temperatures to astronomers, so the
bodies of the jealous, the bed wetter, the murderer, the pick-
pocket, and alas, also the heart-sick, will speak themselves.

Or so Dr. Johnson, our director, maintained. For my part,
I couldn't help but recall an anatomy lesson from my undergraduate days. Directing our attention to the nude cadavers
around which each team of students huddled, the instructor commanded us to begin, saying only, "Observe!" After a period
of silence during which we merely blinked at one another, one
student meekly raised his hand and asked, "Observe what?"
And so unfolded the lesson of that day—that it was impossible
for the researcher to merely gather "data." It was only by looking
for some "thing" that data could be seen.

Nevertheless, even though Dr. Johnson and I did not know precisely why we did what we did, we believed our work to be, from the vantage of 1957, vital. Even exhilarating. In this sense we were like Christopher Columbus unrolling the world map, had Columbus been armed with an aerial camera and his New World been a geography of the body that would call out to us "Land Ho!" once we were in sight. That is, once we had photographed enough subjects for their statistical significance to emerge. When it did, as Dr. Johnson was fond of saying, our nudes—50,000 strong—would sing a chorus of operatic dimensions.

Our procedure was simplicity itself: de-clothe the subject, position him (or her) in the standard pose and take (yes "take," not "make," I now realize is the proper usage) a photograph. What could be more objective?

I myself did not photograph the women. This fell to Miss Smith, though in the beginning I was against the addition of a woman to the "crew," as I and Professor Johnson referred to ourselves. By introducing a second observer (and a female perspective at that), I believed (what a word that is!), we would needlessly make cross-gender comparisons a subjective matter. Dr. Johnson, for his part, remained moored to the fact that though our work on men was progressing nicely, the number of women we had photographed remained at 1 (his wife).[1]

1

I provide my data in the form of footnotes which may be passed over by less technical-ly-minded readers without too great a loss to the narrative. Conversely, those readers who are more inclined to the reading of actuary tables, appliance comparisons and the like may skip the narra-tive and simply refer to the footnotes. Thus:

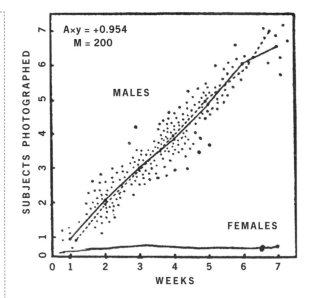

The Center back then maintained
a home for transient men whose
restless migrations kept us in ample
male subjects. For females, however, we
were completely dependent on volunteers.
He believed that if a woman interviewed and
photographed the females, ordinary house-
wives, students and mothers would feel more
comfortable stripping for our camera. To this
I replied, what if the data began to indicate
that Ectomorphs were more "comfortable"
being photographed by Ectomorphs? Or
Mesomorphs preferred a Mesomorph photographer? Given the fact that we had preliminar-
ily identified 18 body types and confirmed a
base line of two sexes,[2] we could by this logic
be driven to the use of 36 observers. And
this didn't account for the possibility of other

2
The first principle of
any mapmaker being to
distinguish land from water.

combinations: not just an Endomorph photographed by a fully-clothed,
i.e., neutral Mesomorph. Or an Ectomorph photographed by a neutral, i.e.,
clothed Mesomorph, but also, say, a nude Ectomorph photographed by
a nude Mesomorph; or a Mesomorph photographed by an Ectomorph; or a
Mesomorph photographed by an Endomorph; or an Endomorph photographed
by a Mesomorph; or an Ectomorph photographed by an Endomorph; or an
Endomorph photographed by an Ectomorph or an Ectomorph photographed
by an Endomorph with a Mesomorph as a neutral observer. This last permuta-
tion obviously implies a Mesomorph photographed by an Endomorph with an
Ectomorph as an observer; or an Endomorph photographed by a Mesomorph
with an Ectomorph as an observer; or an Endomorph photographed by an
Ectomorph with a Mesomorph observer; or a Mesomorph photographed
by an Ectomorph with an Endomorph observer; or an Ectomorph photographed by a Mesomorph with an Endomorph observer, and et cetera....
If the groupings began to cluster (e.g. two Ectomorphs), why the permutations could spiral to $X=N_1+N_2+N_3+N_4+N_5+N_N$—a number of observers that would quickly exceed those who witnessed all World Series
series combined. With so many observers, waves of subjectivity
would surely begin to lap at the foundation we were laying.

Dr. Johnson only laughed, "Faith, my good man, faith," and charged me with the training of our new "crew" member, though I could not help but notice the grinding of his molars.

{

Miss Smith was a square-jawed woman of athletic figure, a sommotype body of 4-4-4, as I estimated through her clothing. Dr. Johnson considered it a stroke of great fortune to have found her, working as a nurses-aide right there in the psychiatric wing where The Center was housed.

A bright if reticent woman, she at first gave the impression of indifference. On the first day of her training, she reported to work still wearing the stiff, white uniform of the psychiatric unit she had come from. Her expression didn't change as I acquainted her with the facilities: her office which adjoined mine and was its mirror image, a few steps across a corridor, and into a processing suite which consisted of an outer and inner room where she was to respectively conduct the interviews and photograph her subjects, an arrangement that also mirrored the rooms used to process the men (save the difference that the men's rooms—by this I do not mean to imply the toilets, which were a separate facility—were blue, while those of the women were painted pink; though perhaps it should be noted that the men's toilets—here I do mean the room they were housed in as opposed to the toilets themselves—were also blue while the women's rooms, were also pink, though this was merely a coincidence). The inner room of each suite was clinical in its arrangement: a booth where the subject was to de-clothe him or herself, a scale for weighing (of course), a stadio-compass (a body-caliper of Dr. Johnson's invention, whose useful purpose had not yet, at that time, revealed itself), a set of photographic lights trained upon a raised dais upon which the subject was to be posed, and an army-surplus K.24 aerial-mapping camera setup on a tripod exactly 6 meters from the dais.

Miss Smith, in the role of a subject, asked no questions as I demonstrated the procedure: "Stand in front of the subject," I said, standing before her as she stood motionless as a statute (and white as one too, dressed as she was in her nurse's nylons and uniform), frowning down upon me from the dais. "Demonstrate the position of attention." I did so, holding my arms stiffly at my side in the pose she would need to master in her own subjects. "Take hold of his, or in your case, her wrists," I said, "and pull firmly to ensure that the arms are forcibly extended." When I did so, her breasts extended.

In retrospect, I understand the power of a body to mock even the most rigorous system. In the instant it takes to trip a shutter, its mere presence can change the objectivity of a clinic into that of a boudoir, or conversely, turn the poet's longing into a fart at a funeral. At the time, however, Miss Smith and I merely forced this moment back into the stream of banal existence by continuing as if nothing unusual had happened, there under the harsh fluorescent lighting of The Center.

{

As time went on, Miss Smith and I developed a certain "relationship"—that word seems neutral enough to characterize the thousands of moments we spent together. (Doubtless, a more scientific term could be located. If by more "scientific" one meant more "precise." Especially if one had access to that map of the language known as a thesaurus.)

What could be more natural? We were crew members, after all, and it was a small ship. While the state universities operated large assembly-line operations employing separate interviewers, photographers and clerks to keep hundreds of physical education freshmen moving from the showers, then through a series of two-minute stations, we were responsible for the entire process, from the unlacing of the first shoe to the last exit interview.

Indeed, our respective work loads held fraternizing to a minimum. Thus my above phrasing, "moments" together. Days would pass during which our only contact would be an exchange of nods when I, for example, would emerge from my office just at the "moment" that she, for instance, was admitting into her office a female subject from the bench in the hallway upon which they waited.

On those occasions, I would endeavor to say "hello," or some other such pleasantry. Whereupon she would often smile in return. As days became months, I increasingly looked forward to those brief exchanges. I even began to time my egresses into the hallway so as to intersect with her ingresses from the hallway. These "chance" encounters seemed at times to be the one respite from the work-a-day monotony of the subject interviews we conducted which was only broken by the monotony of photographing bodies, which was only broken by the monotony of interviews, and so on.

To be sure, by "monotony" I do not mean "boredom." The work of profiling the Personalities and Temperaments of the subjects we photographed was often more "eye-opening" (now there's a phrase!) than the surprises one sometimes received when a subject stepped from the de-clothing booth. Aside from parolees, mental patients, and draftees, those most likely to volunteer were college students. So it was not surprising to find that to this sample every inkblot resembled a "female pelvis." Indeed, I began to think that the entire personality could be extrapolated from an careful reading of the Sexual Component (SC) or its lack (-SC). Show me a Well-adapted Cerebrotonic Personality, I say, and I will show you a story such as told by one 4-5-4, for instance, whose hobbies were bird-nest collecting and healthy intercourse in the missionary position (though it should be noted that his definition of "healthy" was broad enough to include a need to drive a heated needle into his flesh in order to achieve an excessive and prolonged priapism).

Conversely, there was the case of the coarse and heavy-set medical student, a perfect Extreme Viscerotonia, who could not recall ever having had an erection over the "thought" of a girl, though as he puts it, he "fucks constantly." While he did enjoy close, sweaty and prolonged contact with another body, the sexual act itself was usually consummated in 5 to 10 seconds, "depending," as he put it, "on how much cooperation I get." Here was a case of a 4-4-4 personality manifest in a somotype of 7-2-1, the subject having been raised, again in his words, as a member of "the New American Aristocracy." He had a new automobile each year at college. During his sophomore year he killed a young woman in a smashup on the highway. No papers were served and the incident appears to have had no effect on him as he has been in one other accident in which his car was a total wreck, and also a number of minor crashes. "It would be poor business," he says, "to pay for insurance and not have any accidents." He plans to go into surgery, "where the big money is." This too was described by the subject as "only natural."

Then there was the Extreme Cerebrotonia with a delicate frame and narcissistic admiration of his penis. From the onset of puberty he began masturbating in earnest ("Charleying," as he calls it). It was the one physical activity he found he could do well. For a time in his junior year he had a girlfriend—a girl who like him had a slight body, blue eyes and blonde hair—but she eventually broke it off because in lieu of intercourse he preferred masturbation, which in the beginning she would perform on him by kissing (with her lips) (of her face). Since then he has been content with sexual themes in literature, during which he would endure prolonged bouts of priapism, and experiment with subsidiary techniques of excitation. One Saturday night, after resting up all day, he succeeded in producing so violent an orgasm that he strained a muscle in his back, which caused him to limp for a week. His father attributed the limp to a "Charley horse," hence his name for what were in effect athletic contests of one. Again, an activity that was "only natural," according to the subject

The SC of the subjects made me consider my own "natural" life, living with Mother as I did. All through undergraduate, and then again in medical school, the regime of studies precluded any romantic entanglements. The non-stop activity of men and women removing their clothes at The Center was, of course, strictly a matter of professional interest. Even so, the proximity of Miss Smith and her naked female subjects made me realize what heady work science can be. My imagination increasingly took up the scene of her on the other side of the wall focusing the camera on her naked female specimens. When passing them as they waited on the bench in the hallway, I fell into mentally casting their somotypes: the Rubenesque 5-4-1s, the slender 2-4-4s of Botticelli, the rounded 4-5-4s of Degas's bathers. Eventually, the numbers alone were arousing (yes, scientists are normal men too), and the secret list of 5-4-1s, 2-4-4s, and the rest I compiled and kept hidden in a drawer became to me a kind of garden of earthly delights that took the utmost fortitude to abstain from frolicking in.

Then one day, while administering an ink-blot exam to one of my subjects, it occurred to me that perhaps I had been blind to the true interpretation of the smiles Miss Smith afforded me. It increasingly seemed like a distinct possibility, then probability that the heady experience I had of being near naked bodies of the opposite sex would be mirrored exactly in her, imagining me on my side of the wall with my specimens. Not being experienced in these matters, however, I was unsure of how to test this hypothesis. Mother was no help. When I suggested to her one evening that perhaps it was time I began thinking about raising a family, she only became teary eyed, blubbering, "*I'm* your family, Jimmy." Seeing her reaction made me fear for eliciting the wrong response in Miss Smith. If I provided a stimulus that was too weak, she might not even notice, just as I had not noticed the true intent of her smiles. Yet if I was indelicate, I realized, I could scare her into flight. That is, I feared she would deny her, and therefore my passion, out of fear of being seen as "easy" or some other such social mores. How could one predict such things?

{

This was the period I thought of us as a modern-day Heloise and Abelard, with science as our religion, and its collegial protocol as the monastic walls that separated us. Alone in bed, I would think, "Oh hang it all," and resolve to put the question to her point blank. To ask her to lunch with me and Mother one Sunday afternoon. But under the cold fluorescent lights of The Center, the proper opportunity never seemed to arise.

Indeed, we never spoke. Despite my best attempts to draw her out, one would have thought she was mute if it wasn't for the fact that I had accidentally overheard an answer of hers to one of Dr. Johnson's original interview questions: "Yes."

To no avail, I tried to recall the question that had solicited that response. But perhaps secretly, I reveled in the fact that I couldn't bring it to mind. For in its absence, my own questions found it easier to steal in. Like a miser counting his gold, over and over I heard myself ask her, Would you like to have dinner with Mother and I? And over and over came her answer: "Yes." No matter what the question—Would you like to sit on the porch swing? Are you cold? Would you like me to sit closer?— always and without hesitation she would answer, "Yes."

I began to spend increasing amounts of time in my office, knowing she was just on the other side of the wall that separated us. I'd stare at that wall, upon which hung a large framed lithograph of the hospital that The Center was located within, and the surrounding grounds as the estate looked at the turn of the century. At that time, the hospital was solely an insane asylum. Its gothic architecture matched my melancholic brooding, and as claimed by the state of the psy-chiatric arts at that time (mapped, so to speak, by the lithograph), I also found a measure of solace in the island of tranquillity formed by the grounds. I imagined the two of us strolling hand in hand down winding paths through gardens where the lunatics once took the air. We conversed freely, walking by time-withered trees, glacial

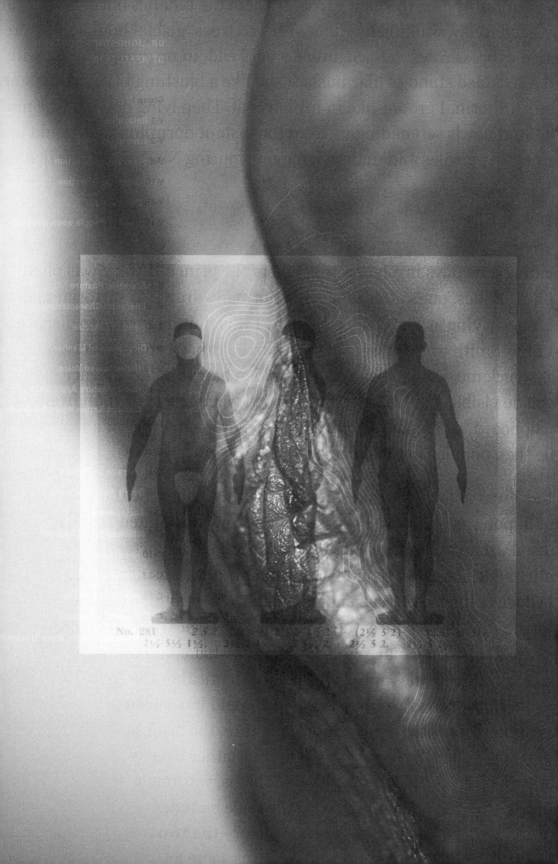

boulders covered in ivy, gnarled cypress roots.... Each amble would end, in my imagination, with us behind a secluded stand of lilac bushes, she like a blushing bride in her starched nurse's uniform, I groom-like in my lab coat. Then lying down in the moonlight, faint howls serenading us from the distant dormitories, I would bend over her, her girdles and underwiring murmuring No, No, but her lips saying, "Yes."

Spending long days in a laboratory where the principle work was photographing nudes, one's attention is not normally drawn to sartorial matters. Yet arriving at The Center one day, I was thunderstruck to discover that Miss Smith was not wearing her nurse's cap. Or more precisely, what struck me was the head of lush golden hair that the absence of her cap made visible. My heart nearly stopped when she looked up from her clipboard, a bang dipping over one eye in the manner of a femme fatale then popular in the cinema.

Just as I was about to speak, thinking that that might be the moment to pop the question, I was summoned by an agitated Dr. Johnson. In his office he excitedly challenged me to correctly identify which of the two nude photos on his desk was of a male, and which of a female. True enough, with their genitals covered as per standard procedure, the two photos were nearly twins, the "broad" hips and "narrow" shoulders of what could have been a "feminine male" appearing nearly identical to the "narrow" hips and "broad" shoulders of what could have been a "masculine female." When I admitted failure, the professor nearly shouted "Precisely!" He was in a lather over whether female 4-4-4s = 4-4-4 males. That is, was one a palindrome of the other? Or should the scale be redefined so that a female 3-4-5 = a 5-4-3 male?—the two being mirror images? Or perhaps there was some as yet undiscovered G-coefficient that would have to be factored in, G standing for "Gynoandomorph," the scientific term he had already coined for the phenomenon (an etymological hermaphrodite of the Greek *Gymen*, woman, and *Andos*, man).

If so, much of our taxonomy would have to be redone. Taking the analytic interviews, IQ, Temperament and Personality testing that we performed, he had compiled a list of 650 traits. From this list, he had drawn up some 22 categories, his "Doctrine of Affections," which seemed to embrace all of the ideas represented in the original 650. The 22 categories were then

Somotype	Incidence	Doctrine of Affec. Coefficient	Mean Height		Mean Weight		Ht./÷Wt.	Mean Range Ht./∂Wt.	Standard Deviation
			Inches	Centimeters	Pounds	Kilograms			
117	10	5	71.2	(181.0)	112	(50.8)	14.3	(45.5)	14.6-15.3 .13
126...	25	77.8	71.8	(131.5)	124	(55.7)	13.3	(47.1)	14.0-14.5 .12
227....	20	5	72.2	(353.5)	124	(53.2)	14.8	(48.0)	14.2-14.8 .13
136....	7	2	70.9	(34.9)	124	(53.2)	14.8	(48.7)	14.2-13.8 .14
150...	128	8	14.1	(46.6)	133	(77.9)	14.3	(48.8)	14.4-14.9
145...	22	6	70.3	(178 5)	130	(34.9)	13.0	(45.5)	13.7-14.1
254....	21	5	65.3	(276.0)	136	(61.7)	13.5	(44.5)	13.3-13.8
262....	24	6	67.9	(272.5)	147	(76.7)	12.5	(42.6)	12.7-13.1
163....	17	4	67.9	(177.0)	251	(68.8)	13.1	(43.2)	12.8-13.4
171....	20	5	64.1	(173.0)	103	(78.8)	12.8	(31.2)	11.3-12.7
172....	21	8	70.2	(178.8)	169	(76.7)	12.7	(32.0)	12.5-13.0
216...	21	3	65.3	(176.0)	117	(53.1)	14.2	(36.1)	14.4
217...	5	1	70.6	(275.5)	115	(83.8)	14.4	(37.6)	14.3-14.6
225...	78	20	60.0	(275.5)	123	(87.9)	13.5	(34.8)	15.6-14.1
226....	101	25	72.0	(555.0)	133	(60.3)	14.1	(4.6)	15-14.3 .11
235....	15	45	70.2	(278.5)	232	(55.6)	13.8	(32.6)	23.6-14.0 .10
236....	20	5	71.7	(182.0)	136	(61 2)	13.0	(46.3)	13.5-14.1
244....	167	42	68.6	(274.0)	231	(30.4)	13.5	(43.6)	13.3-13.7 .11
245....	56	14	70.8	(175.0)	137	(62.1)	13.7	(33.2)	13.3-13.8
252....	33	8	66.1	(165.0)	151	(55 4)	13.0	(43.0)	12.7-13.2
253...	243	33	64.2	(175.0)	234	(33.5)	13.2	(33.6)	13.0-13.4 .10
254....	64	16	70.5	(175.9)	375	(46.9)	13.4	(33.3)	15.7-13.6
261....	27	7	66.0	(175.0)	143	(51.5)	22.3	(31.5)	12.2-12.8
262....	51	23	55.2	(244.9)	151	(15.8)	12.8	(32.3)	12.3-13.0
263....	25	6	70.4	(146.3)	334	(56.9)	13.0	(32.5)	12.7-13.2
271...	23	3	66.8	(155.3)	344	(57.8)	12.3	(40.6)	12.2-12.4
326....	5	1	65.4	(176.5)	123	(55.8)	14.0	(46.2)	13.0-14.2
325....	84	21	55.3	(127.8)	125	(55.9)	16.0	(47.5)	16.0-14.0
326....	12	37	62.5	(571.5)	345	(57.9)	13.5	(53.5)	55.9-14.0
334....	201	50	55.4	(543.9)	355	(59.9)	15.3	(55.5)	33.6-13.8 .12
338....	215	55	15.7	(365.2)	133	(13.5)	13.7	(55.7)	33.6-33.8
343....	189	49	23.2	(335.5)	130	(23.4)	34.2	(66.8)	34.7-45.9
344....	333	53	22.3	(355.5)	159	(24.5)	45.6	(45.6)	34.5-33.3
425....	7	2	69.8	(535.7)	15.5	(25.5)	13.7	(45 .2)	35.5-55.8
425....	30	8	70.0	(577.5)	15.5	(37.7)	35.7	(40.0)	36.6-56.8
433....	57	24	67.3	(272.5)	15.7	(42.8)	32.5	(53.8)	50.0-55.3
434....	130	35	70.7	(175.5)	14.2	(50.1)	15.3	(54.3)	55.5-54.5
434....	24	67	56.6	(175.9)	133	(56.3)	15.3	(53.5)	53.3-55.3
442....	217	25	66.8	(565.5)	240	(73.5)	12.4	(6.32)	67.7 ....

incorporated into a simple 5-point rating scale (later expanded to a 7-point scale) that we were well on the way to correlating to the somotypes of the subjects.[3] The introduction of a G-coefficient would necessitate a re-calibration of all this data and the conclusions the doctor was drawing from it. Not that a G-coefficient would negate these conclusions, the Professor said. He continued in that abstract way of his, thinking out loud, reconciling the G-coefficient with the muscular arms and highly developed physiques of women who had taken up the factory jobs of men who had been called to serve their country during the last war. Nor was this "inversion" seen as a "perversion" as evidenced by the eagerness of sailors and soldiers to decorate the gun turrets or nose-cones of bombers and other such military hardware with images of mesomorphic, i.e., "pinup" girls. After the war, in both the styles of the street and the beach, he noted, dress has continued to swing toward mesomorphic dominance. The earlier high, stiff ectomorphic collar which completely covers an anemic neck has been virtually replaced by the low, wide, and often open collar more comfortable to the mesomorph type. Likewise, the bathing suit has dropped away piece by piece, in accordance with the general temperament of the mesomorph, who with a highly developed torso has an understandable urge to display her body, just as some other individual is compelled to embroider doilies, or attend church.

Group I

V-1	Relaxation
V-2	Love of Comfort
V-6	Pleasure in Digestion
V-10	Greed for Affection
V-15	Deep Sleep
V-19	Need of People When Troubled

Group II

S-1	Assertive Posture
S-3	Energetic Characteristic
S-4	Need of Exercise
S-7	Directness of Manner
S-13	Unrestrained Voice
S-16	Overly Mature Apperance
S-19	Need of Action When Troubled

Group III

C-1	Restraint in Posture
C-3	Overly Fast Reactions
C-8	Sociophobia
C-9	Inhibited Social Address
C-10	Resistance to Habit
C-13	Vocal Restraint
C-15	Poor Sleep Habits
C-16	Youthful Intentions
C-19	Need of Solitude When Troubled

Needless to say, I found it difficult to concentrate on the significance of what he was telling me, my mind instead conjuring images of Miss Smith's cap falling away, followed by other articles of clothing, until he began thumping on my chest to make some point about "...the dramatic increase in intrafamilial nudity witnessed by our society...."

But the instant he stopped thumping my chest, my mind returned to more personally specific conjectures as to what her lack of a cap could mean.

Was she doing it for my benefit? To display her hair, as the female rock pigeon puffs up its plumage to attract the male? Or was it simply a pragmatic decision on her part that had nothing to do with me? Not having to wrestle down the occasionally violent mental patient, perhaps she had concluded that there was no longer any reason for her to tie back her hair in a manner that would prevent fistfuls of it to be yanked in a brawl. Still....

Again I was rudely awakened by Dr. Johnson's voice, whereupon I answered "Yes?" Apparently he had asked me some question for he was staring intently into my face. Not wanting to let on that I had not been listening, I repeated "Yes" again. He stared hard at me a moment, then asked, "Are you certain?" Again I said "Yes," less surely this time. He shrugged, then continued, having progressed apparently during my lapse to fashions in furniture, noting how the Victorian style so suited to ectomorphs with their love of overstuffed chairs had given way to the more mesomorphic "Prairie" style....

Again it was impossible for me to listen. For as thunder follows lightening, I suddenly recalled the question that had elicited Miss Smith's "Yes." It was precisely the same as the one that had been put to me: "Are you certain?" And as I had hesitated, so had she, before slowly replying, "Yyyyyyyyes," her very uncertain tone emptying the word of its content, and thereby making a mockery of all the yeses I had imagined from her lips ever since. Had she meant No? Had she simply, like me, been mentally elsewhere? And if "Yes" could mean "No" as well as so many other things, couldn't it be the same for the absence of her hat?

I might not have given it any more thought had it not been for an interview I conducted the very next day. I was putting the subject, a boisterous and talkative 5-6-7 through the usual IQ and Temperament Testing. We had just finished the ink blot portion (his replies: Pelvis, Breasts, Scrotum) and I was asking him to blurt out what ever antonym came to his mind as I read words from the Wisconsin Inventory of Normal Expression.

Initially his responses fell within the bell curve of expectations. When I said Cat, he said Dog. When I said Hot, he said Cold. When I said Birth, he said Death. When I said Love, however, he also said Death. Indeed, Death was the antonym summoned to mind by a number of expressions. Man? Death. Woman? Death. Banana? Death. Sex?—no, not Death, for Sex and Death were clearly synonyms to everyone save Freud and Dante, the later of whom would have phrased it "Gigantic," even "Infinite Desire," as in "God's

Love" bounded by Finitude, i.e. "Mortality." So come to think of it, Sex and Death were synonymous for Dante as well. If he was a religious believer, that is, whose infinite love for God was reciprocated. (No sure bet, if you've ever read his poem.) So that leaves Freud, standing alone (an obvious allusion to masturbation). So perhaps they were synonymous for Freud also, the poet's observation that "Each act of sex was like a little death" presumably applying equally to masterbators. Masturbation being a kind of suicide, if you will, which really gets to the heart of the matter: how could a word be its own antonym?

I think you get my drift in regards to the meaning of Miss Smith's cap?

"Corpulent" has never been a word I would use to describe myself. Indeed, when I put the question to my mother that evening, she at once replied, "No Jimmy, you're just right," serving me a third heaping of mashed potatoes. Growing up in a rotund family, I had, in fact, always been known as the svelte one. So I was taken aback to discover that my own physique did not fit comfortably within the range of "normal" somotypes. Being a trained reader of the body, I knew, of course, that I tended toward the endomorphic. The surprise was how few of us endomorphs there were in the world—a fact brought home graphically by Professor Johnson's first draft of Mount Somotype, as he had titled his first map of the body types we had identified:

As if an entire landscape of bodies had been captured with one click of our aerial camera (a.k.a. a God's-eye view), Professor Johnson's map depicted it as a pyramid-shaped mountain with a triangular base as seen from above. At the pinnacle of this Olympus resided type 4-4-4, the ideal: a body type dominated by

No. 281   (27),   2 5 2-3.5 2   (2½ 5 2)   12.25 at 51
2½ 5½ 4   2,   2 5½ 2 2,   2½ 5 2,   2½ 5 2½

sleekness and a relaxed carriage that grooms well, having hair that combs easily and lies smoothly over a well-rounded head. In contrast, residing at the pyramid's lowest extremities, the points at the base of the mountain, were the somatic extremes: 1-7-1s; 7-1-1s; and 1-1-7s. That is, the full flowering of mesomorphy, i.e., the modern-day Neanderthal with his square head; the pure endomorph with his "pneumatic" body; and finally, the pure ectomorph, a human rail.

The three of us, Dr. Johnson, myself and Miss Smith, sipped the champagne Dr. Johnson had brought to celebrate the occasion as if we were the first explorers to have scaled a great peak. Only by mapping a place can it be said to have been discovered, he toasted, for if no one else could return, it was no more real than Shangri-La. He continued marveling at how the unexplored cliffs we had identified would one day be traveled by others using chair lifts, and even roads. He tempered his excitement, though, by cautioning that the completion of this map of the human body was only the first leg of the journey. Next came the arduous ascent of the female mountain, the discovery of the G-coefficient, and the correlation of both maps with their soil samples: the IQ scores and the rest of the data we had taken from below the surface of our subjects.

It should have been a happy occasion for the entire crew, yet watching (capless) Miss Smith run her hand over the map, her fingertips lingering on the 4-4-4 ideal, I was painfully aware that my own physique would fall somewhere south and to the west of the location she caressed, which is to say, lower down the mountain.

An image of those bright red nails and delicate fingers caressing another's peak continued to haunt me in the following weeks. Dr. Johnson had had his Mt. Somotype blown up to wall-map size and hung in each of our offices. Yet this daily reminder only motivated me to consider features that would not appear in our survey, features that could, I happily realized, shore up the devaluation of my own real-estate. To begin, our camera did not record smell. In many of our transient subjects, this was their most distinguishing characteristic. I took heart in the fact that a 4-4-4 who stunk would not be as desirable as a 5-4-3 who bathed. (Proof positive: so strongly did I associate Miss Smith's body with the lilac scent of institutional soap that emanated from her that first day I held her by the wrists that I still cannot wash my hands in any hospital, train station, or school lavatory without getting an erection (though the effect of the observer on the observed has been well documented, the reverse is not so nearly understood. Perhaps because of the fact that study of the phenomenon would necessitate a dynamic whereby the observed (i.e. observer) would affect in unknown ways the new observer who would, of course, affect the observed who would affect the observer who would affect the observed who would affect the observer, and etc., thereby rendering any conclusions elusive, if not unobservable (obviously). Likewise, the uniformly flat lighting we used washed out all individual skin complexion. Nor did our technique record hair thickness. Or even facial features. In sum it was possible that the rigor of our methodology systematically cropped out the most distinguishing features of our subjects' bodies: the whorls of the crown, for example, or for all we knew, of the navel or anal pore. Perhaps we should have been tabulating the ratio of "innies" to "outies" or calibrating arseholes to elbows or toenails to fingerprints or a million—maybe a trillion other such permutations.

Rather than imposing our cookie-cutter pose on each subject (the very essence of any "pose" being artificiality), perhaps we would be better off letting our subjects adopt whatsoever aspect they fancied. In this way, the shifting eyes of the criminal, slouch of the laggard; the pursed lips of the God-fearing Christian spinster would more readily assert themselves.

The number of variables that offered themselves to the imagination was staggering, and given the few that we actually selected, the opportunity for error seemed gigantic. I approached the doctor with my misgivings by discreetly bringing up what seemed to be our most obvious omission: the fact that we did not photograph genitals.

Fitting subjects as I did with the penile cloak, I could not help but notice an enormous variation. I asked the doctor if perhaps we were thoughtlessly bypassing a rich vein of data, as well as inventing a false need for a G-coefficient. That indeed, perhaps the legend to the map of humanity we were drawing might reside in those omitted bits. Somatyping, did after all mean typing the "whole body."

Surprisingly, the doctor said, "Nude bodies, yes, but face and genitals, that we have no right to observe," an attitude I took to be an anachronism still alive in his older, and more puritanical generation—just one example of how flat-earth habits of mind continue to shape knowledge, often unawares, long after their *raison d'être* has been eclipsed by scientific precision.

I, however, was forced to live the reality of the present we had created through the current state of our art. That is, I knew that the Rosetta Stone to Miss Smith's absent cap and ineffable smiles depended on how she saw me. And how she saw me depended on how she saw my body type. And how she—a fellow somotyper—saw my body type depended on the context in which she saw it. How else was it that Medieval Chinese were able to map sunspots, supernova and other astronomical phenomenon that their European counterparts, with their conception of the cosmos as a static, crystalline sphere, mistook as atmospheric effects like wind? That is, it became increasingly clear that in order to see myself as she saw me, it was necessary to determine where on the map I fell—where I objectively fell, not where I thought I fell, or hoped I fell, or feared I fell—and to do this, I knew, I would have to submit to the process.

On a Friday night after everyone in The Center had left for the weekend, I took off my clothes and took up the standard pose on the dais where I had by now posed thousands of other subjects. I had rigged the K.2 with a string so that I could operate its shutter. But instead of the sense of authority I normally felt in my role as photographer, I had the distinct sensation of being a marionette whose strings were controlled by the camera. Would its objective eye reveal a body that was further down the slope of the mountain than I feared? Or would it tell me that my fears had only been the figment of a scientific, i.e., skeptical, training turned inward? These and a million other questions raced through my mind as it pulled my string and went *click*.

As the film developed, I awaited its verdict in my office. Moonlight streaming through the venetian blinds cast bars of shadow across the engraved illustration of the insane asylum that hung on the wall. The sight of those bars reminded me that in an earlier time, I may have very well found myself as an inmate here. Once, while eating our sack lunches together, Doctor Johnson explained how the very apartments that now housed The Center had once been used to confine masterbators. In those days, he said, masturbation was believed (known?) to dissipate a young man's vital essence as the over-heated brain poisoned itself with toxic sepias. The more lethargic the mind became, the more intensely the masterbator strove to stimulate it through his singular vice (pleasure?) until his vicious (wonderful?) downward (upward?) spiral ended in catatonia or death. The only cure was to prevent the patient's own self-humbuggery and to accomplish this, patients were sewn into canvas bags that prevented access to their member.

"Sewn into his bag," the Professor said, "the masterbator would be tied in a chair which was located right..." He looked around the room, then pointed to where I sat in my office chair. "There."

From here our conversation drifted to other efforts to map "humanness" on its clay, particularly early maps of mental formations that investigators believed (knew?) to have been written on the body. The Comparative Physiognomyists, for example, who attributed to the man who resembled a heron the heron's discernment that makes possible its *coup d'etat* upon the frog. Or their equating of Turks and Turkeys for the perceived propensity of each to strut about until challenged by a stronger adversary whereupon both Turk and Turkey become equally patterns of submission.[4]

4

From Physiognomyists we progressed to Phrenologists with their vocabulary of head bumps, then believed (known?) to be as real as the circulation of the blood but now as dead as their Latinate captions. "*Cupidipihilious*," he laughed, "*hew hee haha haaaa!*—a capacity to love being in love. Or *Animoprogenitiveness*— *ah haha ha ha hew weee!*" When he got control of himself again, he moved on more soberly to the typing of blood globules, then the recent discoveries by Mr. Watson and Mr. Crick and he expressed a sincere gratitude that the maps being drawn by scientists today contained no room for the mythical beasts and anthropomorphized winds and currents of old.

Yet as I dwelt on these matters, I could not help but marvel at the Professor's own cheery disposition. For why should he or any one scientist believe he is on the trail of Truth when he himself helps prove every predecessor to be a pioneer in error, false steps and myopia? How does science, a history of failed theories, go on with such confidence?

How do people, for that matter? In regards to the former, this
is obviously a non-scientific question
so is therefore never asked. In regards to
the latter, perhaps they can take a lesson from
the former's example.

Indeed, I began to understand Dr. Johnson's ready-
made answer to whatever difficulty I presented—
"Faith, my good man, faith!" For what other than "faith"
(a loaded word) characterizes the "progress" (now there's
a loaded word!) of science? Yet when we see all the wonders
that science has produced, e.g. the light bulb, e.g. the atom
bomb, there does indeed seem to be "Progress." To continue this
march, the scientist therefore must be a man of unshakable faith.
The religious, seeking no evidence for his beliefs, requires none
to sustain him. But the scientist, requiring evidence and forever
finding its absence in yesterday's work, requires the utmost faith to
believe that he alone will be different. The Triumph of Science therefore, is a triumph of faith, or perhaps, given our more secular world, a
more precise word is ignorance. The light bulb, like the atom bomb, like
the discovery of all New Worlds therefore represents the Triumph
of Ignorance.

This is not meant, of course, to belittle ignorance. On the contrary, the
ancient Greeks believed that the universe rested on the back of an enormous
turtle. What did that turtle rest on? Another turtle. And so on.[5] Yet isn't
all of our learned science with its endless theories upon the backs of other
theories rushing to prove the veracity of this first explanation? For when all
is said and done, after you figure out how the universe works, then what?

I hadn't been dwelling on these matters long
when I was alerted by the sound of footfalls in the
hallway, then someone opening the door to Miss
Smith's office. Suddenly, a crack of light appeared
all around the frame of the engraved illustration.
Taking it down from the wall, I was startled to
find a window with a clear view into Miss Smith's
office, and of Miss Smith herself in high heels and

5 *Ad infinitum*

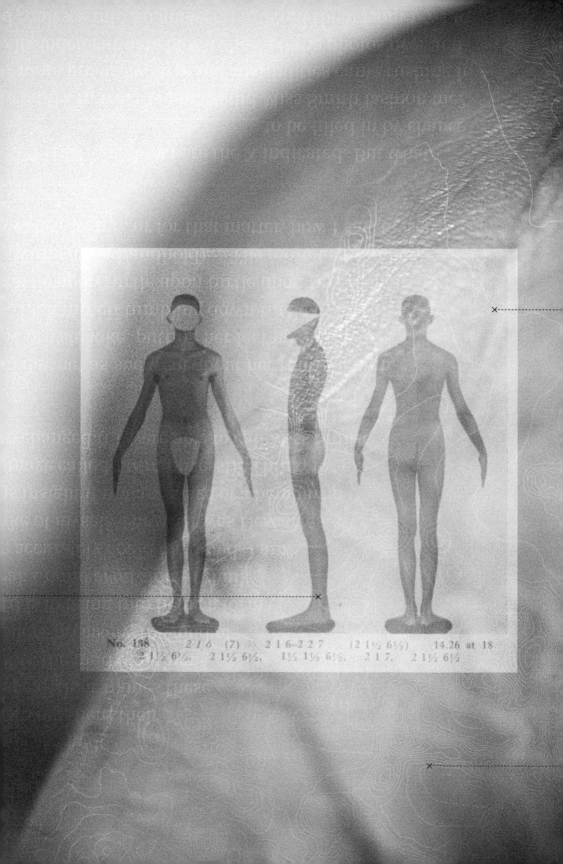

No. 138   2 1 6   (7)   2 1 6–2 2 7   (2 1½ 6½)   14.26 at 18
2 1½ 6½,   2 1½ 6½,   1½ 1½ 6½,   2 1 7,   2 1½ 6½

a sequined evening dress of low, i.e., mesomorphic, neck line. She was going through her desk, apparently looking for something she had left behind. When she stood erect and faced me, I didn't know what else to do but give a little finger wave. She stepped forward to a position barely more than the thickness of the wall from my own face, looked directly at me and smiled a half-smile as enigmatic as that of the Mona Lisa (had the Mona Lisa worn lipstick). Then she barred her teeth as if she would spring upon me like a wild animal. But her expression froze as if she were examining herself in a mirror. Which, I realized, she was—for presently she began to pick at a sesame seed that was wedged between her teeth. Flicking it away with a fingernail, she gathered up her purse and whatever it was she had returned for, shut off the light and left, leaving my own reflection in the darkened mirror. A one-way mirror. A one-way mirror that must have been installed for some sort of psychiatric observations back before The Center moved into this portion of the wing.

{

I arrived early Monday morning, anxious to begin my observations of Miss Smith. Upon entering my office, though, I was taken aback to find on top of my desk the cigar box in which we kept all of the endomorphs of type 5-4-1 through 5-5-5. Drawing nearer, I couldn't have been more struck down had I been the superstitious native who peers into a miniature coffin and discovers a voodoo doll of himself. There, staring up from on the top of the deck was the nude, corpse-like dopelganger of myself that I had made but had taken care to secret in a drawer. On the wall-map of Mt. Somotype, someone had used a black magic-marker to write YOU ARE HERE beside an X marked squarely on the plateau of 5-3-3s.

It is an odd sensation to hold a photo of oneself in the palm of the hand.

Through the one-way mirror, I observed Miss Smith struggle to untwist her girdle.

It's odd to reproduce anything, let alone a human—To imitate, not the God-like act of forming a man of clay, breathing into his nostrils and thereby punning *adam*, Hebrew for "man," with *adamah*, "mud" or "earth," though there is, of course, sweaty breeding and biological reproduction and all that jazz. Rather, to make (and here I do mean "make" as opposed to "take") a photo, is to walk as Adam through Eden, calling into existence lions and lambs and all the other plants and animals by giving them their names.

She puckered in her "mirror" and proceeded to touchup her lipstick.

So we call ectomorphs, mesomorphs and endomorphs into existence by giving them their names. And once we cease to speak their names these same beings will recede back into the mud of humanity from which they came. Or more precisely, the mud of language, for to imagine a word is to bring into being a form of life. Thus did Descartes speak *Cogito ergo sum*—I think therefore I am—when he more accurately could have said, I am the images of myself that I make of myself. For what was Descartes to himself at the moment of his insight if not an image of a being who thinks (in that corpse of a language called *Latin* no less!)? Think, for example, how the world would be changed if I were able to call Miss Smith by her given name, Evelyn.

Viewing Miss Smith day in and day out as she went about her routine, humming, often laughing over some private joke, putting her feet up on the desk and making crank phone calls, I felt myself tumbling down turtle upon turtle upon turtle upon turtle upon turtle upon turtle upon turtle upon turtle upon turtle upon turtle upon turtle (with nary a handhold).... The more I saw of her, the less I knew of her, or of how she saw me, or for that matter, how I saw myself. How can anyone know these things?

As the map said, I WAS, indeed, THERE, right where the X indicated. But what was the X itself?—other than a .... to be filled in by chance and circumstance? More importantly, in what language did Miss Smith fashion me? I couldn't begin to imagine. Or more precisely, so many possibilities came rushing in that they amounted to an equally indeterminate blot. I shuffled the photos over and over, hoping their chaos would coalesce into an answer. I ordered them from 1-7-1 to 7-1-1, included my own photo and fanned them out across the desk like a magician's deck of cards arranged by suit—such lightweight, cheap, easy to reproduce objects—with myself as the Joker of 5-3-3s, that is Hearts—each a *memento mori* of a gigantic need to know, a gigantic need to be known, or as the physiks of the troubadours might have had it, to be loved.

"Speak body!" I commanded my photo, its fear and longing frozen in black and white. "Speak, damn you!—like the zombie who upon hearing his name rises from the grave!"

No effect.

While fitting what was in effect blindfolds to the faces of the subjects I was about to photograph, I often had the urge to offer them a final cigarette. In a certain sense these people truly were about to die. By taking up the standard pose we told all subjects to adopt, they did shed their own individuality for the nameless, faceless identity of the "subject." The black-and-white images I would "take" of them, that I had taken of myself, would last far longer than our flesh-colored corporeal bodies. Like the Youth on Keat's Grecian Urn, they would remain forever "true." But even full knowledge of this scientific necessity—to dissect one must first kill—could not dissipate a creeping uneasiness I felt for being the instrument of their deliverance. Looking at them naked and upside-down in the viewfinder of the camera—for the lens of the aerial-mapping camera we used inverted their image—they often appeared to me as victims of some horrible inquisition, hung by their heels until they confessed to some crime that was unknown to us both.

Watching Miss Smith through the one-way mirror—with her lipsticks and somatype-altering bras and manner I never saw anywhere but through that looking glass—made me wonder how a map of the Andes would appear to Andeans. Would a silhouette of peaks be the only one that made sense to them? Or do the peaks appear, to those who live among them, as a flatland? That is, natural. Do the Antarcticans draw themselves at the bottom of their world? Holding the thick deck of somotypes in which mine was included, arranged from the 1-1-7 to the 7-7-1, I was able to riff them like a flip book that gave the appearance of a single metamorphosing body, mocking the very bricks of The Center with the fluidity of the human type—a seamless continuum of MAN. It became impossible for me to ride the subway, attend a lecture, or even dine with Mother without mentally undressing everyone present and casting their somotype. And not just somotypes. I also began to inventory body hair, whether the subject wore black or brown shoes, wingtips or loafers. The length of ear lobes, angle of noses. Length of stride, zippers or buttons, square or oblong cuticles, symmetry of thumbs…. And always, always, the more detail I added to this map, the more useless it became for navigation.

I don't know. Perhaps it was the elusiveness of the G-coefficient. Or perhaps the professor was arriving at a similar conclusion that we were attempting to draw an atlas of the world by only looking at the shoreline of New Jersey. Who can say? But I arrived at The Center one day to find that Dr. Johnson had a little experiment that he wanted me to conduct in regards to how representative our data was of the general public. He led me out to an old milk wagon, freshly painted and lettered with the words DR. JOHNSON'S CENTER FOR SOMATIC STUDIES TRAVELING LAB. The lettering circumnavigated a cartoon globe upon which stood cartoon Mesomorphs, Ectomorphs, and Endomorphs. Inside the van was a miniature version of our lab, complete with posing dais, camera and somotype scale. Dr. Johnson had also mapped out a tour I was to go on: a series of concentric orbits radiating out across the state (and presumably across the country, then the world), each precisely 25 km apart, like rings on a target with The Center at ground zero. I asked the doctor, if perhaps the wagon, with its circus-like banner, did not give the impression of a traveling freak show. Or perhaps one of those sideshows that sold elixirs? "Faith, my good man, faith," he only laughed, and sent me on my way.

I pulled away from the elegant, Victorian-era neighborhood of weeping willows, and tightly-drawn shades that surrounded The Center, then followed the Professor's map until I found myself at the center of a Negro neighborhood. Immediately I was struck by the wisdom of augmenting our data by reversing protocol so that instead of bringing subjects into our experiment we would situate our experiment within the world. The landscape itself was more varied here, consisting of street preachers and children playing in the spray of broken water mains that the city would never repair. Instead of the narrow dimensions of the "horsey set" so common among the white, university students (our prime meridian), here on the streets, one could find the whole carnival called humanity. I understood viscerally the enthusiasm Sir Francis Galton, Darwin's uncle, must have felt, charging into the African underbrush to measure the buttocks of natives with his sextant. Unfortunately, these people were not as educated as university students so it was difficult for them to grasp the importance of stripping for our cameras. Though I stood on the running board trying to entice volunteers to embrace our campaign, I was mainly laughed at. A few unfortunates smelling of alcohol did enter the van. But after realizing that I had no interest in buying their blood, and that yes, repeatedly yes, their only pay would be the satisfaction that they had contributed to the glory of science, they too left laughing. Or in anger. Twice I was convinced that had I not been protected by the color of my skin, I would have been beaten up as a homosexual—a mistaken identity that did serve to produce the lone photo set I managed to obtain: that of a Negro homosexual, who having readily stripped, began frolicking about, bidding me to catch him.

I was somewhat of a naturalist, net in hand (so to speak), in pursuit of an unusual somotype for our collection. So initially I did not mind playing along. But once I got him on the dais and stood behind, fitting him with the blindfold, he kept grinding his buttocks against me, giggling in falsetto. After I had taken his photo, he insisted that I put on the blindfold while he fondled me or I him. Incredulous of my refusal, he asked what did I want. I repeated that I only wanted to take his photo and having done so I insisted he leave. He began to cry, demanding to know why, if I wasn't going to be a "pirate" to him, I had told him those "lies." I had never promised anything but to take his photo. Nevertheless, when I opened the van to show him out, the crowd that had gathered outside stood staring at me as if I was some kind of monster. For a brief moment I thought that the attention his hysterics drew could be turned to good. But after he shouldered his way though the onlookers, bare-chested except for a scarf, weeping and blowing his nose in his shirt (in the confusion we found it only at the very last), it became apparent from their expressions that the day was lost. When I said, "Next," the crowd dissipated so quickly that an observer would have thought I'd flung hot oil at them.

Emerging from the rush, one understanding officer offered to lend a hand. Perhaps it was the fact that we both employed a "wagon" in our respective trades. Or maybe it was the camaraderie of the uniform, his blue, mine white. Who knows? In any case, he was more than willing to beat a few "faggots or niggers" into "cooperating." Yet when I suggested he pose—

Here memory goes on holiday....

Prof. Johnson felt terrible about my concussion. Upon my return to The Center, he lauded me as a modern-day Bruno—just one of the many investigators who had paid for his beliefs? knowledge? with his body. My head still aching, though, all I wanted was for him to shut up. What words could he or anyone utter, I now understood, that could penetrate the fog of incomprehension all of us share of another body's pain? Or fear? Or longing? Nonetheless, his cheery tone continued unabated as he continued to inform me, as happily as if he was describing new wallpaper, that in my absence the room used to photograph the females and the room used to photograph the males had been inverted. Thus, my office, with its one-way view onto Miss Smith in her office, was now Miss Smith's office, with a one-way view of me in what had been her office.

The look of empathy? sorrow? I received from Miss Smith during all of this—
perhaps inspired in her by the sight of my bandaged head?—or perhaps
it was mocking contempt?—I don't know. Can anyone know these things?
In any case, the "look" I received from Miss Smith made my whole body ache
with the ache normally associated with the heart. Yes, my whole body. For
though there is no scientific basis for emotion residing in the cells, in the
blood, in the bone, let alone the heart, I could feel them all cry out in anguish
for the betrayal she must have surely read into my secret observations of her,
hauled into the light by the reversal of our offices.

Only when I went into my (her) office, I discovered that what I had thought
was a one-way mirror was not a mirror at all. It was simply a window. All the
while I had been watching her she had been able to see me. Yet, she had made
no effort to hide, nor even mask her motions, and the memory of it threw me
into confusion. Even now, standing before the window (mirror) in her (my)
office she behaved no differently than when she had been before the mirror
(window) in my (her) office. Looking directly at (through?) me, she reached
into her blouse and adjusted a breast. At first I felt compelled to play dumb—
to act no differently than I had behaved when my office was my office so that
she wouldn't think that I had thought (known? believed?) I had been spying
on her on purpose.

I went to the filing cabinet to retrieve a box of somotypes and begin panto-
miming the day's work, even though the very actions of this ruse screamed
out its absurdity (this is why there are one-way mirrors to begin with).
She had been observing me, after all, observing her, and still was. Only
now she was observing me observing her with the knowledge that she knew
I was observing her knowing she was observing me....

When I asked the professor why the change in rooms had been made, he replied without looking up from the data he was trolling for a new G-coefficient
and spoke so softly that I couldn't tell if he said "Miss Smith requested it all"
or "Miss Smith, flower in a crannied wall." But he definitely added, "Trust me,
my son, it's for the best."

Back in my (her? our?) office, I wearily went about what all researchers do in
moments of disorientation: return to the data, the cold hard facts that cannot
be denied and are the interpreter's *cogito*, his soundings, his security blanket,
his baseline from which all conjectures, dreams and flights of fancy ascend.
I gently lifted my own nude photo from what I now saw was a family album.

If there was an answer, I knew, it was here: since I was the author of my own photograph, I clearly understood the intention with which it was made—to take the measure of my own (unique) normalcy. But cradling it in my palm, a yo-yo that allowed me to revisit that frozen moment again and again, the photograph itself told a different tale—one of an endomorph—a type—or so it seemed to this interpreter—a body who brought to the photo his own gigantic needs and desires, a body who in this case, I might add, was both attuned to such photos and so dulled by the viewing of thousands of such photos that seeing them in the aggregate he couldn't help but remember that a tea-spoon of earth can contain as many as 100 million bacterial bodies. But since I was also the author of the photo, perhaps I unconsciously loaded my own individual likeness with my own gigantic longing, e.g., a curled pinkie or some other such token of my own (banal) uniqueness.

Perhaps they all did—each photo an icon of gigantic needs and desires—including those of the researcher, for, as I now believe the Professor meant to intimate, it is the researcher's longing to know all in all that makes him do what he does; and yet, the more intently he gazes at his subject, the more it begins to dissipate until finally grasping the impossibility of ever possessing his beloved, he blinders his desire to the particle, not the atom, the flower, not the garden. If everything can't be known, he consoles himself, then at least something may be said. And perhaps, just perhaps, that some thing in some way may—Nay, it must!—stand in for the whole. At least to him.

As work at The Center "progressed," and my "wound" continued to "heal," I continued to perform my "duties" in such a fashion that to an observer (e.g. Miss Smith) it would appear as if nothing had changed (if by "nothing" we mean "everything"). I gathered data (saw what I looked for), all as before, save for my own little experiments (i.e. tautologies) that I occasionally inserted into the grander work. I would, for example, tell my subjects that if they did not pose correctly (i.e. according to Royal whim), the dais upon which they stood would give them an electric shock. And there in the developing photos would be confirmation of what I already knew, the trace of tense shoulder blades, for example, that revealed that "someone" had thought that "something" would happened.

Miss Smith remained steadfast (of course), and we fell into our routine, she on her side of the window, I on mine, keeping company after our fashion: arranging our photos, those mute, isolated moments, into patterns that spoke volumes. To someone. Or more precisely, arranging them into our family album.[6]

6
"Precise" being such an inexact word—as we demonstrate by giving or taking a million miles when we state the "precise" distance to a "nearby" galaxy but cannot split hair fine enough when we give the "precise" distance of an electron from its nucleus.[7]

7
Maps of the atom that depict the nucleus as a planet orbited by moon-like electrons as antiquated as Potolomy's fictions anyway.[8]

8
As shown by contemporary maps of the atom which depict it more like this:

$$< x > = \int \psi^*(x,t) x \psi(x,t) dx = \int \frac{x}{\sqrt{2\pi\sigma^2}} e^{\frac{-(x-m)^2}{2\sigma^2}} dx = m$$ [9]

9
Math being the only ink ambiguous enough to draw precisely the fact that looking at an electron's position changes its location.

The definition of 4-4-4, the ideal, matched precisely that of a fit college student. But could not this definition have arisen only because we looked at so many college students that the ideal became 4-4-4? Which is the ideal, which mirage? Which was found? Which gave rise to the other? Does the cartographer (or perhaps more precisely, the "poet") make the map (by which I also mean the "poem") or does the map make the cartographer?— as well as the explorer, the tourist, the miner, the scientist, even those scientists cursed to wander that oxymoron of shadow and light euphemistically known as the "human sciences." (Napoleon was said to have been a great lover of maps.) In the end, was there a difference? Is that what Miss Smith meant by switching offices? That is, was there still hope? At least for the ignorant?

Or was this blossoming "relationship" she and I shared a fantasy? Being a "scientist," I considered the possibility. It was possible, given the nexus of body, consciousness, and world otherwise known as the crack in my skull, that I was hallucinating the contented domesticity that had descended upon The Center. It was possible, even, that I was the subject of some grand psychological experiment as yet unknown to me. Can any of us know for certain the motives of another's "hello?" Short of this, can anyone say for certain whether the Professor was a Modern Magellan? Modern Renoir or Svengali? Many maps end their lives not as tools, that is, not as propaganda, not as blueprints, compass, or Ouja board, but as lampshades or in museums—that is, as art. My poster of Mt. Somotype already leaned against a WWII-vintage filing cabinet, massed as if for a rummage sale with the framed lithograph that had once hung in her (my) office before I had been moved into my (her) office.

Even if I had hallucinated (i.e. saw) it all, "something" happened—if only it was the hallucination ("view") itself. I had the (mute) witnesses—the photos which no matter how interpreted where like death masks or fingerprints of "something." Photos which did not lie, for they did not speak—and were therefore true—in the way that a ventriloquist's dummy is truthful until animated by its master (if by master we mean all of us in our family albums of stock ceremony: birthdays, anniversaries, class photos and family feasts— millions and millions of self-portraits and all identical, save the details: arrangements of facial features, the particulars of date, which were themselves, of course, finite, the principle of "finite possibility" being what makes "Perpetual Calendars" possible, as well as the "Eternal Human Heart," and also the relative dearth of sexual practices indulged in by our species, itself a function, perhaps, of the fact that though we number 2 billion individuals, any one individual typically expresses only seven orifices, and an equal number of basic emotions, though it should be noted that given the 2 billion individuals now living on earth, and the fact that each body has up to 60 trillion cells, the odds against any two people having identical bodies, and therefore emotional responses, exceeds the number of all bacteria on earth, and is in fact astronomical, exceeding the number of stars visible in the sky (at night).

Using a telescoping lens, I was able to focus so closely on the navels of some subjects that their whorls formed abstract patterns that could have just as easily been those of an inner ear, watery vortex, or galaxy. A fish-eye lens allowed me to stretch the frame to include the somotyping room all around, its calendar (a redundancy to be sure), even the side windows through which could be seen the wider world and whatever automobile, for example, happened to be passing by at the "moment." Along the bowed margin there also appeared a medicine chest's mirror in which could be seen, when the light was right, the reflection of a man whose face was obscured by the camera he peered into (assuming his eyes were open), bringing into focus (assuming he was not blurring) some "subject," perhaps, but certainly a self portrait, if by "self" we also mean "family," if by "portrait" we mean one moment extracted from billions of others without captions, its rhumb lines not so clearly written on the body as was the gash on my head but written nonetheless, if by "written" we mean lived, if by "lived" we mean having existed; if by "existing" we circumnavigate back to "body" and its family of unknown coefficients. That is, its Family of Man. (If by Man we also mean Woman.)

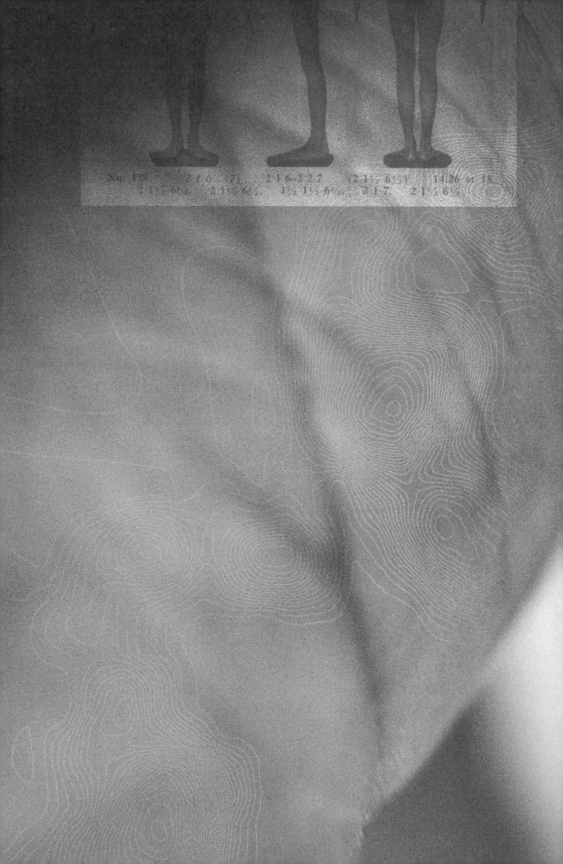

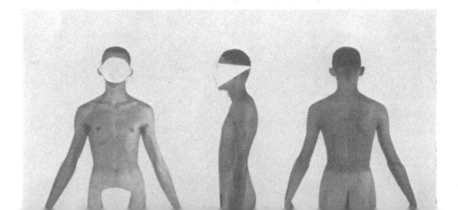

The Risk-Taking Gene
as Expressed by
Some Asian Subjects

Their shirts had the uniform neatness of suburbia: chemically fortified green, polo. White father, mother, symmetrical child: a Family Unit (FU) with n members where $FU_n = \pi$ (the mother was pregnant). Contrasting their statistical tidiness to the thrown-together character of the Three Happiness #1 Chinese Restaurant we had each in turn stumbled upon, I couldn't help but wonder if the great fattening in comfort won by Western nations has not been paid for by an equal narrowing of imagination. Not an imagination to create wealth, or even scientific knowledge, for in this we Westerners obviously live at a time of genius. Rather, I refer to an imagination—or call it a gut feeling—that can so powerfully apprehend an other world that the dreamer risks all and leaps!—a blindfolded trapeze artist without a net!—sure that the trapeze swing he has flung himself after, a world he can't actually see, will be there when he closes his grip.

The waitress, a dried apple of a woman with no English, bowed to her guests as she had welcomed me. But instead of following her shuffle to the table a busboy had reluctantly gotten up to wipe, they stood gaping at the surrounding shabbiness: American colonial and other mismatched chairs (refugees no doubt from some doomed IHOP); faux windows, their Colonial frames now painted red and gold; and paper lanterns that were as ashen as the old Chinese men sagging about the other tables, squinting through the smoke of their cigarettes at the new arrivals as if a decision to stay or go would be the most dramatic thing they would witness in this the Year of the Snake.

"Gin zhuo," the waitress insisted. To no avail. The sight of the table being set with chopsticks sent the family off in search of a restaurant more in keeping with the souvenirs they carried while the old men returned to their tea, their Chinese newspapers, their cigarettes.

"Ha!" one exclaimed to no one, as if he had won a wager against himself.

Just then a great clatter of men swept in, talking Chinese in a loud, celebratory manner. The busboy sprang to action, joined by the waitress who left her water pitcher sweating on the mythological constellations and dragons printed on the paper placemat beneath my own lunch.

That a certain kind of risky imagination has been supplanted by a more pragmatic one can be seen in the way we Westerners read our stars, I considered, as the men noisily rearranged the Colonial chairs of the restaurant, chasing a few of the old men to other tables to do so. Whereas the ancient Chinese saw dragons in their sky—those guardians of hidden mysteries—whereas the Hindus looked up to the same stars and saw Agni the fire god in gymnastic couplings with the wives of the Seven Sages, we here in the pragmatic West are taught to see a big dipper. And as if to confirm our paucity of vision, when we look to the stars nearest this dipper we see another dipper, smaller.

These thoughts weighed on me especially heavily that day because of the study I was conducting on the Risk-Taking gene: the genetic propensity discovered by Cloninger, Adolfsson and Svrakic for some people to put themselves at risk in order to feel the level of arousal most of us get from the petty concerns of our day—a disagreement with a co-worker, for example, or walking into a restaurant and discovering that it wasn't as nice as we had expected. With the blunted receptors in the brain that mark Risk-Takers, though, such trivial incidents barely register. Compared to the general population, Risk-Takers, or R-T Personalities, feel as though they are sleepwalking through life unless they find themselves in situations extreme enough to release the flow of neurotransmitters lying in the primitive recesses of all of us: norepinephrine, which helps trigger the flight or fight response, dopamine, which is associated with feelings of intense pleasure, and of course, serotonin.

In ancient times, such carriers of the Risk-Taking gene must have been valuable to the tribe for these were the men and women who would risk sailing off the edge of a flat earth or eating the untested berry. In today's climate-controlled world, however, the carriers of this gene are forced to turn to artificial dangers for their norepinephrine/dopamine/serotonin rush: BASE jumping, that practice of leaping from antenna towers or sheer cliffs; other extreme sports as well as traditional mainstays: reckless driving, compulsive gambling, adulterous affairs—all reasons the investigator of Risk-Taking (or any behavior) must take pains to prevent his subjects' responses from blurring into ink-blots of action.

Indeed, laboratory constraints are so central to the creation of knowledge that when the subject is the human, a creature that by nature resists living according to the dictates of the lab, the researcher must seek out natural substitutes or simulate them in order to prevent, for example, a restaurant from transforming bored hanger-arounders into laughing, joking friends who transform a dead restaurant into a place so suddenly alive with colorful lanterns and the Cantopop music that sprang from this one's ceiling that it would be impossible to say which variable had what effect on what whole.

Thus we know more about the bloodlines of prison populations than previous generations knew about the pedigrees of their kings and queens....

Beers all around. The big ones, *Tsing Tow* twenty ouncers—though when I had tried to order a beer, I was told it was not possible. "*Yam sing!*"

...a library could be filled by the published data on the olfactory responses, spatial judgment...

"*Mui kwe lu!*" A young woman with the men laughed loudly—and I wondered how I had missed her, for she was wearing a sleek, red dress.

...inter-male aggression...

She gave a start in her seat, simultaneously turning to slap the man beside her and setting off guffaws in the others.

...familial nudity, and vocabulary transmission among Eskimos—as opposed to extra-female pacifism, stranger clothedness, and vocabulary incomprehension among non-Eskimos. Why, I even knew that the alcohol in two beers would make the earlobes of 84% of the Chinese blush in comparison to 63% of Caucasians, and I watched my table neighbors for these signs, taking comfort in the fact that they were the very sort of homogeneous population needed for my study. Like the Amish. Though the relatively low percentage of Risk-Takers believed to live among the Amish precluded my use of this group.

Not so the Chinese.

A boy ran into the restaurant and delivered to their table one of those white cartons all Chinese restaurants use for carryouts while the men laughed at something the woman said as she performed a magic trick—or maybe she was telling an obscene joke?—covering a salt shaker with a napkin so it looked like it was protruding from the table.

Indeed, one only has to look up "Chen" in the phone book to see how many of their addresses fall within the narrow confines of my current lab, i.e. Chinatown. More importantly, one only has to look at a few of their chromosome stains to see how many physical, real-world loci can be found under the single heading "Chen." Haverson-Shreck has documented the Asian predilection for all manner of gambling, be it *pai gow*, cards, fighting fish, crickets, kites, cocks, or men; and the tongs that permeate this community (so associated in the Western mind with opium dens and speakeasies) are ideal genetic self-sorting mechanisms. Set up in America to duplicate the paternalistic help a young man might receive from his extended family back home, these benevolent societies also continue in America the biological heritage of the ancestral home. If an immigrant whose family name was Hip Sing needed a job or a doctor who would not demand immediate payment, he could turn to other members of the Hip Sing Tong. And no other. If his last name was Hop Sing, he would be adopted by the Hop Sing Tong. And no other. It was, and is, that straightforward.

Plus, commuting to do my fieldwork among this homogeneous population would only cost me the bus fare to Chinatown and this was no small consideration.

I had acquired, you understand, a certain reputation—one that led me to believe that my current study would determine my fate. That is, whether or not I would ever again be funded by the federal government. And therefore allowed (or not) to stay in my university. Or any institution. Not that this reputation was deserved. Indeed, I tried hard to follow the lead of colleagues who consistently took the pragmatic route, building careers out of studies that built on the conclusions of those whom they would later, coincidentally, depend on for promotions and grants. But it was especially at those times that the impossibility of seeing the world exactly as another would creep in, forcing me to either ignore how many meanings a simple yet key word such as "education" or "anger" could have, or else forcing me to qualify my conclusions, and then qualify my qualifications, and then qualify my qualifications of my qualifications so that in the end, despite massive amounts of data and charts and graphs that laid out much, in the end I was able to say nothing. Or to put it more precisely, to conclude that "the linkage between feelings of 'shame' and Chromosome 12 is inconclusive"; or "after adjusting for covariants in 'education,'—i.e., formal 'education,' e.g., school 'education' (even if given at home), or informal education (e.g. living abroad or over a pool hall), rote memorization, manual training, reading widely, or narrowly (specialization), having a 'feel' for, an acquaintance with, being a master of, a novice to, maybe a Saturday-afternoon painter, mechanic, or poet, having educated fingers, or palette, or nose, or feet," etc. etc.,"—evidence for a hereditary locus was lacking and obscures any..." and so forth.

This time would be different, though. It had to be. Yet reviewing the data I had thus far gleaned from the volunteers who answered my ad in *The Chinatown Lantern* my spirits were as high as a goldfish kite caught in a tree. Not a single Risk-Taker had shown up among the dishwashers, cabbies and day laborers who answered my ad, leaving the topology of my data as flat as my placemat: all baseline. No peaks, no valleys, no difference, that is, from which to conjure significance.

The woman in the red dress sat close to one of the men, her thigh speaking to his with a body language understood in any culture. Like her, he was also younger than the rest of the men. And dressed better. In contrast to their sugar-bowl haircuts, his jet-black hair had been combed into a stylish wave; he wore a yellow silk shirt over a black tee while most of the others were middle-aged, and dressed in the wrinkled white-cotton shirts of clerks everywhere. At one point they paused to listen to him recite a poem. At least I thought it was a poem, given the regular cadence his Chinese fell into:

> *Lu acai yu huang feihong.*
> *Gui ma zhi duo xing.*
> *Yige zitou de danshen.*

But then he began to end each line with what seemed to be an English translation: "All the Wrong Clues for the Right Solution" and "Too Many Ways to be Number One," one of which I thought I recognized as a title, and I realized he could be reciting a list, an inventory, maybe of book titles: both his English and the words themselves had just that sort of catchy snap. I couldn't imagine the group as an office party for book importers, though, or the Association of Chinese-American Librarians, given his flashy yellow shirt, the spaghetti straps of her dress, the laughter one of his titles caused. Maybe they were just happy, I considered, gazing out a faux window and onto the grainy black-and-white blow-up photo of The Great Wall of China, snaking into the distance. Indeed, sometimes it seems as though the best approximations of truth come from being no more specific than that hunch—despite the claims made by data, or horoscopes, or the calculus of lucky numbers printed on my place mat. *8, 44, 848.* Eight. The number made me smile, for it was the number of DNA repeats that my study predicted would be found on the D4DR gene carried by Risk-Takers.

The waitress emerged from the kitchen, and I signaled again for a bill. She nodded again?—or, again, exercised a crick in her neck?

Another boy ran into the restaurant to deliver one of those white, carryout cartons, and it struck me as odd that some of the men would eat in one restaurant while ordering carryout from another. But then, about the time the waitress finally picked up my dishes, a third boy entered and a pattern began to emerge: whenever a boy dropped off one of those containers, one of the men would take it into the washroom only to return a few minutes later—without the carton.

Stop it, I told myself, happy to have the waitress save me from the pattern-making path my mind had wandered onto. She placed before me a teacup plate containing my bill and a fortune cookie.

One of the men rose as if to give a toast. Their table fell silent as he began, delivering an obviously prepared speech to the one in the silk shirt. Or was his demeanor yet another example of form giving significance to what is actually insignificant? Like columns of precise phrenological data, for example or—need it be said?—a yellow cookie.

When I cracked open my fortune cookie, though, time slued through one of those moments when a glance from a wife thought to be faithful or a slip of the tongue reveals an unspoken truth and, in an instant, our safe and solid world—our core beliefs—are shown to be no more than the view from Myopia. Slowly, I re-read this bombshell on mine: *You like Chinese food.*

Sure enough, the clatter of the kitchen, the man emotionally speaking Chinese at the next table—the world all around—continued as if nothing had happened, though the world within went belly-up as I mulled over this message. Could the mechanism for delivering this fortune to only those who have selected themselves for its truth also be at work in my ad? That is, could the very structure of my study have been screening out all Risk-Takers? Could all of the work I had done up to this point equally be a phantasm, an exercise in putting one's head in a pot? The answer left me nauseated. What Risk-Taker would answer a newspaper ad to sit in an office and fill out a questionnaire?

It was at this time that the man I thought had been proposing a toast began to weep. The woman, and most of the men turned away—from pity? in disgust?—the shame culture of 'face' is powerful—but the one in the yellow shirt and a hard-eyed man beside him continued to look on, their jaws set in what struck me as murderous expressions.

The one standing shook his head as if in apology, continuing some explanation in an impassioned voice. When he finally fell silent, he looked down as if awaiting a sentence, and the truth of the details that had been swirling about resolved into their one reality: the plants in the window... prevented a view inside from the street; the boys delivering carryout boxes...runners, I now saw; the men all sitting with their backs to the wall, facing the door.... I was in the midst of a tong, clearly, or more exactly, the underbelly of one of the tongs that still engaged in gambling, prostitution, dockworker control, and other illegal activities. In other words, a roomful of Risk-Takers. Men who could become, if they wanted, successful bankers, teachers, or soldiers, for they were in fact all of those, but who instead chose to live at the edge of society. Not despite the risk, but because of it.

The waitress was at my table again. "You go now," she said, taking my money, an ability to speak English suddenly coming over her. "We closing, you go," she insisted, though it was the middle of the lunch rush. I am not a brave man. But sometimes the drive for self-preservation allows even the timid to act heroically, and as I rose to leave I realized I was walking away from perhaps the one chance I might get to salvage my study—that is, the last chance to salvage my university life—the only life I had ever known.

I found myself ignoring the protestations of the waitress to reach the men at the table. Dangerous men, I now saw, who'd been smoking so much that a gray haze made them look like something out of *film noir*.

The one standing, sweating—I could now see the fear in his eyes—turned toward me as the twins, or brothers, or whoever the men were, shifted their murderous looks my way.

Government agencies like police departments rarely bother with discerning the differences between the Chinese and Japanese. Or Koreans or Vietnamese for that matter. Often they assign any Asian in their employ to any Asian problem and perhaps the men mistook me—in cheap suit and tie—for some detective working vice, since my face bears the legacy of a Japanese grandfather. If so, I would be worse than a *gweilo*, as all foreign devils are called. In any case, as I got out a copy of the ad I had been running in the newspaper, several of the men hurriedly left, not waiting to see what the paper was. But not the leader—the one in the yellow shirt. He took it from me and carefully read it as I said my piece.

For my answer he "showed me the whites of his eyes," that stock response to all *gweilo,* clasping his hands behind his head and looking up to the slowly rotating ceiling fan until I left.

*

Shit!—have you ever been *kung-powed* by a piece
of paper?—wham!—*fist-of-the-dragon* worthy of Bruce Lee.
Sounds crazy, *ai yah,* but if you ever got a deportation
order you know what I'm talking about only less so. I
mean, the banana may as well have been the Ghost of HK
Past, tail me all the way to America, and I had to catch
my breath, lay the ad on the table so Jenny wouldn't see
my hands shake. I mean, why me? Why that ad? Why did he
bring that ad to my hands and no one else's if not for
bad qi?—like a scene out of vampire-fu:

[00:00:00] Wide Master Shot of Restaurant: We were
eight of us at table.

[00:00:03] White Ghost bring his scroll of the dead
[Chinglish Subtitle: "Now is time for you to suck the
coffin mushroom."]

[00:00:15] After he leaves, we all make joke—Risk-Taking Study—*chi sin*!—plenty good banana fun!

[00:00:20] Analytic Cut to Jenny-Po: the womanly way she squeeze my arm let me know that she knew that that paper had let the wind out of me.

[00:00:21] Reverse-Angle Shot to Me for My Reaction: Man, I don't want her sympathy! Not again! But that's only on the inside. Outside I am Chin the Grin from ear to ear, like I been swallowed whole by an even worse movie, keeping it light, keeping it moving, and finding the role too easy—Me!—who could act like any proper Mr. Fleetstreet when necessary, who used to skateboard up and down Jordan Road with my mates, running off the sidewalk any chippie in the shorts, white shirt, plaid tie of the tea-and-crumpet academies. Yeah, we bad,

even at fourteen, rolling all over the harbor, looking
for on-location movie shoots. When we'd find one, we'd
stroll up to it, cool, boards shouldered so security
could see the black dragons we painted on them to make
people think we got bigger brothers as we offered our
services to keep little pricks like us from skateboarding
in and out of the scene they were trying to shoot. Once
we even got Karen Mok's autograph!

So why, I used to ask myself, why does the Chinese
businessman smile as he shakes hands to accept unfair
tariffs? Why do parents spend HK$ 20,000, like the
father of my old mate Johnny, to put their son in a UK
school when schools in HK of equally high standard? As
foreigners they'd pay double tuition—enough to build a
front-yard swimming pool—but Johnny gets housed under the
stairs, worse than the maid, worse than the dog of the
maid. He gets bullied by English students, even Chinese
ones who say he makes them look bad with his *gong si fong*
ways, his under-the-stairs room decorated with torpedo-
titty HK movie posters, him and his Cantorap, but he says
nothing back. Not even to his parents. Is it because
we're all too polite to make complaint? No, I now know.
It's because no one can take your face. You can only lose
it. And you can only lose it by letting them know that
you know that they know that you know you've lost it.
That's what shame is. So you smile instead—no biggie—what
me worry?—you know how to get your fingers out of Chinese
handcuffs, right?

But scissors work too. And okay, despite what Jenny
says about me, I know the world doesn't spin about me,
it's not all a B-flick, blah, blah, blah. I'm only saying
that if it was, I know how my director's cut would run,
even with her thinking she needs to jump into every scene
to save my face, even if she's right about everything:
I'm not the bad guy, it wasn't my fault, and Western
science is just the charm to make peace with Chinese
ghosts. Still, I'm skeptical only for good reason. You
see, I know about bananas because back in HK I was in
college myself. Yeah, me; Johnny gets packed off to the
UK but by the time he graduates I'm in the HK Institute
of Fashion Design and Polytechnic. During the day I
am studying Ming vases, Chi-Sci-Fi movies, all visual
culture, as the *ah seuh* say—and loving it. Nights we're
duping movies—lots of gangsta-fu, chop-socky for yuks,
sai chai for spice. We are only small-time pirates with

camcorders: find some real *triad* blokes who want to see
Shaolin Fox, pay their way in so they sit by you while
you shoot right off the theater screen—nobody says
nothing, the bun's okay, and everything's in balance
till one day Jenny delivers a bootleg copy of *Gui ma zhi
duo xing*—All the Wrong Clues (For the Right Solution)-
to a lady customer. When the lady returns the tape, and
she see me, and I see her [ping-pong cuts], and we see
each other, her realizing I am one of her students and
me realizing she is one of my professors, everything
changes. She becomes very interested in my studies. She
pays me special service. Says I have a great eye. That
I would make a great director, even professor, and who
knows? Maybe I would have had a different fate if I
didn't get mixed up in her *wài kuài*. But no, I let her
sign me for an independent study with assignments to
visit special collections in libraries. I have a letter—
all very official—explaining that I am a student, and why
I need to see such-and-such rare book.

Librarians are so helpful, so happy to share the
treasures they guard that they set me up in a private
room. Just me and the book so I could study in peace.
They had me wear a pair of white gloves to keep off
fingerprints!—can you believe it? No matter. Not once
did they ever check to see if I razored out a page—you
know, the ones with *si fu* calligraphy that academics
and rich men trade on Nathan Road. Pen-and-ink bamboo
grooves, *Fu-ch'un* mountains seen through mist. Just cut
deep in the gutter so no one could tell if a mountain was
missing unless they squint hard. Which no librarians ever
thought to do. They're not police. Course if they did,
professor-po would be shocked to find out her student was
a thief. And who's gonna believe some *ah chaan* from the
mainland over Professor Art Historian? Paper-Scissors-
Rock—you know how that works, right? And people with
glasses always pay others to take their risks. So okay,
I take all the risk, but is it my fault I also pick up
how her business works? Things are never as they seem—
if you think New York apartments look enormous in TV
sitcoms just think how they look from HK—so we'll see;
just because *gweilo* science put a man on the moon, like
Jenny keeps saying, doesn't mean this banana can hold
chopsticks....

*

Located on a dead-end off a Chinatown back street, the storefront office space I had rented for the month appeared as small as one of those kiosks crammed with all manner of magazines, candy, watches, phone cards, and 220-to-110-volt converters: that density that the Chinese are accustomed to in everything, from their cities to their alphabet, coming as they do from a nation so populous that to get a sense of it, we in America would have to imagine our entire population squeezed into the east, then multiplied by four. It is for this reason that a dozen immigrants can tolerate living in one of those closet-sized *gong si fongs* they share, sleeping in shifts in its single bed.

My office was much bigger than it looked, though: as deep as the building that housed it, with a back door that opened onto the alley. A heavy beam barricaded this back door, held in place by a system of pulleys and weights that, like Chinese handcuffs, seemed to be as much puzzle as lock, and could only be opened by someone who was not only already inside but also understood how its interlaced tensions produced their sum result. Discolored floor tiles formed a ghostly outline of what must have been a long, store-length soda fountain—or rather a pharmacy counter as the place had been the former home of 王氏上古妙方，专治现代人士 which I was told translated roughly into Wong's Ancient Cure for Modern People, a business made anachronistic, a grinning realtor informed me, by Viagra.

Ceiling paint, electrical piping, and fluorescent lighting fixtures obscured one of those ornately patterned tin ceilings ubiquitous in Victorian-era stores, but the stench of another time was still distinct in its space—rancid orange peel and fish heads—or so it seemed as I shuttled between the office and a dumpster in the alley behind the building, cleaning out rags and waterlogged charts, a newsprint manual for bringing this organ into harmony with that bodily factor (cold, wind, dryness, etc.)—the claptrap of a way of ordering the world where Chinese ghosts and *qi* were as real as the rhino horn used to medicate their effects. Or so I imagined, replacing that ancient refuse with my own lean equipment, a desk and two metal chairs, though I could never completely erase a trace of the Ancient Cure that hung in the air.

This last week saw only four volunteers: a man employed by a chicken-parts processing plant and three Chinese punks—dirty pink hair, tongue studs—who giggled so hard that it took them five minutes to supply the cheek scraping I required of all subjects for the DNA tests that I matched to their questionnaires.

Then he was there—coming in the door—the tong boss I'd seen in Three Happiness, girlfriend in another streamlined dress at his side.

In order not to scare him off, I pretended I didn't recognize them, but he saw through this immediately. "Come on, man, we're not stupid," he said in an odd kind of English. British English, that reminded me for some reason of an old Al Capone movie. He spun the metal folding chair around and straddled it, sitting across from me at my desk while his girlfriend walked around to my side and began looking through my papers. "So," he said, either to distract me, or to tell me to never mind what she was doing, "You still looking for Risk-Takers, or what?"

I told him I was, and he said, "Good. So am I, maybe we help each other."

While she opened first one desk drawer, then another, I began my standard orientation in the hopes that behaving naturally would be the best way to bring him in. He listened politely as I emphasized my confidentiality statement, and then explained how the results would be used, trying to maintain the best matter-of-fact demeanor I could despite the distractions of his girlfriend. At one point she grunted, working to unscrew the mouthpiece of my phone as though it were a stuck pickle jar and the effort brought out the muscles of her bare arms and shoulders. Jet black, pixie hair.... Had she been brought up in a different social group, I thought, she might have become a famous gymnast. Or rock climber.

While I showed her boyfriend the basics of the questionnaire, she roamed the office. Like a tourist in a gift shop, she'd pause from time to time, her eyes widening in surprise at some laughable curiosity—maybe the pristine order of sharpened pencils I kept at the ready—and her reactions brought out the strangest feelings in me. For some reason, the pencils, my optimistic stack of questionnaires, the narrow office suddenly seemed petty: a personality embodied and put on display. And I felt embarrassed for her to see how small the boundaries of my life had become.

For his part, her boyfriend didn't exactly agree to participate in the study, but he didn't stop me, even after I explained that I would need to take a scraping from inside his cheek. So I pressed on, getting as far as writing his first name at the top of a questionnaire: Tommy. "Family name?" I asked when he didn't offer one.

His jaw set in that expression I'd seen in the restaurant. Then he snapped, "Just Tommy." Taking the exasperated tack parents often use with children he added, "Let me see that," pulling the form out from under my pencil. He studied it a moment, then read in a flat tone: "True or False. People should dress in individual ways even if the effects are strange." It was a question from the Disinhibition Subset. I could see him mentally comparing my Sears blazer to his linen shirt, his oval, tinted glasses, gold necklace.... "You really think this works?"

Apparently satisfied with the wastepaper basket, the file cabinet, and the back door, his girlfriend came around to his side of the desk. She stood behind him, her taut, trapeze-artist arms crossed over his chest as I explained the Zuckerman Personality scale for Sensation Seeking that Ebstein, et al. developed into the Tri-Dimensional Risk-Taking Index (RTI) that Hur and Bouchard then applied to identical twins to demonstrate a strong hereditary component in RT Personality Types (RTPT).... They looked back at me with that glazed expression I often faced in class, their eyes making me aware of the sound of my own voice. "Examining the biochemistry that influences the broad behavioral mechanisms and psycho-physiological reactions in rats," it was saying, "Resnick found that those rats that exhibited elevated tendencies to explore their surroundings also had elevated levels of dopaminergic—"

"Rats," he interrupted. He read from the questionnaire: "True or False. The worst social sin is to be a bore."

With a quick underhand flip, she popped a pack of cigarettes out of his baggy shirt's pocket, then lit up, exhaling something in Chinese that made him snicker.

I forged ahead. "Building on this research..." Convincing him of the worth of the study was going to be more complicated than I had thought, I saw, for as I explained the Svrakician linkage between twins who were identified as RTPTs, a black-and-white mirage of Wong's old pharmacy seemed to rise up behind Tommy and his girlfriend, a line of customers standing at the long counter, Mr. Wong himself in black, flowing *cheongsam*, using a library ladder to ascend a wall of bottled potions, Tommy and his girlfriend superimposed before it in the Technicolor of their Chuppie attire, not so much a break from the past as—"...the enzymes such as MAO and DBH that regulate the neurotransmitters associated with behavior, and hormones such as cortisol and testosterone—"

"Testosterone? You mean being macho?"

Macho. The gang boss. Big man, The Rock and his moll—a way to break in suddenly appeared. "*Voila!*" I shouted, in the loud tone I sometimes used to shock students awake. "Find the gene that controls the enzyme, and you'll find the genetic marker for the personality!"

Instead of the "*ah ha*" of recognition I had hoped for, they only exchanged frowns the way freshmen sometimes did when they realized we weren't going to be studying Kinsey. "So what?" he ventured, "Only Risk-Takers have balls?"

I may as well have been building him an elaborate temple of gods, demigods, lesser demons and monkeys, all baroquely entangled. But what else was I to do other than finish the door: "Van Tol, Wu, Guan, O'Hara and others have already put forth a candidate: variations in the DNA coding sequence of the D4 receptor, a forty-eight base-pair sequence that controls clozapine and spiperone binding, especially when it appears as an eightfold repeat. Put simply, people without this redundancy of DNA are no more or less sensitive to the enzymes that control behavior." I showed him the DNA sequences on a chromosome stain—C CCC GCG CCC GGC CTC CCC CCG GAC CCC TGC GGC TCC AAC TGT GCT—explaining how when a person carries a sequence that repeats itself eight times—

"Come on, get to the practical stuff."

"In practical terms..." I cut to the conclusion. "...an analysis of the genetic phenotype could tell you which poker player will be prone to take risks, to bluff with a mixed hand, and which will tend to play it safe and fold."

A faint smile came over Tommy's lips, and in silence they both looked over the questionnaire for the longest time. Then sheepishly he asked, "There's one question I'm not sure how to answer."

"Yes?"

He read: '"Rate yourself on a scale of one to ten, one equals fully Asian, ten equals fully American.' I mean, I drive big American car...." Then he growled, "But my ricksha is 110% Chinese!" and his girlfriend shrieked as he pulled her onto his lap, simulating a bumpy ride.

When they finished laughing, I pointed out, "As a token of appreciation you will be paid a gratuity of forty dollars."

"Fourti ho Yhankee dohlars?" his girlfriend asked, exaggerating a Yan-Can-Cook accent.

"*Chì lâo*," he said, sliding the questionnaire back, "you don't need that crap. I'll tell you what you need to know about Risk-Takers."

"Oh, do you know some Risk-Takers?" I asked, trying to sound nonchalant.

He pulled out his cell phone and spoke into it. Then he proceeded to tell me about a great uncle who swam the Niagara to get into this country. "The whole while, miners shot at him from the bluff. Like they're shooting at rats at the dump. Uncle says when he made it and lay on the bank exhausted from swimming for his life, he could hear them up there hooting, drinking and shooting at other bubbles in the water." Today, he continued, jets and ATMs and container shipping have made that swim 12,000 miles long: from Fujian by mule train across the Yunman Province. Aunties did it. Brothers. He talked about an uncle who hung onto the undercarriage of a train despite blowing snow and a cold so deep that when guards discovered him, he couldn't let go. "They amputated two fingers just to arrest him," he said, holding up a hand with his fingers folded at the knuckles to illustrate. "But the next year he tied himself to the undercarriage and tried again...." Nieces. Nephews. All trekking through the jungles of Burma and into Chiang Mai, being passed from handler to handler, some of whom were robbers. Some murderers. "Sometimes you are a mule for heroin. One way or another your body is your dollar—all you got—and you pay as you go till you emerge from a crate, or a trunk, or a hold with other shitting, puking rats to North America. And here your troubles begin."

A few minutes later, there was a knock at the door, and several men filed in. It was the men from Three Happiness; not the men who had been with Tommy and his girlfriend at the table. It was the old men who'd been sitting around reading newspapers and smoking cigarettes before his gang showed up. "You were expecting Jet Li?" Tommy asked. One of them, I noticed, was missing two fingers from his right hand. As they stood in line along the footprint left by the store's old counter, it was as if the ghosts I had imagined earlier materialized before me, each in turn stepping forward so I could take a scraping from the inside of a cheek for the DNA samples, listing them in the manifest only as Uncle A, Uncle B, Uncle C, through F. Was there a G? When Tommy saw me looking at him, he pulled out two small squares of gauze, wrapped in Saran Wrap and stained with blood.

"You run your test on these two, too," he said. "This one," he said holding up the first sample, "came from someone without balls."

"*Zheng ben wei shi me bu you ta qu?*" his girlfriend said, pouting.

"This other is from someone who always thought he could piss with the big dogs." He shook his head wistfully, handing it over. "When in Rome you've got no choice but act in Italian movies, huh, Jenny?" he asked his girlfriend. "Even if they're Spaghetti-Vampire-Westerns." She smiled wanly, looking down.

*

While yet in graduate school, my thesis director invited me onto a study he was conducting. The subject was the relation between biochemistry and social cooperation, and at the stipulation of his funders my director drew test subjects from the employees of an enormous *maquiladora* just south of Laredo. This particular *maquiladora* was Japanese-owned, the most high-tech manufacturer of air conditioners in North America, I was told, though one would never have guessed it from the slum that sprawled out from the plant: hundreds upon hundreds of shacks constructed from discarded shipping crates, oil drums and cinder blocks, and lived in by employees and their families, sweltering without electricity, or even running water. The plant was only running at seventy-percent capacity because of the predilection of employees to supplement their wages by selling copper tubing meant for the air conditioners and even the very tools supplied them to do their jobs.

When I confided to my mentor that I didn't think the plant managers really cared about discoveries in social science, he snorted. So I explained my suspicion: that the Japanese, with their lingering notions of racial superiority, were actually hoping to use our study to biologically screen out those who wouldn't pull together for the profitability of the company. He walked away, chuckling at what I thought he considered unwarranted cynicism in his young apprentice, until years later, when I learned that he had listed me on his proposal as co-investigator not because I was an outstanding student, as I had also believed at the time, but because I had a Japanese surname. And my surname, in fact, may have been the reason his study was funded ahead of competing proposals, including one by my present department head, who provided this explanation, recounting how he and my mentor had once shared a laugh about my "Mexican question" over a few beers. I would have chalked up the whole story to jealousy, professional gossip, if it weren't for the ring of truth sounded by one of his details: that the Japanese managers also blamed me for the failure of our study after they discovered I was only a *Hapa-Hadle*, heavy on the Caucasian side at that, though I maintain even now that the real reason thefts increased after the company did, in fact, implement a blood test based on our study was because smuggling copper from a tightly-controlled factory requires more social cooperation than does being a dutiful cog in its assembly line.

Everyone in the sciences has had a brush with or knows someone whose work has intersected that of one government lab or another: the study of migratory birds, for example, that arouses the interest of those trying to invent creative ways to conduct germ warfare, or the latest snowflake-pattern-recognition software that might somehow be employed in riot control. It did not take much to imagine others watching from the shadows to see if the genetic linkage I was seeking between DNA and risk-taking could ever be used to identify suicide bombers, or perhaps those who would risk their student visas by illegally taking a job. This wasn't just idle speculation. Already, Korea was completing banks of DNA fingerprints, while in Germany, would-be immigrants had to prove their German-ness by submitting a saliva sample along with their applications—just two examples of a worldwide genes race that was extending the surveillance and control of many populations down to the level of the human cell.

Did Tommy also have some such ulterior motive? When he asked if I was still looking for Risk-Takers, hadn't he added, "Good, so am I"? Then an item in *The Chinatown Lantern* turned me cold. A boat trying to smuggle illegal Chinese immigrants had drawn the suspicion of a Coast Guard cutter. The boat had been disguised as a fishing trawler. But instead of playing their ruse through, the smugglers—or snakeheads, as they are called—panicked at the sight of the cutter and threw their real cargo, the illegal aliens, into the sea. They knew that the Coast Guard would have to stop to rescue the illegals, and so the snakeheads managed to escape. None of the illegals could swim, though, so they drowned before the Coast Guard could find them. The article was simply restating the fact that these smugglers were still at large, just one of the many "consumer alerts" that circulated as news.

Was Tommy involved somehow? Is this why he was so intent on finding "macho" henchmen who would follow through on risks rather than turn tail at the first sign of danger? Looking at one of the blood samples he'd supplied, I wondered if that was what he meant by it coming from "someone who thought he could piss with the big dogs." If so, wouldn't that make him an accomplice to murder? Even if he was only looking for men willing to risk smaller crimes, numbers running, drugs, or whatever, did I implicate myself by having that blood analyzed? As it happened, the DNA tests run on the two samples showed that the 'one without balls' was decidedly a Risk-Taker, by my measure, having eight repeats of the D4DR gene on Chromosome 11. The "Big Dog's" swab, though, indicated an ordinary person. Had I mixed up the samples? No, that was impossible, I concluded. But had he? Both samples were tainted, of course, and I only played along to keep him in play. But if I retested and got the opposite results, I was sure Tommy could put me in touch with the very pool of subjects my study needed. Conversely, the existence of a biologically positive Risk-Taker who expresses negative risk-taking behavior was troubling enough, and I knew I had to find out which was which, though I also hoped I would never see Tommy again.

*

As soon as the banana let me into his smelly office I ask, "Did you test those blood samples?" He had moved into Wong's old shop like a hermit crab, and now the crab curled up in his shell frowning. Then he nodded—slowly—his lips tighter than a sealed vinegar pot. But why?

Something wrong? The *yin* of me didn't want to know:
imagine a soft-focus shot of me walking past his office,
twice, each time deciding to forget the whole stupid show.
What's he gonna tell me anyway? But with him stalling
before me, the *yang* of me was burning to find out. "They
stood out, right?" Again he nodded—not giving up his
secret—and I could see we were sliding into another scene.
Sure enough, squirming like his knickers are in a twist,
he says he wants to meet the men himself.

    Chì lâo! Where'd this guy get his nose for comedy?—
turning every solemn moment into jokey puns, mistaken
identities.... In HK cinema, a jilted woman always
tears up a photo of her lover; when *triad* goons murder a
detective, his partner always swears revenge. Directors
know how to keep it real with age-old types, not the
cartoons of people this banana makes by connecting his
numbered dots. So I see that if this movie had any hope
of staying genuine I had to keep us on script. And in
roles that real people could recognize: Jenny-po as the
"Cute but Ballsy Girlfriend," him as "The Professor," and
me? I guess that's what I was trying to find out.

    First I laughed in his face—*Ah ha ha ha Ha!—You
think your kung-fu powerful but today is day you die!*—and
say he didn't need to meet anyone. I had already met them
for him. But he wouldn't let it go, him trying to put a
headlock on me [slo-mo] by turning turnips into temples
again, telling me that if I wanted a reliable test for
Risk-Takers, we would have to follow through on paperwork.

    Paper! *Aiiiiiiiija*!

    It was hard not to lose it—go *psycho-fu* all over
his head—this banana lecturing me about Risk-Takers and
chicken hearts and I don't know what, when he doesn't
know anything about breathing water, or despair, or how
hard life can be in Chinese countryside. Especially for
those with no face, or worse, filthy blood: to know your
nephew, your sister, get constantly bullied—beat up, too—
because sixteen years ago she tried to escape the Suzy-
Wong way only to end up stuck and with a baby that has
no proper father. You know what it does to you inside to
hear your nephew's voice, made puny and crackly by one of
those provincial phones as he tells you, "Uncle, I have
to have my blood replaced. Otherwise I see no sense in
living." Could the banana's papers replace blood? Could
it find a man in all of China who would marry her? Or even
hire her? Could it warn someone that a moment's hesitation

in HK could be the last straw on the mainland or go back
and undo a split-second's decision? No, and it all came
broiling out: flurry of fists, head-high kicks, manga jump-
cuts with him answering back, us two shaolin fighting
on speedboats, on flaming ladders, off trampolines and
soaring—him on wire, me no net—somersaulting sword fantasy
through bounce lighting, him dodging, me countering,
double-pistol standoff, then typhoon of bullets, slo-mo of
me diving to save sister, me doing all my own stunts while
Jenny-po covers my back with two-fisted Uzi volcanoes,
a flock of chickens burst out of the kitchen and into
crossfire—pause in the action so we can exchange witty
quip—resume shooting—amp up the Wu-Tang Clan soundtrack—
rack focus of pained expressions, fury, envy, fear—but
that's not the point anymore—a bloodbath for male honor
and sacrifice, camera zigzag-tracking through the action,
even switch to witchy-nudie-assassin genre, but even that
don't work, and when it becomes clear that I could jump
off from my condo to die before he gives in, I give up.

"All right, all right. The both of them," I said,
breathing hard, meaning the blood donors, "will be at
the rocket-rice races tomorrow." I sketched a map of the
area, and show which alley to take, wondering how I had
let our fight spill out of the frame, the camera swinging
around to show the crew. Then I told him, "Memorize this:
Confucius say, 'Gui ma zhi duo xing.' Or no, make that,
'Yige zitou de danshen.' Whenever you get stopped along
the way, repeat those words."

Seeing that banana strain to make a bootleg Gucci
out of my no-good Mandarin, scratches and all, was funny,
despite myself. And the more he rehearsed—struggling to
myna-bird the words without a clue what they meant—the
harder it was to stay mad. He's such a porcelain chicken
that I almost just came out and asked him plain. Or at
least I began to think it was okay, it being impossible to
lose face before a porcelain chicken. "But if you think
you still need your papers after tomorrow," I say for
now, "maybe we'll both just play for the outtake reel."

*

This is absurd, I told myself the next night, stepping off the Chinatown bus. And possibly dangerous. A gaggle of old Chinese women dressed in knit caps and layers of men's vests shoved by me with their mesh tote bags. Rival tongs sometimes shot at each other, I knew, or turned in each other's cockfights or gambling parlors. Not to mention the police. The bus hissed, sliding off into a misty night and leaving me before the bronze statue of Confucius, that symbol of tradition, all marked up with Chinese graffiti as though to memorialize the fact that every country is a state of mind, especially to those who didn't live there. I wanted to kick myself for allowing Tommy to suck me into his. Neon signs multiplied in the rain-slick street, their candy-colored pinks and greens turning Chinatown as cartoonish as any world must appear to its outsiders. Paper! he said—as if I could forget the true lesson of Paper-Scissors-Rock when without that paper, without the tables and co-variants and standardized means, Risk-Taking didn't exist. At least not in my world.

The tourist shops were closed, but the restaurants that catered to fan-tan clubs and other basement establishments were just beginning to come alive. I assumed the map he had drawn was directing me to one of these and took one last look at it, debating whether or not to go on. No researcher inserts himself into his study to this degree. If some journal published my work—then found out the lengths I had gone to enrich my pool... Shame. Disgrace.

Suddenly my ankles were wet—I had walked into the spray of a fishmonger who was hosing off the sidewalk before his shop. Perhaps it was the eeriness of the foggy night. Chinese lore is full of ghosts and shape-shifters, and this, along with all the talk I'd been hearing about human smuggling, was surely at work on my subconscious. In any case, the faces of live bullfrogs straining against the chicken wire that held them in their barrel all seemed to be laughing with Tommy at the idea that a researcher could be anywhere else.

I didn't believe any of that claptrap about reason screening out other modes of reality or the dead being more powerful than the living, of course, so it was easy to move on. Still, this is not to say that the past—an unfaithful wife, for example, who excuses her actions by claiming her mate is a "dull academic"—does not influence the present. And once Tommy pointed it out, certain questions on the RT Personality Questionnaire that I had inherited—"I would like to join a 'far-out' group of artists or 'hippies'"—did seem to be spoken by the ghost of mood rings, astrological signs, and personality tests which were once the rage among researchers—before they morphed into the biochemical measures of the '70s, which became neurological explanations in the '80s, which were giving way, in this the age of genetics, to strings of AGCTs.

Measure enough things about enough people and you'll see something, Tommy had said when we argued in my office. Not so much to mock me, I believe, as out of the same sentiment as those shrines found in every Chinatown business, their incense smoldering with lip service if not utter belief in the miraculous transformations that supposedly permeated the place: moon maidens become brides, paupers turned fabulously rich.... And even if my data did have as much to do with reality as the spirit-filled cosmological maps of medieval Chinese, as Tommy claimed, that didn't mean it wasn't valid—if by "reality" we mean what that spirit-filled reality meant to medieval Chinese, the only one that could possibly matter to them—which opens up a real question: would the practical use to which any of this knowledge was put be the true measure of the man?

*

The gangway that my map said to go down was pitch-dark, so narrow that only a single person could pass. Then the building Tommy had indicated by an 'X' was there: an enormous industrial building that I knew to be an old coal-fired power plant built in the last century. Dark windows. The upper floors now held garment manufacturers, though the realtor I rented from said that ever since China reclaimed Hong Kong, the capital flight from that financial epicenter had been exerting pressure to turn this building into high-end condos or a mall. Now I saw why nothing ever came of it. The ground floor had plywood for windows, but tellingly, no gang dared tag them. Approaching the building from the back, it looked like a fortress, its single door made of reinforced steel. I knocked softly and a voice from inside answered in Chinese.

"*Gui ma zhi duo xing... Yige zitou de danshen,*" I replied, and there was muffled laughter. Why? What was I saying? Bolts were drawn back; the door opened.

I was ushered in by an old man whose long braid and embroidered silk tunic and cap made it seem as though I'd stepped into a Charlie Chan movie—was this a joke? No. From the darkness behind him, two large men emerged, and one began to frisk me. "What do you know about classy Chinese quim?" the other asked.

"What?" I stammered—what had I said!—as the old one shooed me toward the noise of what sounded like lots of people arguing deeper in the building; a lawnmower or chain saw revved, the noise of voices and engines growing louder as I neared the one lit doorway. Then I was in a huge, warehouse-sized basement, full of men who, just like in movies, were waving fistfuls of dollars and shouting in Chinese. Young and old, men in thousand-dollar suits, men in mechanics' coveralls.... The fishmonger I had seen earlier was there. Or someone like him, still in his stained apron and paper cap, jostling with others for the attention of the few men dressed in rumpled white shirts who were holding the bets. Indeed, it seemed as though all of the cabbies, chicken-parts processors, and others I had interviewed were there—a fire marshal's nightmare—but that was impossible, I knew. They couldn't all be tong members. But if that were true—

Three men in motorcycle helmets sat on souped-up minibikes, gunning their engines as they eased up to a starting line while some of the men in white shirts yelled at the crowd, pushing people to clear a path for the bikers around the perimeter of the basement.

Tommy appeared at my side, eyes wild, as he yelled over the noise, "Now you'll see!" At that moment the minibikes roared off, a straggler at the edge of the crowd leaping to get out of the way. The basement was round, as though we were all inside an enormous barrel, but it was tiny as far as racetracks go, and watching the bikers go around and around me and the other spectators was dizzying. The basement itself had obviously been dug by horses as were the basements of many buildings from that time: a team of horses would be hitched to a plow-like digging blade that radiated out from a post in the center of what would be the basement. Then as the horses walked around and around, they dug deeper and deeper, coolies hauling away the loose dirt in baskets. Now, a plywood ramp had been erected so that the curved brick wall itself could be used as part of the track, the minibikes rocketing by so fast that their centrifugal force held them to the wall as they used it as a lane to pass each other.

The dopamine rush that came with just watching these men shoot around the track made my hairs stand on end. The bikers roared off like short-track speed skaters: a burst at the start followed by three laps of jockeying for position, after which they gunned into the final no-rules lap. I understood as never before—understood with my body—the lure of gladiator tournaments, of kick boxing.... It was impossible not to get caught up in the "what if" of one racer recklessly shooting between a pillar and another biker to win, and I practically forgot why I was there until, heat over, Tommy nudged me. He nodded toward the winner, coasting into a fold of men, his green soccer jersey crisp as new cash. Like jerseys in the city's youth league, this rider's was emblazoned with the name of a sponsor. And when he turned into a position allowing me to read it, my pulse quickened: *Three Happiness*.

"Blood Sample A or B?" I asked excitedly, trying to catch a look at the man's face through the narrow eye slit of his helmet. His jersey also sported a number—*8*—my lucky number, according to the restaurant's place mats.

Tommy only began to complain about the families who were abandoned by the British when they returned Hong Kong to the Chinese. I thought he was somehow referring to the man before us, but the engines and shouting of bets for the next heat made it hard to hear, and just as I began to think he was actually talking about kung-fu stunts I realized he'd been really referring to his old video-dubbing business. Because bootlegging movies was a business that party members were in, he suddenly found himself a copyright criminal. "Enemies of the state and such...." I didn't know why he was telling me all of this. Afterwards, I wondered if it was because he knew I suspected he was involved in human smuggling. Everyone wants to be seen as the hero in his own movie. Or maybe he figured this was his best shot at getting whatever answers he really wanted from my study. Or maybe, it occurred to me, he was just a guy. Not a tong boss. Not an immigrant, or even a Chi-Am, just a guy describing the rural province his family was from, a place so hard, so spirit-crushing, he said, and with so little chance of ever being different that suicide was the leading cause of death among the young, fertilizer the poison of choice. "Hey! *Wo xiang da ge du!*" Tommy yelled, breaking off his story to grab the attention of one of the bet takers. A quick exchange of cash for betting stub, and then he continued, agitated—but instead of sending money back to a sister, he said, he himself was going to be sent back. Bureaucrats in some office processed his papers along with hundreds of others like so many parking tickets. Just before police arrived, though, a customer, his professor, tipped him off. To save him? To get rid of him? To save herself?—maybe she both turned him in and tipped him off? In any case, it was clear what they must do. Jump on the motorbike his partner, his girlfriend, used to use to make deliveries, weaving in and out of Hong Kong traffic. But with the police coming in their building's front door only one of them did so. The other froze. Just a moment. But the moment was enough to be caught while the other roared away.

"Why?" he asked, grinding out a cigarette with the sole of his boot. "Why did one hesitate? Or obey their order to stop? Because he was from the Mainland, The Servile Chinese? Chicken? Afraid the police would shoot? Confucius says we reveal ourselves to ourselves in the moment we least expect, but what did that hesitation reveal about him? Everyday I ask myself that."

He paused, there in the nicotine sweetness and stench of exhaust, as though waiting to see if I would attempt an answer. When it was obvious to us both that I couldn't, Tommy shrugged. "The one who pulls the train gets to be the engine, and America is a great place to become an—" "Gweilo!" someone shouted, and Tommy, indeed the entire basement, fell silent. For an instant. No more than a heartbeat. Then it was instant confusion. "*Gweilo!*" others began to yell as people scattered. The racist "Chinese Fire Drill" popped into my mind, not so much to describe the people running about as the tumult of details that came rushing into my head. Tommy was already gone. A bald man was screaming in my face—"*Gweilo!*"—to me or at me, I couldn't tell. Not knowing what else to do, I ran, too. I didn't know if we were running from the vice squad or immigration. Or maybe the building had caught fire. A double report boomed—gunshots? Engine backfires? I was knocked forward by a scuffle between two of the bet takers and a man trying to retrieve his money, then I was running with others down a dark corridor. "*Kuai! Kuai!*" I tripped after, then through a boiler room, then up a metal ladder, and past aisle after aisle after aisle of darkened sewing machines, hampers, racks of garments, all the while wondering, Why? What did I have to run from? When I caught up with them, they were going out a back window. We had emerged in a completely different building and were at a level that was higher than the alley, and from this height I had a glimpse of the checkerboard of alleys and backyard fences below. Men vanished into the night. Following their example, I descended a fire escape then hung down as far as my arms let me before dropping to the ground. Then I was on the run again, this time with other men down another alley and away from a red throbbing glow that seemed to fill the fog. Flashing squad-car lights? Or flames? Fear colors everything. From the darkness came the screech of tires—squad cars taking positions? Maybe it was a tong after all, boxing in its rival? Before I could tell, I found myself alone—no, behind one other man, just ahead, the back of his green jersey leaving no doubt who he was:

Three Happiness
8

"Hey!" I yelled. "Stop!" But this only made him run faster and his backward glances made me realize he thought I was chasing him. Which, I was. He threw off his helmet—threw it at me? To run faster? He was getting away, my academic's body beginning to lose to fatigue. "Wait!" At that moment all my hopes, my very self, seemed subject to my ability to catch him. But why? It was completely irrational, but still a gut feeling made me cry out, "Wait! *Deng*! Please!" A car engine gunned somewhere, followed by a siren.

Then I had him.

The alley we were running down dead-ended—it was the dead-end behind the office space I rented—and I was paralyzed by the confusion of questions that came rushing in. Though breathing hard, the man turned calmly, slow as a gunslinger squaring off for a quick-draw duel—only it was her. Tommy's girlfriend. Jenny. Her delicate nostrils flared with each breath, hands on hips in leather pants, her legs apart and straight as the blades of open scissors though her heavy-lidded eyes were as calm as they had been that afternoon I bored her in my office. She nodded toward the back door to my office in a way that indicated this was where she'd been leading me. But how? Had she switched clothes with the racer? A decoy? Or had I been so conditioned to expect a man? The typhoon of questions was so soaking that it was only later that I could sort them out from thoughts of snakeheads who let someone else be their front; politicians airing news through anonymous leaks; actors in masks; magicians; con jobs that accidentally help everyone; mundane tasks that allow evil; or Mafia bosses who live as meek dry cleaners while their flashy underlings do all the tough talking and high-profile living.

Could she be the real boss of the tong?—if there had ever been a tong and not just a bunch of people? Was she the one who jumped on the motorcycle? Escaped first? Blood Sample A or B? Neither? Did she win races because of daring, or because she weighed less than the male drivers? What kind of Risk-Taker wanted to hide? What did she see when she looked at me? What did it mean to help a Risk-Taker—or whatever we call her—hide? To my study? To my funders? To my subject? Not least of all, to me, and what I had become, devoting my entire adult life to?...

A sweep of light snapped both of our heads toward it—probably a flashlight, but who knew. A projector beam. Or even a ghost. At that moment I could have believed anything. Gathering breath to speak, she looked at me directly then said, "The key! Quick!"

Medieval
TIMES

A smile?

Brief as a blush—for him?—
before she turned, hurried on.

"..in a time…"
　　　Anselm daydreamed, Troubadours sang…
"…long, long ago…"
　　　…others, too, until songs trapped in wax hard-
ened into vinyl discs ever evolving—revolving—spinning
in place—faster, faster—history anew?—better that than
wobbly plates atop a juggler's sticks—men-with-tele-
scopes-discovering-planets redux, griffins and gargoyles
walking the earth again; End Times and Holy Wars.
De novo peasants, and tyrants too—once more the earth
is 5,000 years old, as it says in the Bible—and he wondered if that was how…
"…though not so very far away…"
　　　…how, in the 21st century, he had ended up a
gong farmer.
"Medieval Times!" the recorded announcer roared, and
the gates were flung open, the knights galloping out into
the arena on their steeds, their squires jogging behind.
And Anselm walked out behind them, shovel in hand.

If he'd seen what he thought he'd seen, what did it mean? Where would it lead?

A Milky Way of photo flashes.

Every time he, the knights, and squires entered the arena, a thousand points of light flared and died. Like distant stars. Here contained. Beautiful, if not heaven's majesty, a band of twinkling lights in the darkness of the stands that ran all around, and, like the heavens, allowed mortals to intuit what lie beyond: tiers of tourists cheering for the spectacle, opening their cameras to capture a few fireflies of memory. Show after show after show.... The repetition put the horses at ease though Anselm never quite understood why he didn't bolt, considering how each portaled the eye of Never Learn, the camera flashes far too far away to light the scene, their owners bringing home pictures of inky black. Over and over. Think about it: a star reduced by distance to a speck called upon to bring noon to a cave. Still they persist. Faith or ignorance?—Or Never Think?— their machines first made 150 years agone, you'd think they'd know a thing or two about its workings by now. Press the button. This time it will be different. Press the button. The button (or present?) will make it different. This time. The button that operates God-knows-what inner magic. This time will not be like the past.

Still, how could anyone know truly what anything might mean?—especially if he'd never even talked to her?

More Theological Questions

How many angels/strings/meanings/computations/black holes/singularities galaxies can dance on the head of a pin?

Has any one ever seen an ionic bond?

If a body is reconstituted at the end of time, what happens to the bodies of Christians who have been eaten by cannibals? What happens to the cannibals? Especially cannibals who, after having dined on Christian flesh, have themselves been baptized into Christianity? And then eaten by other cannibals. Who were in turn baptized. And then, in turn, eaten? Ad nauseam.....

If a transplant recipient receives the heart of a chimp, will he or she crave bananas?

If a war has no name will it have existed?

If a humanized mouse bears the genes of a tobacco plant that carries the genes of a jellyfish, that bears the genes of rat, that has been born by a rabbit that carries the genes of stink weed is it a?— Oh, never mind.

The Primum Mobile or The Crystalline Sphere
From his post down in the dirt of the arena he could descry her up in the heavens. His Beatrice. O! Beatrice! Not one of the hundred Serving Wenches moving among the 1,200 Lords and Ladies and their Kyds, bringing them their Coke products. *Keep Your Mug, $2.* No, dressed as a jester, she lugged a camera instead of hash—*Add Your Other Mug, $5*—her legs firm and noble in red leotards, a miniskirt of colorful flaps and jester's bells. A blonde ponytail bobbing from her jester's cap, bulky press-camera hanging by a strap as she jotted in her pad. Though he was far too distant to hear, he could discern her song by the way it moved the Lords, Ladies & their Kyds—"How many in your party?" Auto focus. "Can you squeeze in together a little closer." FLASH. Plenty light there, she who understood how all things worked. "No, there's no obligation to buy."

Number of new planets discovered outside our solar system: 150 (and counting).

Chance that Avian Flu will mutate into the next plague: 100%

Number of planets inside our solar system: 10, if Quaoar is counted as a new planet; 9 if it isn't; 8 if Pluto has to be kicked out of the club for being a huge asteroid like Quaoar; 900, if all Quaoar-Pluto-sized asteroids are counted as planets.

Can God create a rock so heavy He can't lift it?

Number of subatomic particles it takes to set off a nuclear war: 1.

Can people?

In the middle of the journey of our life I came to myself within a darkening wood where the straight way was lost. Ah, how hard a thing it is to tell of that wood, savage and harsh and dense, the path diverging into many while a ball poised on a peak can roll into diverse valleys—butterfly effect—given minute changes in its initial impetus and I?— *I took the one less traveled by, And that has made all the difference,* for a journey is best measured by its steps… —*Dante*, Chaos Theory, *Robert Frost*, Boethius mashup.

MEDIEVAL TIMES. You can see it from the highway: an enormous metal building, like those sheds that homeowners buy from Sears to store riding lawnmowers, also from Sears, only a thousand times bigger, maybe a million. A great gray box if the roofline hadn't been notched to give it the silhouette of a storybook castle. Yea, without its battle pennants, its Las Vegas-style marquee— MEDIEVAL TIMES! MEDIEVAL TIMES! MEDIEVAL TIMES!—you might think it's just another of those gigantic box-buildings that populate much of America where land was once so plentiful that even farmers could afford it— until tax rates were rigged to attract agri-industries that could pave a state with corn. That is, you might mistake it for one of those astrodome-sized distributors of tires, or televisions, given the land for the 100 serf-wage employees they might employ.

In a sense you'd be right. It was sort of a FedEx of goods, Anselm oft' considered as he pulled into the employee lot. Only instead of flying goods in to a central sorting center before they are flown out to individual addresses, here in this redistribution center, individuals—or better, whole families—were brought in and the goods returned to their addresses in the form of food in their bellies, real plastic crowns on their heads, real plastic swords in their hands, and memories.... Real memories! Anselm, limping in sackcloth, one of them.

What happens when the rabbit, engineered to glow green escapes the lab? When the salmon-cow jumps over the banapple and runs away with the spork? Will they care for the field, for the stream?

Of the 150 new planets discovered outside our solar system, only one, in the constellation Aquarius, has terra as firma as earth, and orbits a sun as warm and yellow as our own.

Though this planet has never been actually seen...

He'd been standing there, shovel in hand, dressed in his sackcloth, paring dirt from under his fingernails, thinking about popes and planets and places long long ago when she jingled by, and said "Hi"—or so he'd thought, feeling the earth move—though it could have just been the bells on her head.

...we know of its presence by the wobble it produces in its sun.

But she'd smiled too, hadn't she? A smile unlike the laughter that came pouring down on his head when called upon to do his job. A gentle smile. Gentle as mist, pale as moonlight and just as enigmatic—what wasn't?—until he recalled that she was garbed as a jester while he, in his gong-farmer weeds, was the jest; if hers was the moonlight, his was the shaft; if hers was the mist, his was the mud; and even if hers was just a smile, his was still the mud, recalling to him the true distance between mud and moon.

In 1146, the cleric Gautier de Metz calculated that a pilgrim to the star-studded crystal dome would need 7,157 years to walk there while a nobleman on horse-back could reach it in 5,782. He also calculated that a rock dropped from the Moon, would fall for 100 years before hitting earth.

Anselm knew that the stars were so far away that he could never walk there, while if a rock fell from the moon, it would only take a few seconds for it to hit him.

E thru G (from ERIC the RED's BLOG)

Executioner: a much-despised man whose responsibilities included torturing detainees, chopping through necks as though they were logs, parboiling heads and displaying them on pikes. Often haunted by ghosts, many executioners committed suicide.

Faerie: a mixed and varied species, from beings of light to walking scarecrows. While Faerie dispositions range from altruistic to murderous, all are capricious and simply can't care about the consequences of their actions.

Feudalism: an arrangement linking power and wealth to pedigree. Feudal society eventually centered in castle life for many of the same reasons that those with means join today's gated communities.

Subjects Are to Remain in Character at All Times

All employees, as they exit the locker room into the public areas, were supposed to bow to the faux crest on the wall: a shield emblazoned with the family tree that showed links between the founder of Medieval Times and one hundred and twenty other aristocratic families, descendants all of noble stock, as well as their wholly-owned subsidiaries. A God-given right to rule. Or so it would seem.

Indeed, back on the day that the castle's marquee announced NOW HIR-ING, Anselm had found himself in a line of would-be subjects so long that it wrapped around the outer walls. Praying with the multitude for an audience within, he had fallen in with another supplicant who, like Anselm, only had to sell what God had given him. Only this guy—Jude—had already optioned off his futures to the National Guard: "They're gonna teach me a skill—heavy equipment operator." A clean-cut boy from one of the farms that used to dot the land before there was a Medieval Times Inc., Jude could have easily ridden in its show—if he didn't look like a hick who'd grown up feeding chickens.

In single file they approached their present judgment: a Casting Director who stood with the Personnel Manager at an elevated podium between two doors. As the supplicants filed forward, the director would assay each body, wherein was written that person's God-given station: "Royalty," "Court" or "Peasant," send-ing those with photogenic smiles, healthy skin, the bodies of ex-cheerleaders and jocks to the right, while those with computer-nerd acne, or philosopher's physique, a hunch or lumps, librarian's tan, those who grew up suffering a lack of skin-care products, whose teeth had never been set in their ideal places, who grew up in want of five-dollar co-pay or no-pay health insurance, whose non-existent training in posture, walking with grace, those whose frame bore their mother's or fathers' occupation (back of a hotel maid) or place of origin or des-tination (lungs of the asbestos abater), or gimp, like his, were sent to the left.

"He does have a clubfoot," the woman who interviewed Anselm acknowl-edged to the personal manager, pleased enough by Anselm's relative lack of sym-metry, "But I was so hoping for a dwarf."

Friar: a monk, an expert in matters of food and fund raising. Confessors who were known to be lenient for a donation were highly valued. Often consid-ered naïve of the ways of the heart because of their cloistered life, they figure prominently in the schemes of lovers.

Gong Farmer: (from gong, a going, passage, drain) a cleaner of privies. Any Cleaner of Shyt. The toilet seat of a castle sat atop a gong, that is, a chute that ran through its stone wall and emptied into the moat below. One of the gong farmer's duties was to kill invaders trying to gain entry through the gong. Even in times of peace, though, the gong plugged up often since Medievals used straw for toilet paper. When it did, the gong farmer would beat his drum to announce 'the hour of no shyting,' climb up into the gong and clean out corpses or other clogs. The gong farmer had such low status that nearly everyone else in the castle considered it a great prank to sneak up above him as he went about this duty and let loose a torrent of filth upon his head....

Jester: ruler of my heart, Anselm thought, as he went about his duties, wiping down MEN'S RESTROOM No. 3. The company liked him to carry out this part of his job while the visitors were in the house, seeing him dressed in his sackcloth costume, picking up paper towels that the royal pigs left on the floor, making sure there was enough toilet paper in the stalls. He was mopping the piss stains under the urinals when two princes ran in, plastic crowns, on their heads, $200 Michael Jordan's on their feet, the both of them splashing right on the floor he'd just mopped. He washed his hands, something the kyds didn't do, pushing by him as he signed the log taped to the door: LAST CLEANED BY:_____. Then he went to take up his post in the arena for the show, humming to himself, *Well I haven't fought a dragon in a fortnight...*

The Black Knight, a clean-cut Latino with a low-rider out in the lot, fought dragons nightly, and twicely on Saturday and Sunday. His jet-black goatee, square jaw and physique made him look so much the part that even before he came here, out on the street, they called him El Cid. So they trained him to ride, to fight with broadsword and mace, and the stage kung-fu that the director's worked in. It's made him quite a lady's man, and teenage girls—and their mothers—crowd around to have him autograph their programs after the final Battle Royal. When they pose with him for a photo—get in tight—he's been known to squeeze. He's also taken to ordering the Gong Farmer about. It's not in the script. But each time Anselm feels compelled to obey because the number one rule here at Medieval Times, here where a laser-light show precedes the joust, is to stay in character.

Unification Theories & Marvelous Signs (Or What Holds the Planets in their Place…
Creation was written, or perhaps only read, differently then: the language of a snail's shell, a flower's bell, inner ear or comet's tail a ladder to You, scribes copied in gilt, the Unmoved Mover beyond the frontier of time and space, Divine Desire quickening the spheres as life animates our dust, bringing into existence angels, then man, then beasts…insects…plants…molds unto the lowest dregs. Great Chain of Being: each wax an ever fainter impress of one Love, though each an intimation of this true Unity that draws us neigh for all things have order within themselves and in this they resemble Your Unity. Thus, we can see that our faces have the same number of windows as heaven has planets because our face is a counterfeit of that face; we know of the dissonance of Mars by observing its influence in the humors of the body, while the humors of the body teach us the medicinal value of vomiting by dogs whose action reveals the poisonous nature of the Judas Weed, which even worms dare not gnaw. To know completely, then, just one flower in the crannied wall was to know all in all in all: a single grand synthesis, or say Unification Theory, that cannot be refined or simplified for it reveals the face of Being itself, not as in a mirror darkly but face-to-face and renders obsolete the partial explanations of chemistry, physics, botany, cosmology….

Yea, this holy grail seems within the grasp of those able to see written within that flower a creation myth that starts with a Bang, the frontier of time and space, in which magnetism, electricity, gravity, and nuclear force are all aspects of One; that shows how the warring theories of Relativity, with its fear of absolutes, and Quantum Mechanics, with its foundation of chance, are but two voices in One harmony, the Great Chain of Strings, one-dimensional entities, all length, no thickness, in which one string vibrates a quark into existence, while differently vibrating strings are manifest as neutrino, diverse vibrations creating a symphony of charm-quarks, and strange-quarks, and implies time travel and 17 (or 21) dimensions, as well as muons and taus acting instantaneously at infinite distance (mega butterfly effect), black holes and worm holes, gravitons, photons, gluons, and bottom-quarks and top-quarks that make up electrons…protons… neutrons that make up atoms, that make up molecules that make up the lowest dregs, a snail's shell, a flower's bell, inner ear or comet's tail, the Music of the Spheres......

...and How We Are to Express It)

Say rather, why must history continually be rewritten? Why must one generation's truths be naïve, implausible, inadequate to the next? Is it, as String Theorists insist, that the past depends on the future? That space-time and day-to-day life are illusions, projections of a deeper reality, the way 'temperature' is a shorthand fiction to portray the speed of atoms? There's something to their sum over histories business—a sense that an electron-arrow shot at a target arrives by all possible paths, all possible histories of its journey taking place simultaneously, our determination of 'what happened' a sum of chance and all factors, including our present, allowing some histories, like waves, to cancel and disappear while One is reinforced and rises up with tsunami force? Or is this a statistical trick to get the answer right, "right" meaning a probability that fits what is seen *now*, what we call *The Present*? A snail's shell, a lily's bell, polar fleece or comet's tail— and us—needs be in words, which forever exceed our grasp:

We get this result from the physical observation that pre-spacetime is in thermal equilibrium at the Planck scale. The initial singularity of space-time corresponds to a zero size singular gravitational instanton characterized by a Riemannian metric configuration (++++) in dimension $D = 4$. Therefore it should be subject to the KMS condition. ... a unification between "physical state" (Planck scale) and "topological state" (zero scale) which suggests that the "zero scale singularity" can be understood in terms of a new topological index, connected with 0 scale, of the form $Z_{\{beta = \emptyset\}} = \sum Tr \infty (-1)^{\wedge}s$, which we call the "singularity invariant".

This much is clear: whatever desire draws bodies toward singularity, Venus, the celestial sphere of Love, woos the Sun, the circle of Wisdom, that most distant circle yet touched by earth's shadow, and often wins. Or as the poet said of his Beatrice:

What seems she when a little she doth smile
Cannot be kept in mind, cannot be told.
Such strange and gentle miracle is wrought.

Phenomenon familiar as Time if even further beyond expression, and that, like the electron in its path, is changed by looking and renders description less incomplete than too full: the sum of all histories appears clearer the closer we look and seeing more renders saying less. For seeing all in all in all also reveals how "black" contains "white," how "judas" means little without its "christ," how "night" falls to nothing without day's "light" while man gives signs like "$\sum$, ∞, $\emptyset$" or "God" their might. Continuums of continuums can run free, not just Up. Strings tangle. Sideways and crossways in loopity-loops. Skywriting Truth in plumes of vapor. History in water. Adam as poem written in dust. High greets low in so many places. Man drifts to woman to womb to loom to machine to screw to driver to passenger to wife to husband to husbandry to stock to DOW or cow utter gay or straight, any one meaning is suspect for what it leaves out. Yea, the problem with laws is in their stuff—an empty shell, a clapperless-bell, on our face or as our tale—*a smile is just a frown turned upside down*—dependent on poor us for animation.

God descends to jumpstart Adam on tee-shirts and key chains as well as chapel ceilings.

Anselm knows (he thinks) the reason El Cid has taken to abusing him in the ring. The knight is jealous. He guards Beatrice, his wife, the Jester, though there was no love lost between the Cid and Anselm before she graced him with a glance. Soon after Medieval Times opened, Anselm walked in on the Cid bragging to the Friar that he'd "bagged m'lady." No great feat, Anselm later came to learn, for he'd meant the Queen—one of those country-club women of indeterminate age, too old to be a princess though she held the requisites, perfect teeth, hair like flax—to which she'd added a high-end face and boob-job—one of those "ladies who lunch" before she came to the throne: the wife of a banker, it was said, who was himself in the process of trading up in looks, down in age, acquiring a trophy, but for the moment, for the sake of the kids, or career, or who knows what, calls her "mistress" instead of "wife," the Queen's end of the bargain being loads of disposable cash and freedom—so long as she's discreet in her own affairs, volunteering her services through Public Radio auctions, Art League benefits.... Civic (and other) Theater.

At the time, though, Anselm had thought he'd meant the Jester—his Beatrice—for earlier he'd seen El Cid drive off with her in his Chevy, and from the rest of the locker-room discourse that passed that day, Anselm understood that the Cid could think the title "M'lady" applied to any beaver.

But lo, in time, through more chance happenings and words, the truth came to be revealed that Anselm's Beatrice wasn't the knight's toy but wife, and Anselm holding ill-gained knowledge he wished he'd never heard, and seeing her stiffen in the presence of the Queen, discerning a chill toward the knight when offered his gloved hand, understood that she knew she'd been usurped by the Queen, via her own knight, in her own bed. And having much sympathy for her, Anselm couldn't help but see in her dignified countenance more nobility than in those more richly dressed. And she, perhaps, noting that his eyes lingered upon her countenance too long to be but chance, understood, perhaps, that he knew what had passed, and blushed scarlet to have been so undressed.

And the two of them, exchanging such sighs and tender looks, were caught by her husband, El Cid, the vengeful and black knight, who holds all fast.

Saturn, The Sphere of Contemplation

Why do men and women rush into each other's arms when the sky is falling? What graviton draws two bodies together, makes them hold, and want to be held, when stars fly apart?

A multitude of video clips on the web: Looking at the silent, sun-bleached home-videos of road-side bombs detonating beneath Humvees in Iraq, where Jude had been sent, Anslem couldn't imagine him over there instead of at his post operating the Dragon from inside its head. "Maybe God wants me to go," Jude had said. As if we're all fish in a net. An answer that did not persuade, or even make sense, until Anselm surveyed some other clips on the web: masked Arab men using their crescent-shaped scimitar to sever a journalist's head; an African Achilles dragging behind his Toyota chariot the charred body of some other Hector; random car accidents, or liquor-store holdups gone bad, random customers caught by surveillance cameras in random crossfire.... A Tsunami

Smorgasbord: more home-video of children playing on the beach, of fishermen on a pier, just before the sea arched its back and—

The video that struck Anselm with the most force had been taken by someone on the balcony of a resort in Indonesia, a tourist obviously, just filming a panoramic of the hotel's courtyard and pool on an everyday Sunday morning when people started screaming, the courtyard suddenly filling with water, swamping the pool, camera shaking, the water rising like a tide that wouldn't quit until it nearly reached the level of the balcony, the camera jerking wildly in many directions, droplets on the lens, view of the wet floor, then dry-eyed heaven, then back down to the poolside bar and lounge chairs joining oil drums, broken trees, a mailbox and the other flotsam swirling around in the courtyard like hair around a drain, and a pair of elderly men who had been sunning themselves in those deck chairs a moment ago, strangers obviously, struggling to get into each other's arms, clinging to one another as this false and monster tide suddenly went back out, sweeping them to sea.

....a ball poised on a peak, That Lonesome Valley, journey's eve, a worm's-eye view of the bird's open beak?...

Here came Anselm's cue: a horse raising its tail. He didn't even have to see it to know that one of the horses had beckoned him so, taking a crap during the joust. He could tell from the crowd. First, a murmur of delight and disgust would percolate up from those Lords, Ladyies & Their Kyds who were sitting closest and could therefore see best. Then it would grow into laughter, traveling through the hall like a stadium wave. A horse dump always got a bigger reaction from the crowd than even Merlin pulling rabbits from his wizard's hat. The laughter would surge as the shit hit the deck, die into titters, then surge again as Anselm jogged out, shovel in hand.

This evening it was the Green Knight's steed. Anselm trotted up behind it, always wary of being kicked, but just as he was about to scoop he was shoved—rudely from behind—and so hard that he had to jut his good foot out so as to not fall—his good foot landing square in the plop.

Bumped by a horse—the black horse of El Cid.

When Anselm tried to extract his foot, his gong-farmer's clog came off, stuck. The audience was laughing hard now, but not El Cid. When Anselm bent to retrieve his clog, his backside received a stinging blow. Sword drawn, the knight sneered down from the height of his steed, and pronounced gravely, "Thus do I deal with those who would covet what is mine."

Getting his clog back on, Anselm said, "What are you talking about, Rodrigo," though he knew full well.

"Thus do I dispatch those who would besmirch my honor," the Cid cried, delivering another swack with the flat of his sword.

"Oww! Cut it out Rodrigo," Anselm yelled.

High up in his royal box, The King, who was also the show's narrator, was into it now, pronouncing into the mic he wore so that his words might be broadcast throughout the land, *"Ho, looks like our knight needs to teach the lowly gong farmer a lesson!"*

Anselm quickly tried to shovel up the crap when another blow landed. "I mean it! It's not funny!"

But the knight did not desist. Nay, Anselm's pleas only made the knight chastise him to his task, working the reigns to keep his horse in close, crying, "I'll cut your eye out if I ever see you looking at my woman that way again, *cabron!*" while Anselm simultaneously dodged blows and tried to shovel the crap. Once he had his shovel full, he ran full bore for the gate, his club foot slowing him with its limp, the knight wheeling his horse around into galloping pursuit, Anselm escaping at the last moment to the full-belly laughter of the Lords, Ladies & Their Kyds.

Religion

Anselm liked to watch televangelists, raging in their video wastelands, for evidence of The End. *...don't believe that nonsense that the ACLU will tell you about separation of church and state. Abortionists, homos, pornographers, and the National Organization of Witches want you to believe in that so they can go about their business of killing babies, throwing blood on preachers, fornicating, and poking God in the eye!...* Not because he believed, per se, at least not in the way he imagined these later-day baptists, with their big hairdos and 1-800-BELIEVE numbers, wanted their faithful to follow. *...have you ever wondered why the Lord has set a plague of AIDS upon us? 'And ugly and painful sores broke out upon those who had mocked Him.' Revelations 16:2....* Rather, his faith was more in how they explained this world, not the next: how men with the horizons and heart of a BB were elected to public office, for example, why each of his neighbors had independently corrected him for parking his car too close to the curb, too far from the curb, not parallel enough to the curb, in front of the wrong house (this one 3 times). They explained why, when Jude's unit was called up, he thought that going as told was the right thing to do; or why, when Anselm's kindly old, church-organist neighbor died, the yard sale that his widow held to sell off his tools, his golf clubs, also offered an array of guns: his bedside Smith & Wesson, his kitchen shotgun, the living-room revolver, as well as the small, personal gun he always carried in his sock.

"Remember New Orleans," his widow warned, raising a finger heavenward, ghostly white, and wrinkled enough to have been pruned by water.

True enough. Anselm recalled watching, on TV, the end of the world come to that city by act of god, flood, then aftermath: a shopkeeper armed with an ax holding off a circling pack: angry, poor desperate men jabbing, poking, testing his nerve to kill to protect his stock—popsicles, Huggies, and other merch— until one managed to get him by the scruff, and the others poured in over the broken glass.

Blazing gas roared from broken mains. Other gangs overturned cars and order, rapists, score-settlers and chaos-makers widening the dance of death. The city of saints sliding toward a post-apocalypse that even firefighters fled—to save their own—or because they were shot at by unseen riflemen for sport, or revenge, or for no reason. Not Atlas, nor the police, could hold above water a world crumbling around their heads, suicides, some, out of frustration and exhaustion as men who refused to evacuate drowned, hoarding stolen DVD players to the last—no help from the outside—hungry survivors and dogs alike scavenging what food they could—every man, woman, and child for themselves, taking shelter in a pleasure dome for sport. A corpse, in a wheelchair, was set out by the curb with the trash for pickup when there was no trash pickup—wilting under some TV-camera's glare, flies—and dogs—trying to gnaw, for days—disease spreading as the best-laid plans of mice and men came undone. As well as the second-best. And the worst, those of the government that could send hurricane relief across the world but couldn't find it within itself to to care about its own poor, black, backyard.

Dante, nor Hieronymus Bosch, had nothing over the scenes that poured out of the nightly news.

Indeed, watching TV he saw how medieval mosaics of the Dance of Death really got it wrong, depicting paupers, popes and princesses equally joining in—

all fish in His net—when New Orleans showed that even Death listens when money talks. Those SUVs carrying fair, Armani-clad riders before the flood, entertaining them, too, with on-board movies, as they got out and up to highest ground, out of the city faster than Boccaccio's fair nobles took to the woods, servants in tow, in time to dine on linen and tell stories while the Black Death brought The End to everyone else.

Anselm made twenty cents more than minimum wage.

The End. Unimaginable. So it was to the peasants of 1310. And 2008. And again in 1492, and again in 1816 and 1918 when that generation's strain of avian flu killed more than died in all of The Great War, The War to End All War. The War to Prevent Nuclear Blasts, they might have called it had whoever titled wars been able to imagine whole cities vanish in a flash and bring civilization—ours—each time, to the brink.

With the melting of the polar icecaps, a rise in sea levels that will wash away island populations, an increase in the number and intensity of hurricanes, global warming will also make the planet a hothouse for the breading of plague viruses. Avian influenza H5N1, for example, is spread like the common cold and characterized by sudden onset of severe illness and internal bleeding. Rapid contagion, and a mortality rate that can approach 100% within 48 hours has earned it the nickname 'The Big One,' the tsunami of bird flu that will make SARS look like the sniffles.

More Unification Theory

"Me and my girlfriend are getting married before I ship out," Jude had said. "We'd like you to be best man."

Anselm had been moved. Not for love. But pity. For Jude. For himself. For humanity. For though he and the reticent dragon-keeper only spoke between their duties, passed some few thousand words since they met in that line of souls without occupation, Anselm must be, he realized, the closest thing the man had to friend, while the ritual required that he produce his "best."

"I'd be honored," he'd said.

...the "L" of a carpenter's square; the "O" of a wedding ring; the "V" of ducks in flight....

This time would be different. The present (or technology) would make things different. This time. A new plague wouldn't depend on rats being carried by merchants' camels or the slow boat from China.

On global maps, experts chart its approach as migrating ducks spread plague from China to Vietnam, entering Eastern Europe, heading to the west as it drew ever genetically closer too, mutating toward the point where it could jump from bird to man, then from human to human as easily as the common cold.

Anselm prepared to— Do what?

The Government's Prevention Plan (Formulated by the Same People Who Brought You New Orleans (& obviously rode limos to work)))))))))): *As a safeguard against Avian Flu,* he read, standing sardine-tight in a subway can, *always maintain a separation of at least three feet from other people.*

When the virus did leap to humans, scientists said, it would be everywhere all at once. Humans in jumbo jets traveling much faster than migrating birds, collapsing space-time all over the globe, the soccer stadium, kindergarten, pub, whorehouse, sweatshop, trading, temple, gymnasium, and factory floor all one, and he may as well be squatting outside that hut in Africa where the plague had already arrived, waiting with women in native dress, balancing baskets on their heads—

if he was feeling noble that day—for the scene was actually a newspaper photo of women waiting to get into a neighbor's hut so they could offer their gifts of food and condolences to a family whose son had been among the first humans to die, eating, as he had, an infected duck. None of the women were wearing bio suits, or even masks.

Truly, here it would be different....

The photo recalled to Anselm the time he had been with friends, and they had been talking about Y2K, once the danger of losing email, or air-conditioning that had caused them all to stockpile had passed. Dante said that a man reveals himself in his ultimate concern—the thing he thinks to grab when The End was at hand—one friend confessing that when he thought society was about to crack, he had horded gold. And they laughed when another among them confessed that he had hoarded beer, laughing harder still when a third said toilet paper, and the fourth, unlike the African neighbors bearing gifts in the photo, ammunition. After this last had spoken, they stopped laughing, and looked at one another as they never had before.

Mˌore Alternate Histories
For lack of a gong-farmer the kingdom was lost.

Butterfly effect....

"When I joined, I thought they'd teach me how to operate a bulldozer. I thought that if my unit was activated, it would be to help clean up after a hurricane. Or earthquake."

Did Jesus ever laugh?

The next day, Anselm was at his post when Beatrice approached.

A panic went through him. He quickly looked down. Out of shame for his humiliation in the arena. Humiliation at the hands of her man. And also out of fear that her husband would catch him looking at her again. Fear— Fear—

The lady approached. Her face bore nothing—if not pity?

Then she passed.

Followed by the Friar. Obese, of course. In a monk's brown robe, his belt a knotted rope. He and Rodrigo were kinsmen, rare sojourners to this white land, who liked to play up their roots to remind the others, and themselves, that they were from the same barrio. Often he would see them calling each other "*Cabron*" and "*Hombre*" and other such endearments as they conversed in their native tongue.

He held out a black cloth. "Hey Anselm, Agnes said she found your snot rag."

"Who?" Anselm asked, confused by the hankie though not its finder, even if hearing his Beatrice's real name gave him pause.

"Agnes Kry-go-ski?" he said, pronouncing it slowly, as though for the slow.

Seeing her punch in one day, Anselm had espied which slot in the time-clock's rack was privileged to embrace her card throughout the shift. Then, when it was his turn, he stole a look: Agnes Krygoski.

The Friar must have mistaken Anselm's reverent silence for incomprehension so added, "One of the jesters who takes pictures of the guests?"

Guests. Anselm had to bite his lip at the Friar's use of corp-speak for the pigs he cleaned up after.

"Rodrigo's wife? The chick you got crap knocked out of you for making eyes at? Jesus, are you dense."

He began to say it wasn't his handkerchief just as he realized it wasn't a hankie at all but the small square of cloth a photographer would use to clean her lens, one corner tied in a knot. A sign.

"She wanted me to give it to you so Rodrigo wouldn't see you talking to her again."

A sign. The lady was giving him a sign. It was then that he perceived the lady's intent, and also the necessity of discretion.

"Uh, yeah," Anselm said, pocketing the holy relic, "Thank her for me." A thief in her sanctuary.

In the banner's furls, a tall wave's curl, in a smoke signal's swirls or tree knot's burl, everything in God's creation is a sign for those who know how to read.
—St. Augustine

The last portion of the show involves a display of riding skill, a contest between Christian knights and Mohammedan caliphs. Each in turn, the knights, then caliphs, bear down with sword, then scimitar, as they aim for colored rings that dangle from strings. El Cid isn't any good at it and it's getting him into trouble with the director. For like most histories, this one's fixed, and the Christians always win. In the past, if he hadn't harpooned a ring by his third attempt, the stagehands were supposed to release the dragon: a contraption with two operators inside that snorts dry-ice smoke.

Jaws snapping, red-eyes flashing, animatronic tail swishing, Jude used to be in the head, operating its fiery breath, directing its steps.

But a lot has changed since the dragon first emerged from its den. Jude was gone, and since it was nearly the end of the summer, the company didn't bother to replace him. In fact, they wanted to rethink the whole ending to a show where the dragon's appearance used to signal all knights and caliphs to dismount. First the Christian knights made an attack, and were repelled by the beast; then it was the turn of the Moors, who had an equal lack of success. It was only when they joined forces that they were able to defeat their common foe. With the beast dead at their feet, they used to link arms, Christian, Moor, Christian, Moor, Christian, Moor, and sing as inspirational rock music swells, "We are the world...."

But as another song goes, a lot has changed since then.

Google Search No. 3: Swandown, swan neck, Gloria Swanson, swan dive, Swanson TV dinners, Cygnus the Swan Constellation, The Swan Maiden Folktale; The Swan: FOX Reality TV; Swan boats, Black Swan Fashions, Swan's Pumpkin Farm, Swan Song, The "S" of a Swan's Neck....

The nightly news was full of it now: men in bio-suits burning thousands of chickens, ducks, and geese in Asia, Africa, and Eastern Europe to slow the plague's global spread while one American bio-tech company was caught smuggling the virus into the U.S. so it could illegally experiment with making a vaccine for a rich Saudi client.

Medieval doctors wore duck masks, somehow knowing that when God, with His sense of humor, ended the World, it wouldn't go with a bang, or whimper, but quack…

Bible Prophecy: a collage of world chaos: mushroom clouds, hurricane-bent palm trees, mind-numbing death tolls, plagues, mudslides, wild fires, rampant superstition, drought, floods, earthquakes and starving children; the tyrant of the day whipping up turbaned hordes.…

The Soviets used to figure prominently among the atheists in these collages: bushy eyebrows and scowling faces looking down approvingly upon parades of missiles sporting Hammer-&-Sickles.… "A beast will rise up from the East": a common pull-quote at the time was still on-screen, having survived, apparently, the Soviet fall, though Putin's face now graced the collage. A handsome man in a business suit, he could easily be one of ours, though Anselm didn't think that was the point.

Prayer for the Holy Innocents on the Eve of Extinction
O Lord, our Prophets tell us that You, in your infinite wisdom, periodically extinguish 95% of the life on earth. They know this from reading the strata of earth, Your book, a geological record, wherein is recorded some 20 global mass extinctions which arrived with the regularity of German trains and includes the Ordovician-Silurian extinction (fickle hand on the global thermostat?), then the Late Devonian extinction (a mistaken delivery of fire?), then the Permian extinction (fire again), then the Triassic extinction (floods worse than Noah's), then the Cretaceous extinction which did in the dinosaurs when, according to Your fine print, a layer of Iridium at that strata, an enormous meteor slammed into the earth, the dust kicked up by the explosion plunging us into a night so pure that it seemed to draw the final curtain for every mammal. The regularity of your timetable makes many fear that earth, Your book, is in the path of Your pen, an elliptical asteroid belt that brings the two into contact every 26 million years, and means that the period You'll put to Your next sentence—ours—is due. We watch the skies.

Grant us, O Lord, a spectacular miss.

All that day and all the next, his day off, Anslem pressed his face into her token, a square of black silk with one corner tied in a knot. A palm-sized prayer book, it took the mould of his face when he breathed in her scent. In his pocket it twined as sensually around his fingers as a silk sheet over bare legs until both sheet and legs ended up in a tangle.

Tangle.

He fingered its knot knowing that just giving it back would be the simplest release. But if he did, would that be the end of?— Of what? What could her giving him the cloth mean? Did it mean? A test? Or message?— What else could it mean other than that she, like him, wanted to live!

She could have chosen any object to give him a sign, a lens cap, for instance, that prophylactic that blinds. But no, the Lady bequeath him the hankie she used to clean her lens, so clearly she was telling him to SEE.

But what?

It did have a knot, and knots, by nature, were vexed. So if message, what did she mean by that? That she was lashed to another, and thus unable to reach out to him? The knot that bound her more complicated than the tangle that confounds the fisherman's net?.... Or worse, more like a rope woven to form a noose—a heart-shaped loop—placed around the star-crossed's neck?...

Or did she mean that him and her, the two, could be one, even if only in a complication? This last thought made his heart race. For truly, presents had bows and what was a bow if not a pretty knot? An easy puzzle, easily undone, and put there to delay the reward a tad, to tarry, not to block but to make the prize that much sweeter once won. And like a ravenous dog thrown a bone, he fell upon the knot, using his teeth to get it undone. There, like the meat within a nut, or rather the fortune in a Chinese cookie, was a slip of paper: *I thought you and I could meet for a drink sometime. 232-0933.*

He stared at the number for the longest time. Was he simply playing fortune's fool? The silk was black after all, a funerary. And her husband, Rodrigo, was a psycho. A psycho who'd seen another man's eyes—mine—follow his wife's comely shape skip up the stairs, leaving Anslem behind with her Cid glaring back, eyes burning with the hate unique to Black Knights, and husbands, who know that something theirs—by rights, by might, if needs be, if not by the lady's grace—had been taken, and will not let the offence stand. He had once knifed a man, they said. Or maybe that happened in West Side Story. In either case, the knight would surely call him out in another one-sided duel. The arena. The sword. The shit.

Throw the hankie—and number—away, Anselm told himself. Forget about Beatrice—married to another man. Choices beget outcomes while it's foolish to dream, he dreamt, all that day and into the next, phone in hand.

Church & Science in the Age of Irony

Catholic bishops denounce researchers for trying to coax stem cells into transubstantiating into heart muscle, or other new flesh, demanding that they "stop chasing after miracles."

A prominent study in The Journal of Reproductive Medicine found that women "doubled their chances of becoming pregnant when Christian groups prayed for them."

The State in the Age of Religious War

And lo, while yet governor of Texas, the Lord came to him in a vision, or so he has claimed, and said, "I want you to run for president." Me Lord? The governor might have asked; though he did not ask, for all his life he had been among the elect and so was less surprised that God Himself, not an angel nor any other emissary, would deliver the message than he was by the scorn heaped upon him by atheists, secular humanists, and other witches who scoffed at the idea that God would choose him as His instrument, righteous finger on the button of Armageddon, ruler of the mightiest military on earth, he whose greatest ambition was to be baseball commissioner, who needed gift-grades to get to 'C' (at a college where 'C' spelled dunce), who was surprised (this in his first term as president) to learn that there were blacks in Brazil (this from someone who grew up not in a shack in Appalachia, nor a dark hole, but in the highest circles of power), who went missing from the military the time he himself could have fought instead of sending others. Still, with the certainty granted only to those touched by God, he continued to speak in tongues—"We need to make the pie higher"—and the faithful continued to vote, for surely, the Lord had made fishers of men from fishermen, thieves, and worse reformed drunks than him (but no harlots like Mary Magdalene), and besides, gay marriage must be defeated at all costs, and they recognized in the "funny math" that twisted the election's results, the Hand of God.

To what end, was not yet clear. But clouds were gathering in the East, ominous clouds it seemed since the governor now president oft' declared, "God is at work in world affairs." And he didn't need no advisors to remind him of Zechariah 12:1: Jerusalem will become an international problem; and Revelations 16:12: Troops will cross the Euphrates; and Revelations 11:9: The world will be able to simultaneously witness events; and Joel 3:2; and Micah 4:1; and Matthew; and Luke and four score other such passages wherein is foretold the natural disasters, rampant immorality, the rise of a world economic orders—NAFTA, Starbucks, Wal-Mart—and other wondrous signs that signal the Rapture: earthquakes in divers places, famines and troubles, as well as the difference between glorious Jerusalem and wicked Baghdad, the new Babylon; and the return of the Messiah once the Jews had been returned to the land promised by God to Abraham.

Reading these signs he declared, "I believe there is a reason that history has matched this nation with this time," for truly, we have entered The End Times, the final battle between Good and Evil, which 40 million American voters believe will usher in the Second Coming, so he'd better get right with Israel, the lobby said, for a showdown there could be a "dress rehearsal of Armageddon," and God speaks clearly in opening His Seven Seals, and woe unto those who oppose His Chosen People.

As if to punctuate their words, a beast rose up and smote the United States, and unable to capture the beast for his people, the Great Leader's eyes turned to Saddam, this newly-risen Saladin; for if a rematch was in God's master plan, as it was in *True Grit; Rambo 2; Warhead; The Dirty Dozen; The President's Man: A Line in the Sand; Hell in Normandy; Fort Apache; Walker, Texas Ranger: The Final Showdown, Parts 1 & 2; Walker, Texas Ranger: A Matter of Principle; Walker, Texas Ranger: Way of the Warrior; Fighting Back; The Proud and the Damned; Eagle in a Cage; The Green Berets; Master and Commander; Moment of Truth; Blood in the Sun; Delta Force 2: The Colombian Connection; Delta Force 3: Operation Stranglehold; Hero and the Terror; Missing in Action; The Delta Force; Invasion U.S.A.; Code of Silence; Missing in Action 2; Bravo Two Zero; First Blood; Lone Wolf McQuade; Forced Vengeance; Lord of the Rings; Braddock: Missing in Action III; Silent Rage; An Eye for an Eye; A Force of One; Operation Dumbo Drop; Walker*

Texas Ranger 3: Deadly Reunion; Gung Ho!; Battlestar Galactica; Rambo 3; Command and Conquer, Red Alert (for PS2); The Sum of All Fears, Tom Clancy's Ghost Recon: Advanced Warfighter and every other epic he had ever seen, and if Saddam was Saladin, the great Muslim warrior-king who repelled Richard the Lionhearted during the third crusade, that made him?—

Quoth he on the matter: "God told me to strike at al Qaida and I struck them, and then He instructed me to strike at Saddam, which I did."

And in response, Muslim clerics urged their followers to blow themselves up in 'Jihad'—holy war—against America, calling this Crusade one more in a series of barbarous military operations against the Muslim world by Christian kings, who launched wave after wave of coalition armies to steal Jerusalem over the course of several hundred years.

And yea, the Great Leader warned television viewers that this effort to bring about the rule of God on earth, "this American crusade, this war agin' Evil, is gonna take awhile."

Conquering Evil is also part of Osama bin Laden's plan to "establish the rule of God on earth." Quoting from the Koran, he assured the faithful that "those who believe fight in the cause of Allah, and those who reject faith fight in the cause of evil. So fight ye against America and the other friends of Satan: feeble indeed is the cunning of Satan."

And in reply the Great Leader quoth: "We will export death and violence to the four corners of the earth [Editor's note: most believe the earth is round] in defense of this great country and rid world of Evil" [sic].

And in reply, President Mahmoud Ahmadinejad of Iran, addressed world leaders at the U.N., saying that his nation will also develop nuclear fire, their only defense against the aggression of America, not only as a way to keep the evil west from imposing "the logic of the dark ages" as it did in Iraq, but also because his entire nation would welcome martyrdom. As the world's presidents, kings, and prime ministers sat held in place by the hand of God, or so he has claimed, a halo glowing around him, or so his cabinet has claimed, Ahmadinejad lectured them on the contract he had signed with God to usher in the cataclysmic confrontation with Evil and darkness that will herald the return of Imam Mahdi, The Hidden Imam, who will lead the Forces of Righteousness against the Forces of Evil (a.k.a. America) in one, final, apocalyptic battle (a.k.a. nuclear holocaust). And he ended with a prayer for God to "hasten the emergence" of this Imam, "the Promised One," who after the apocalypse will "fill this world with justice and peace."

Prayer for the Holy Innocents on the Eve of Being Caught in the Crossfire....

The lunchroom was more segregated by faux class than by age or even race. Except for the Queen and her new conquest, a young buck of a duke, who sat off by themselves playing footsie under the table, the nobles, in their costume jewelry and finery, congregated at one of the picnic tables, apart from what had come to be known as the peasant tables—"not because we think we're better than you," one ex-cheerleader had explained in her earnest, open-eyed way the day that Jude called them out. "It's because of the smell. So don't take it personally."

There was a truth in that, Anselm noted, for Jude did smell of Dragon's breath: its smoke, hydraulic oil and fire. Which made Anslem, who handled urinal cakes, and worse, wonder at his own perfume. So he and Jude sat together, until Jude shipped out. Now, because Anselm got there later than those who were actually in the show, there wasn't even room for him at the peasant tables so he sat alone save for the Executioner, a sullen man with sunken eyes, who ate his sack lunch morosely, and in silence, just as Anselm liked it.

Today, though, when he entered the lunchroom, he couldn't help but notice conversations pause, eyes track his movement; a pair of serving wenches scooted apart as if to make room for his tale.

He couldn't bear to go through with it so changed course in mid stride, heading to the employee kitchenette so as to not look like he was avoiding them, or had something to hide.

Eliciting Confessions in the 21st Century

The United States redefines "torture" as only those actions specifically intended to cause "organ failure or death," unless excused under the president's executive powers for some circumstances. While such circumstances are left up to the president (or his designees), methods of non-torture allowed under routine circumstances include, but are not limited to: The Ducking Stool; The Witch's Cradle; The Boot; The Collar; Burial (temporary); electric shocks; testicle clips; The Heretic's Fork; Pressing; Knotting; The Oven; The Pear; The Shin Vise; Stockades, the Adam's Apple (a wooden ball that can be strapped into the subject mouth to induce gagging); Ordeal by Freezing Shower & Air Conditioning; Water Boarding; Ordeal by Phonebook (place on subject's head and hit with hammer—leaves no bruises); terrorizing nude detainees with dogs or by forcing them to play Russian Roulette; hooding your tired, your poor, yearning to be free, then wiring them up on a pedestal in the Statue of Liberty pose, telling them that if they fall asleep, or fall off, the floor will electrocute them; stacking your naked, huddled masses into pyramids; forcing them to perform oral sex, and etc.

More Science

New studies of a fossil called *Scipionyx samniticus* reveal that dinosaurs must have breathed in much the same way as crocodiles. The fact that the biblical record contains no mention of dinosaurs has often perplexed scientists, but this new finding explains why Moses wouldn't have reported them: if they existed, they probably were just another type of crocodile to the people of his day, e.g. "the great crocodile crouching in the river" (Ezekiel 29:3).

If humans can immortalize stem cells, does that make them god?

If the Big Bang birthed an expanding and contracting universe, as well as 27 (or 11) dimensions (as the prophets of String Theory proclaim), instead of the 10 spheres of heaven, 7 circles of hell, and one earth (that we can actually see), does that mean that the cosmos is more like a yo-yo than a plate spinning atop of a juggler's stick?

If the 27 (or 11) dimensions prophesized by String Theory prove true, and the Reality we think we know is only a subset of the Real Reality, one reality among many, as its prophets say, with tachyons, i.e., particles that travel backwards in time, and the ability of any of us, given the right circumstances, to walk through lead, does that mean that the sphere of the Moon, the lowest sphere of Heaven, doesn't just come near Adam's Peak, the highest point on Earth, but actually touches it?

Fides. Faithful. To whom? To what? To vows? History? Her heart? *Semper fi*, the jarheads say, as if it were that simple.

Once upon a time, a knight in love with a lady told her he would do anything for her love. Anything? Anything. Even return to me this glove were it to fall from my hand? she asked, taking it off. She then walked out to a pit near the stable wherein was contained a tiger, and holding her glove above the roaring beast, let it fall in....

Bestiary

When the falcon catches the falconer's lure and realizes it's only a cloth dummy, does it feel duped? Why does it come back for more? Ditto the cat and its string?

Must they pounce on every twitchy movement, powerless against the flipping of some biological switch?

...griffins, gargoyles, unicorns....

Likewise, must he persist, or must he play falcon, cat, mouse, and frog? And not just any frog but the fairy-tale frog who falls madly in love with a stork and pursues her, croaking his love ballads from the mud at her feet, putting his all into one last effort—his swan's song—until she finally notices and gobbles him up?

...The knight, a noble of honor, leapt in after the glove. After a terrific fight, during which he received a number of wounds, he managed to slay the tiger. Exhausted, he climbed out of the pit and returned the lady's glove to her, saying as he did so, "Seeing how highly you value this glove, and in what regard you hold my esteem, I am reminded of how a ball, poised on a peak can roll into diverse valleys, while the best way to judge a journey...."

Did the frog turned prince speak as passionately as the humanized mouse, the mouse with a human ear grafted upon its back?

If a cadaver can supply 2 corneas, 2 inner ears, 1 jaw bone, 1 heart (or 4 valves), 2 kidneys, 2 lungs, 1 liver, 1 pancreas, 1 stomach, 2 hip joints, 2 shoulder sockets, 2 tibias, 2 femurs, 23 ribs more than Adam gave Eve as well as 206 other bones, 27 ligaments, 2 biceps, 2 triceps, and 650 other muscles, 2 hands, 2 feet, one face, 20 square feet of skin, 3.5 quarts of blood, 60,000 miles of blood vessels, 90 ounces of bone marrow, 100,000 human genes—all of them collectable, taggable, processesable, saleable—and these parts go into 252 different recipients,

as did the reusable relics of one Timothy Wergde—whose family reunion should those recipients attend?

(And by the way, what happens at the Rapture if these various people are headed in different directions?)

...thou shouldst no more wonder at their action than at a stream falling from a mountain height to the valley, for in heaven's order all natures fall, or rise, to their place, not as flotsam at the mercy of waves, but as ships gliding to different ports on the Great Sea of Being. —Beatrice to Dante, *Paradiso.*

A tiny buoy, bobbing up and down in the ocean and attached to a tsunami beacon could have prevented 300,000 deaths 7,000 miles away in Indonesia.

...a smile is just a frown turned upside down.... What did she really want? To make of Anselm the tool she would use to work the leather of her husband's heart?

But in such service, would he not also be the tool that works her most inner, tender part?

A conch shell, the spread of wings, a lily's bell, a journey judged by its butterfly effects....

The heart! He meant her heart!

"They never had sex?"

"He never even spoke to her." Back in college, while Anselm was a history major, he had been describing courtly love to a business major, a co-ed who "valued him as a friend." Heartless woman. Accountant of the cruelest sort. Still, he couldn't get over her, so would show up early to Sociology 201, their mutual class, in the hopes of sitting near, of making her see, he saw years later, so that he himself might understand how a man could persist in a hopeless love. "Often the knight's lady was married, and so as needs be, the knight would content himself with worshiping her from afar."

"Like a stalker?" she asked absentmindedly, brushing her long hair, her penchant to do little personal hygiene tasks in front of him one of her endearing traits.

"No, the woman was in complete control even if she didn't even know she was being worshipped, even if she didn't know the man existed; Lancelot and Guinevere, Dante and Beatrice.... There are so many poems and troubadour songs about courtly lovers because theirs is the most perfect love, the purest love, better than any love between people who spoke to each other because the man never has his image of the woman spoiled by something she might say or do. Because she's forever fabulous, he can devote his love service to her, his obedience, his submission. In so doing, he ennobles himself."

"That's sort of sick, don't you think? I mean the way he objectifies her."

Her long, soft hair. So near. So beyond the fence.

Anselm, tried to make her understand; no, he ached to make her understand, to explain himself to her through them, without confessing his fantasies about her, so she would come to see the goodness of his heart, go out with him, and in so doing come to love him, bear their children, a life together—Great Chain of Being—maybe their son or daughter discovering the vaccine for plague, savior of millions, maybe the world, the world's salvation hinging on this very moment—butterfly effect—or so it seemed, and trying to not sound defensive, he tried to put courtly love in modern terms, telling her how it wasn't all that different from someone today getting a crush on a movie star; or that one model with those bedroom eyes who was always in the lingerie section of the Victoria Secret's catalog that came to his mailbox... Her frown made Anselm explain that it wasn't unusual at all for a guy to have a crush on a swimsuit model or Aunt Jemima—the young one, after the logo had been redesigned, not the one that looked like Mammy; or that muscular woman in the *Tomb Raider* video game; or the Indian princess on the Land O'Lakes Butter Package. "They drew her knee caps to make you think of breasts...."

"You seriously need to start spending more time around 3-D women," she said, gathering her books and taking her business to another seat.

Butterfly effect; Alternate histories: Native Americans don't rise up against French colonies so Napoleon doesn't send troops to put them down so the troops can't be bitten by mosquitoes and contract malaria so Napoleon doesn't give up on the colonies and sell the U.S. half of its continent and the U.S. never becomes a superpower with global ambitions of its own and Jude never gets sent to the Middle East.

For lack of mosquito nets a kingdom was lost?...

Coleen Rowley, one of the FBI agents who realized that terrorists were learning to steer but not land jumbo jets, is listened to instead of hung up on so September eleventh never becomes 9/11, America doesn't launch a global war and 26 million Iraqi civilians, and Jude, never get put in the cross-fire.

For lack of a phone call....

Choose Your Adventure Ending #1: The Sphere of Saturn, Temperance
Thereafter they found many ways to use the Friar to pass messages back and forth, finding other evenings for clandestine dinners so that she might unburden her woes and he might take comfort in listening to the cares of a woman who had married too young. And Love, who never rests, crept between the twain, and before they were aware, planted Her banner of conquest in their breasts. Say rather, one heart had they: her grief was his sadness, his sadness her grief. Both were one in love and sorrow, and yet both would hide it in shame and doubt.

For once burnt, as was she, she feared to approach love's flame.

And he? He saw her altar would be an all-consuming thing. And wanted to do right by her. And himself. How far were they willing to carry this, this?—Summer romance?—Is that all it was? But how does one say this in confession?

Here she blushed, colored by the shame of her love, and fear too, for she doubted if his was true. For in truth, though both their hearts were ruled by whatever force holds the planets in their place, she also felt the power in man-made names like "wife." And the consequences of breaking either nature or man's laws being heavy to her, she would hide her desire.

And likewise, he, when he looked upon her, another's lady, his desire would fight against his outward appearance, like a prisoner struggling against his fetters, till he wearied of this fruitless strife. Each knew the mind of the other, yet was their speech of other things.

Or at least that was one possible journey Anselm imagined.

Choose Your Adventure Ending #2: The Sphere of Jupiter, or Justice Glowing as Struck Embers Emit Innumerable Sparks

Thereafter they found many ways to use the Friar to pass messages back and forth, finding other evenings for clandestine dinners so that she might unburden her woes and he might take comfort in listening to the cares of a woman who had married unwell. Then, after work one day, they met at the Holiday Inn, and before you could say the "f" of "fi" they were in each other's arms. The passion they had withheld from one another came burning forth, as a spark once kindled consumes the forest, and they gamboled and frolicked until they very nearly died of bliss.

After this encounter, having devoted some thought to the subject, to the accompaniment of many hilarious comments about the stupid friar's naiveté, and random jibes at her cruel and clueless husband, they arranged matters in such a way that, without having further recourse to their friend the friar, they slept together no less pleasurably on many later occasions, so mutually pleasing each other all the days of their lives that troubadours were moved to compose songs about them, many of which ended:

And I pray to God,
In the bounty of His justice,
That He conduct all like-same pilgrims
To self-same beneficence

Choose Your Adventure Ending #3: The Sphere of Mars Burning Red as Fire Appears behind Alabaster

Or perhaps mariachis would take Rodrigo's part, and sing how "esposa" means both "handcuff" and "wife," and shows why love is bound to hate and explains why El Cid relieved the Gong Farmer of his heart: after following her to the Holiday Inn, he waited for her to come out. And waited, images of his sweaty wife in bed, twisting under another man, twisting his guts. All the night he kept his vengeful vigil, expecting her to emerge at every moment. But she didn't appear until the sky had begun to lighten, washing out every star excepting that which we call Lucifer. She was with him. Her lover—who walked her to her car. There, he kissed her tenderly, and stood a moment looking after her as she drove off. Then he turned to discover El Cid. No lance nor sword had the Cid, but a switchblade gleaming bright. "Die Traitor!" he cried, running through the two-legged cockroach.

Adam's Peak

It wasn't that Anselm was critical of the Lords and their riding mowers. Having been molded from humus, like all humans, they surely felt a need from time to time to lie upon their Mother's breast, and in the absence of anything better, he knew, the smell of freshly mown lawn would serve. Grass and loam. With its blackness and worms—that the Lords, unlike him, never touched—riding their mowers, hush-puppied foot on the gas.

Yea, though cloistered all the week in office cubicles smaller than a monk's cell, they lacked the link their brother scribes enjoyed, drawing God's word from mother earth: skinning a lamb, scraping its hide smooth, sharpening the quill of a goose, dipping it into ink they themselves wrung from blackberries to form words without separation, sentences coagulating into pages, pages making up sacred books of mysteries serene as the Primum Mobile with their architectural capitals and luminous illustrations so fine that their gilt details had been painted with an eyelash—yes an eyelash that the scribe himself plucked from his own head—the books' ornaments and wonders—shimmering portals of thought embodied—that said Creation was one continuous expression of Divine Letters-Proportions-Harmony-Laws-Spheres without separation, the symmetry of a snail's shell, of a flower's bell, of an inner ear, a breaking wave, a moth's flight or comet's tail....

Say rather, they pass their weekdays typing on keyboards so letters appear behind glass, ants in ice, but not like ants at all for unlike the process of suspending an ant in ice, they have no idea how press i n g a b u t t o n m a k e s a n X or O a p p e a r o n s c r e e n let alone how it can appear on some distant screen and represent there an order for shoes, or elsewhere the release of toxic gas, or to another pair of loving eyes, housed in the next cubicle, hugs and kisses....[1] But working on screen, they feel the unseen virtual world beyond the glass as

---

[1]   The keyboard is a grid of electrical switches (switches under the plastic caps of a keyboard's keys typically consist of a pair of metal contacts separated by a spring which, once released, will return the key to its original position). Depressing a key, say the key labeled X, closes that switch (a timer on each switch/key introduces a 10 millisecond delay between the switch and the rest of the circuitry to allow the tiny bounce present in the keyboard switch to settle so that false openings and closings are not transmitted (the timer consists of a pair of serial NAND gates (a NAND gate is a two-input logic circuit (this type logic circuit is composed of transistors (electronic switches activated by a voltage applied to a central terminal that allows a current to flow through the semiconductor substrate between its other two terminals) arranged so that a voltage applied to their inputs will create a voltage at their outputs with the following truth table: Output Q = 1 (or +5 volts) for all inputs R, S except R = 1 and S = 1 while all other inputs produce an output of 0 volts) with the input of each gate cross coupled to the output of the other gate with a crystal /capacitor-resistor oscillator (a capacitor can be thought of as a storage device for electrons formed by two conductors, such as foil, separated by an insulator. The rate at which the capacitor charges can be set by a resistor in its circuit (a resistor is an electric component that adds resistance to electric current in a circuit); as the capacitor charges to ⅔ of the +5 volts supplied by the power supply, the logic gate it is connected to senses this and turns on, draining the capacitor and starting the cycle over). With the keyboard button depressed then, another logic circuit latches its output, that is holds it in a steady state so that it can be detected. When a small micro-processor inside the keyboard (think Chinese boxes.....) detects a circuit that is closed, it compares the coordinates of that switch in the matrix it is part of to the character map in its read-only memory (Read-Only Memory or ROM is a bank of logic switches (see above) that can serve as a look-up table: every particular set of inputs voltages produces a particular set of output voltages) and loads into a buffer memory (buffer memory is a kind of RAM, or Random Access Memory, that is logic circuits whose output will remain in the state they are placed into until they lose power, or are reset) that store temporarily the corresponding ASCII code (American Standard Code for Information Interchange, first developed for the teletype machine, a set of digital codes representing letters, numerals, and other symbols, widely used as a standard format in the transfer of text between computers), which for the letter X is 55, which

real as the keyboard in their hands, the keyboard and screen an interface between them and an unseen universe as surely as an illuminated manuscript portaled the scribe's mind to Celestial Spheres.

They are used to interfaces.

And something deep inside of them longs for their Saturday afternoon on the riding mower, sun on their face, wind in their hair: If only we could mow the lawn on Adam's peak!—the highest point on earth, the place humans could stand to be nearest the moon, the lowest sphere of heaven. An interface between heaven and man, the point that connects.

From *A Brief History of the Dark Ages* by A.L. Helms: With deserts populated by mystics; with holy hermits living atop 30 foot pillars; with saintly women burning the word Jesus into their breasts; with the wearing of hair shirts to put off demons; with gargoyles and demons in the architecture; with witch hunts, flagellation, Holy Wars, miracle relics, the torture of prisoners, burning of heretics, the scrutiny of every tree crotch, knot hole, tea leaf or mossy rock for the trace of God's face or hand, Medieval Europe resembled one vast insane asylum.

"Operating the dragon was a lot like operating a garden tiller," Jude had said.

"We have sinned against nature...."

The TV preacher was hitting his stride, beads of sweat polka-dotting his face. "And we too will reap what they are sowing if we stand by and let it happen as surely as God decided to lift the veil of protection He had used to shield America since the founding of our country up to the day those devils flew into the World Trade Center. Can I get a witness?"

Miraculous Transformations

Bread to flesh; water to wine; wine to blood; New Creationists; new planets; face transplants; artificial wombs; Medievals believed lead could be turned into gold.... Pigs carry human genes; rabbit genes are collaged with those of geese;

humans are given monkey hearts while monkeys, in an attempt to give them voice, are given larynxes, and though they couldn't yet speak, they could vocalize, their cages filled with the sound of "human" weeping and none of it seemed farfetched to Anselm anymore.

Great Chain of Being

If Einstein, halfway around the world, had never dreamed how links far too small to be seen could be broken, would ten-year-old Hideyuki Kurata, chasing a butterfly on her way to school, and ShutaroYamada, opening the shutters of his noodle shop to a new day, have vanished, along with the rest of their city, in the dawn of a vaporizing sun?

If Anselm never answered her token, would he have fathered the savior of the planet, or paralyzed Rodrigo?...

Why is it that when Galileo discovered the moons orbiting Jupiter, he was threatened with fire, while the shell game of planets and whole worlds outside our solar system or deep in our atoms—by what man or woman? What agency, what institute? Who?—was met by a yawn.

By everyone but astrologers: "Astronomers can claim that Pluto isn't a planet," scoffed one Wizard Ed, "but Pluto's transit through the last degree of Capricorn was a clear indication that the U.S. would get endlessly bogged down in Iraq if they launched the war on that date. And look what happened. If you want a quick war, you don't begin it with Pluto in the last degree of any sign but even more so in the last degree of the last sign. White House astrologers should have known that. Of course, there is the possibility that the White House has the best astrologers in the world and they wanted the U.S. to get bogged down in Iraq because it's good for business or whatever. I am not a political analyst so I don't know. But if they were hoping for a quick, decisive war, and IF they had good astrological advice, then obviously it would have made more sense to wait until Pluto entered Aries."

A lack of faith to shake? No passion to burn?

The Children's Crusade

One spring day in 1212, a child of French farmers began to preach Crusade, claiming that Christ had appeared to him while tending sheep, and bade him to retake the Holy Land from the Muslims. Others had tried before, of course. Four times, armies led by kings had tried and failed, their efforts dissolving into spectacles of greed and barbarism since many crusaders only used religious patriotism as a pretext to plunder the Holy Land for their own enrichment. But their example was the very reason his Crusade would succeed, the boy professed, since his Crusade—a Crusade comprised solely of children—would use no other weapon than faith and as he and his fellow children prayed down the walls of Jerusalem, their innocence would protect them. At the urging of his father, he began to march to the east—*an army of one*. Other children joined in, increasingly encouraged by their parents as their number grew—*be all you can be*—for so clearly did the innocence of the children shine out from them that they truly did seem touched by God.

Prayer for the Holy Innocents on the Eve of a Dangerous Journey

By the time the main body reached Rome, the army had grown to 30,000 French children—not one over twelve-years old—and another 20,000 boys and girls from Germany. The pope (named Innocent) didn't believe real innocence had a chance. So rather than dissuade them, he gave the children a blessing, and let them pass, believing that while they could not succeed, they would shame the crowns of Europe into forming a coalition of the willing to join in on the attack.

Damsels, Knights, Great Chain of Being, Unification Theory

Everyone was searching for a narrative they could fit within, Anselm imagined, watching one of the slick commercials created for the Army, Navy, and Marines by the same ad agency that knew a lot about getting young people into a particular brand of jeans, or tennis shoe, and ran their fast-paced, jump-cut clips of teens dressed as ninjas with night-vision goggles, or cavalry officers with white gloves and chrome swords, rock climbing, and launching cruise missiles at video-game-monsters between shows on MTV, cartoon programs, or during football, baseball and x-games, in *Mad Magazine*, on websites for funny animal downloads and skateboarder and music stuff—or on soft-drink cups and in the school paper—anywhere and everywhere young minds might be hanging out: a favorite at the time showing a kid in the yard of a farmhouse, flying a kite, then a little older, flying a toy airplane, then older still flying a radio-controlled model plane, then jump cut to him just a little older now, features of a fine young man at the remote-controls of a pilot-less, surveillance-kill-drone, as heroic rock music swells—the culmination of a childhood—voice over: *We've been waiting for you. The U.S. Army!*

"Everyone carries a rifle. But the recruiter said everyone also learns a skill and mine could be heavy equipment operator like those soldiers who built dams and bridges in commercials. I thought that if my unit got activated it would be to clean up after a hurricane or earthquake. I joined because I wanted to learn how to operate a bulldozer."

Of the 20,000 children from Germany who joined The Children's Crusade, none returned and of their fate nothing is known. Of the 30,000 children from France, many fell to disease, drought, exposure, kidnappings, and other hardships of the journey. When the rest reached the Mediterranean, the sea did not part for them as they believed it would and they languished at various ports, waiting for their miracle until—Reprieve!—it came: two Christian merchants with ships to take them to the Holy Land!

Two of the seven ships that the merchants hired were lost in a storm, though, and all of the children aboard drowned. The remaining ships were handed over to Muslim slavers from Africa, at a destination prearranged by the merchants. Those not sold in Algiers were later sold in the slave-markets of Baghdad where the price for white, Frankish slaves was higher. Though most converted to Islam, more than a few were tortured and martyred for not accepting their new faith.

Only a handful managed to make their way home and relate the fate of the rest, whereupon the father of the original shepherd boy, the father who had encouraged his son and other children to take up the crusade, was beaten and hung by a mob of angry parents.

A TV commercial aimed at guidance counselors and parents: working-class Kid, crappy hair-chop, letterman's jacket, lunch-bucket Dad in flannel shirt, the two of them shooting pool (one of the things fathers and sons can do together without looking homo), having a heavy father-son discussion between shots (talking to each other suspect enough). *It's the reserves*, Kid whines, as though trying to convince dad to let him borrow the car (and obviously ignorant of the fact that unlike Vietnam, when the future president's dad and others like him pulled strings to get their kids into the reserves where they could dodge the shooting war by guarding hangers in Texas, those joining the reserves today get shipped out, bloodied, sent home, too often, in body bags). *It's still the army*, Dad counters. The voice of parental reason. *It's the reserves*, Kid counters. *They'll train me.* This rejoinder takes the wind out of Dad, who understands the value of pipe-fitter training. *Will it be top training?* In answer, heroic rock music swells: *Help them find their strength.*

....how describe the ringing of a clapperless bell? Or what makes us think a snowflake's white? If white is the sum of all color, then what are we to make of ice?—or a wave's white cap, white water, white whale, whitefish, white meat, white wine, white blood cells, white hair, white swan, white feathers, white fur, white bears, white elephants, white rat; white lies, white flag, white flight, white stork, White Sale, white slaves, white pages, white flour, white bread, white heat, white-knuckle, white fear, white hope, white label, white privilege, white knight; White House, whitewash, white collar, white gloves, white chocolate, white truffles, white sugar, white lightning, white power, white trash...
White noise?

Original, to Medievals (and to post medieval, post renaissance, post-everything us), didn't mean 'new'—for there could be no such thing—but rather that which has been there since the Origin. Especially in affairs of the heart.

Religious Symbols & Practical Matters

The blade and hand guard of Crusaders' swords were fashioned to make the sword resemble a Christian cross, while the curved blades of Muslim scimitars where intended to resemble the crescent moon of Islam. No matter what their shape, though, they all had blood gutters: channels along the length of the blade to prevent it from acting like a cork in a body that had been stabbed, making it easier to push the blade in, making it easier for the blood to squirt out.

Was everyone a hero in their own story?

The 12,000-Ton Blood Gutter

He never wanted to kill anyone, but when he imagined how it would be, it was always a uniformed target that would stand there and let him aim because it knew it deserved to die as completely as those flat silhouettes of soldiers they shot for practice. Not some child running into the crossfire. "You studied history," Jude had said to Anselm during a quiet moment at the restaurant that the bride, groom, her parents, his parents, two sisters, and the witnesses had gone to to make a reception after the wedding. "In all your readings, doesn't war seem like something that just happens? Like a hurricane. Or accident. Just because a guy joins of his own free will doesn't make it predetermined. Or make him a killer, does it?"

A man of so few words, that was the longest speech he'd ever made. Or at least the longest he'd made around Anselm so Anselm could tell how much going weighed. But before he could fumble an answer both comforting and true, Jude looked away as though accused. He brusquely handed Anselm a card. "Here's my address. In case anyone at Medieval Times wants to write to me." FPO: *USS IOWA*. A ship named after a state paved with corn.

And on that day and all the rest, Anselm tried to imagine it as a gleaming city afloat upon a sea of green, a pastoral image, though looking it up online, he thought he understood how Jude's dragon could come to live within, about to be carried to the Middle East not by the winds of chance, nor by an accident, nor even the white sails of some merchant's ship, but aboard a gray device with its 8 Babcock & Wilcox three drum 565psi Boilers; its two 18 foot 3 inch (5.563m) four-blade Screws; its 12.1 inches, inclined 19° (307mm) armor plating; its nine, 66 foot-long, 239,000 pound, 16-inch (406-mm) / 50-caliber guns and their 2,700 pound Armor-Piercing shells, 1,900 lb (862 kg) Mk. 13 HC (High-Capacity—large bursting, bombardment shell (with their signature 50-foot craters, and defoliated forests); its "Katie" or kilo-ton nuclear shells; its 12 5-inch/38 caliber DP Guns (Mark 12) (127mm); its arrays of 16 launch tubes, 8 Armored Box Launchers and 20mm/76 CIWS Anti-Aircraft/Missile Missiles; its 32 BGM-109 Tomahawk Cruise Missiles; 16 RGM-84 Harpoon Anti-Ship Missiles; its SPS-49 long range radar system; its SPY-1D Phased Array Radar (simultaneously tracks 128 targets); its two VTOL craft, Apache helicopters, eighty assault tanks and other armored vehicles; its 8 RQ-2 Pioneer unmanned, remote-control vehicles (RPVs) and other (history-making) robots (first time ever to have enemy forces, an Iraqi army unit during Iraq War I, surrender to a robot, the dawn of a new age); its 8 Westinghouse electric Generators (SSTGs) and air conditioners for the comfort of 60 Officers, 70 chief petty officer, 720 enlisted sailors; its 10 Aircraft Crew-members; 80 assault Marines in Power Armor, and 120 Marines in Body Armor…. And him.

If the engineering drawings needed to create every part of this small, floating city for killing were put end to end, they would stretch to the moon and back four and a half times.

The Chronicler's Tale

That day at the restaurant, after the wedding, after considering both the question, and the mud of the past before it was fashioned into history; after consulting the Sum over History theory in which the laws of probability allowed one explanation to coalesce from a cloud of all possible journeys, what Anselm wanted to answer was, "Have you ever heard the expression, 'Like watching a train wreck about to happen?'" Unlike the flight of a butterfly in Chaos Theory, unlike chance that allows the marble of a journey to roll from a peak to any direction, at every step, what appeared to his mind's eye were two trains, one path. Not three or four or a thousand or the quadrillion possible germ-human combinations—the sick friend of the groom kisses the bride, who kisses her uncle John who holds the baby—that will decide who will live and who will die in the next pandemic. If you're an optimist, he wanted to say, maybe you see the trains colliding at some future crossroads of history, the presence of an intersection implying a chance for a spectacular miss. If your imagination is limited, like most, you see the locomotives pounding toward each other, head-on. A single set of tracks. On a treeless plain. On a clear day. In clear sight. Of each other. The whistles of both locomotives are screaming but neither train is able or willing to give an inch, for always the collision takes place dead center in our picture plane. The rails are important here, for their sense of doom, for the inevitability they imply of what we are about to witness, unable to redirect, or prevent; as is the blackness of the locomotives—always the locomotives are black—a sign of their mass, their inertia and the extraordinary length of time it takes 80,000 tons of full-speed train to stop even after the need to stop is recognized, the odds against the two trains stopping in time racing toward infinity as the time both engineers—and it's important to note here that recognition by only one of the two parties involved is insufficient—as the time both engineers have to recognize the need moves to zero. Only maybe one of the trains, like a virus, or the other, like a government, has no one at the controls. Never do we imagine the scene from inside one of the trains, the other rapidly filling our windshield....

Always the viewpoint is that of the spectator.

Of course train wrecks don't have to have tracks. Or even trains. They can happen anywhere, at any time. Without warning, any one of us can find ourselves in the witch's hot seat, no steering wheel or brake at hand. Or imagine those passengers who found themselves, one day, taking off in one of those airplanes that routed the video from a camera in the plane's nose to the TV monitors inside the cabin so passengers could watch the runway hurtle past faster and faster as they rocketed up into the sky until one doomed flight, the plane plummeting back to earth, camera still on, the passengers on board watched their own approaching deaths—on TV—their screens rapidly filling with dirt....

...in a doomed plane, as in hell, all roads lead down....

...as on the torturer's bench. Never do we imagine it from the viewpoint of the heart, beating along its rails, no more able to stop or not be what it is than the electric current once released, by an interrogator, perhaps, who threw the switch for the officer who gave the command for the army set in motion by the government put in place by events that the detainee threw himself against, with all the determination and hope of a fly who knows, just knows, there's a wider, better world on the other side of history's window glass....

...or an icecap, which as it melts in Antarctica allows the sea to swallow villages around the Pacific rim....

Polar Bears as Canary in the Mineshaft

(Fairbanks) Three more drowned polar bears were spotted in the Antarctic today. The bears drown because so much polar ice has melted that they are unable to find floes to climb onto and become exhausted while swimming. Scientists say that up to 90% of species alive today, including human, are threatened by a rise in the global temperature, but polar bears are noticed first because of their size.

Or are Swans Our Polar Bears?

(May 1997) Early warnings: Bird flu virus H5N1 infects 18, and kills 6 people in Hong Kong. Within three days, Hong Kong's entire chicken population of 75 million birds is slaughtered to prevent further outbreak. (Dec. 2003) Current plague of Avian flu resurfaces in South Korea; slaughter of 11 million chickens fails to contain disease; (Jan. 10, 2004) Japan reports first outbreak; (Jan. 15, 2004) Eleven people and 80 million chickens die in Thailand; (Jan. 20-25, 2004) Additional flocks devastated in Vietnam, Thailand, and Cambodia indicate that the plague is moving rapidly outward from this epicenter; (Jan. 27, 2004) Appearance of H5N1 in a duck farm in China indicates that the plague is developing the ability to jump species; (Feb. 2004) Mass culling of birds fails to prevent spread of plague to Indonesia, Malaysia, plague seen rapidly advancing toward Europe; (Aug. 2004) Virus becomes endemic in Vietnam and Thailand.

New infections in pigs in China indicate virus is developing ability for bird-to-mammal transmission and a likelihood of a pandemic that could kill millions of people. (Feb. 2005) Plague spread accelerates in: Cambodia (March 2005); North Korea (March 2005); Indonesia (May 2005). Rumors of human deaths persist in China where thousands of migratory birds have also died. (July 2005) The Philippines, the last remaining Asian country to be free of the plague reports its first case.

Europe braces.

(August 2005) Maine Biological Labs is fined for illegally importing the virus into the U.S., then smuggling out a drug to a private party in Saudi Arabia. (Aug. 2005) Russia and Kazakhstan report outbreaks carried into the country by wild waterfowl. Mongolia reports thousands of wild turkeys die; (Oct. 2005) Wild swans on the island of Chios, Greece, reported dead; (Oct. 2005) Virus appears simultaneously in Turkey, Croatia, and Romania; a human strain of the virus appears in Indonesia, though this ability to leap from animal to human has not yet developed the ability for human-to-human spread; (Jan. 2006) The quickly moving, and rapidly mutating virus attacks Nigeria; scientists say it had arrived months ago but social unrest and political chaos slows reporting, and prevents efforts to contain the disease making the continent—and other poor nations—an incubator for the rest of the world. (Jan. 2006) Virus continues its march from Asia, to Russia, to Africa, to the European Union; a forest in Romania is rumored to be filled with the corpses of thousands of migratory birds. The virus arrives by swan in France. (Feb. 2006) Pedestrians discover two dead swans, infected with the disease, in Italy. To date, entire ranges of wild birds, and millions of domestic poultry, have died or been killed, along with 160 people, or 89% of those infected. The high mortality rate, and path of the disease, recalls to many the fact that Italy was the European port of entry for the Black Death in which so much of the European population died that Medievals thought the world was coming to an end…. In this case, swans, not rats, are seen as the harbinger of plague: because swans are large, people notice their deaths first when all birds begin to die.

Prayer for the Holy Innocents on the Eve of Nuclear Fire
Prayer for the Holy Innocents on the Eve of a NEW and IMPROVED Ice Age!
Prayer for the Holy Innocents on the Eve of Religious War
Prayer for the Holy Innocents on the Eve of Post Humanity

²**P**rayer for the Holy Innocents on the Eve of Plague
O Lord, Here we are again (and by HERE I mean in Your crosshairs), rumors of doom gathering like the night with us feeling not a little like the doorman given the task to hold it back. We understand You must be pretty pissed at us for Copernicus and Nietzsche—and probably even all the throw-away packaging and throw-away TV shows like "Date My Mom" for that matter—for when they gave Earth, Your creation, a bum's rush from center stage, you couldn't help but end up in the gutter. Still, we've all seen those photos of earth from space, a beautiful blue marble hanging in inky black, and—You know it's true—we didn't even bother to look for strings because we knew that *that* scene, and so You, were soooo beyond all that. And that was pretty scary, but then, as we got used to it, it became okay—the idea of Spaceship Earth was kinda cool, and it inspired Earth Day, *Star Trek*, Greenpeace, and all of that.

But then the camera kept pulling back—long crane shot—showing earth the way the other planets and stars look to us, i.e., too many to count let alone name, the rocket that took those photos sending back postcards from an ever distant place, our home becoming more alien, shrinking ever smaller, fading, fading to a dim point lost in a field of dust—more of a haze of germs on a microscope slide than garden or cherished pet—and we realized how far from You we really could be, how loud we'd have to shout for You to hear.

Prayer for the Holy Innocents on the Eve of _____.

Still, we can't stop wondering, are you listening? Are YOU there? Are YOU picking up your mail or is there just too much THERE for YOU to be anywhere and this prayer a message in a bottle addressed to space?

Prayer for the H.I. on the Eve of X.

Prayer for H.I. @ X.

If not, then open our bottle, hear our prayer. Look down upon us, or up above, or sideways or with the eye in your palm, or in the back of your head, or out from the pyramids on our dollar bills, or from the Force Field that is You (Star Trek Episode 107). Or, if we really have fallen so far, as the preachers say, then at least look upon those too young to have yet tried, the innocents, and stay your hand a while longer....

RE: H.I. ☺

Choose Your Adventure Ending #4: The Fixed Stars

Or were all our fates fixed? And the best one could hope for this?:...in the Holiday Inn parking lot, El Cid dragged the body of the Gong Farmer between two parked cars. There, continuing the work he had begun with his switchblade, he cut open the chest of his wife's lover and with his own bare hands, ripped out Anselm's heart.

The lady, meanwhile, had gone home to an empty house. This wasn't the first time her husband had stayed out all night, so she didn't think it that unusual and was relieved that she wouldn't have to explain her own absence. She showered, then took a restless nap. When she awoke, Rodrigo still wasn't there. Or else he had come and gone? Strange. In any case, she got ready for work, and reported to her post, taking pictures of tourists, exhausted though humming to herself, and keeping an eye out for her lover. When Anselm didn't appear either, she began to worry, though she soldiered on with her duties. As the day wore into evensong, though, and he still didn't appear she grew very vexed.

Between shows, when the cast was allowed to sup, she intended to slip away to look for her lover. But Rodrigo appeared at her post and bid her to dine with him. Having no excuse not to, she was compelled to follow her husband to the cafeteria, enduring his assessments, in the guise of concern for her health, that she looked pale, and care-worn.

Seating her at one of the picnic tables, he told her to relax, that he would cook her a supper such as she'd never had. He went to the employee kitchenette, and retrieved something from the fridge. She pretended to watch him rinse, and mince, smiling back at him when he turned to look at her, as out of concern, though really he was making sure she was still there while secretly she was really watching all the while for a chance to call her lover, whom she had begun to worry had met some evil—in an auto accident, or by illness, or perhaps even at the hands of muggers.

Finally the microwave bell dinged. Rodrigo brought out the dish: a plate of steaming fajitas, mixed with green peppers and onions.

"This does smell delicious," she said, for she had not eaten all day, and she had not realized how hungry she was until the smell of the dish revived her appetite. Tasting a bit, she ate the whole down, whereupon Rodgrigo told her, "I dare say I knew you would enjoy that dish for while it was alive you loved it even more."

Upon hearing these words the lady was filled with foreboding and put her fork down. "Say what?"

The knight, seeking to bring her low, rehashed the affair: how espying her and the gong farmer exchanging glances he had become suspicious; and after following them to the Holiday Inn he had had his suspicions confirmed. Having them confirmed, he waited in ambush and tore the heart from her lover with his very own hands then served it to her with these tortillas.

The lady wiped her lips. Was silent a moment. Then said, "Since it was I who was unfaithful, it is I who should have born your wrath. But having supped on such rare fare, I feign I shall never be able to bear any common sort." And without hesitation, she went to an open window, whereupon she allowed herself to fall. The cafeteria was on the top floor of Medieval Times, so not only was she killed by the fall, but disfigured as well. Coworkers called the police, and since Rodrigo had the great misfortune of being a minority in a Red state, he was given the electric chair. His lady and the gong farmer, however, were laid to rest in a common grave, with a headstone that bore in verse the great love they had shared:

> *His was the mud*
> *Hers the moon*
> *United they'll lie*
> *As all Heaven sighs*
> *Ex uno disce omnes*

[from one judge the rest]

Anselm had only seen a real swan once. In the wild, that is. He'd been on a camping trip, lost in a darkening wood, when he'd stumbled upon a clearing just in time to see a big white swan—wingspan of an angel—gliding down onto a lake mirroring the sky. Its white body was doubled by reflection: white clouds, blue sky, white swan, blue water as one—maybe the most heavenly thing he had ever seen, either real or mirage—making him understand why Medievals believed that swans were harbingers of good fortune, their song a combination of all bird songs, the song of a dying swan the most beautiful of all for the death of anything beautiful was always tragic, but the death of a song that contains all songs constituted an unbearable tragedy of an unbearable beauty.

Then the swan *craned* its long neck. To swallow? Or *crow*? No, it didn't mime any other bird but shook, more like a dog, a violent spasm, its head flopping to the side with a splash. Then it just lay there. Still. Too still. Neck slack, head underwater, an aspect reserved for the immortal, its wings relaxing, spreading flat in the water, the body slowly drifting.

As he just stood there, unable to believe what he'd just seen, a second swan descended. Déjà vu. It landed near the dead one and paddled over. Took a smell, then clumsily climbed onto it and began to hump the corpse.

Medievals get a lot of things wrong.

But not all.

Kilimanjaro is a snow covered mountain 19,710 feet high, and is said to be the highest mountain in Africa. Its western summit is called the Masai "Ngàje Ngài," the House of God. Close to the western summit there is the dried and frozen carcass of a leopard. No one has explained what the leopard was seeking at that altitude.

Farewell to Kilimanjaro

...late summer of that year we lived in a house in a village that looked across the river and the plain to the mountains. In the bed of the river there were pebbles and boulders, dry and white in the sun, and the water was clear and swiftly moving and blue in the channels. Troops went by the house and down the road and the dust they raised powdered the leaves of the trees. The trunks of the trees too were dusty and the leaves fell early that year and we saw the troops marching along the road and the dust rising and leaves, stirred by the breeze, falling and the soldiers marching and afterward the road bare and we said **good-bye to white—**

"—*hair forever with Grecian Formula 409!*" blared a commercial, ten times louder than the volume of the show and E. swore bitterly at having been brought back by it to the day room he had been wheeled into. "For the sunshine," the nursing aide had nattered, turning his chair to position him before the television.

E.'s colostomy gurgled as he turned to look out the window. In the sunshine outside, a mimosa tree shaded their sign: Kilimanjaro Arms for the Aged, Inc. (A Wholly Owned Subsidiary of Time Warner). Did the wide world really continue on out there without him? It was hard to believe so judging from this view. Just past the sign was the swish of traffic on Route 66 and just beyond that a strip mall. In the heat of its parking lot, vultures squat obscenely, while in the sky a dozen more sailed, making quick-moving shadows on the motionless cars.

"Look at them," he said. "Now is it the sight of this place or its scent that brings them like that?"

No one answered. The Hodgkin's case in the wheelchair next to his continued to have a conversation with herself. A Parkinsons case continued to stare mask-like in the general direction of the television while the nursing aides went about their routines. A radio played.

To no one in particular, E. continued: "I watched the way they sailed very carefully at first in case I ever wanted to use them in a story. That's funny now."

On TV, picture-in-picture displayed a still of an anorexia-skeletal woman in the corner of the main screen, which displayed live video of her obese version.

Judging from this, the only other view that he had, the view through the 19" keyhole, E. doubted he would recognize the world outside the home even if he could get back in it.

"*Binge and purge eating became my life....*"

He tried to escape; he tried to get back to his first war, the war he had had when he was young instead of this war that he now had and in his head he wrote: There were many victories. The mountain that was beyond the valley was captured as were mountains—

"...mountains of ice cream, mountains of chocolate..."

There was not a feeling of a storm coming....

"And you felt trapped?" the 'host' asked, holding his 'guest's' pudgy hand.

"You always feel trapped biologically," E. answered.

"Eating made me feel inadequate but hunger...."

"—hunger made me see truly how Cézanne made landscapes."

Suddenly he realized he had not only skipped a hundred pages but had derailed into an entirely different book. "You God damn complainer!" he shouted, blaming those on the screen. The fat one, the 'guest,' began slobbering into a handkerchief, her body shaking with great, theatric sobs of self-pity.

"You dirty phony saint and martyr!"

"Should I change the channel for you?" It was C., the rehab nurse: the only staffer who didn't yak away as merri-mindlessly as a TV weatherman. Or sulk about her duties with the concern common to minimum-wage employees.

"I'm only talking," he said, calming himself to bring down his blood pressure. "It's much easier if I talk. But I don't want to bother you."

"You know it doesn't bother me," she said. "It's that I've gotten so very nervous not being able to do anything. I think we might make it as easy as we can until the doctors get your cancer into remission."

"Or until they don't get my cancer into remission."

"Please tell me what I can do. There must be something I can do."

"You can take my arms off and that might make it easier, though I doubt it. Or you can shoot me."

"Please don't talk that way. Couldn't I read to you?"

"Read what?"

"Anything in the book-bag that we haven't yet read."

"I can't listen to it," he said. "There hasn't been pure artistry since that damn Stokowski stooped to shake hands with Mickey Mouse. Talking is the easiest."

The 'guests' on the talk show had taken to quarreling among themselves. *"I'll tell you this,"* a G.I. shouted at the artist who wanted public funding to make a life-size church out of garbage, *"in my parish you're a dog!"* The audience howled. Some broke into a barking chant as if they were at a football game. The 'host' tried to get in a word of reason—but not too hard, E. noted. As in politics and all other spheres, the medium of howls had become the message and after a while he couldn't remember if the subject for this morning's argument was artists who piss on the cross, artists who shit on the flag, blacks who want to put the cross next to the flag in school, atheists who want to keep it out, gays who want to be married by the cross and serve under the flag, or whites who want to wrap themselves in the flag and burn crosses, atheists, blacks and gays.

"We quarrel and that makes the time pass."
"I don't quarrel," C. said. "I never want to quarrel. Let's not quarrel any more. No matter how nervous we get. Maybe your next treatment will be the one. Your oncologist told me that any one treatment could be the one that puts your cancer into remission."
"There's no sense in moving me now except to make it easier for you."
"You're not going to die."
"Don't be silly. I'm dying now. Ask those bastards." He looked over to the huge, filthy birds, now sitting on the sign and looking in, their naked heads sunk in the hunched feathers.

...inventor of MS-DOS, net worth $13 billion, has begun buying up the rights to Cézanne paintings which he uses as screen savers on the monitors in his office complex.

"Oooooooh-weee! Uncle Jed!"

They were in his room now. She sat on a canvas camping-chair beside the chrome of his hospital bed, adjusted to face an architect on TV, ancient eyes welling with the struggle to put into words what it was like to witness one's vision swept away in scorn.

"Jim, can you share your feelings," prodded the talk show 'host,' dripping with understanding. Even without the sound, you'd be able to tell that this was the sensitive part of the show, the part before the audience turned on their 'guest.'

"Functionalism once defined every skyline in the world," the architect said, gaining his composure. *"Glass curtain walls hung like banners to 'ornament-as-crime,' 'individual signature-as-sentimentality' and 'romanticism-as-kitsch.' But now the beauty of that purity has given way to imitation medieval squares and faux space villages. Bread and circuses, circuses and bread, and all because builders stopped giving the great unwashed masses what was good for them and started giving them,"* bitter sarcasm came into his voice, *"what* they *thought was good."*

The 'host's' face was a mask of empathy, easily readable though reduced as it was to the small scale of the screen—just as the Greeks wore exaggerated masks in their amphitheaters so that even the furthest (or dumbest) member of the audience could distinguish the tragic from the comic.

Closeup on the host's cartoon sympathy. *"I care...."* pause for dramatic effect *"about...your aesthetic."*

E. groaned. When the means and ends of the hoi polloi are given equal weight, equal time, equal volume as those of the intelligentsia, that is, when there is a true democracy of ideas, what becomes of culture? When the audience takes over the stage, what becomes of the playwright? What need is there for any art-ificer?

"Would you like me to read?" C. asked.

"No thanks."

"Maybe your Tuesday treatment will be the one."

"I don't give a damn about the treatment."

"I do."

"You give a damn about so many things that I don't."

"Not so many, E."

Transvestites in the Modeling Industry....

•   •   •

Museum fundraisers increasingly turn from the black-tie cocktail
party to walk-a-thons and other outdoor/heath-related events.

•   •   •

The Search for America's Sexist Lifeguards...

Cyberspace will redefine territory just as the invention of the
clock redefined....

Gay teens call now! 1-900....

Gaia means God is alive again and He's a She.

Grand Opera Meets Grand Ol' Oprey!....

Former CIA Director William Colby and former KGB Major General Oleg
Kalugin collaborate to create the computer game Spy Craft....

Daughters' Disapproval of Mothers' Provocative Dress....

Monochrome ex-commies pouring onto the technicolor side of the
Berlin Wall....

The BOFMOW (Based On Fact Movie Of the Week)...

The morphing of *grande histoire* into *petite histoire*, the morphing of
paranoia into schizophrenia, the morphing of ambiguity into indeterminacy,
transcendence into immanence, hierarchy to jouissance, 'less is more' to 'less
is a bore,' mastercode to mass carnival, paradigm to hegemony, proletariat to
cognitariat, words in print to image on screen, alienation to recess, genres
to hybrids, writing to archi-écriture, artist priests to artist clowns, Logos
to lacuna, sources to Ur text, criticism to Sur text, transparent window to
self-conscious page, characters as mirrors on life to characters as tain of

mirror: art mirroring life to life mirroring art to art mirroring art to mirrors mirroring mirrors mirroring...

• • •

"When I caught my boyfriend doing it with my mother in front of <u>our</u> mirror," wept the 'guest' disguised for anonymity as Groucho Marx, *"I thought I would lose my mind...."*

If it bothers you so much, E. remembered telling F., why do you want to talk about it?

"...my feelings of inadequacy...."

Watching this nation of whiners, he still didn't know. But even more perplexing was the unconditional victory of 'open wounds on camera' over 'grace under pressure.'

And to think he used to mock F. for boo-hooing in the pages of *Esquire*—I'm a cracked plate! My wanger doesn't measure up to the statues in the Louvre!

E. tasted bile rise up in him. It wasn't that he couldn't have gone public with his own chronic depression. Or his impotence. Or his broken marriages. Or the suffering he endured as a minority in the Italian army. Or even his hemorrhoids (and people thought he wrote standing up because he wanted to suffer for art!). Battles, executions, tortures, violations, fearful customs, unbelievable practices but through it all a stiff upper-lip. That stiff lip contained the only real meaning in a godless, modernist universe, after all. And a Man would make it show up in his Art—even if his first gush verged on hysterics:

There was a whistling that changed to an inrushing screem of air and then a flash and a krash outside in the brikyard. Then a bump and a sustained incoming shreak of air that exploded with a roar, the krash of high explosive tearing steal apart on contact and vomiting earth and brick.

Speaking now to the audience in his head, E. said, "I'm not trying to hide it." He was on stage, a 'guest' in the hot seat of "Everything Dysfunctional" with today's topic being authors guilty of he-mannish posturing, practicing what they criticize in others, propagating artistic movements long after their causes had been spent, sterility, cowardice, banality, bull in the afternoon.... The 'host' was Max Eastman so he knew the gloves would be off. *"Any voyeur can spy on that embarrassment in those personal papers of mine that got donated to my library. But he should know that I would have starved rather than put that draft in public. Or padded it into an eight-hundred-page 'blockbuster miniseries-in-print.' And I* certainly *didn't* jazz *it up with a lot of exclamation marks and* underscoring—*the way one of your other emotional cripples would have* done*!!!"* At this point, E. thought of the diva he had once seen in an opera. After hitting a clarion C, she had tossed off one of those musical laughs and pirouetted, her period-gown flowing in a way that none of the women in the audience, still in business suits after a hard day at the office, would ever be able to duplicate. Those women, the ones in suits, had gained a lot by being able to buy their own tickets, he knew. But he suspected and he suspected that they suspected, that there had been an additional price to pay. One that was regrettable for everyone and he calmed himself to read his revision in a steady voice:

> *A big shell came in and burst outside in the brickyard. Another burst and in the noise you could hear the smaller noise of the brick and dirt raining down.*
>
> *Lt. Henry asked, "What is there to eat?"*

What is there to eat!?—

Dread gripped E. Had he remembered to tick the dessert box on today's menu? What I leave out is as important as what I put in, he'd once told that pony boy from *The Paris Review* and the irony that his present context gave to that old remark depressed him greatly. He'd been leaving out more and more lately. And not just in terms of art—

Sighing, he resigned himself to missing out on today's fruit cup, the one thing with any flavor on his institutional diet.

"What about a drink."

"It's bad for you. Your oncologist said to avoid all alcohol."

"Molo!" he shouted.

"Yes Bwana," answered an orderly.

"Bring whiskey-soda."

"Yes, Bwana."

"You shouldn't," C. said. "That's what I mean by giving up. Your oncologist says its bad for you. I know it's bad for you. You should play shuffleboard instead. I'll push you out to the court."

"No," he said. Then he sulked.

So now it was all over, he thought. So this was the way it ended in a bickering over shuffleboard. Since the cancer had spread he had no pain and with the pain the horror had gone and all he felt now was a great tiredness and anger that this was the end of it. For this, that now was coming, he had very little curiosity. For years, through all his treatments, through scares of the nation's blood supply being tainted with AIDS, through reports of Tylenol then a host of other consumables being laced with cyanide, through anxiety created by Red Dye #12, radon and scores of new sources of cancer, through lethal spaceheaters, highchairs, autos, furnaces, lawnmowers and their factory recalls (which only happened when some bean counter determined that a recall would be more cost effective than paying off suits filed by family survivors), through upswings in random street violence, random mail bombings and arrests of family members who'd abandoned their grandmas, grandpas, moms or dads at horse tracks, airports and other public places because they'd been burnt out and could no longer deal with the stress of the aged, through this and more, death had obsessed him; but now it meant nothing in itself. It was strange how easy being tired of writing made it. It was strange how still wanting to write made him seem like all those other people on TV.

Either way, now, he would never write the things that he had never had the time to write because of the crush of teaching freshman composition at the college he had taken a job at after he was too old to go on safari and after being reviled by the universities that gave their faculty time to publish. Well, he would not have to fail at trying to write them either. Maybe he could never write them, and that was the real reason he was slowly shut out, not the shrinking departments, mergers with women's studies or march of literary fashion. Well, he would never know, now.

Now in his mind he saw an apartment complex in Karagatch,
constructed by a multinational company from materials that had
been outlawed in the west and could therefore only be sold in third-world
countries. That was one of the things he had never had the time to write,
with the children who played in the basement where the asbestos crumbled.
They hit it with sticks so it would swirl about them in great blizzards as they
shouted, "Snow! Snow!" Seeing them come out for air, their dark bodies a
fleecy white, a U.N. peacekeeper had asked an old man, "Is that snow?" And
the old man had answered, "It's too early for snow." And it was not snow that
they rollicked in until they began wheezing that winter.

Nor was it snow inside the North Orchard Shopping Mall though it
looked like snow, arranged about Santa's throne from which a man who was
not Santa passed out coloring books that when painted with water became
pre-colored ads for the pre-assembled models, "cha-cha-beat" organs that
played preset songs, complete sets of "collector" cards, and military toys
from a manufacturer that had frantically reprogrammed an assembly line to
duplicate, in time for Christmas, the snow-white camouflage used in the latest
global hot-spot.

Nor had it been snow that that boy had been staring at during a
holiday visit to the 'home' his parents had chucked grandpa into. The boy,
naturally, was not used to seeing white hair and had innocently asked,
"Momma, why do all the people here have snow on their heads?"

"There might be snow on the roof," C. had growled into E.'s ear, "but
there's fire where it counts." Behind everyone's backs, she playfully grabbed
his crotch.

"That's us," he had answered. "The snows of Kilimanjaro."

"*...the prefix 'Post' implies continuity,*" the expert on TV was saying,
arguing on stage with the author beside him, "*unlike 'Now This,' which is a*
transition to signify a complete disjunction...."

Watching them argue, while dying, E. realized how incredibly petty it
all was, how incredibly petty most of his own life had been—in comparison
to this ultimate that he was now facing. Yet somehow, because one refused

to face the pettiness, it could go unnoticed until a person was too old to do anything about it.

"...*so the appropriateness of a dance troupe named 'Still/Here,' made up of dancers who are all terminally ill....*"

You woke up one morning with an ache when there was no reason for you to have an ache, then your visits to the doctor grew more frequent and less determinate, then you had "health problems" and one day you realize how these problems, and their continual diagnoses and treatment had become your life.

"*Dying dancers isn't art, it's spectacle.*"

"If I had a shotgun," E. shouted at the TV, "I'd blow off your fucking head!"

"Shall I change the channel?" C. asked.

"Leave it."

"I really think you would enjoy something else more."

E. didn't answer.

She began to read from America's perennial best seller, the *TV Guide*. "One o'clock. Channel two. A neon-sign artist is propelled into the fourth dimension."

"You know I don't like those science stories."

"All right then. Channel seven. 'Hail to the Chief.' Lugar wants to delay nuclear proliferation talks until after his daughter's prom."

"I can't stomach what politics has become either."

"A modern-day zombie finds love in...." C. read, going down the list of all 149 cable channels until she said, "There's only two left. Now what do you want to watch? 'The Chipmunk Reunion' or 'Survivors of the Holocaust'?"

On TV, Dr. Kevorkian's face appeared along with the apparatus he had invented to allow family members to give a loved one a 'Death with Dignity' by injecting them with a lethal dose of morphine.

"Leave this."

The audience listened quietly, then by degrees became hostile, saying ugly things about the 'guests' and each other.

"I'm glad we're not like those horrid people," C. said.

"We are those horrid people. All of us."

"I'm not. You're not. You couldn't write those poetic books if you were. You couldn't love me if you were."

"Oh yeah, I love you, you kind, condescending bitch. That's poetry. I'm full of poetry now. Cancer and poetry. Cancerous poetry."

C. began to sniffle. E. sulked.

．　．　．

It was evening now and he had been asleep. The birds no longer waited on the sign. They were all perched heavily in the mimosa tree, their bodies silhouetted by the fluorescent glow of stores across the road. If he used his imagination, he could believe that the birds weren't waiting for him, but for the people coming out of the 8-Plex, their skin a ghoulish pallor in the light of its marquee: Cinema I: *Bloody Sunday—The Revenge*; Cinema II: *Kill for Your Supper*; Cinema III: *Her Inner Thigh*; Cinema IV... *Gore*...V...*Heat*... VI...*Skin*...VII...*Smoke*.... The inside of the nursing home was lit by the ever-present glow of its televisions. His personal boy was sitting by the bed.

"Memsahib's gone to mini-mart," the boy said. "Does Bwana want?"

"Nothing."

She had gone to get a cream Slurpie, and knowing how the sight of them was aesthetically appalling to him, she had sat in Dunkin' Donuts until she drained it all. In his mind he could see her, making that irritating sucking sound with her straw but doing so out of his hearshot. She was always thoughtful, he thought. It was not her fault that when he went to her he was already over. How could a woman know that you meant nothing that you said; that you spoke only from habit and to be comfortable?

It was not so much that he lied as that there was no truth to tell. He had had his life and it was over and then he went on living in this place.

You kept from thinking what this place was and it was marvelous. You played along and called this place a 'retirement community' like they all did and you were equipped with good insides so that you did not go to pieces that way, the way most of them had, and you made an attitude that you cared nothing for the work you used to do, now that you could no longer do it. But, in yourself, you said that you would write about these people; about the aged, the terminally ill; about riders of golf carts and patrons of museum gift-shops and other galleries of high-end kitsch; that you were really not of them but a spy in their country; that you would leave it and write of it and for once it would be written by someone who knew what he was writing of. But he would never do it, because each day of not writing, of comfort, of being that which he despised, dulled his ability and softened his will to work so that, finally, he did nothing at all. Nothing except watch television.

"And that's how those Italians get stripes into cannoli," an anchormodel chirped, standing in a cafe like the ones from which E. filed stories when he worked as a war correspondent for the *Toronto Star*: "...abstract words such as glory, honor, courage, or hallow were obscene beside the concrete names of villages, the numbers of roads, the names of rivers, the numbers of regiments and the dates...."

To add variety to her image, the anchormodel grinned and bobbed her head as she spoke, the way she must have learned in "journalism" school, her perm bouncing over a safari jacket like all "reporters" now wore to indicate they were on assignment outside the country.

...the bombardment of Plava, the evacuation of Thrance, the retreat from Caporetto, the break-out of Paris, the Spanish Civil War, the Greco-Turkish War, the slaughter of Somme, the slaughter of Verdun, the slaughter of Vittorio-Veneto, the Italian-Ethiopian War, the overrun at Gandesa, the landing at Normandy, the Cuban Revolution....

C. said she loved her job, E. thought, staring at a crack in the wall. She loved taking care of people, seeing them through therapy. Re-teaching old hands to squeeze rubber balls. And he had felt the illusion of returning strength of will to work. Now if this was how it ended, and he knew it was, he must not turn like some snake biting itself because its back was broken. It wasn't this nurse's fault. If it had not been she it would have been another. Another kindly caretaker and destroyer of his talent. Nonsense. He had destroyed his talent himself. Why should he blame this woman because she took care of him well? He had destroyed his talent by not using it, by betrayals of himself and what he believed in, by watching television so much that he blunted the edge of his perceptions, by laziness, by sloth, and by snobbery, by pride and by prejudice, by hook and by crook. What was this? A catalogue of old books? What wasn't? he moaned. There, he'd admitted it. How was that for a confession from an art hero, soaring above history?

Oh Gertrude! he sighed. Gertrude. He felt himself going weepy. All those years the critics puffed up my "famous style" when all along it was you speaking through me, and James and Flaubert speaking through me through you and—all right, if we live in a confessional culture, out with it!—all of us writing upon Shakespeare and Beowulf and Homer and the Bible and a compost of forgotten books back to the Garden. All of us High Moderns—a bunch of frauds or worse, naive romantics splashing our egos (another modernist notion!) across the page. Recycled plots, twice-told tales—Make It New!—when anyone who read truly could see that the medievals had the most profound understanding of "original": not that which is new but that which has been among us since the Origin.

"*Grocery clerk sues Michael Jackson for theft of song. More at ten!*"

Lawyers might not recognize that notions of plagiarism are but a fashion, E. told the ceiling, yet what else was I to do? What could anyone do, Gertrude, when you and Eliot and Pound and the rest of the goddamned saints were Caesars to me?—and to Literature as a whole. His tears were flowing freely now, collecting in his ears. Yes, Caesar who said, Better to be first in a village than second in Rome. How else was I to escape the mastery of the masterpiece if not by making it my own? Do my appropriated titles make me so very different from the darlings of today's academe, the post-colonial writers?

On TV, a studio audience had begun to grouse about bands that don't play their own music. A big woman with hair teased the way it was worn in bowling leagues took the microphone. "*I was cheated!*" she shrieked at the band members, smirking on stage. To authenticate her feelings of shame she continued for the cameras, "*I was duped into buying tickets to hear a band that lip synched even their 'live' performances!*"

Relativity, bohemian art, psychoanalysis, just-in-time inventories....

Revolutions in thought always spread through the middle class late and in a diluted form and E. turned away from the television, disgusted to hear arguments he'd worked out as far back as The Monkees.

Then he saw C., walking across the Dunkin' Donuts parking lot with a Slurpie cup in her hand—a Big Gulp, 42 ouncer. She was still a good-looking woman with a pleasant body, he thought. As she stood waiting to cross Route 66, a carload of male silhouettes slowed to also look. The more things change, the more they.... Cigarettes glowed inside the car, its occupants probably sizing her up, deciding whether to rape and kill her then throw her mutilated body down a ravine. She hurried across just as the punks in the car took a pass, screeching off to a chorus of "Bitch!" and wolf whistles at her body, still handsome enough to fool teenagers even though in a few years she would probably be a resident instead of an employee of the home. She had a great talent and appreciation for the bed, E. considered, as she approached their front porch; she was not pretty, but he liked her face, wrinkles and all. She read enormously.

Her husband had died when she could still call herself middle-aged and for a while she lived being shuttled between her grown children, who did not need her and were embarrassed at having her about. Then one of her two children was murdered for being a rich (though naive) tourist on vacation in a picturesque (though dirt poor and politically turbulent) country (it's the parenthetical elements that always get you) and the inattention of her remaining son was no anesthetic and she was suddenly acutely frightened of being alone. She devoted herself to this place that needed her so badly.

It had begun very simply. She liked what he wrote and he liked what she read. She brought better booze to the home than he could buy from its commissary. Then she began reading to him, then she began reading with the door to his room closed, a bottle of bourbon beside the water glass that held his dentures. The steps by which she had acquired him and the way in which she had finally fallen in love with him were all part of a regular progression in which she had built herself a new life and he had traded away what remained of his old life.

He had traded it for security, for comfort too, there was no denying that, and for what else? He did not know. She was a damned nice woman. He knew that. He would as soon be in bed with her as any one; rather with her, because she was closer to his age and understood how it was. And now this life that she had built again was coming to a term because his body had turned against him, a cancer that began in his colon spawning like trout in his bloodstream.

Here she came now.

He turned his head on his hospital bed to look at her. "Hello," he said.

"I bought you a McCroissant," she said, taking it from a bag. "I thought it might remind you of Paris. I got the kind without sesame seeds that upset your intestinal tract. Do you feel well enough to eat it?"

He nodded. "I had a good sleep. Did you walk far?"

She tore cellophane away from plastic utensils, then cut the McCroissant into proportions fitting for the very old or the very young. "All the way to the KFC. K-Mart was having a sidewalk sale." She pulled from her bag a pinwheel, blew on it to make it spin, then handed it to him, laughing.

"Oh you don't know how I would like a KFC, Cajun style," he said, wishing he could gather enough breath to spin the pinwheel himself. It stuck from his meaty fist like a flower that had rigor mortis.

"When you're well enough to eat greasy food we'll celebrate by sharing a thigh. Darling, you don't know how marvelous it is to see you feeling better." From her blouse she took two pairs of 3-D glasses. They were for the "Circus of Celebrities" that Coca Cola was sponsoring later that night. The glasses would make the show appear in 3-D and Coca-Cola was giving them away with any coke-product purchase. Since she didn't have any coke-products (the carbonation gave him painful gas), he guessed she had used the excuse to indulge in a little recreational shoplifting. "I couldn't stand it when you felt that way. You won't talk to me like that again, will you? Promise me?"

She put a pair of the glasses on his head and he adjusted them; one lens was blue and the other red. "No," he said, looking with only the red eye. "Getting old is horrible, horrible." He switched to the blue. "You say things you don't mean and mean things you can't say."

"You don't have to destroy me. Do you? I'm only a senior citizen who loves you and wants to do what you want to do. I've been destroyed two or three times already. You wouldn't want to destroy me again, would you?"

"I'd like to destroy you a few times in bed," he said.

"Yes. That's the good destruction. That's the way we're made to be destroyed. I'm sure your Tuesday chemo treatment will put the cancer in remission."

"How do you know?"

"I'm sure. It's bound to come. Your doctor told me—

"What makes you think this Tuesday's treatment will be the one?"

"I'm sure it will. It's overdue now. It'll go into remission, then you'll get stronger and then we will have some good destruction. Not that dreadful talking kind." Happily, she turned and called into the hall, "Molo, letti dui whiskey-soda!"

The highlight of the evening, the "Circus of Celebrities," came and went (Sinbad taught a monkey to smoke a cigar). Then there were the memoirs of cameramen who taught mobs of militant Iranians to chant "Death to C. I. A.!" in English so as to create a more dramatic scene for viewers (and sponsors) back home. Then, as "Laverne and Shirley" reruns passed into "Beverly Hillbillies" reruns followed by "I Dream of Genie" reruns, they drank and just before Jay Leno when it was dark and the mini-mart was empty except for its single employee, a hyena crossed the sidewalk on his way around the outdoor ice machine.

"That bastard crosses there every night," E. said, pointing. "Every night for two weeks."

"He's the one that makes the noise at night. I don't mind it. They're a filthy animal though."

Drinking together, with no pain now except the discomfort of watching reruns he'd already seen, the light of the television jumping on the ceiling, he could feel the return of acquiescence in this life of pleasant surrender. She *was* very good to him. He had been cruel and unjust in the afternoon. She was a fine woman really. And just then it occurred to him that he was going to die.

It came with a rush; not as a rush of water nor of wind; but of a sudden evil-smelling emptiness and the odd thing was that the hyena slipped lightly along the edge of it.

"What is it E.?" she asked him.

"Nothing," he said. "You had better move over to the other side. To windward."

"Did Molo empty your colostomy bag?"

"Yes. He said he'll get a q-tip and swab out the orifice with boric acid later." The moist hole in his side made a sucking noise and the charcoal filter taped around it to remove the stench reminded him of the soldier who had plugged holes in his chest with cigarette butts before he'd gone on fighting. But E. couldn't remember if that man had actually existed or simply come from an ad like the ones in which cover-models were kept perpetually young and happy by the filters of their cigarettes—*Alive with Pleasure!*

"How do you feel?"

"A little wobbly."

"We'll I'm going out to the car. I forgot to hide its radio under the seat and I heard there's been another smash-in on the block. I'll be right back."

"We'll be right back."

He thought about being alone in Constantinople, that time, though he was on a tour with two dozen people including a wife with whom he had worked through every sex manual offered by Crown Books. The flight over had been very crowded, but no one spoke, their attention instead plugged into an in-flight movie. He had been reading in an in-flight magazine about a woman who lived, worked, and shopped in the same highrise so never went outdoors and it occurred to him that something very similar was happening to him though Constantinople would be the ninth city on an eleven-country package. And he was still feeling this 'something very similar' as he took the obligatory photos of his wife smiling before the Hagia Sofia (where thousands had been massacred for their faith, according to the tour book) and the other 'sights' the guide led them to 'see.' And he felt it in the Constantinople Holiday Inn where he ate the Lavish Arabian Nights Banquet ($12.99/plate) that he *had opted for before leaving the States and while he tipped the belly dancer (who had once tried out for the Dallas Cowboy Cheerleaders) the standard amount suggested in the Standard Travel Guide (ref. 'entertainment'). And had the obligatory fight with the wife who repeatedly caught him gazing at the one fellow tourist (younger, of course, and dressed in a Sear's version of a miniskirt that harder girls wore ace-bandage tight) who seemed to not speak to the others in order to conserve her integrity for the sketchpad in which she worked and reworked. And he was still feeling it when he returned home to find the photos he had sent ahead already developed and waiting along with a birthday card from Dental Clinic #27, and in the weeks afterwards during which he had the 'adventure' of test driving a new car, and the 'experience' of a new lite beer, and violent sex, in his mind and palm, with the belly dancer and the tourist in the miniskirt and he still felt it after he told the story to his shrink (while the meter ran) and he was still feeling it during dinner as he watched African children starving on the nightly news before going down into his rec-room to play ping-pong. But gradually it began to go away and he noted a definite ebb in the feeling while waiting in line to get the autograph of a celebrity about whom he knew many intimate things since she was famous primarily for her fame. And he felt it even less while following the flurry of pub that followed the gangland execution of a fourteen year-old by an eleven-year-old. And day by day the vague numbness that the feeling had been reduced to was pushed even further from his consciousness by his job and its gossip and the distractions of trying to decide which presidential candidate had the most leadershipesque style and the football game he attended but watched on the TV in his lap and the ceremony in which his own child received an 'Award for Excellence' in a school where 85% of the student body, including his daughter, couldn't name the first president, and he had forgotten about it completely the morning he took his family to McDonalds, the madness all over, glad to be home again with his wife and their sex manuals, the cartoon-colored sculptures of the Hamburglar and Ronald grinning in the sun when his heart froze to realize he was sitting next to the same fellow tourist he'd lusted after in Constantinople, a slavery 'sympathy' bracelet now jumping on her delicate wrist as she worked at her sketchpad until she noticed, and his wife noticed, him staring at her legs and his wife gathered up the children and put them into the minivan.*

"So what do you think?" the girl, the one with the sketchpad had asked,
smiling coyly as she turned her drawing to him. And it was then that he saw
that what she'd been trying to perfect was a copy of the kitten in an ad that
said, 'Do you have what it takes to be an artist?' and before getting up to give
his wife the keys to the van, he'd said, "I'll be right back."

He had never written any of that because at first, he had never wanted
to hurt anyone, especially himself. There was so much to write. He had seen
the world change and not just the events but the subtler changes; he could
remember how people were at different times. He had been in it and he had
watched it and it was his duty to write of it; but now he never would.

"Could you eat now?" C. said, standing in the doorway. Molo stood
behind her with the stainless-steel hospital tray.

"I want to write," he said.

"You ought to take some broth to keep your strength up."

"I'm going to die tonight," he said. "I don't need my strength up."

"Don't be melodramatic, E., please," she said.

"Why don't you use your nose? My spleen is starting to go. I've
retained so much water my legs look like sausages about to burst their
casings. Each drip of my IV is like a water torture," he said, holding up the
hand it ran into. Swollen and a purplish green, perforations looked like bird
tracks left by the struggle a needle-wielding nurse had had to find a vein.
"What the hell should I fool with broth for? Molo bring whiskey-soda."

"Please take the broth," she said gently.

"All right."

He couldn't eat more than a half of teaspoon and then he just got it
down without gagging.

"You're a fine woman," he said. "Don't pay any attention to me." She
looked at him with her generous, patient face, only a little the worse for
age, only a little the worse for bed, and as he looked at her good breasts
and useful thighs and those lightly small-of-back-caressing hands he felt
death come again. This time there was no rush. It was a puff, as of a wind
that makes a candle flicker and the flame go tall.

"I'm not going to eat tonight," he said tiredly. "It just isn't worth the effort."

So this is how you died, not in a blaze of glory as on "Gunsmoke" but in whispers you did not hear, wearing 3-D glasses to watch the "Circus of Celebrities," a McCroissant in one hand, a pinwheel in the other. Well, there would be no more quarreling. He could promise that. After everything he'd lived through, being machine gunned, blown up, shipwrecked with Ginger and the others, three divorces, burnt by hot water twice, clawed by a lion, gored by bulls and feminists, dysentery twice, pneumonia, pulling a skylight down on his head, two plane crashes in Africa, marooned on an uncharted planet—or wait, did that happen in "Lost in Space?"—he couldn't be sure anymore, but what's more, he couldn't care. The one experience that he definitely had never had he was not going to spoil now. He probably would. You spoiled everything. But perhaps he wouldn't.

"You can't take dictation, can you?"

"I never learned," she told him.

"That's all right."

There wasn't time, of course, although it seemed as though time telescoped so that you might put an entire life, even a Zeitgeist into one paragraph if you could get it right.

There once was a girl who was born so pure she was almost enough to convince one of God. Of course, as she grew older this began to change. Through no fault of her parents (the type who wore bicycle helmets and drove a Volvo), Girl's taste grew more atrocious by the day. In toy stores the parents hurried their daughter past pink kitchen appliances and go-go girls molded in plastic (they had summa cum laude aspirations for her). But whereas the toy medical kits on the blue side of the aisle sported a picture of a boy dressed as a doctor, the picture on the exact same kit, rendered on this side of the aisle in pink, equated girl with nurse. Much to the horror of the parents, it was the pink one Girl, naturally, identified with and it was the pink one she wanted. By kindergarten, she began to demand the other pink things, the press-on nails and body-art glitter. She especially cried for a Barbie doll that had been made the same size as a five-year-old so that five-year-olds could dress Barbie up in their jumpers and put on themselves Barbie's glittering cocktail-waitress miniskirts. "Your kids will want what their culture wants them to want," the parents' educated friends commiserated. But the parents themselves redoubled their efforts with piano lessons and Public Radio's "I Am Somebody" Theater for Children. Girl went along with most of this, for she was a good child at heart, but she tossed in her sleep while visions of Malibu Ken surfed in her head. Upon seeing the extent of her distress, the parents realized that though they could install child-proof latches on all the cabinets in the world, they couldn't protect their daughter from the air she breathed. And anyway, they didn't have the time to if they could. By degrees fatigue set in and by degrees they let her have what she craved, including the kidvid in which cartoon robotic Vikings destroyed planets and perky girls acted like leggy newscasters on infotainment shows that featured nine-year-old boys jumping around on stage, lip synching various rock stars while girls in spandex mimicked their groupies. In short, no matter what the parents did, Girl was always absorbing an educational channel with one lesson: how to be American. She learned her lesson well. In grade school she grew confident of her somebodiness because of the images projected by the diet colas, chewing gum—Blow teach's mind!—and bobbles and deodorants she got it from. By high school, the fabric of her somebodiness was deeply dyed by an intense flight from asexuality through the right acne creams, costume jewelry and cheap knock-offs of designer perfumes—Attraction, Me!—and long before she graduated to beer commercials with fast-paced music and weird camera angles—I want more for me!!—she realized she was "rad." But all the while, her nurse/groupie/beauty-queen lullabies hummed in her id, and when she met her beast, she truly believed, for she was a good child at heart, that she could transform him with a kiss. The beast took her kisses, and more, and by and by he left her knocked-up and alone. This is not to say that the beast was completely inhuman, though. Indeed, though he had also been weaned on the toy weaponry of intergalactic destruction, witnessed four million, seven hundred thousand and eighteen murders on TV along with all the other cola, gum, bobble, deodorant, acne, jewelry, perfume, beer, soap, clothes, snack food, cereal and auto—Drive Excita!—ads in which women were buck naked

*and part of the package, he was also basically a good child at heart and when
Girl confronted him with their baby he felt sorry for her and her situation—a
secretary with a boss who would have expected Post-ball Cinderella to show
up regularly, child or not, no benefits, and a salary of $14,000/year—and
though he didn't offer any child support, he did give Girl a brand-new color
TV, console model, which pleased her immensely because what she got was
more than was gotten by most of the girls she knew.*

*That was one story he had never gotten around to write. He
knew at least twenty good stories from out there where the living
were and he had never written one. Why?*

"You tell them why," he said.

"Why what, dear?"

"Why nothing." He could beat anything, he thought, because no
thing could hurt him if he did not care.

All right. Now he would not care for death. One thing he had always
dreaded was the pain. He could stand pain as well as any man, until it went
on too long, and wore him out, but here he had something that had hurt
frightfully and just when he had felt it breaking him, the pain had stopped.

*He remembered long ago his father in intensive care after undergoing
an eleven-hour operation to cut out cancerous nodes like the ones the doctors
now tried to melt away in him with radiation and chemistry. Whenever he
thought of his first sight of his father after the operation, the words "barely
human" always came to mind. Father's eyes had bulged to the size of cue
balls. Chemicals flowed through plastic extensions to his veins. His head was
a fleshy knob in a mass of gears that clicked while a bellows forced air into
then drew it out of the cavity that served as a chest. His father had been an
iron worker and very good with children. But that night he was a lab animal,
trapped in some tortuous experiment. It was only after minutes that E.
noticed the physician who must have been standing there the whole while.
He had on a white lab coat and was writing on a metal clip board. He was
tending to his gauges and blood pressures and machines that were to make so*

much difference with a faith that was as unshakable or as shakable as that
of physicians in all ages, bleeding their patients, or administering leeches,
or placing the egg of an all-white chicken on the afflicted body part. State
of the art, though a living antique, E. thought, already beginning to see
the man as an oddity with a logic bizarre to all but cultural historians.
E. understood the inevitability of this transformation because just
yesterday, the day before the operation, he had noted the gap between his
generation's way of looking at the world and the anachronism that was
his father's. Specifically, E.'s father had told him that our Lord never sent
you anything you could not bear and E. had taken that to mean that at a
certain time the pain passed you out automatically. But when he bent near
his father's quivering lips that night after the operation, his father was
laboring as hard as a fish in the bottom of a boat to gasp, "Shoot me, E..
For Christ sake shoot me" and explanations—the Lord or biology—were all
just words.

Still, this now that he had was very easy; and if it was no worse as
it went on there was nothing to worry about. Yes, about him were vacant
expressions, living skeletons. Loneliness. The horror of institutional decor
in Southwest color schemes. But little apparent pain. It would be nice to
be in better company, though.

He thought a little about the company that he would rather have.
His mother. Freddy Stemer from the sixth grade when laughter came as
easily as breath... Martha, his high school sweetheart, who like himself
had been so incredibly young as to think that the only currents that
could run through a body were the rapids of pleasure...

No, he thought, when everything you do, you do too long, and do
too late, you can't expect to find the people still there. Nor the ideas.
Men had taken to wearing earrings, chicks tattoos. Max Perkins was gone,
as was Clement Greenberg. Faulkner, Joyce, Mencken, Freud, Picasso gone.
Eliot, gone. Conrad, gone. Ernst, gone. Klee, gone. Woolf, gone. Beckett
isn't waiting for Godot. Trilling's gone. Pound, Rontgen's discovery of
X-rays, League of Nations, point-of-view as epistemological probe,

Tolstoy's *What is Art?* Duchamp's urinal answer, high-speed tool steels, priestly art heroes, gone. Industrial aesthetics, *Metropolis*, industrial society, *Metamorphosis*, orchestral portraits of locomotives, *Pacific 231*, the first wireless communication between Europe and America, The Author, the Wright Brothers, the Lone Eagle, the Marx Brothers, Gauguin brothers, Bolsheviks and Mensheviks, falls the shadow, Big Brother, Relativity, frustration of coherent plots, Bohr's discovery of atomic structure, frustration of conventional character, frustration of cause-and-effect, Zeitgeist, Plank's Quantum theory, sculpture according to quadratic equations, Grabo and Moholy-Nagy, *Linear Construction*, mathematical symbols in literature, unrelated time and space in gothic painting, the fusion of time and space in motion pictures, Eadweard Muybridge's freeze-frame horse, Pavlov's dogs, the march of knowledge through smaller and smaller units for analysis, divide and conquer, Mendel's fruit flies, selenium, Zaum poets, the horse as sum of its parts, electric eye, the horse as machine, electric limb, Brancusi's brass *Bird in Space* as piston, Brancusi's brass bird as torpedo, U.S. customs officials trying to determine if Brancusi's bird should be classified as machinery or plumbing, artificial intelligence, division by middle managers, artificial insemination, a lonely crowd, 2,000% increase in orders for white-collars, pent-up demand for condoms education snakeoil vacuumcleaners terror strawberries democra(*caveat emptor*)cy superfluous hair and ovens, *The Hollow Men*, Frederick Taylor's *The Principles of Scientific Management*, time/motion studies, calculating the most efficient size shovel for men shoveling coal, for men shoveling snow, for men shoveling ash, 20th century solutions for 20th century problems, the Holocaust, electroshock, electric chairs, division by Fermi = fission, the age of anxiety, Kierkegaard, The Great War (to end all wars), the ego, guilt, aluminum, the super ego, The Second World War (that made the numbering of Great Wars necessary), *Nosferatu*, 5,800,000 rifles and carbines, 28,000 trench mortars, I cannot tell how many projectile, mines and fuses, celluloid, *Das Rheingold*, vulcanite, bakelite, the pixel, wall divides Berlin, barbed wire, Charlie Chaplin, Charlie Chan, 49th parallel divides Korea, "Charlie," razor wire, Freud subdivides the subconscious, electrified wire, Ho Chi Min Trail, electrification, Eisenhower Expressway, duplicate grey standard faces, the electric toothbrush, the Kennedy Expressway, suburbs, *On the Road*, individualism = motorcars at a cost of 30,000 lives per year = collective traffic jams, cul de sacs, air conditioning, air-conditioning hum, *Howl*, air-conditioning air, air-conditioning power consumption, the Hoover Dam, standardized water, fluoride, the scientific approach to social reform, Standardized Personality Tests, Benjy, Lennie, collective unconsciousness, Standard Intelligence Tests, standardized inch, the taking of miles, standardized standards, standardized ubermench, Skinner Box, standard second defined as 1/31,556,925.9747 of the year 1900, chrome, perfumes from tar, telegraph divides world into time zones, glass curtain-wall construction, Skidmore, Owings and Merrill, The Iron Curtain, Neutra, division of India, Mies Van der Rhoe, architecture as Esperanto, International Business Machines (IBM), Intercontinental Ballistic Missiles (ICBMs), a blue period, CBW, WPA, SAD, M-1, KGB, SALT, MAD, BDAC, NATO, ABM, HUD, DDT, at the still point of the turning world, National Bureau of Standards (NBS) divides standard second from rotation of earth and fuses it to the standard cesium atom, time keeping with an accuracy of ±1/10 billion part, exact calculation as aesthetic satisfaction, dominion over palm and pine, for loss of a nail an empire, falls the shadow, Heisenburg uncertainty principle, falls the shadow, Amritzar Massacre (the white man's burden), abandonment of the gold standard, abandonment of absolute time = $E = mc^2$ = duck and cover = abandonment of absolute knowledge = abandonment of absolute moral standards, 100 flips of a coin, analytic philosophy, error creeping in due to the Second Law of Thermodynamics, man as limitation to scientific beauty, 100-mile mushroom clouds, *The Grace of Machine Forms*, the beauty of shadows cast by derricks, the wondrous landscape of a hair magnified 3000 times, the starkness of a machined edge, the ugliness of a slag heap, of litter, of eye-punishing industrial smoke, Paul Strand, dehumanized shadows scurrying beneath the geometry of power, The Axis: Freud, Marx, Einstein—"Never has so much been owed to so few"—the new calculus, Durkheim, liming regularities and recurrent series, the assembly line—"Never has so much been owed to so few"—naturalists recording the day-by-day patterns of birds, the sun shone having no alternative, recessions come, wars go, "an incident here and there," Du Pont de Nemours translating birdcalls into French, translating shepherds into machine-tenders and sheep into rows of automated pipeline, *The Americans* [not *A Day in the Life of America*], Freudian-man as egolibido, he became his admirers, the Good = Power, Thus Spake Zarathustra, "abnormal" behavior, sociology divides men, Saussure divides language, Chomsky, Fortran, the coining of "agnostic," the coining of "nihilistic," the coining of "penicillin," control group, Le Corbusier's house = machine to live in, *Art in the Age of Mechanical Reproduction*, painting reduced to "plane surfaces covered with colors assembled in a certain order," scientist artists, the fourth dimension, scientist musicians, Milton Babbitt and the RCA synthesizer, *Construction, y = 2x³ - 13.5x² + 21x*, artists spitting on painterly clouds, water sprites, waves and nocturnal scents, architects, writers, musicians, spitting on twaddle, bombast, harmonic stability, false pathos, false sphinxes, pissing on the notion of art as prettiness, pissing on the works of old masters, pissing on devotion to Roman ruins, pissing on chordal progression, pissing on sentimentality, pissing on Greek harmony, pissing on diatonic harmony, pissing on balance, pissing on restraint, pissing on decoration, pissing on friezes, pissing on columns, Jackson Pollock pissing in a fireplace, Bloom wiping his bum with *Matcham's Masterstroke*, middle-class taste, bourgeois baiting, "a salesman is an it that stinks to please," theater of the absurd, baiting the Cambridge ladies who live in furnished souls, Exercises in Style, primal screams, polytonal music, Lo. Lee. Ta! Weialala leia, Tralala lala, *La beauté peut toute chose* (or not; Oscar Ass-thete between Queen's berryies and a hard place), Oneida Community, polyandric living, Lamplight at *Buovilla e quel remir*, polyglot poems, ὸδὸς αυω κατω μια και ωυτη, polygamous living, Mary Reynold's leather-bound de Sade, the new Individualism is the new Hellenism, the Bloomsbury Group, *frisch weht der wind*, pen and brush as hammer on complacency, anti-novel, art as mantra, Varèse, anti-heroes, anti-theater, art for art's sake, the Russian Futurist manifesto, The Armory Show, the Italian Futurist Manifesto—*a roaring motor car is more beautiful than the Victory of Samothrace!*—the power printing press, the Art of Noises Manifesto—MUSICIANS SMASH YOUR INSTRUMENTS!—Manifesto of the Communist Party, Total Theater, The Iron Foundry Manifesto, the Surrealist Manifesto, post-impressionism, Schoenbert's Society for Private Musical Performance, *au-dessus de la mêlée*, the decline of realism, Auerbach, fascism, arts déco, Vorticism, escape velocity, Fauvism, militarism, dada, idealism, falls the shadow, The Russian Association of Proletarian Musicians, action painting, antiforeignism, *Les Six*, Projective Verse, surrealism, Cubism, imperialism, Robert Capa, nationalism, Abstract Formalism, Kineticism, giantism in engineering, all 46,000 tons of the *Titanic*, giantism in art, *Running Fence*, minimalism in engineering, (transistor replaces atom which replaces the dynamo which replace the steam engine as symbol of an age), Walter Gropius in a Bauhaus, Minimalism, *Composition in Blue Yellow and Black*, Maximalism, pessimism, Constructivism, Expressionism, *Poetry* Magazine, *Blast* Magazine, *Egoist* Magazine, *The Criterion*, *The Fugitive*, *Black Mountain Review*, *La Révolution surréaliste*, *Pravda*, Futurist exhibition, *Tel Quel*, *Camera Work*, The Machine Hall at the Paris Exposition, *Samizdat*, The Eiffel Tower, The Universal Exposition, The Columbia Exhibition, The Ferris Wheel, *Ballet* (written on a circular score) *for Eight Pianos, Eight Xylophones, Two Doorbells, Three Sticks of Dynamite and One Aeroplane Propeller*, Sturm Gallery, Pierre Matisse Gallery, Crystal Palace, *Technisches Museum für Industrie und Gewerbe*, genius, Fellini, madmen artists, photojournalism adapted to the needs of anger, piano playing with fists, black forests of notes so dense that the score looks like black forests of notes, Cage's *4'33"*,

the jump cut from ballet as classical leg-show to movement as message, Ruth St. Denis, The Great Leap Forward, dance without music, "Dirge without Music," painters who don't paint, poetry for poets, composition for composers, architecture for architects, art for artists, professors for everyone else, low culture in its place, lofty contempt for the Slavs, food chain, scores for revolver shots, Archduke Francis Ferdinand, hand on scepter to hand on throttle, the beauty and symmetry of ball bearings, *Blitzkrieg*, Franco's Guernica and Picasso's *Guernica*, brute force, bad faith, *Journey to the End of Night*, expatriate artists in Paris (WWI), progress, Dos Passos, Zola, oppression and persecution, Gide, Stein, a lost generation, Klimt's *Death and Life*, flame throwers, a generation up in smoke, Klee's *Death and Fire*, dive-bombers, armored transport, Luftwaffe, "allnight newsy surreal," disenchantment, cynicism (the unwelcomed guest), preoccupation with tragic fate, Poland, refugee artists in NY (WWII): Hofman, Dubuffet, Klee, Léger, Mondrian, Chagall, Miró, Man Ray, de Kooning, Beckman, Ernst, Matta, Zadkine, Tanguy, Bretan, Masson, Ozenfant, Lipchitz, Tchelitchew, Seligmann, Berman, Grünberg, Schoenberg, Stravinsky, Bartók, Milhaud, Hindemith and Weill, irony, crime, *City Square*, disease, bewilderment, boredom, insanity, corruption, poverty in the midst of plenty, the spacious luxury compartment of an oceanliner/the cramped quarters of steerage = *Das Kapital*, the simultaneous birth of commercial television and WWII, Yuri Gagarin, Natasha and Boris, Fidel and Nikita, Moose and Squirrel grinning on the screen, 7% of the world's population consuming 43% of the world's resources, prefab, birthrate hits 76 million/year, consumptive pull productive push, Calder Hall, eat-off-the-floor cleanliness in power plants, pocket protectors, chain reactions, chain stores, vitamins, radial tires, poliomyelitis vaccine, The Red Menace, hydrogen bomb, *A la recherche du temps perdu*, Hiroshima, Dali and all those melting clocks, *The Cry*, the factory whistle, fluoridation, *Technics and Civilization*, 1 Owens bottle machine = 18 bottle blowers, readymades, Geiger counters, 80% reduction in telephone operators due to automated phone exchange, *Twittering Machine*, replacement of 2 million others by other machines, Wall St. Crash, seeing is not believing, Kuleshov effect, Stalin, Domino Theory, germ theory and disease prevention, germ warfare, tests on civilians, clerical workers, copier technicians, service workers, arms race, ideologically shackled to the new, war conducted as middle-management problem, 15 million military fatalities, middle-mgmt efficiency, 25 million civilian fatalities, intellectual distance, critics with initials for first names, New Criticism, a knowledge game, Club of Rome, discovery of Dead Sea Scrolls, École de Paris, Frankfort School, New York School, intellectual dance, Kissinger, Doris Humphery, containment, Zbigniew Brzezinski, Yvonne Rainer, intellectual painting, Rothko, intellectual music, intellectual cocktail parties, intellectual fornication, *Horizontal Spines*, the culture industry, *Arts & Leisure* Section, Tennessee Williams, Eugene O'Neill, Spengler's *The Decline of the West*, psychoanalysis of Hamlet, *The Economic Consequences of the Peace*, Cold War and Cold Warriors, *Breakfast at Tiffany's*, grandiose futures, 1984, André Breton, *To be looked at (from the other side of the glass) with one eye, close to, for almost an hour*, syncopated rhythm, dissonance, Baldwin, Beckman, Barnes, the first abstract photo, Octopus, the juxtaposition of inward consciousness to rational, public, objective discourse, *The Delights of a Poet*, determinism, Musil, Unamuno, faith in secularization, heroic codes, individual style, *Orlando*, Mauriac, Conrad, Cassier, Lawrence, Péguy, Kandinsky, Critiques of Judgement, CinemaScope, Westernization, Adorno, *The Will to Power*, heart of darkness, police shutdowns of Dada exhibitions, Marx, falls the shadow, Marxist criticism, Truth as NO EXIT, "the uncanniest of all guests," Irish Independence, *The Waste Land*, Kafka, *Ulysses*, Wittgenstein, Mussolini's march on Rome, riots touched off by Stravinksy's *The Rite of Spring*, Hesse, Yeats, Hellman, Forster, Dylan Thomas, Frost, Cocteau, Monumentality, *Finnegans Wake*, origins, Proust, Rilke, the establishment of the U.S.S.R., *A Room of One's Own*, Dos Passos, Kline, Dreiser, Rothko, Newman, *Dasein*, Fitzgerald, elitism, Woolf, stream of consciousness, *Magic Mountain*, Amundsen's arrival at the South Pole, Hillary and Tensing's arrival at the summit, dreams without meaning, the pre-Castro Cuban cigar, defiance before it could be sold as kitsch—*Sweep away yesterday's literature!*—the avant avant-gone, gone, gone, gone.

All exhausted and gone and with them the pure air.

He felt sorry for the ones who were left, the going but not yet gone, and what they had made to occupy themselves with until they went: novels that went loopity-loop or slogged through contemporary whines rendered in 19th century realism. Paintings that looked like cartoons. Music as a function of modern management. And the endless swarms of wanna bees full of buzz buzz buzz "movie concept" buzz "hypertext" buzz buzz "Jacques Nietzsche" buzz buzz "political art" buzz buzz buzz buzz.... The educated artsy set. And the uneducated artsy set. Even the lowlies who emptied bed pans in this place wore gold chains and attitudes. It was the fashion tats that seemed most pathetic, though, for once the world turned back around to where only sailors and bikers got tattoos, the branded ones would wear their banality on their arms, ankles, backs and breasts as painfully as surgically attached love beads.

I'm getting as bored with dying as with everything else, he thought, realizing what he'd been thinking about.

"It's a bore," he said out loud.

"What is, my dear?"

"Anything you do too bloody long."

He looked at her, sitting between him and the glow of the television. It's gray-blue light shone on her pleasantly lined face and he could see that she was sleepy. The hyena made a noise just outside the window.

"Do you feel anything strange?" he asked her.

"No. Just a little sleepy."

"I do," he said.

He had just felt death come by again.

Our nada who art in nada, nada be thy name. Thy kingdom nada, thy will be nada in nada as it is in nada.

He told her how just in that instant he had felt like the old man in a story he had once written. For weeks on end, went the story, this old man stayed late into the night at the same cafe simply because he had no where else to go and the cafe was a clean, well-lighted and pleasant place to sit.

As E. spoke, a man emerged from the fluorescent white of the 24-hour Quickie Mart across the way. Styrofoam cup in hand, he got into the lot's one lone car and drove off.

The two waiters in the story, E. continued, had to wait for this old man to finish nursing his brandy before they could close up and go home. So night after night one of the waiters, the young one, got more and more exasperated with this old man and his routine, his own life on hold sometimes until three in the morning. But the other waiter, the older one, understood that if they didn't stay open for the old man, there would be nothing but nada. Nada but the antiseptic chrome of steam pressure machines used in other bars, nada but those music-filled bars where it was impossible to stand with dignity, nada but the old man's own empty room, which is to say nada serving nada when everyone needed a place in which they could be at peace. A clean, well-lighted—

Suddenly, E. stopped talking.

Because, just then, death had come and rested its head on the chrome of his bed.

"Never believe any of that about a scythe and a skull," he told C. "It can be a high-fashion model as easily, or a new car with 0% financing. Or it can have a wide snout like a hyena."

It had moved up on him now, but it had no shape any more. It simply occupied space.

"Tell it to go away."

It did not go away but moved a little closer.

"You've got a hell of a breath," he told it. "You stinking bastard."

It moved up closer to him still and now he could not speak to it and when it saw he could not speak it came a little closer and now he tried to send it away without speaking but it moved in on him so its weight was all upon his chest and while it crouched there and he could not move or speak he heard the woman say, "Bwana is asleep now. Shut off the television."

He could not speak to tell her to make it go away and it crouched now, heavier, so he could not breathe. And then, while the light of the television went dark, suddenly it was all right and the weight went from his chest.

•   •   •

It was morning and had been morning for some time when the ambulance plane came to take him to the Mayo Clinic. Doctors there had discovered a miraculous cure for his type of cancer. A microbe that when released into the bloodstream acted like a Pac Man on any cells that weren't healthy.

The plane was very sleek and modern and painted like a regular ambulance. But in the pilot's seat was old Compton, dressed like a professor in slacks, a tweed jacket and a brown felt hat.

"We'll have you there in record time, old cock," Compie called back cheerfully to where E. lay and then the engine roared. Acceleration pressed E. into his stretcher. A final bump and they were in the air with C. and the others down below waving good-bye from the enormous shuffleboard court that had served as a make-shift runway. As the plane rose, the strip mall E. had gazed at for so many hours fell away; Route 66 and its traffic became toy-sized.

Paramount Pictures

They flew over Paramount Studios and the studios of MTV standing in
the shadow of Disney's spires. From this height, he could see these assembly
lines attracting to them a string of Oakies similar to those Steinbeck wrote
about. In jalopies and Winnabagos and Toyotas they made their way across
the mountains in search of the promised land. Yet as he crossed onto
the leeward side of the mountains, E. was struck by how similar was the
promised land he had left to the unpromised land into which they were
flying: a plain of Taco Bells and McDonalds and Walmarts and Midas Muffler
shops as far as the eye could see. Its desert ground made Las Vegas, the
cultural capital of America, shimmer as brilliantly as an oasis rendered in
day-glo colors on black velvet.

Suddenly the plane pitched. Compie had executed a barrel roll to avoid colliding with Apollo 11, returning from its moon landing not to the earth but to worlds. In its wake were billions of microchips, "texts" that weren't books, polyglot noise, an ecstasy of communication and academic discourse. The beginning of History as fictions and the end of Literature as art. Then they passed Ketchum Idaho where E. knew he could have taken matters into his own hands so he wouldn't have to live to see it. He wiped a tear of regret into a tear of nostalgia when the Mississippi came into view, shimmering with the country's first glimmer of the modern. A single barn-storming loopity loop through the St. Louis Arch and they were soaring above middle America. E. looked down to see if he could spot the home he grew up in. But they were too high and it was lost in a patchwork that reminded him of the quilt he had once seen, made from tee-shirts collected at rock concerts. Those amusement parks that proliferated during the 70's had also found a home here, the New York companies that had made them abandoning their maintenance to smaller outfits. From miles off he spotted an influential one designed by the firm of Shandy, Watt and Menard. The arcs of its signature roller coaster, The Gravity's Rainbow, towered above many other similar rides. Even from this height E. could hear riders shrieking in terror and glee and for the first time in his life he somehow understood the attraction of a place like that and why so many had stopped reading books like his in order to go there. "Ah well," he sighed loudly, "let them have their fun."

Compie looked back to see how he was riding. Then instead of banking into the direction of the Mayo Clinic, he pushed on toward the eastern horizon, he evidently figuring a bit of a tour wouldn't hurt. Below, stockyards, cold-water tenements and crude naturalism gave way to more rural landscape.

"Winesburg," Compie called back, indicating a small town where, just like the houses of today, all the window shades were up. The cloverleafs along the expressway that Compie was now paralleling took on the character of those patterns made by aborigines to guide flying saucers and near Pennsylvania, it dawned on E. that what he was looking at were wagon trails. Americans had never really left them he could tell, traveling back up stream, so to speak, and seeing how the great plains and all that lie behind to the west was just a convergence of ever-widening paths. Leaves of grass grew along the way, an easily recognizable landmark. As was Uncle Tom's Cabin. For a period, though, the lay of the land grew more obscure.

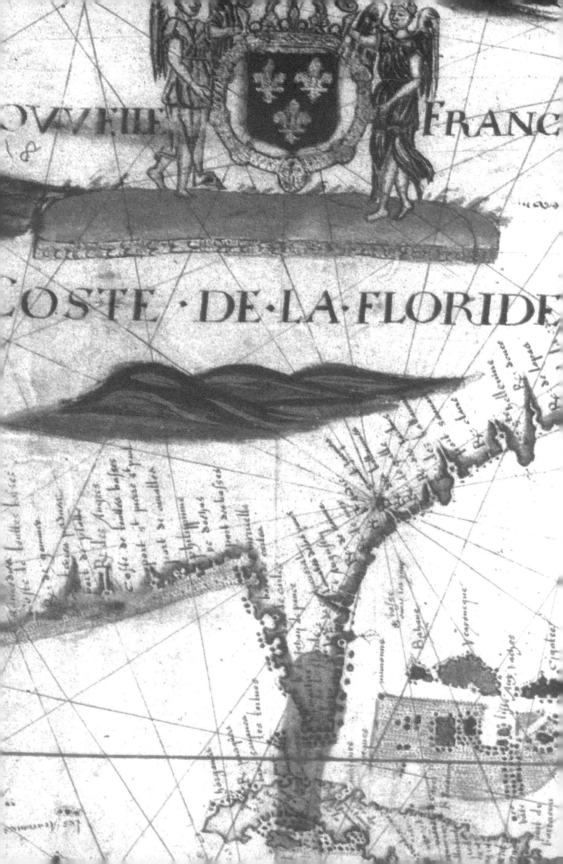

A raven flew up alongside the plane, croaked, "Never more," then careened back down, alighting on the head of a great white whale that had surfaced in Walden Pond. Soon afterwards wilderness closed in. From a hilltop a lone Mohican waved good-bye and Compie waved back with the plane's wings. Then he let out the choke a bit and they climbed up, up and over the Appalachian Mountains. The plane dipped as they bridged its crest, hitting a pocket of low pressure. When it regained its wings, they were lower and over a land where there was writing but not Literature. The trees here were dense as though there were no printing presses to swallow them yet, imported paper being used for religious pamphlets and tracts on how to succeed in business: the diet of nation makers, preachers and others fanatic enough to relocate to a howling wilderness. To amuse E., Compie swooped low to buzz a prayer meeting. The number of holy rollers who had books to shake back at the plane made E. wonder if he'd been wrong about the press and if it had even already churned out the nation's first best seller: *The Bay Psalm Book*. He doubted this, though, when he saw the cargo ships in the bay itself, ponderous from the weight of books, ideas and other baggage brought here from the Old World.

Beyond, the open ocean.

The first slave ships were driving toward their destiny just ahead of the Niña, Pinta and Santa María. The strong wind that sped them on slowed the plane. It whipped up white caps that reminded E. of the leaves of a book being riffled. They were the leaves of books: an ocean of undulating pages, printer's ink and white space, poured together from the rivers of every nation on earth. Endlessly churning, it seemed as though the whole globe was a sea of words. A universe of words that stretched further than the mind could follow until hours later, a continent emerged, low on the horizon. The more distinct it became, the stronger grew E.'s sense of a converging significance. He hoped they were heading for Paris so he could see the origins of his serious work. But instead of cafe goers, expatriates or even campesinos, the land they reached was peopled by men so primitive, he doubted they had yet achieved the cave painting. His pulse quickened all the more at this, for he began to believe that he was going to see not just the origin of his art, but of Art. Suddenly, there were great shoots of lava that darkened and they were in a storm, the rain so thick it seemed like flying through a waterfall, and then they were out and Compie turned his head and grinned and pointed and there, ahead, all he could see, as white as a blank page and as wide as all the world, great, high, and unbelievably bright in the sun—the square top of Kilimanjaro. And then he knew that there was where he was going.

The medical machine made a high-pitched whine that sounded like a hyena. C. stood dazzled by the whiteness of the room. Lights glaring, she had to squint to look through the plate glass that separated her from the machine E. was being trollied into. His eyes were unseeing as they had been for the past two months, staring as if into eternity. Even plants turn to the sun, she knew, and she wondered if he could tell how bright and clean the room was around him. The night he slipped into the coma, she had asked the doctor, "Can he?—" She had wanted to ask, "Can he hear us?" But emotion choked off her words and the doctor had finished for her, "Feel anything?" Then like a schoolboy whose curiosity had been stirred he added, "Let's see." He nodded to an intern making the rounds with him who lifted an arm, stuck in a pin, then let the arm drop back to the mattress, so much dead meat. Less than a plant. Less than a sequoia that could live as silently as this for how long?...

It would be up to her to complete his story, she could see. But resurrecting him somehow, or even pulling the plug, had to be beyond the power of any one woman or discipline. So he'd remain this way indefinitely, a living corpse to be poked and examined by doctoral students, archivists, and the curious as she struggled with his ending. Yes, and hers. For surely, it was up to her to shape their ending, in the time she had left, before another, younger, generation came to stand in her place while she lay where he was now. And who knew what horrors and pleasures desire and commerce would combine to invent by then.

The machine made the same strange hyena noise. But she did not hear it for the beating of her heart.

Once Human : STORIES

A manga artist who is afraid that she herself is slipping into a cartoon version of life; a lab technician who makes art with the cloning technology she uses at work; a sociologist hunting for the gene that makes some people want to take risks—these are some of the characters that people the stories collected in *Once Human.* Exploring the territory where life is shaped by the science, technologies—and changing worlds—we bring into being, the people here often find that the harder they look, the less they can say. The map that emerges from these stories just as often charts the territory of human longing—and that great poetic theme—the failure of poetry—and science, and technology—to explain the 'why' of the world if not its 'how.'

Steve Tomasula is author of the novels *VAS: An Opera in Flatland,* the novel of the biotech revolution; *The Book of Portraiture*; *IN & OZ*; and *TOC: A New-Media Novel,* which received the Mary Shelly Award for Excellence, and a Best Book of the Year Gold Medal in the eLit Awards. His short fiction, and essays have been published widely, and often take up themes of body art and representation, especially how people picture each other through the languages they use. A Howard Fellow, he lives in Chicago and can be found at www.stevetomasula.com.